C000079696

Dragon

A Story from the Oakenfall Chronicles

By Damien Tiller

Publishing

A Black Flag Publication
Dragon's Blight
A Story from the Oakenfall Chronicles
by Damien Tiller

Copyright © 2011 Damien Tiller
The right of Damien Tiller to be identified as the Author of the work has
been asserted by them in accordance with the Copyright, Designs and
Patents Act 1988.
First published in Great Britain in 2012 by Doodle Rat Publishing
Second Edition published in Great Britain in 2019 by Black Flag Publishing

ISBN: 978-0-9573986-7-2

Northern Neeska in the year 87AB as depicted by Aaron Fenton-Blake

Prologue – Fireworks and Fate

Our story starts — as many a good story does — in the dark of night above a bustling coastal city...

The moon was hidden behind the brilliant glow of its Centennial Fireworks. A torrent of pigments cascaded down in brilliant bursts of color, like paint flicked onto a black canvas and running down. Their glow caressed the festival crowd below. Music pulsing from various bards, bands, and taverns resonated so loudly, that the combined revelry almost masked the bombardment of explosions from the night sky. Decorative banners stretched between the tall stone buildings marking the freedom of the north, the end of slavery in the City of Oakenfall.

The cobbled streets were filled with revelers of every class and creed in celebration of the end of the Dragon's Blight. It had been one hundred years to the day since the last scaled beast had fallen in the Scorched Lands, and humans had been freed from their slavery. Well, <u>free</u> might be too strong a word... where the beasts once ruled, the cruelty of man had soon filled the void. Regardless, this did not stop the people of Oakenfall from celebrating, aided, in no small way, by the flow of good food and strong ales.

With this alcoholic lubrication for this one special night, class did not matter. Noble or commoner, baker or shipwright, once the ale hit the stomach, all were the same. Life in Oakenfall — no matter a person's standing — was not always perfect, but for this evening no one cared. Jugglers and entertainers danced in the streets, and music blared from the marching band parading through the city.

People drank, and food seemed aplenty even in a time of poverty. The streets were lined with silver birch tables topped with spoils from the local farmlands...

potatoes, leeks and meat. The meats were fresh and hung to perfection, deer, lamb and the juiciest of pork! The celebrations marked the end of the worst battle in recent history but even during this drunken merriment, whispers of a new war were not far away.

Oakenfall was a jewel in the north and a prize sought by many. Its rulers had been brave and driven, its budding development had driven growth and hunger for resources and caused it to be at war — in one way or another — almost since the moment the last armor-clad dragon body had slammed into the ashen earth and mankind's oppression had ended.

Oakenfall was one of the largest cities in the Northern Kingdoms, known as Northern Neeska, and sat on the east coast in an area of lush farmlands, calm seas and bountiful soil. The Hanson family had been rulers of Oakenfall ever since their ancestor had led the defeat of the dragons. The city was protected by treacherous mountains to the south, an ocean to the east, and miles of fortified lands to the north and west — all of which secured the family's leadership for generations. The Hanson Kingdom had once covered all the lands north of the Northern Neeska border, but civil war had fractured their peaceful rule and new boundaries had been drawn on their old lands.

The country itself took its name from an old dragon-kind word, "Neeska," which roughly translated to "the nest." It was made up of many peoples, elves, and dwarves, who called it home. Most of them had once been slaves, but their common hardship had done little to cement lasting trust.

Although the city celebrated peace and freedom once a year, many of its families were missing loved ones and did not know peace. The city was still waging war with three of Oakenfall's neighboring kingdoms, and many wondered if it would ever truly be calm.

The closest military position was that of the White Flags, who called White Isle home. This was the smaller of the two islands that lined the coast of Northern Neeska close to Oakenfall. It had become home to a collective of pirates who directly opposed the Hanson family and their right to rule. However, unlike most pirates, that were disorganized and haphazard brigands at best, this group had fallen behind one flag, and in the last few years had amassed quite an armada behind their cause of creating a free people.

The second closest battlefront was on the island just south of White Isle, this larger landmass being known as the Alienage. This was home of the elf race, a peaceful druidic people that had come seeking refuge in 450DB (During the Blight), and had been at peace with Oakenfall, even being in alliance with them during the Great War. In 2AB (After the Blight). It had then become another warfront for Oakenfall, because the elves living there refused to allow the Hanson family to plunder its resources.

These two islands were only a few miles out to sea and could have posed a real threat to Oakenfall, but they were held in check by the intervening waters — it was more a war of words, with no side actively seeking conflict. However, this could not be said for the third and perhaps most fierce enemy of Oakenfall's peace.

Towards the western edge of Northern Neeska stood the Northern Mountains and Western Reaches, a place of poor soil, hard stone, and even hardier people. Neeska as a continent was home to both civilized modern humans and nomadic barbarian tribes. One of those tribes had come to be known as the Poles, because of their unique poleaxes, made from the abundant black iron in the mountains.

Because they remained in small tribes and were habitually battling each other, the barbarians of Neeska used to present little more than an inconvenience — stealing from the odd trade caravan or pillaging a homestead. That was until around ten years ago… when something changed. The Poles began to grow in numbers and before the Hansons truly understood the threat facing them, they had lost the City of Northholm.

Northholm had once been part of the Hanson Kingdom and sat in the mouth of a natural harbor at the very northern tip of Neeska. It had fallen to barbarian rule and now stood as a constant source of outrage to the Royal Court. The occupied city stood behind what was the most volatile battlefront, which had been held at a stalemate for years. The war to keep the Poles at bay had lasted for almost a decade. The line drawn on the map in the Hanson Castle's war room, marking the battle lines barely moved an inch per season back or forth over the small town of Briers Hill, a trek of only some days north of Oakenfall.

To some hearing this, it seemed like all the north was in turmoil, but that was not true, and even within the chaos pockets of peace were to be found. On the border between Northern Neeska and the free states of Middle Neeska were the Ashmore Mountains, whose rocky peaks hid a magnitude of tunnels that were home to several small collectives of dwarves. The largest of these was the Goldhorn Kingdom that stretched for miles throughout the mountains. The peace they enjoyed was largely due to the fact that the dwarves had shut their mammoth gates and sealed themselves off from the topside world at the end of the Great War — and opened them just rarely for trade.

Adjacent to the snow-capped Ashmore Mountains, and sitting between Hanson Kingdom and the Scorched Lands was the small and peaceful low-lying countryside known as the Tower Plains. Its views to the horizon were barely broken by the sight of a tree or bush, however it had one shadow that was cast against the sky for miles, a magnificent tower. The tower was home to the magic-wielding Mages of Neeska.

Magic was dangerous, and those blessed — or cursed with it — scared those without it. Although mages had been vital in the defeat of the dragons, during the so-called peace that followed the Great War, to avoid the fear and talk of witch-hunters, the mages had established their own place of learning away from cultivated lands.

The Mages Tower looked out over all the plains of the north and they had the best view of the mysterious Scorched Lands. Those ash cloud covered lands that had been the front for the Great War were used by parents for scaring their children... and secretly still scared the parents in their own hearts. Few alive had seen the battles, but tales of the burnt bodies of thousands of men, the lost cities and the charred forests that fell for the freedom of man haunted the dreams of many.

It had been such an event in the world that it changed the very calendar that the civilized races used for tracking the years. Tonight, was not just an anniversary, it was the turning of a century. This night marked 100AB, the first century of freedom, and this is where our story starts just beneath the fireworks...

Watching from a white stone balcony in the noble district of Oakenfall, a lone figure stood.

Chapter One – Celebration for a Lonely Heart

The lone figure was that of Darcy Dean, a noble by birth and heir to the Dean Estate. He watched the excitement playing out on the cobbled streets below with disinterest.

Darcy, as was common for him, could not enjoy the festivities. It wasn't that he was busy, in fact his evening had been one of loneliness and boredom. Its highlight before the fireworks had been to watch a single bead of wax drip down the side of a candle.

Life in the city could be lonely at the best of times with everyone rushing around in their own lives. The city never slept, as they say, and the average person had little time to spare for others but for Darcy the isolation seemed magnified. It had been with him for so long now it almost felt natural… as if it was meant to be.

He felt as if loneliness had become his friend. Some might have asked how someone who was born into finery and luxury, a guest of nobles and a partaker of feasts, could feel so terribly alone. The answer was simple — other than the short time he spent with his house-hands and crew each day, Darcy spent most of his time alone.

He was the heir to an estate given by the King himself to Darcy's father and it was a wealthy one at that. However, the feasts he went to were for business, the luxuries were not his own but belonged to his father and mother. Darcy did nothing for himself and everything in service of the estate.

Darcy had spent his childhood alone, catered for by servants but without the companionship of other children. Now as an adult, he could not enjoy the benefits of his privileged position in life. With his parents absent, it fell on him to run every aspect of the family estate —the shipyards, imports and exports, shipwrights, council, functions and more bootlicking than the average leather obsessed mill-worm could manage in its short existence.

Darcy was young for his age. He was twenty-seven but had lived a somewhat sheltered life. He wished his father could be there with him just to take some of the pressure off and allow him to experience life.

However, his father, a great hero and soldier, was stationed not far from Briers Hill in a fort known as Hallows Fort, and with no end in sight for the war with the Poles, Darcy didn't know if he would ever see his father again.

Briers Hill was a small town flying the Hanson flag close to the borders of the Western Reaches. Before Northholm fell it was the halfway mark for traders by land. For a small village it had been prosperous, but with the encroachment of the Poles from the west, trade by land had all but died, and now the only people who passed through its quaint streets were the army led by Darcy's father.

The town now stood as the last resistance. Many feared that if it was to fall, then Oakenfall would not last for long. The Poles had moved slowly to start with, unsure if the rumors of freedom in Neeska were true. However, as they gathered in numbers, once their sight was set on the City of Northholm, it fell quickly, as none were prepared for an attack from the west.

Darcy's father was Knight Commander at Hallows Fort. He had been stationed there for the last ten years and in all that time Darcy had not seen him. Darcy only had word from the odd scout and trader that his father was still alive.

Darcy knew his father had work to do for the King, but that did not mean he had to like it. The Poles rarely went more than a few days without trying to breach the defenses of the Hanson Kingdom. Normally they came in small groups and each time they fought inhumanely and violently, as if they were possessed by demons.

It was Darcy's father, Sir Malcolm Dean who had to hold the line so that Oakenfall could remain free and have these celebrations — but that was the very reason there was no way that Darcy could find merriment in them.

A blast from another firework snapped Darcy from his thoughts and he watched it as it flowered into a bright blue lit up by the moon. Darcy took one last look at the dancing crowd and stepped back inside his father's noble home.

He wasn't in the mood for partying and he had been summoned by the King — Harvey Hanson III — to hold a private audience in the morning far earlier than he would have liked.

Darcy's family had not always been noble. For his service to the army, Darcy's father Malcolm had been granted several trading ships and a knighthood, and since he'd been away at Hallows Fort, Darcy had stepped in to be the steward of the fleet — a thankless task that seemed never ending even in these times of economic downturn.

Darcy hated the falseness of attending court at the best of times, but his mood was even less buoyant than usual tonight, because he feared that the King suspected him of withholding tithe… and to be fair, he had been.

Trading had been poor over the last few months but after the so-called "losses" from one of his ships around White Isle, Darcy had agreed to pay for safe passage out into the White Sea. Paying the pirates was an illegal act in theory but widely practiced. Very few ships made it out to the open ocean without their cargo being taken by the White Flags, unless they paid the illegal shipping tax.

The White Flags were fair pirates, if such a thing truly existed. Almost too fair and they had allies amongst the nobles of Oakenfall because of it. They wanted independence in the kingdom and the right to vote for whoever was in charge, rather than have a monarchial birthright which they viewed as barely different to Dragon rule.

The White Flags openly used the protection money and spoils to directly challenge the King. Because of this, submitting to piracy — that is, paying illegal taxation — had been declared as a crime against the Crown and could be punished by hanging.

As tired of his existence as he was, Darcy still hoped that he would not feel the coarse edge of the hangman's rope in the morning, although he did wonder if that would be preferable to continuing to manage the estate single-handed.

The stress of leading a fleet as large as his father's had become much more than he could tolerate. It was Darcy's opinion that, with wars on every front, the times had been bad for the city and if he didn't pay the pirates, then not enough cargo would get through the blockades to pay his men. It was no secret that much of the city had no love for their King and would not sail without pay. If they did not sail, then the King would get none of his tithe at all.

As he made his way from the balcony and shut the large maple door, Darcy resigned himself to his fate, whatever that might be and prayed that sleep would take him quickly. The room was dark and cold, but Darcy knew it well. He shuffled his feet slowly across the dark wooden floor taking in the chill of the moistened wood as he made his way towards the lavish but oddly uncomfortable bed.

The bed often felt damp with the sea not being far away, and the cold Nylar nights being a breeding ground for condensation. As Darcy sank into the biting iciness of the bed, he blew out the last remaining candle that rested inside a candle holder made of solid, beautifully engraved silver on the walnut bedside table that had once belonged to his grandfather.

Darcy pulled the silken and goose feather filled pillow over his head. He knew he would only get a few hours' sleep before his house maid awoke him — if he managed to sleep at all, between the drunken singing, explosions and the biting cold, that is.

Dawn came with light rain tapping on the dirty glass of the Dean Estate windows. The sound of the last die-hard revelers still celebrating outside could just be heard over the pitter-pattering of the raindrops on handblown glass. Darcy opened his eyes and his blurry vision settled on Granny's smiling old face.

Granny, as she was lovingly known, had been a servant in the Dean household since she was fifteen, when she'd started as a kitchen hand. She'd remained loyal and worked her fingers to leather and fifty-two years later she was head maid and as close to family as an employee can come. She was the closest thing Darcy had to a friend — or family, for that matter.

"Morning to you, dear," she said with a voice sounding worn out. "I've set you a bowl on your side table," she continued and even through the warble, Darcy could make out her normal caring tone.

Granny was a haggard old woman whose face closely resembled the side of a cliff covered in chalk that did little to hide how depleted she'd become.

Little wisps of hair poked out from her chin like disgusting oases in the desert. Her body was hunched from years of servitude, and her knees clicked like the loose wheels of a wagon, each time she moved. She was skinny, and her tattered clothes hung from her adding ten years to her appearance. To look at she was a crone in every sense of the word, but she had a heart of gold and her voice that had begun breaking with age still hinted at the sweetness, she must have carried her whole life.

"Hurry before it cools too much," she continued as she placed a plain teak bowl onto the dark walnut side table, and sloshed water down its side as usual.

Darcy pulled himself up the bed to rest his head against the headboard. The wood felt cold even through his long dark brown hair. He let his tired eyes focus on the room around him. It was typical for the grandeur of the estate and had remained unchanged since he was a young boy. The walls were covered with thick white clay that had turned yellowish in the sun of the brief summer months. All the furniture was made of similar dark woods, walnuts and stained oaks, that matched the hardwood floor. There was one island of warmth on the floor... a white and brown rug that was made of a series of sheepskins sown together and decorated to look like flowers. Small paintings by artists Darcy had never heard of cluttered the walls. Strange spiky plants brought in from far-off shores sat in vases scattered around, most of which had turned a strange brown color while desperately waiting the sunnier weather. The windows behind his bed let in hardly any light at the best of times, let alone as the cold days of Winnan gave way to the dark mornings of Nylar, the month of the great freeze.

Darcy didn't really know why he stayed in this room. It was one of the smaller ones in the house and the only one without a fireplace. His parents' room would have been far warmer and away from last night's noise, but even with their absence it would have felt wrong. Darcy was sure he must have first been put into this room as a punishment for something when he was young. There was no other explanation he could see for his being in such a bitterly cold room. His father had probably arranged for one of the maids to stick him there for a night or so as punishment. Then when his father had disappeared off to war Darcy had remained stuck in this *ninth level of hell* as he called it. As to why he still remained in it? Perhaps it suited his melancholy.

The room was a picture of beauty to look at but looks can be, and often are, misleading. Even with his disturbed sleep and tired mind the first thing to drop into it was his appointment with the King, and Darcy wanted to just pull the covers back over his head.

When Lady Elizabeth Dean, Darcy's mother, had been sent off overseas on diplomatic missions, Granny had become Darcy's guardian. She had been around the nobles of Oakenfall for long enough to have almost a better understanding of their twisted nature than the King himself, and even after ten years in charge of the estate Darcy still often sought her counsel.

"Granny, do you know where I put those shipping documents? I fear that the King will have questions about the drop in profits," Darcy said as he slid to the edge of the quilted white silken sheets.

The room remained silent as Darcy reached for the bowl Granny had left on the side table, washing away the sleep from the night before. He could not remember his dreams but the beads of sweat coating his face revealed that they had probably been restless nightmares brought on by stress and the noise of the fireworks and shouting from outside his window.

"They're in the library I believe, Sire. You had them with you when you were entertaining that rather plump gentleman from the Traders Guild," Granny said rather diplomatically for her. She was a woman who spoke her mind — so much so that Darcy always felt that his parents would have sacked her years ago for her impudence, if they had spent more time in the household. He however was personally quite fond of her eccentric little ways. She was old fashioned and spoke her mind to the point of being rude.

"Ah yes … I remember now. That's just one more thing to sort out, isn't it," he sighed. It seemed like he was always trying to balance spinning plates in a scrum of fat angry traders, metaphorically of course. "Granny, if the worst happens today and I don't return, the key for the safe is under the cushion of the older chair in the study," Darcy said as he slid on his chamber wear.

His outfit had been prepared by Granny, and was made up of a white silken shirt, red checked waist coat and black linen trousers. Darcy pulled the shirt tight up to his throat and suddenly felt considerably uncomfortable, as he saw the hangman's mask grinning down at him in his imagination. He shook the idea away as he slipped his feet into his sheepskin slippers. He had to remain confident — the King might not even have realized Darcy was giving away ten percent of his cargo to the White Flags.

"Don't be silly, Sire! You're coming home soon enough… and I moved that key a few weeks ago. I was fed up with the damn thing digging into my arse every time I sat there to darn your socks. It's under your mattress," Granny said with a sneaky smile showing her gapping teeth.

Granny knew that Darcy barely knew what was happening inside the estate and it had been the same for years. She was glad how things worked out, as they often allowed her to buy the best pork from the markets, rather than just cheap trotters or loin — and more than was needed at that. It allowed her to take some home and have some extra for the orphanage. The city was full of parentless children, casualties of war and the sad irony of it was that the children themselves were conscripted into the army as soon as they came of age. The men that is… the women, much like Granny would end up as servants.

"Do remember your place Granny," Darcy said, but he knew his warning held about as much weight as one from a starving field mouse.

When his words were met with a raised abundantly-bushy and white eyebrow, Darcy felt ill at ease — suddenly feeling like he was a seven-year-old again — and he followed up quickly with: "Right… yes… good to know the key is still safe, I suppose. Anyway, I'm not so sure Granny… I've just got a bad feeling about today."

Darcy took a brush to his long brown hair and tried to tame it. A trend had started to keep one's hair cut short, but Darcy rejected it. He could barely remember the face of his father, but he could remember his hair. They both shared long thick locks of it and Darcy grew his to keep a little of his father with him — not that he would ever admit that even to himself.

"You've always got a bad feeling about it," Granny said shrugging her shoulders in a blasé manner. "So, you're paying those pirates a few golds for a ship! At least they're getting out of the bloody harbor. Better that than being added to the reef. If His Majesty is that worried about people paying the White Flags, why doesn't he leave the poor elves alone and send those men to get back some order in the White Isle?" Granny remonstrated as she pulled up the sheets in a huff, making the bed behind Darcy.

She was one of the many people who disagreed with the war over the Alienage Isle. During the Blight, the time the dragons had ruled Neeska, a fleet of elves had docked on Alienage Isle and colonized it. They had helped heal and nurse many of the sick and wounded people during the later years of the Great War, but within one year of its end, King Harvey Hanson II (the current King's father) had grown envious of elven magic and their mystical forest and the resources the isle held, and declared war on the elves!

Most of the soldiers the King had sent to this war did not want to fight the people who'd saved their parents a few years before. This made for a slow battle and diplomatic stalemate that was still ongoing almost a century later! If you could say nothing else about the people of the Hanson Kingdom — they knew how to be persistent when it came to stupid grievances.

"I wish he'd call my father back from the front line and send him against the White Isle. At least he'd be closer to home," Darcy said staring into the oval mirror above his dresser table.

Although Darcy couldn't remember his father's face, he was almost his double. He shared the same slim yet square jaw that did not grow facial hair well, the same flat forehead and equally horizontal hairline. Darcy was well groomed and found time in his busy schedule to pluck his eyebrows into shape and oil his skin. He was after all a noble and did have to look the part. He was as far from rugged as you could get without wearing lipstick.

"Your father was never one for diplomacy, Sire. And I don't think even he could kill every pirate sailing the White Sea single-handedly."

Darcy suspected that Granny was right. The war with the White Flags would need to be settled with words not swords. If the Hanson Kingdom openly attacked them, they could disperse and once again sail under hundreds of different flags. At least while they were under the banner of the White Flag some lives were being saved. The White Sea was a harsh mistress.

"Don't forget to take a coat, Sire. The gods are trying to clear the sky of smoke and the streets of drunkards with that downpour," Granny said flicking a scrawny finger towards the windows which showed black outside, as if the sun itself had been dowsed by the rain.

The view from the Dean Estate was not the best in the city but normally they could at least overlook the street below. With the rain now falling hard and the sky so dark, the light creeping in from the corridor outside Darcy's room hit the window and turned the glass into a shifting mirror of wetness.

"You're probably right at that," Darcy said with a smile.

Some of the sadness from the night before had faded from him and he felt a little more lighthearted, but he could not remember when he'd last been completely happy — if he had ever been — but it was hardest for him during times of celebration.

Darcy wanted for nothing. His home was lavishly decorated and he had servants for almost any eventuality, but he was still miserable most of the waking day. His tasks of managing the fleet and estate meant he did not often get to leave the family home. His mother came and went from one baronetcy to another. She was often away for months at a time doing the diplomatic work that his father would have done during times of peace, but was unable to because of the never-ending battle against the Poles.

Darcy's father had been gone for so long that if it wasn't for the fact that Darcy was an almost exact copy of him, he would not have remembered what his father had looked like. As it was, he was told almost daily by someone how similar to his father he looked. The only portrait of Sir Dean in the estate had been painted before Darcy was even born and hung in the main chamber. Visiting guests to the estate often mistook it for Darcy, and he had grown so accustomed to it, that he didn't even bother correcting their mistake.

Somehow Granny's rather unique view of the kingdom made things seem a little easier. He loved her visits and would employ her just to sit and chat with him when he finally took over the estate for himself. He would sell off some of the ships, sell the townhouse and buy something smaller and more relaxed and have time to make friends. At least that was his dream for when the day came... it would be his home and not his fathers. That was not today though, and Darcy braced himself to face the King.

The streets of Oakenfall were filled with litter from the previous night's celebrations. Ribbons and confetti clogged the drainage ditches and the Dunny Men had not yet cleared the sewerage floating in the many canals intersecting the main roads.

The severe rain that had been pouring down for the last few hours had quickly begun to flood the streets and made the silvery-stone cobbles even more treacherously slippery than usual. Darcy almost tripped as an empty bottle sailed under his feet on a torrent of water, before it bounced off his shoe and rushed down towards the harbor with a satisfying splash as it leapt off the brink of a stairwell on a makeshift waterfall.

Oakenfall was the largest city in Northern Neeska. The next closest in size was Northholm but even that was a mile or so smaller. Oakenfall was a trading hub and had been even in the time of the Blight. It had been built on a very distinctive ridge which ran almost directly downhill towards the harbor, jutting out past the many canals on carved natural rock formations.

The many canals and sloping hills allowed it to be an unusually clean city. All the waste was washed downhill and out to sea. Sailors often jested that the White Sea should be renamed because of the sewage that filled their ocean path. It was probably the reason the nobles had placed themselves at the far western edge at the top of the hill.

The City of Oakenfall was made up of very distinct districts, the first of which was the castle at the top of the hill, which was surrounded by raised mounds of earth and a natural pool that came from an underground spring and fed the canals. Along the main road running north-east from the castle gate down to the sea were the other districts. At its upper end were the homes of the nobles and rich traders. These were large stone buildings made of brilliant white slabs of rock. They had once been extensively decorated and sculpted. In previous times, many of them outshone the grandeur of the castle, but now they were shabby from heavy wear.

Just a gnat's breath further towards the harbor were the markets and Celebration Square — a hub of eastern architecture, domes, statues, and waterfalls — which had sprung up towards the end of the dragon's reign.

Further north were the common homes, simple wooden houses, some multi-story, some tenements, all of them held together with shoestring and prayers.

The city as it was now seemed to have been built almost in two. The parts south of the market were all stone and tall and had been there since before the end of the Blight. Most of them had once sported gargoyles of dragons and other statues honoring the human's masters — the great black dragons — but these had mostly been hacked off at the end of the war, giving the nobles' homes an almost weathered look that particularly seemed to please the pigeon population that had colonized the area.

The width of the streets showed the city's dragon heritage. The noble part of the city had large streets wide enough for dragons, but the closer to the docks you went, the thinner the streets got as only human slaves lived there, but even at their thinnest there were still several yards between both curbs. The roadways of the noble district were far wider than needed for just carts to rattle on by — they'd allowed the huge beasts to easily walk or even take off without trouble. The common and most eastern parts of the city were built after the Blight and therefore did not need to be have been made of stone. Instead hundreds of little wooden houses had popped up.

The wide streets had been broken into tiny side alleys and were often changing as dictated by the harbor. For as long as Darcy could remember barely a month had passed in which a hovel wasn't left empty — its family moving to another part of the town — so wax could be shipped out or spices shipped in. One week, a smithy would be on the eastern road — the next week, the building would be filled with apple cider being stored on its transit across the world.

At the city's furthest point was the harbor itself made up of warehouses, stores and strange empty buildings that were torn down and put back up in obscure positions to assist with trade. The effect was like picking up a forest of trees and dropping it randomly into the shadows. The harbor area was dark, damp and desolate, home to the city's unfortunates. It was commonly said that all shit was swept towards the harbor — and that did not just refer to sewage.

Moving away from poverty towards the noble district was Celebration Square. It sat at the heart of the city and was a stark contrast to the city's degenerate parts. It had once been the site of the temple where the first born chosen by the dragons were offered up in sacrifice to feed the dragons. There is still a rumor in the city that a huge labyrinth was built below the temple for entertaining the dragons and housing their gold and slaves, but no sign of this had been found since the end of the 800 Years War. Only rumor and unspecified books hinted at a lost entrance, though it is said that some of the cellars of nobles' homes had breached parts of the maze and hundreds of would-be-adventurers had gone missing in the darkness hunting for the lost treasure.

Celebration Square — as it ended up being known as — had been used as a hospital during the 800 Years

War and had seen thousands of dead and dying. When the Great War ended the crypts were closed and the temple was torn down, and in its place statues of war heroes were erected. It was a place of worship and remembrance for the people.

The gleaming green marble of the Square looked black in the morning rain and already people were out clearing the trash from around the statues.

Darcy left his estate at the very edge of the noble district. The hill that climbed up from his home to the castle was awash with water and forced him to shield his face from the splatter. It was only a matter of passing three other estates and a small alleyway before Darcy reached the palace walls, but with the steep slope and heavy rain it was a hard slug that left him soaked.

On reaching the palace wall Darcy looked back across the city while catching his breath and turning away from the rain. His hair was stuck to his head in heavy locks. His white shirt was almost transparent, and he felt as if someone somewhere — one of the many gods — was having a laugh at his expense.

He looked back over the city and could just make out the mast of the *Cassandra,* his father's flagship at the dock. It had been due to leave a week before with supplies for Port Lust, but the King had requested it be halted in the docks for repair and improvements. This was something Darcy knew meant that he would be losing it from his fleet in the battle against the Poles.

It had become common practice for the King to claim ships from nobles to use in the war. Very few ever returned and even fewer nobles were compensated for the loss. Most of the battle was being fought at the two forts on the Briers Hills, but after years of stalemate King Harvey Hanson and taken to using ships to blast Northholm directly from the ocean — a tactic that was as pointless as it was costly, but Darcy knew the King had to be seen to be doing something to reclaim Northholm, or lose what little respect he still had with the people of Oakenfall.

King Harvey was not a loved figurehead. He led by the luck of birth, rather than any man's choice. He couldn't afford to give the White Flags any more ammunition to use against him in their propaganda campaign or it would surely lead to civil war.

A small glimmer of hope passed through Darcy's mind. It might just be that the King would announce that Darcy was down to five ships now, as he would be losing the *Cassandra*. It was a long shot, but it was better than thinking of the alternative. If anything, it would be easier for Darcy if the King reclaimed all six ships, he'd given the Dean family — hell he might even suggest it!

Darcy passed through the pitted walls of the outer keep. The walls had once been filled with precious gems and stones, but King Harvey had issued the command to remove them all to inflate his treasury and fund the battle against the Poles — a decision that had outraged the city.

The huge stone walls blocked a lot of the rain and let Darcy raise his head for the first time since stepping outside his front door. The guards inside the courtyard looked a little worse for wear and Darcy could tell that even they had enjoyed a few strong ales during the night's celebration.

Darcy had to fight the urge to smirk at the sight of rain dripping off their noses poking out from below their steel helmets. The wobbly guards made Darcy wonder as he passed through the large garden courtyard, whether he really was the only person who did not feel up to celebrating. It seemed like that, when one of the guards who was patrolling the perimeter tried grabbing the wall unsuccessfully to keep his balance, before he fell over with a splat into what Darcy presumed was a cold puddle by the way he leapt back up with a curse and shot a look at Darcy that could kill.

Fighting even harder not to laugh Darcy busied his mind. He'd been the castle a few times in recent months and one thing he had noticed was that the castle was built poorly in the traditional defensive sense. The walls were weak, and the gateway would take only a few men to be breached. The inner courtyard was huge and seemed a massive waste of space. There was no internal well or storehouse per se. The actual tower keep poked up and had few windows, but its roof was raised almost a floor higher than its walls, clearly showing who it had been built for. It had not needed to be massively strong or defendable, as it would have been home to the Dragon Lord. It only needed to have a large courtyard for stocking livestock, or slaves, or both, and a large raised roof to let the beast easily fly into its throne room.

Once inside the keep and after an annoyingly long wait in a small and dusty private room, Darcy was summoned to the throne room. He remembered being struck by how unimpressive it was, when he'd first been called to there in his father's absence.

The room was huge but very bare — another sign that at one time it would have been the lair of a Dragon Lord. The entrance corridor opened into the throne room, a vast rectangle easily the width of a large galleon and of about the same height.

The roof high above was supported by massive beams that ran between the window frames. The craftsmanship and style almost looked Dwarfish even after years of neglect. The pillars holding up the roof would have been decorated with dragon propaganda once, but they had been chiseled down to within an inch of their lives.

Darcy wondered for a moment where all the mounds of destroyed dragon sculpting had been piled. Was there a hill somewhere outside town full of dragon heads and broken wings, or were they all kept down in the dungeon?

The throne was not stone or precious metal as you might expect but plain and wooden — not the grand or comfortable throne you would assume for royalty. It looked like it didn't get all that much use either. It had obviously been brought in after the collapse of the Dragon Empire and had started to show signs of aging. It was yet another reminder about Oakenfall's unstable economy. Oddly, it reminded Darcy of the chairs from the class he had attended as a boy.

The huge windows that ran around above holding up the roof had been filled in with glass, but at one time they would have been open to allow the dragons to come and go easily. Now the only access point to the roof-top ramparts was one small trap door in the roof and a sturdy metal ladder.

The only real object of note, apart from the throne, was a table that was set in the middle of the room. This in contrast to the abandoned feel of the rest of the space showed signs of excessive wear and the aged wood seemed to creak and moan as if it held a life of its own.

The legs of the table didn't match; two seemed to be pine, one was some dark wood that remained a mystery, and the last looked like cedar. You could tell at a glance that the table had taken a few beatings over the years. Its top had been painted to be an exact replica of Northern Neeska and tiny — almost child-like — toy soldiers were scattered across its top.

The paint of the now Scorched Lands had flaked and peeled off in places. It did not take a detective's mind to realize that this table had been used for at least some of the Great War to plan the human campaign against the dragons.

King Harvey was standing next to the table with a stern and worn-out face which strangely seemed to match the tired and aged wood around him. His skin was dry and flaky, just like the tabletop, and deep red, almost purple, signaling a heavy drinker. However, he seemed strong on his feet for an older man, and beneath the layers of quilted clothing and fat a strong man could possibly be hiding.

Harvey barely looked up as Darcy timidly approached. He had a lot on his mind and was distracted as he stared at the table in front of him, with his leather-like hand hovering above different playing pieces on the miniature Neeska.

Darcy tried to calm himself by making Harvey seem less scary, which was easy since Harvey looked strangely like a fruit in his orange and red fleece with his deep red tights poking out the bottom. His rotund build only added to the fruity mirage. It gave him the appearance of an old and oddly angry, if somewhat squashed, tangerine. Darcy had to bite his lip not to chuckle to himself once again. With the guard toppling over and these fruity thoughts maybe today wouldn't be as bad as he'd thought. If nothing else, it gave him something to talk to Granny about that evening.

When a minute had passed, and Harvey had still not even acknowledged Darcy's entrance, Darcy became more and more uncomfortable. The fruit-like fantasy could only go so far in calming his mind. He nervously looked down towards his feet and could see the fading color in the floor around the base of the table.

The dark wood had been worn almost white from the current — and no doubt previous— King's almost constant wandering around. Darcy had only had a few meetings with the King in all his time as steward for the

Dean Estate, but he had the impression that the constant threat of war had left Harvey more than a little unhinged.

The King was a man obsessed. That was the reason the city was in the poor state it was. Any profits made from the rich trade routes were piled into the soldiers and wasted bloodshed that Darcy's father sat in the middle of. Darcy was one of the few people in the city who believed that, in his own way, the King did mean well for his people.

"Ah, Young Darcy! Welcome!" Harvey said when he finally realized he was not alone in the room, and sent a rather weak smile in Darcy's direction before turning back to his obsession, the table.

After another ten or more uncomfortable seconds of Harvey just staring blankly at the table, he suddenly remembered Darcy was there and continued, "Come closer and tell me what you see here," while pointing towards an area to the far south of Northern Neeska, the Scorched Lands, or in this case the small and poorly painted tabletop version of them.

The area in question was a point on the board that still had some faded green paint to simulate the hills and mountains, unlike the real world which now lay in ruin. The Scorched Land had once been part of the Hanson Kingdom. Back before the time of the dragons, it had once held several villages and a lot of Neeskan farmlands — but that was before the war with the dragons. Now the once green and fertile land, which had taken the name of the Scorched Lands, looked like hell itself.

The ground was black with ash and scorched bone, both humanoid and draconian. The stone houses and towns that had survived the blazes remained empty... a stark and ghostly scene. A few of the large trees that had not been completely turned to ash stood out as singed stubs which bony fingers clawing at the sky. No plant seemed to want to grow within the shifting clouds of ash and even the birds flew around it, hundreds of miles away from their migration routes, rather than risk the chocking black clouds of ash. Only a handful of crazed adventures or outlaws dared to try to call the place home and no one ever heard again from those who'd walked too deep into its ashen landscape.

The Scorched Lands split the very continent in two very distinct halves and the map on the table showed a time that no one alive remembered. A time before the breeze that blew from the southwest carried the stench of death.

Because of its greenery, it took a naive Darcy a moment of staring at the table to recognize the land. He'd never left the city and had only seen it on maps in his downtime within his library. This looked very different.

"They're the Scorched Lands, I think. Why do you ask?" Darcy asked as he moved closer to Harvey. Darcy was a little taken aback by the strange question. He had no idea what this had to do with him — unless the Poles had made a move into those lands, and maybe the King planned for him to follow in his father's footsteps and set up a fort to hold them in a stalemate there. Darcy sighed internally… well that was better than the gallows, but barely.

"Why do I ask?" Harvey said looking up at Darcy, as if it should have made perfect sense.

Harvey Hanson was a history buff. When he wasn't sending men to their needless deaths in battle, he was studying the history of his ancestors. The Hansons were the ones who'd started the rebellion against the dragon's rule and sparked the 800 Years War.

"What do you know about the last dragon that fell?" Harvey asked, as he playfully pushed a figure from Oakenfall towards the middle of the map. Darcy was surprised he hadn't noticed it before, as the sculpture was very out of place on the board. It was an elegant stone statue about the size of a fist depicting a dragon in flight. Its flat and misshapen back showed that it had probably belonged on a wall or maybe even one of the pillars from inside the throne room before it was broken off.

"Not all that much Your Majesty. I was never really a history enthusiast," Darcy said, fixated on the dragon. "It seems to depend which book you read as to what really happened. Half of it is badly remembered, and the other half is fantasy, I'm sure," Darcy paused as he watched Harvey prodding the sculpture with his finger and rocking it back and forth. When the King gave no reply, the pressure grew too much for Darcy to cope with. "Sire, I must ask. What does this have to do with me?"

"Why be in such a rush to get to that point, Darcy. Anyone would think you don't feel comfortable in the presence of your King," Harvey said looking away from the table and at Darcy with a smile that oozed with confidence. If the conversation had been a poker match Harvey would have had a handful of aces, whereas Darcy would have been lucky with a high two.

"We'll get to your part in this in just a moment, Darcy. For now, I'll tell you a little story. That is unless you have to be elsewhere maybe?" Harvey asked, but Darcy could sense he was not expecting an answer. It seemed he was right, when almost without taking breath Harvey carried on talking. "No, quite as I thought. Do remember! You're only busy by my say so," as he adjusted the rim of his cloth crown.

Darcy, as uneasy as he felt, took some solace in how ridiculous that hat really was. It was stupidly big and surrounded by white down feathers. It looked as if one of the seagulls from the dock had decided to set up nest on the red peak that was Harvey's head. Fruit and seagulls — if Harvey had even suspected what was going through Darcy's mind, he'd have ended up in a dungeon for sure... or worse.

Completely unaware of the disdain his guest felt for his taste in clothes Harvey carried on with his monologue: "Out of all the different accounts of the Great War the story I like the best is the one which says that when the last dragon fell, he knew that the reign of the Dragon Lords ended with him. He was after all the biggest and strongest of their brood."

Darcy wondered if Harvey saw himself in the same light as this all-powerful Dragon Lord. The way he'd said it, it seemed so — biggest maybe, Darcy thought to himself while growing more and more disillusioned with Harvey.

Still unaware of the belittling his nervous guest was conducting within his own mind, Harvey continued telling his story, his hand never leaving the white stone of the miniature dragon.

"You realize Darcy that he had once occupied this very castle until he was forced out by my family?" Harvey said sidetracking a little from his story. "We pushed them back to the mountains; thousands died, but because of my ancestors the dragon's lordship was finally ended; and when the ballistas began dropping dragons out of the sky like leaves, the last dragon summoned up all the power he could. He literally sucked the magic out of the mages fighting him." Harvey continued pushing the small stone fragment around the board fighting imaginary people on the board below.

Darcy could not help but notice the obsession in Harvey's eyes. This was a battle that had happened sixty-five years before the King was even born, but in that moment, Darcy was sure Harvey thought that little board was the battlefield from a century ago. Darcy wondered if the King had finally snapped. Rumors were ripe among the nobles that the stress had finally pushed him over the edge, but all this dragon talk confirmed it. Harvey had been waging war with every other kingdom since he was old enough to lead, and now it seemed he wanted to start a war with the dragons that had all died over a hundred years before!

As if unaware of the questioning eyes on him Harvey continued his tale: "When the mages' power failed, the sky itself turned red with ash and forced the power deep down inside the beast. The bards say that the Dragon King shone hot white like steel on a smith's anvil. He'd planned to crash into the earth and release this power all at once to shatter the whole continent into nothing more than sand to wash up onto distant shores," Harvey said smashing the stone figure onto the board and denting the wood with an almighty thud that sent Darcy stepping back in shock.

After yet another dramatic pause, Harvey continued. "If the Dragon Lords couldn't have the land, then no one would," he stated, the excitement in his tired eyes as evident as the nose on his face.

Darcy was not sure what scared him more — the King seemingly trying to re-live a moment like that from the past, or viewing himself in the same light as the dragon. Would the King really destroy Neeska, rather than admit the Poles had won!? Darcy almost wished he had been called in for the White Flag tax. At least he knew how that would end, whereas, the King's story — the passion in his cold eyes — scared Darcy. He half expected him to leap from a window and try to take flight... or tell Darcy that the city was about to be set ablaze.

Harvey now cupped the dragon stature in both hands and bent down over it, as if he could see something in it that Darcy could not. "It would have worked too, but as the dragon began to dive towards the ground the Arch Mage cast a spell so powerful that it cost him his own life. From the very peak of the Mages Tower he sacrificed himself to freeze the dragon solid. Its body crashed into the earth and turned to a frosty powder. Nothing remained of it. There was no trace of the beast in the ruins of the battlefield," Harvey said and finally let go of the dragon. Turning to face Darcy now that the battle was over, he seemed more present — more aware of the room around him.

"Do you understand magic, Darcy?" Harvey asked.

"No Sire, and I still don't see what this has to do with me… I am no mage," Darcy said trying not to be rude — not to risk his neck — but desperate to either get answers or get out of what had started as an uncomfortable meeting and had been rapidly getting worse.

"Magic uses power; it takes energy, practice and strength. It is no different to muscle. If you over-stretch yourself, you need to rest. Some say the Arch Mage must have made a deal with demons for us to win the war, as that was the only way a mortal could summon that kind of power. They say it took the power of a demon pouring through the Mage to freeze the dragon and that was why the Mage died," Harvey said getting out of breath, as the excitement was too much for his keg-shaped body.

Darcy thought Harvey might stop but he didn't. Instead Harvey collected a second small figure from the middle of the map, this time a little tin painted human from the area around the Mages Tower and pushed it towards the Scorched Lands.

Struggling for breath Harvey continued with sweat forming on his forehead. "Anyway, they're all things you can read in a history book. I'm sure your library is full of them with what I pay your family," Harvey said this time not bothering to look around.

There was that dig again. Darcy knew the King well enough to know the conversation was drawing to an end. When Harvey began using threats you knew it was nearly the point in time when he'd ask you politely what he wanted you to do.

"What they don't tell you is that the Dragon Heart didn't lose its power. The magic the dragon summoned was too strong to dissipate and when the beast crashed into the ashen ground and shattered, the Heart was freed. It's buried, lost in the Scorched Lands and is still there somewhere. The mages knew this, but they kept it secret. After all it could still destroy whole region of Neeska in the wrong hands," Harvey said, and Darcy couldn't help but think that those wrong hands were most likely Harvey's.

"So, they left it. They destroyed all records of its survival — well most of them. You see the King at the time, my great grandfather kept a diary of his own. So, I know it's still there," Harvey said pressing a hand against his rotund chest.

For a moment Darcy thought the excitement had become too much and Harvey was going to keel over — that was until he noticed the outline of what looked like a book under Harvey's fleece. Harvey and his father had sold off most of the kingdom in their two reigns to pay for the ongoing war. Whatever it was in that book must have been worth a fortune in sentimental value, or it would have been traded long ago. Taking his hand away from the hidden pages Harvey carried on with his sermon: "At the time it would have been a bad thing to fall into anyone's hands, but I think now is as good a time as any to get it, before all the magic leaks out from it, that is. Although it was too strong to disperse, it will have weakened over time I'm guessing." Harvey paused and looked at Darcy expectantly.

"I'm sorry Your Majesty but I still don't see what this has to do with me. I thought you'd called me here about the *Cassandra*," Darcy said no longer caring why he was summoned, but still not wanting to mention the White Flags needlessly. Harvey seemed unhinged enough as it was.

"The *Cassandra*?" Harvey said wrinkling his fat forehead. "Oh, your father's ship. Yes, well I suppose that will be used in this slightly. As you know we are at war with the Poles and have been for some time," Harvey walked towards Darcy and leant in close.

Darcy tried to pull back away from the smell of gingivitis, but Harvey leant in further. Darcy could feel the fat man's belly pressing against him and wondered if there was any way he could feel any more uncomfortable. He hazarded a guess he would feel less worried wearing a dress on a long sea voyage with a crew of nymphomaniacs.

"What I tell you now Darcy cannot leave the throne room. I will hold you to this under threat of death," Harvey said. He coughed and waved a hand towards the exit. The two burly guards by the entrance hall took their leave. Darcy suddenly felt very alone. Yes, he would feel a lot safer on the before-mentioned ship.

"Your Majesty, you're scaring me," Darcy said. The hangman's noose would probably be the easiest thing to come out of this meeting. Darcy had heard rumors trickling through the noble district that the King had been asking nobles to do strange things as of late — and that many of them had never returned… or those that did were often found dead in their beds a few nights after their return to the city. Whatever the King wanted from him, Darcy knew he had no choice… saying *no* would be suicide.

"The coffers are empty Darcy… we're spent. The city barely has the funds to hold Briers Hill for another month. If that falls, then it will only be a matter of weeks before the Poles fall against our city and how long do you think we can hold out against them?" Harvey paused, not expecting an answer.

"The city was not built for war. We do not have walls around it and those around the keep are damn near falling over without cannon fire. We do not have the people stationed here to hold them back. The Poles would march straight into the throne room." Harvey dramatically knocked over the soldier pieces placed on Oakenfall.

"So Darcy, you see we cannot hold out. I am not a fool. I know the people are sick of war. They have lost respect for what my family did for them. Once a few weeks' pay doesn't reach the soldiers at Briers Hill most will turncoat and join the Poles."

"My father would never —" Darcy started but was cut short. It seemed Harvey was in no mood for listening.

"We need the Dragon Heart. With it we can push the Poles back and reclaim Northholm and the mines close to it. Not to mention the trade possibilities! The disunited barbarians would crumble, and we could reunite trade with them. It is our only hope of bringing gold back into our coffers," Harvey said whispering the words, so inquisitive ears in the corridor outside the throne room could not hear them.

"I still don't understand what this has to do with me. My father is the knight, not I… and I know nothing of archaeology, so what use would I be in finding the Heart?" Darcy asked. He could understand that the Heart might turn the tide of battle — its power could be used to destroy some of the Pole army — but why Harvey had called him in was still a mystery.

"I need someone I can trust to travel to the Mages Tower. We'll need their magic to find the Heart. The Scorched Lands are about sixty miles square. Just hunting blind would take years and we're pushed for weeks … a month at most," Harvey paused and wiped sweat from his forehead.

"If I am honest young Master Dean, you were not my first choice, but times have grown dire indeed. I doubt you will be back before word gets out that the city is bankrupt, so I need something to offer the people. I would normally summon your father, but he is the only man I trust to hold out at Briers Hill and by time he got here, it might be too late." Harvey paused and looked back to the board.

"Unlike the rest of those dogs, he won't just swap sides because the coin stops, and hopefully enough men will be loyal to him that it will buy us extra time." Harvey backed away from Darcy and leant against a nearby window.

"Your ships will be claimed to launch a lasting attack against Northholm to keep the Poles busy. Hopefully it will buy you more time while you travel to the Mages Tower. With any luck the Poles will pull some of their men back from Briers Hill to defend Northholm meaning that there would be fewer battles at Briers Hill. That should mean there's more time your father's men can hold out."

"Do I have any say in this?" Darcy asked hopefully, but he already knew he didn't. Harvey wasn't known as a man of gray — it was always black or white. You either did what he wanted, or you didn't do much at all… apart from maybe make some worms fat.

"Do any of us have any say in times like this Darcy? I don't think you understand what will happen when people realize the coffers are empty. The city will tear itself apart.

"Look Darcy, I picked you as your family has always given their all for the service of the kingdom. Your grandfather fought in the Great War and your father has been fighting the Poles for as long as I can remember. Your mother is off polishing some posh foreigner somewhere to make trade easier and maybe save the city in her own way. I had hoped after the sheltered life you'd been given by them, that you might want to make a name for yourself. Not to mention that, if you're swift enough, you might even be in time to save your father," Harvey said, with spittle forming on his lips. He was controlling his anger but barely. Darcy knew he would have to watch his words carefully if he wanted to avoid the dungeon.

"What about the estate here?" Darcy asked, hoping that might be his saving grace and he could stay.

"The ships will be claimed until this damnable war is over, and the housekeepers can manage the running of the estate. I know normally that if a household is left man-less it will be returned to the kingdom's estate, but you have my word it will remain in your mothers' occupancy.

"Look Darcy, my time is scarce. This is a simple mission and will possibly save the blasted kingdom. At dawn in two days' time a caravan will leave, and you'll be on it as a diplomat. All you have to do is carry a letter to the Head Mage at the Tower.

"Now if you'll excuse me, I have an appointment with the Tax Office at the harbor. More ships haven't been paying their full tithe." Harvey turned from his window and with a look that more than confirmed his next few words, and froze Darcy to the spot. "Oh yes, if you keep this between you and me Darcy, your ship receipts might get lost when you return… there's been a lot of rain damage after all."

This was something Darcy could have done without. Any chance he had at talking his way out of the harsh travel across the rough roads to the Mages Tower was gone.

"Your will is my command," Darcy said with a bow as he turned and made for the throne room exit.

Once outside the castle walls Darcy stopped, his stomach was churning… he needed to rest. Standing in the cold wind and drizzle Darcy thought back over what he'd just heard.

The kingdom couldn't run for more than a few days without gold and if that news became common knowledge it would give the White Flags the ammunition they needed to finally over-throw centuries of monarchy and replace it with the republic they wanted. After all, the treasury on White Isles was plump and bloated with stolen cargo. Darcy had been raised to respect the monarchy, as it had led the battle against the dragons. However, in his experience, it seemed that King Harvey put his own needs before those of the kingdom. The high tax increases and the almost weekly introduction of new laws, blackmail and new battle plans against one or other of the other races inhabiting the North of Neeska had started to make him wonder if handing power over to the White Flags wouldn't be such a bad thing.

But the civil war that would rage would take many lives and weeks, or years to settle down. During that time the Poles would raid the city. Darcy shook those thoughts from his mind — he couldn't think of them or he'd be overwhelmed. He'd been saying for weeks that he wanted the stress of running the estate taken away from him, but he didn't realize he would be freed from one hellish duty by being given something even worse.

With the rain at his back Darcy staggered home in shock. The next two days were filled with rushed packing and trips to the market.

Oakenfall market was something to behold. Traders came from as far away as Lashkar Gah to the north and even the Greenstone Isles of the Tropical Bounding to the east. They traded in everything from fruit and vegetables to weird animals and brightly-colored and noisy birds. None of these interested Darcy now, as he was searching for the essentials he would need for his journey.

Darcy had never been further than the city gates. Even though he was strictly speaking in command of a small fleet of ships, he had never been out to sea, so he was completely petrified of the journey ahead of him. His dreams, or rather nightmares, were filled with endless plains, walking around lost, barbarian raiding parties and battles.

A knock at the bedroom door awoke Darcy. He opened his eyes and they blurred into darkness. It was around an hour before dawn and the rain outside had flared up again. It seemed as if it had barely stopped since the celebrations. The season of Winnan, the freeze, wanted to stake its last claim before some brighter days started creeping in. They were now a few days into Nylar, the first month of the Brilanka Calendar, and known as the planting. These were the months when warmer weather started to walk out over Neeska, but it looked like it would be late this year.

The knock came again and this time the door slid open slowly. Granny walked in carrying the same wooden wash bowl as always at arm's length. Darcy noticed that for an old woman she still had a lot of strength. Her arms barely shook and the water inside the bowl was as still as a mill pond, which is more than could be said for the sea outside. Darcy could hear the waves crashing against the docks even from this distance. He could make out the sounds of ships struggling in the harbor with the ropes tethering them straining and creaking. The preparations had begun, and the fleet of trading ships had been emptied of all but the essentials. The smiths at the harbor were loading them with iron balls and shot instead.

Granny placed the bowl down next to the bed and reached inside her gown, which Darcy noticed was extra woolly today and lined with thick wolf fur. The weather outside must be truly bitter, as the old woman seldom seemed to feel the cold. From her inner pocket Granny pulled out two small sticks that she clicked together. They gave off a warming yellow light that slowly filled the room.

Because of the shortage of wood in Northern Neeska the mages had begun making flash sticks. They enchanted two small sticks with the essence of fire and when put together they gently released light much like a roaring fire would but using much less wood. Since the Scorched Land covered most of Northern Neeska, wood was rarer than it had once been. That was the reason for first invading the elven lands of Alienage. They were some of the very few people who could grow a thick forest of strong wood, since most of the country's woodland had been obliterated by the Scorched Lands.

The fire sticks lit the room better than a candle and warmed it better than a fire. It wasn't long before the chill faded from the room and by the time Granny returned for the second time with a steaming mug to ward off the last of the cold, it didn't feel all that bad at all. It was a shame the traders from the Tower didn't bring many to the city, as Darcy would have kept them burning permanently in his room, if they weren't always running out of them. After the usual morning routine of waking up, Darcy turned to Granny.

"Granny do you think you'll be alright with this place alone?" Darcy asked as he slurped a hot mug of milk. He asked the question purely out of nicety, because anyone who knew the Dean Estate at all, knew that Granny ran it. She would be glad of the rest if anything. Darcy imagined her with her feet up in his slippers flicking through the many books that lined the library enjoying some well-deserved time off.

"Sire, my life will be a darn sight easier with the house empty," Granny said bluntly but with a smile. Servant as she was, she still needed to stamp her authority over the Deans sometimes and this seemed as good a time as any. Granny wanted Darcy to remember he couldn't do without her. Afterall, she was getting old and it would not be long before she could not carry out the tasks, she was required to do, and the Deans would be looking for a new head maid. Before that happened, Granny had to make sure she would be looked after in her old age and not left to rot away on bread and water. "This isn't really about me anyway, is it?" she continued, shaking the image from her mind of the spinster sitting alone in her dank little hovel by the harbor.

"I do care for you Granny," Darcy replied lamely. "But no, I guess not. I am just scared," Darcy admitted, both to himself and to her.

"There's nothing to be scared about out there. You'll be travelling with a well-armed caravan and from here to Briers Hill. The scariest thing you'll face is the odd roaming wolf pack and as long as you stick to the roads, they avoid them anyway," Granny said as she made the bed… looking quite like an old wolf herself in that coat, what with her gray hair hanging over it.

"I guess you're right, although I hope we don't get to see any wolves. Sir Mel's dog scares me enough and that thing is supposedly tame," Darcy said before he finished off the last of the warm mug and placed it next to his wash bowl. "We'll be gone for just over a fortnight. It'll take just under three days to reach Briers Hill, where the caravan will unload and another day to reach the Tower. I'm not planning to be there long," Darcy said and then pulled his shirt on and buttoned it up to the neck.

"Just how is it you know about the road anyway?" Darcy asked, partly interested and halfheartedly just trying to prolong the time before he left.

He wasn't sure what he was most scared of — the trip itself or meeting his father after so long. It had taken just over a day for Darcy to realize that he would be stopping in Briers Hill just west of Hallow Fort, where his father was stationed but as soon as he had, his nerves had flared. He knew he shouldn't be scared about seeing his father — they were family after all —but it had been so long that the man was a stranger to him now. He had even thought about sneaking through without taking the time out to see him… but then, if what the King said was true? It might be his last chance.

"I haven't always been in Oakenfall, Darcy. I only came here when I was fifteen. Your Grandfather hired, well saved me really from a group of slavers heading in from the Western Reaches," Granny said openly, though Darcy could tell she hesitated.

"So, you were a slave. I'm sorry to hear that. I wish I could do something," Darcy said with the almost automatic response people had whenever they heard the word "slave."

"Do you, Sire? Being a slave and a servant isn't all that different," Granny said as she picked the empty mug back up. "I was relatively happy. I grew up travelling around the Reaches. I got to see a lot of wonderful things — some terrible, but that's part of life. Female slaves have a rough time of it in the most civil parts of the world let alone out in a barbarian camp," Granny said, and a cold mask fell over her face, and Darcy could guess what she meant even with his sheltered upbringing.

"You were… are a Pole then?" Darcy said trying desperately to relieve the awkward feeling that had flooded the room.

"We weren't called Poles back then. I was a slave to the barbarians, but aye, basically that's right, Sire. Don't worry I don't plan to murder you in your sleep! That's something the people here forget. The Poles aren't some two headed dragons just looking to eat children. We're people too… trying to improve our lives. A lot of the Western Reaches are mountains, so there is not much in the way of plains for growing food and becoming civilized. That's why they're heading this way I think. Anyway, I was just lucky to have been bought by your grandfather," Granny said, and Darcy saw her almost sag slightly in the dim light of the bedroom. She was old and always had a slight sagginess and a hump, but this conversation seemed to remind her of just how much she had aged.

"I'm... I'm sorry, Granny," Darcy said. He didn't know what he was sorry the most for — the fact he had known Granny for the whole of his twenty-seven years and had never bothered to find out more about her, or the fact that he now had.

"I told you what I'm being sent for, didn't I?" Darcy said changing the subject.

"I know, Sire. It'll destroy a lot of the Poles, but I've been here for so long I don't know if anyone I knew is still alive. If they'd got hold of it, they would have done the same to you. It's in our nature it seems. I sometimes wonder if things wouldn't be better under the dragons," Granny said as she helped secure a fine fur satchel to Darcy's back.

"Look lad, I'll see you in a couple of weeks. Get going before you miss the bloody caravan and I have the King prancing in here with his dirty boots. I take pride in these floors you know," Granny joked, and they said their goodbyes.

Chapter Two – An Unwitting Buffoon

While Darcy was preparing to depart on his journey, he was unaware of events transpiring that would change his life forever. His preparations were being watched. The observer would lead to steps being put in place that would change Darcy's life forever. Clueless, Darcy was worried about wolves, when he should have been worried about old men and buffoons.

Standing at the heart of the Tower Plains against all logic was the Mages Tower. Its occupants probably had one of the best views of events across all Northern Neeska. The tower was almost as tall as the mountains that covered the lands to the south and its denizens extended their gaze with magic and seeing stones.

The turret itself stood as a warning to any that would approach and was visible for many miles in all directions. The monument of a construction was made of stones blessed with magic which allowed for its tremendous height. It contained the living quarters for all the wielders of magic who were outcast in Neeska. The stone giant of a tower stood as the last bastion before the Scorched Lands and was as much a prison as it was a fortification.

Sometime shortly after the Great War, a countrywide fear of magic and all mages began. It had started because in their desperation mages had turned to consorting with demons to rid the world of dragons, but this choice would haunt them for over a century.

As mages fled from ostracization, they made their way to the tower, and wanting to learn to defend themselves, a university of sorts developed at the tower's base.

The tower seemed to grow slightly taller with each year as more and more space was needed. The tower itself was made of a mismatch of stones from the surrounding area giving its outer surface an almost wild charm. The higher up the tower a mage found his chamber, the more important he was.

The university that had developed at its base was made up of two large stone buildings made of the same shambling stone type as the tower itself. The ragged rocks coated in ivy and other climbing plants made the building look ancient and alive… like a sleeping colossus.

As the number of mages that flocked to the tower had grown, so did the need to feed and supply them. Overtime a massive garden was created which stretched a mile from the gates of the tower out to a stone wall that was there to both protect those inside the walls from the prejudices outside, but also to prevent the escape of magically inclined experiments.

It was from within this stone tower that eyes had been cast on Darcy, the eyes being those of the Arch Mage. He had plans for the young man who was making his way slowly from Oakenfall. These plans would rely on a mage, one Calvin Clark.

Calvin was a modest man of simple tastes, who was cursed with almost comical misfortune. He was growing old and thought all chances for adventure were long behind him.

At the age of sixty-three Calvin was starting to find that he was getting tired more and more often. He spent his days either teaching or trying desperately to find a quiet nook to rest in.

It was not easy to find somewhere to repose in a tower full of magic, so relaxation in the tower was seldom peaceful. Calvin believed it was almost guaranteed that the Arch Mage would find something that needed doing, and if he didn't then a student would accidently set fire to a dorm while trying to light his pipe with magic or worse.

Calvin had found that living and teaching in the tower was full of surprises — few of them welcome — and this had led to him growing tired of teaching years before. He would have left the tower if he had anywhere else to go. The only thing that really kept him there were the large and often excessive meals.

Calvin was a cumbersome man, who would not likely have been a successful person had the Tower not existed. However, his natural talent for serendipity and magic, combined with his grumpy disposition, had meant he was a perfect teacher… he hated doing it, but Calvin was a good teacher.

As deputy head, Calvin spent his time teaching the young mages that joined the Tower. Magic was something that came naturally to the "blessed" and could not be taught to everyone.

In those who could summon spells, the extent to which they could do it depended hugely on two factors — the connection mages held to the Spirit Realm, and the more importantly training to focus their minds, if they wanted to avoid something from the Spirit Realm using their life force for its own gain.

The Spirit Realm was a place where living essence flowed through everything, from rock to animal. Its energy was used to give life to new-born babies and was released back into the flow when something died. It was the realm next to the Mortal Realm and sat between death and rebirth.

This Spirit Realm was a place of dreams. The life energy there made almost anything possible. It was the building block for the world. Mages grabbed small handfuls of the "anything" there and used it to make fireballs out of air. It was the place where both life and dreams were manifested.

Calvin had first discovered he had connections to the Spirit Realm and found his powers when he was eight years old. He had been an orphan in Northholm before its occupancy.

In Calvin's case he had started his mage career with a minor catastrophe without the need of a demon. He was just <u>that</u> kind of person and because of it, he could understand why some people feared mages.

During a rather heated nightmare Calvin had awoken in what he thought was a cold sweat. During his slumber he had managed to set fire to the boy's bunk above his own.

The boy had leaped from the bunk, as could be expected, calling young Calvin every name under the sun and a few more beside.

In Calvin's panic to put out the fire he managed to summon a Wind Wisp, a small ball of air-creature that normally remained hidden from human view and caused havoc moving storms out at sea.

This creature pulled from its normal habitat delighted in gathering the burning sheets and spinning them around the room like a white cotton tornado.

Escaping the fire, children were chased out of the orphanage by dancing empty dressing gowns and floating tables that were smoldering as the Wisp took great pleasure in the new environment it found itself in.

The two days it took for the Mages Tower to send someone to collect Calvin and stop the escaped spirit proved to be a very interesting time in Northholm indeed.

The streets were filled with flying underwear. Horses and carts soared through the air, which at times created an exciting turn of events and made for a change of scenery for the muck clearers and a few unfortunate pigeons on the roof tops that got a rather large dollop of their own medicine.

After a less than routine initiation into the Magic Circle, once inside the tower Calvin learned everything, he could quickly to control his gift. He was gifted and learned magic like most people learned to read. The known world's magic was broken down into five main schoolings.

The first schooling taught was Elemental Magic, which is as it says, about control of the elements. Considering Calvin's event at the orphanage he took a real interest in this schooling and had almost mastered its higher tiers within two years.

The second was Curative Magic, the hardest of all magics to master. The Life-force that mages use from the Spirit Realm prefers to go into creating new life, not preserving current ones.

The last skill the Tower University taught was Arcane Magic. This is your odd job magic — anything from turning invisible to telecommunication was under this umbrella and it was often the last the Tower taught to its would-be students. Students overall do not need to ability to vanish to get into mischief... it just adds to their toolkit of misdemeanors.

The last two types of magic were banned: Necromancy — raising the dead or prolonging one's life — and Blood Magic — consorting with demons and using either the blood or the life-force of the caster, or someone else, to cast strong and extremely destructive magic.

During his teen years, Calvin had almost been expelled from the school for his transgressions using the abilities he mastered in the Arcane arts.

This was the outcome most mages dreaded. The best they could hope for in the real world outside the gates of the tower was a small hut somewhere making poultices or potions to put the spring back into brewer's step... until the local villagers drove them away.

However, Calvin had been lucky, and cemented his path to leadership on a rather unremarkable day when the tower cat at the time, Mr. Fiddles, slipped from the tower's uppermost window and very nearly hit Calvin, who was tending the gardens below. The forty-story drop had left a slightly distorted red cat-shaped splat on the tower steps. Calvin managed, without thinking, to heal the cat's wounds by casting a strong curative spell.

The level of power needed to cast such a spell didn't go unnoticed by the faculty and although the Tower had few rules, it did have a code.

All mages had to become either teachers, care takers or collectors. Calvin hadn't fancied the open road as a collector — they were mages that travelled around the world finding young mages and fixing the issues they caused.

Calvin enjoyed tending the garden but was too slow to really work the fields of the massive garden. So, he settled for teaching.

It was shortly after Calvin saved Mr. Fiddles — who went on to live for another exciting few weeks before he made the same trip to again the ground after leaping at a sparrow (nine lives are not enough for some cats) — that Calvin was given his own class to train and had been doing that ever since.

Unaware of the Arch Mage's plans for him, Calvin was about to head to bed after a rather exhausting and late-running Arcane class. Calvin had planned to get an early night — maybe to wax his beard — but as he turned the bend into the teachers' dorm, he was met by an overwhelming headache he recognized as a physic connection.

"Calvin, can you hear me," the Arch Mage whispered directly into Calvin's head. It was an odd sensation like having someone nagging inside his skull accompanied by a pulsating headache.

"Yes," Calvin replied to the empty corridor. He hated it when the Arch Mage used physic communication, as it always gave him a nosebleed.

It was a source of bafflement to Calvin why the Arch Mage couldn't just walk down one flight of stairs and come speak to him like a normal person. The Arch Mage expected them to climb thirty-nine flights at times to go to him, but hell would freeze over before he dragged his wrinkled backside down even one set of twisting stairs.

"Can you come to my room? I've seen someone coming in the crystal and I want to discuss with you what we're going to do about it." The headache faded, and Calvin wiped the blood from his nose onto the long brown sleeves of his robe.

If there was one thing Calvin hated more than short bursts of telecommunication with the Arch Mage, it was when he had to talk with him for any length of time. The man had spent far too much time looking into the future and had lost the grip on the present.

Unlike the rest of the hoi polloi that lived like packed rats in the thirty-nine floors below, the Arch Mage's floor comprised only two rooms for him alone — a whole floor for his living quarters and his personal library!

Inside the Arch Mage's library Calvin sat waiting surrounded by elegance. As he gazed across the room his eyes were drawn to the statues of the long passed Arch Mages that looked down with steely faces from alcoves all around the edges of the room.

Just below them were more stone and lifeless faces of heroes from the Dragon's Blight that seemed to watch the proceedings with an air of dissatisfaction and a heavy weight of boredom.

Surrounding the jury of statues, were grey walls, contrasting with the long bright red and golden rug that covered the floor's stone tiles.

Several imitation gold candelabra hung from the roof with the same swirly-cherry-blossom effect as that of the rug.

Directly opposite from the entrance ran a long table cluttered with books and magical paraphernalia, skulls, bowls and strangely glowing glass flasks.

Running next to the table were the Arch Mage's bookcases, whose out-stretched legs looked like those of a wooden millipede. The books inside held some of the most powerful spells in all Neeska and even from long-lost history before the Age of the Dragons. Almost all literature in Neeska from before that time had been long lost, but what did remain was either hidden in buried tombs or here inside the tower.

After a few minutes of silence only broken by the odd echo of shuffling feet from one of the many alleyways between the books, Calvin grew bored with waiting.

"Arch Mage!" he shouted as he leant against a bookshelf… he had learnt not to bother hunting for the Arch Mage.

The library was not massive but once you proceeded into the corridors of books that ran like fingers from the center of the room it turned into a maze. The corridors seemed to expand well beyond the space that should have been available within the room.

Its secluded alcoves were so isolated that some students had started the rumor that there was a tribe of small pixies living within the library that hadn't seen a human in over a generation. How true that was Calvin didn't know, but he did know that the last time he tried to find the Arch Mage it took him and hour and a half to find his way back to the foul-smelling concoctions on the table in the middle of the room, and he was sure his shoes had gotten woodworm.

"It took you long enough to get up here," the Arch Mage said as he popped out from behind a bookshelf like a bearded old mole carrying a huge tome that had seen better days. The book strangely enough matched the cream moth eaten robe the Arch Mage was wearing.

"I came —" Calvin started, but didn't get to finish the sentence, as patience was not one of the Arch Mage's characteristics. Senility, an odd cabbage odor, and a hunch you could use to draw a perfect semi-circle yes... but not patience.

"Yes, yes Calvin. No time to talk, so just listen," the Arch Mage instructed waggling his bushy eyebrows like two grey weasels dancing. "Some wet-behind-the-ear knight or some-such is prancing in from Oakenfall as we speak. He'll be here within a day or so, maybe three if he stops at Briers Hill — and we have to act." The Arch Mage dropped the heavy book onto the table with a thud sending a cloud of dust into the air.

"Act on what exactly?" Calvin asked as he walked closer to the Arch Mage hoping that the book would shed some light on affairs.

Calvin knew from experience that the Arch Mage often presumed the person he was speaking to had as strong a power of future divination as the Arch Mage himself had. This often led to rather muddled and brief conversations that left younger and less-experienced mages completely clueless as to what they had been asked to do — and in some instances with punishment for conversations that they had not yet even had!

"The Second Blight my boy, keep up will you. We'll need a Warrior Mage, we will. That'll help this little noble squid-wrangler from Oakenfall to survive the apocalyptic ruins of the Scorched Lands," the Arch Mage said shooting Calvin a disappointed look.

"Wait, Second Blight as in dragons, Scorched Lands? What are you on about?" Calvin asked.

It was possible that the Arch Mage had been staring into the crystals too long again and this was something that had already happened... or would not happen for another thousand years.

Either that or he had spent too long playing with herbs in the many jars scattered around the room and he'd just had a bad dream, however, when it came to dragons, it was never wise to be complacent.

"Yes, big scaly things, breathe fire, not so good for freedom," the Arch Mage said and looked confused, obviously struggling to tell if it was something that had already happened or would indeed happen.

"Are the dragons returning?" asked Calvin.

"Why else would we need the Dragon Heart? Look here," the Arch Mage said opening the dusty tome with a flick of his wrist to the exact page somewhere near the middle.

"Dragon Heart? As in the myth from the Scorched Lands?" Calvin asked, still confused as to what was transpiring.

"Yes, Yes, and Warrior Mages, just like the old days. Oh, they would have been something to behold in the last war with the dragons."

"Are you sure you saw dragons returning? What does this have to do with me?" Calvin asked becoming steadily more uneasy.

"Well someone will need to do it. Did you know they say some of the Warrior Mages could even divine their elemental skills to the point where they could boil the water in a human body? That's one way to steam Shrivel armor isn't it?" The Arch Mage made a rather explosive hand gesture followed by an excited chirrup.

For an old man he seemed full of life and easily excitable — probably something to do with the fact he was never truly in one-time frame and was often exposed to chemicals.

"I'm not sure I like where this is going Arch Mage. You realize that after the Great War ended the Warrior Mages were disbanded? Not one of them survived without a demon from the Spirit Realm corrupting them. It was too dangerous, for everyone. There is a reason magic like that is banned," Calvin said remembering the stories of mages returning from the war, going insane and murdering their loved ones, neighbors and quite often themselves.

Most demons liked to return to the Spirit Realm shortly after they arrived in the Mortal Realm as they found its physics quite dull, but the odd one enjoyed the whole mortal experience and took it to new gruesome levels.

"Yes, but if it is just one… you. I mean you're getting on a bit now, then we'd know who to watch out for and it's better than letting some big scaly lizard burn the rest of Neeska. It seems simple enough. You become a Warrior Mage, find the Heart and save the world. All I have to do is cast this spell at you, and you wake up in the Spirit Realm to find a spirit to make a pact with." With that the Arch Mage flicked his stubby hands and a bright white light hit Calvin like a mountain troll's sledgehammer.

When Calvin opened his eyes the world around him had a shifty white glow and he lay in the middle of a beautiful forest clearing.

To his left huge mountains climbed towards the sky and water cascaded off them in ever shifting colors that seemed to change at will.

Behind him lay a desert filled with walking cacti, and to his right snow and blizzards. The three very different landscapes met at the forest clearing and at the heart of it was an old stone pedestal right by Calvin's feet.

Atop the pedestal was a thick book that was writing itself. The quill floated above it magically scribbling quickly. As much as Calvin wanted to pull himself up to read what was being written his attention was swept elsewhere as bright wisps of light like those Calvin had heard blessed the elves darted around from area to area.

As the wisps zoomed past his ears they seemed to carry the sounds of people from the mortal world — either moaning of a hard winter, if the wisp had darted from the frozen wastes, or spring-time passion and love-lust, if the wisp had just finished a swim in the amazing waterfalls that seemed to fall forever from the heights of the mountains.

Because of his study and strong connection to the Spirit Realm, Calvin knew where he had landed.

This was the Place of Dreams, where people went when they slept. Calvin tried to focus directly on one of the wisps and without moving his feet Calvin felt the sensation of motion, of the world moving around him. He was suddenly travelling hundreds of miles in the blink of the eye.

The spirit world disappeared by him as he whipped through the air and when it stopped Calvin found himself sitting deep in a forest. He was still dizzy from the speed of passing continents and the odd hollow feeling that everything had.

Calvin hadn't thought he would ever find anything more nauseating than telepathic communication with the Arch Mage, but he now knew he was wrong... this was far worse. There were more wisps in the forest and Calvin was sure he could see reflections inside them of the settlement just northeast of Oakenfall.

The world seemed to shake again and this time his feet left the ground and he shot upwards into the great white glow above. There in the clouds he saw thousands of people running around in what could be considered normal lives. They paid him no attention and Calvin knew it was the dead he could see.

The world had been damaged long ago and many lives that should have returned to the world hadn't. They should have faded into the Life Stream, the power that made all known life in the world. As one thing died it came back as something else. Think of mixing fruit in a blender and pouring it out into a tree. However, the flow had once been stopped by a demon who'd tried to enter the world, and it looked like those who'd died during that time had congregated here and for a moment Calvin wondered if they had just continued their lives in this place, but before he could call out to ask, the shift came again and he was falling.

Calvin splashed into the sea and travelled a million depths down into darkness. He knew if this was the Mortal Realm, he would be choking to death, but here he could breathe fine. Calvin had a strange feeling that he was being pulled towards something. Whatever spell the Arch Mage had cast was sending Calvin somewhere specific within the Spirit Realm. Calvin was alone apart from a single golden fish that swam towards him. It seemed to smile as it grew closer and the world shifted once more. Fire and brimstone replaced the beauty of the ocean floor as Calvin was summoned into a demon's presence. The same white glow filled the valley that Calvin now found himself accustomed to, but the wisps were nowhere to be seen. There was no way to leave the demon's small kingdom of dreams unless it gave you the right to leave.

"Well, a human here and a live one too! It must be a century or more since one of you came poking around in our domain. I can feel that you're not here dreaming, so what brings you here?" a voice called out in a hundred voices — male and female, old and young and tones no mortal ear would be able to hear.

The voice belonged to what looked like a young woman who sat cradling the decomposing body of the fish. Her skin seemed to shimmer and looked too perfect. She had not even the slightest flaw to her figure and many a man might have fallen for her even with the outlandish voice, but Calvin could sense the magic dripping from the beast that hid itself behind the illusion.

Demons spent eternity sailing on the Life Stream that flowed through the Spirit Realm. They knew how to control it and its powers and could use it to craft any realm they wanted and shift it around themselves to make themselves whatever they wanted to be. If they wanted to be old, they could. If they wanted to have wings or be as small as an ant it was only a matter of crafting the energy. They could build great rolling plains, or like this demon, molten filled volcanoes.

"Dragons —" Calvin went to start but found himself cut short with a wave of the demon's hand. It seemed that demons were just as rude as the Arch Mage.

"I know all about dragons," the demon said, as she transformed into a huge and powerful golden dragon within the blink of an eye.

That was a demon's biggest threat in the Spirit Realm. They could pretend to be anything, and they often used this to possess the unwary, by offering bargains or trades. Often, they'd approach and prey on the more lustful, transforming themselves into beautiful women and offering up favors for a trip into the real world.

"I know you're not a dragon, demon," Calvin said struggling to fight the effects of the illusion spell. He found himself wanting to believe but that was a dangerous path to go down.

"I never said I was. That's the thing with you humans, always think you know everything. It has been that way ever since the first of your lot crawled out of the caves and saw the sky. You thought you knew it all. You forgot us and thought you could handle the world alone. You forgot your mother, your creator," the demon said as it trawled through Calvin's mind seeking out any weakness it could use.

"You're using the wrong illusion for that, demon. Do not pretend you care for humans or that you gave birth to us," Calvin said trying his hardest to fight the feelings washing over him. He'd been an orphan, hadn't known his parents and could sense the demon was trying to play to that side of his emotions.

"Yes, of course! You all believe in false gods that supposedly created everything. You don't realize it was just another realm for demons to play in! They grew bored with you and forgot about you. That is the truth of it," the demon said, and Calvin found himself wondering if it was true. After all he had seen the desert and forest here, and they had seemed so real. It was not impossible that the real world did not exist but was instead the creation of a bored and twisted mind.

"You try to lie to me, demon. If that were true more demons would have come," Calvin said finding his mind awash with doubt but doing his best to fight it. The Arch Mage really must have lost his mind if he thought a creature like this would help matters if the dragons were really coming back.

"One demon cannot just waltz into the realm of another uninvited. But believe what you will … mother knows best," the demon said with an eerie smile.

"I doubt you're even a female demon," Calvin said finding himself able to feel the magic of the beast again. If he stayed focused on it, he could sense the spell trying to wash over him.

"Maybe you're smarter than most mortals, so I might just let you live… if it so pleases me. Now I know why you're here. Your little mind is as easy to read as a children's book. You're here to beg me to join you. To save your pathetic people and you expect me to do this for nothing."

"I never asked for any of this," Calvin said defiantly to the huge dragon-shaped demon in front of him.

It was the first time Calvin had seen a dragon — the first time anyone had since the end of the war when they'd all vanished. If what the demon was portraying was real, then the beasts were far scarier than any illustration in any book in Neeska.

"No. True, I suppose. You're just a tool following orders. A hammer to hit a nail, but without my help your world is doomed. Would you pay any cost to save it? Would it be so bad if at the end of me saving your sad little world I got to enjoy it a little?" the demon asked shape-shifting back into the women Calvin had seen to start with.

She shot Calvin a beautiful smile below the purest eyes he had ever seen. Calvin found himself wanting to agree with the demon. To do anything for her, to please her, to satisfy her, to succumb to her. Focusing again he fought it off.

"I'm not falling for your trickery, demon. By 'enjoy the world' you mean kill people, or worse," Calvin said as the demon changed form once more this time into a swarm of wasps that buzzed around him. He could feel the demon's anger.

"I personally don't enjoy the killing part, but I suppose you mortals do often die when I peel your insides out through your pores," the demon laughed from a hundred little mouths and it was a sound Calvin would be happy to never hear again.

"Forget it, demon, send me home," Calvin demanded knowing he could not return to the Mortal Realm now without the demon's say so and he did not fancy an eternity in its company.

"Do you seriously believe that is a likely outcome? No, I don't think you're that foolish. How about I make you an offer you'll find fair. I grow tired of dragons. The time of the dragons is long over, and it would be fun to kill something new. Like in the old days, evil gods and lost kingdoms not just ash. It gets everywhere," the demon said shifting back into female form. The beast had realized this was the one Calvin found hardest to refuse. "You need to find the Heart. If you promise to destroy it, I'll help you. I'll give you the magic you so desperately need and then I'll slip back here to play with my little fishy without even a goodbye. How does that sound?"

"Far too easy to me, if I'm honest," Calvin said. Demons were renowned for being less than honest. If the demon wanted this Heart destroyed, there was a reason behind that.

"Oh, you really are a smart human, aren't you? Let's just say that once this little task is done some fun will arrive, that we've been wanting for a long time. Wait! I recognize you?! The orphanage! Ah yes… that fire was oh such fun! Well, you don't have a choice little human. I had not realized, it was that time already," the demon said.

"Do I have a choice?" Calvin asked but he never received his answer.

Instead the white light blinded him a second time and he found himself crashing to the floor in the Arch Mage's room blood oozing from his nose. He didn't know at the time, but the demon had been waiting for a new chapter in history to start and Calvin was going to have his part to play in it.

Chapter Three – Reunion at Hallows Fort

Darcy Dean's journey was relatively easy — it had none of the wolf attacks or bandits of his dreams — and the only danger was from getting water-logged in the continual drizzle that had cursed them since they'd left the gates of Oakenfall.

The roads were reasonably well maintained, far better than Darcy had expected what with the war and the city's crippled economy. The cobbled roads leading out from the city broke off into dirt tracks not far from the city, but these were kept clear of the shrubs and hedges that lined the edges of the grass lands. Gullies worn into the landscape by caravan wheels ran in almost perfect curves over the hills and farmland towards Briers Hill. They were broken from view only at the crests of the hills and bottoms of the dales. Little fences marked the borders of the sprawling fields that lay waiting for the finer weather. Bushes showing signs that they would soon start to sprout leaves marked out the fields and farms they passed during their journey.

The ride was stable, and the horses moved quickly from dawn to dusk. At night they pulled off the road and made camp. The horses, glad of the rest, made short work of the shrubs that seemed to grow waist high all along the roadside. While they made camp, the caravan was left unguarded. It was very plain looking, all painted white. Its four small windows, one in each of its sides, were surrounded by wooden arches that matched the rest of the caravan's decoration. It was warm but the curved roof did little to stop the rain seeping into the cabin itself. The wheels looked new compared to the weathered body — Darcy wondered why they would have replaced them for such a short journey as this. It occurred to him that the caravan looked more like a traveler's caravan than an envoy from the King. He knew not to expect much with Oakenfall finances being the way they were, but it was far too small for a trader, let alone for a five-man team, and had probably been hired from a noble. The hooks pressed into the rear porch hinted at its normal use for hunting.

The driver was the only one to sleep inside the caravan. Darcy and the three guards slept close by under cleverly-made sheepskin tents. The outside was waterproof and the inside fluffy and warm. Darcy had brought a couple of fire sticks from his estate and they made the camping trip quite enjoyable. Camping was something Darcy would loved to have done with his father when he was a boy but, in his father's absence, never had. The closest he'd got was pulling his sheets over the cabinet in his bedroom, which he'd got thoroughly chastised for when Granny had found "the mess" as she had called it.

Just as the cold wind and rain had washed any remaining enjoyment out of camping and Darcy had heard about as many stories as he could bear about the "one that got away" from the would-be poachers, it seemed their journey was reaching its mid-point.

It was around noon on the third day when Briers Hill appeared on the horizon. Darcy had decided to sit up front that day with the driver, as they could see the sun for the first time in days, and although it was still cold it was a pleasant day. There were still plenty of clouds in the sky, but they were white and fluffy not like the angry gray mass that seemed to hang around since the Centennial Celebrations.

It looked like the gods had finally convinced themselves that the smoke was cleared from the heavens. As Darcy looked out across the rolling rocky plains, the town of Briers Hill seemed tiny in comparison to

Oakenfall and Darcy could barely believe how people could live in somewhere so small.

They entered town on the south-eastern road, one of the four roads out of Briers Hill which was built around a crossroads. Darcy had thought the town looked small from a distance compared the city he'd always called home, but as they left the countryside behind and settled back onto cobbled lanes, he could see for the first time just how small it really was.

Briers Hill was made up of seven to ten small red thatched houses which gathered around the well in its center, plus a handful of shops on its western road. The windmill's huge blades sitting above the baker shop were the most noticeable thing in the whole village. The slow spinning of the blades fascinated Darcy and the small blue jay that kept hopping from one to the next showing signs of annoyance at its moving perch added to the strange charm of the village. When the bird seemed to give in and fly off, Darcy's eyes were drawn away from the windmill.

Aside from the small houses and shops the only other building for miles was a tavern where the caravan stopped. Unlike Oakenfall that was made largely of sloped slate roofs Briers Hill was thatched. Most of the slate in Neeska came from the dwarves of the Goldhorn Kingdom and the road from there led straight to Oakenfall. Since the dwarves had sealed off their mountain years ago what little slate was left at Oakenfall had been kept there, so the people of Briers Hill had replaced their slate roofs with thatch from the fields around town. Although the countryside around about was littered with rocky outcrops that stuck up through the brush, the quality of local stone was poor. A sign of how far Briers Hill was from a decent supply of stone was that all the buildings had been made with clay. It was easy to see timber frames beneath the red uneven and often flaking clay.

A unique trait of the Briers Hill area was that all the sandstone and clay had a natural reddish tint. The story went that the blood of the warriors who'd died in the Scorched Lands had seeped into the clay as it was making its way to the sea, but the truth was it had always been red. The area was very rich in iron and even some crops and plants had a slightly red tint to them because of that.

This was the reason Northholm had been built in the first place — a mine had been opened towards the west coast around a day and a half's travel from Briers Hill. The miners had started to head to the coast there to ship the ore back to Oakenfall, and over time a city, Northholm, grew around them.

The tavern that the caravan had stopped outside was known as The Dragon's Blood Inn, which was very appropriate. The building was as red as every other building in the town, apart from the huge white balcony that stuck out from its front like a dragon's mouth. The second reason was that the hops used to make its ale were grown locally, so the beer had a very metallic taste, like blood, as well as a slightly red coloring.

From the outside the inn looked extremely busy for such a small town. Darcy was no mathematician but with only eleven buildings in the town realistically there could only be seventy people in the town at a push, and unless they were all in the small yet very packed inn, a lot of the guards from the fort up the road must have been frequenting it too.

Darcy suddenly felt very sick as he realized that he might be walking in to meet his father much sooner than he'd expected. He struggled with his fine fur satchel wishing Granny was around to help him strap it on. She had a knack for getting the brass clip not to snap back and crush her fingers which Darcy seemed to lack. Rubbing his sore fingers Darcy followed the guards into the inn nervously.

The inside of the Dragon's Blood Inn was pretty much as he expected. You could just see dark wooden tables poking out under people's arms or between their standing legs. There was barely enough room to sidestep towards the bar as Darcy followed his guards.

The guards nodded towards the innkeeper and then left Darcy to it. They suddenly seemed very interested in the barmaid, or more precisely the burgundy ale she was serving up.

Darcy struggled on past a few more drunken elbows and clinking glasses and rowdy bearded faces, until he finally made it to the bar where an elderly man stood behind it looking angrily at the crowd of guards.

"You want a drink go see me daughter," the old man snorted through a mess of rotten teeth as Darcy grew close. The smell almost knocked Darcy back a step — or it would have, if there was room to step backwards in the crowded bar.

"I'm actually interested in a room for the night, or two to be precise," Darcy said knowing it would come out of his own coffers, but he'd already shared two nights of stories from some rather uncouth guards and wanted a room of his own.

"Payment up front, twenty-five coppers a room. Thirty if you want breakfast," the old man grunted, again sending another wave of stale ale and smoke with a hint of what could have been kipper towards Darcy.

"That seems a little steep," Darcy said as he was used to the finer things in life, but even he wouldn't charge that for one of his rooms let alone some lice-ridden bed in a place where he felt it would be a miracle if he could sleep.

Granny had told him stories of common life and he had even seen a little of it as he'd made his trips to the docks in Oakenfall, but the realism of it was more than he had expected.

"Aye, that it is but I need to make some money somehow and there isn't another bed for sale for miles, so take it or leave it," the innkeeper finally looked at Darcy. "You don't look like one of this lot. You might even pay your tab," he laughed, and his moustache wiggled like a fox wagging its tail. "Tell you what, you tell me what you're doing here, and I'll do you a deal. Fifty all in for the two plus breakfast and I'll start you a tab for your friends' drinks over there." The old bar keeper pointed towards Darcy's guards who were already onto their second flagon.

"They aren't my friends. I am just travelling with them," Darcy said feeling the need to separate himself from the cackling beer-swilling guards. "Why would you want to know?" Darcy asked wondering. It was probably paranoia, but he suddenly suspected this was some test from the King. He knew it was probably nothing, but with so many nobles going missing lately, maybe they had let something slip about the King's plan.

"Just you're not the first person coming in from the direction of Oakenfall in the last few months. Are you off to the Scorched Lands too?" the innkeeper asked seemingly with no malice or hidden agenda. It was commonly known that innkeepers knew more gossip from the lands than the King's own advisors and this was probably more of the same, drunken nosiness.

"No, we're off to see the mages, private business. I hope you understand," Darcy said, and he paused. Who were these men that went off to the Scorched Lands? Was this mission as straight forward as Harvey had made it out to be? The envelope inside his jerkin suddenly grew heavy and Darcy felt an urge to open it and see exactly what the King had written to the Arch Mage. He knew he couldn't. If word got back to the King that the wax seal had been broken, then Darcy's little indiscretion with the White Flags might not go away.

"These men you mentioned; do you know who they were?" Darcy asked, trying to cover his tracks and find out more of the King's true intentions at the same time.

"I don't know much, lad. Just a few new faces coming into town that were not just soldiers for the fort. I asked them just like I did you. What they were up to and they said they were off to the Scorched Lands. Crazy bastards, if you ask me, there's nout there but ash and death," the innkeeper said and even Darcy with his lack of people skills could tell he wanted to break into a story, but Darcy did not have time to listen to some drunken story about dragons. It had been bad enough having to listen to Harvey's retelling of the tale.

"Did any of them say what they were after?" Darcy asked ignoring the signs and breaking the innkeepers' chance at starting whatever tale he had planned. Darcy could see the red-faced man's look of disappointment, but he didn't have time for it.

"No, they wouldn't say… well one did say something after a few too many Dragon Blood ales." The old bar keeper laughed, and Darcy had to fight the urge to faint from the bellow of stench that poured from his mouth. It seemed the hygiene of the city had not made it out as far as this village.

"What did he say?" Darcy said once he could catch his breath. He knew this would probably be the chance the innkeeper was after to drop into one story or another. The man seemed to have little else to occupy his time. His daughter seemed to be running around tending to the needs of the patrons and the fat innkeeper did little more than slowly drink himself to death.

"The fella was on a mission for the King himself, something about finally beating the bloody Poles. Good thing too. I don't think we can take any more attacks from them. So, I say good luck to the crazy cow prodder — next morn, he headed off into the ash," the innkeeper said lifting his cloudy glass in a lame toast before supping it dry. "Oi Maria! Another one over here!" he called out to what Darcy had presumed was his daughter.

"In a minute Frank, I'm kind of busy here," Maria called out from the other end of the bar, as she struggled to balance a tower of glass tankards as she waded her way through drunken soldiers.

"That's 'dad' to you," the innkeeper called back, and his fox tail-like moustache sagged. "Want my advice posh pants? Never have kids. They're nothing but bloody trouble," the old innkeeper, that Darcy now knew to be called Frank, said.

"I can imagine she's quite the handful," Darcy said innocently but the gaze Frank shot him made Darcy fluster. The young lady did seem to have ample assets but that was not what Darcy had meant at all. "*Um*, thank you for the information. It sounds a little farfetched, but you never know, I guess. Now about these rooms, we'll need them for tonight only," Darcy said desperately trying to change the subject from the young barmaid as he reached for his coin purse.

With the rooms booked Darcy decided to make the most of the fair weather and the hours before the sun would set. He could just make out the fort a mile or so in the distance beyond the wheat farms and curiosity won the battle. He had to go see his father. He could be there and back within a few hours and there was no sound of battle in the distance, so he should be safe.

The road was a gradual climb, but it was still tiring and the wind zipping across the open farmland didn't seem to make it any easier. The sky seemed to be clearing in the strong westerly wind and Darcy was thankful that it brought the smell of the countryside.

As he grew close enough to see the high walls of the fort, he could see the Poles' fort in the distance, which drove home to Darcy just how constant the battles must be. The two forts must have been no more than two furlongs apart and a decent archer could easily fire an arrow that far, so neither side could spend much time outside unless they really had to.

The serene views of rocky outcrops and fields faded, and the thick brush reclaimed the land near the fort. Upturned wagons littered both sides of the road and confirmed the stories Darcy had heard of constant raids from the Poles.

The wagons were not the only litter around — rusted weapons of both Pole and Oakenfall craftsmanship lay discarded in the hedgerows from countless battles. It was a pleasant surprise to Darcy that neither side seemed to leave their dead on the battlefield, as there were no corpses left rotting that he could see or smell, though a huge mound of earth at the side of the fort gave a hint of a mass burial below.

The huge wooden gate to the fort was sealed shut and Darcy was met by a pointy headed guard staring at him through a slit in the smaller door inside the large one as he approached.

The fort itself loomed above with its towers pressing into the sky like the hunched shoulders of a giant mossy beast. What windows there were in the walls were secured, and with thick iron crisscrosses it looked like it would take an army of giants just to rattle them. The stone walls were thick — three or four feet thick — but showed signs of wear and looked like they had begun to crumble.

"State your business or do one," the rather grumpy owner of the eyes growled at him from behind the door in a voice that sounded like a badger chewing on a bag of nuts and bolts.

"I'm here to see my father, Sir Dean," Darcy said nervously, as he wasn't sure if the guard would believe him.

It was strange really. Darcy was the son of a war hero and a renowned soldier, but he'd never really had to speak to anyone in the army. The harsh tone and discipline of the old man's accent made him nervous, but that was not a strange emotion for Darcy who always seemed to be running on his nerves. The hatch in the huge door was slammed shut and after several minutes of silence Darcy heard the metal latch being slid aside and the fort door being opened.

"Come with me," the short man in front of Darcy with the coarse voice said. The old man walked with a hobble and could probably have benefited from a cane, but he still looked like he would have been strong in his youth.

It occurred to Darcy that the man was probably retired from the army because of his age, but he was still within Hallows Fort for some reason. Because he was of an age when he would be freed from the army, but still chose to remain at the battlement, it looked like the old man had nothing in the world to go home for. So, he did the only job he was fit for now and watched the gate. It was a sad thought but one that was only fleeting as Darcy's attention was drawn to the fort around him.

The inner courtyard was empty of people as he'd expected. The realization that an arrow could fall from the sky at any moment made Darcy suddenly feel very uncomfortable. Several closed doors led off into the stone keep. The only thing of real note inside the clearing apart from the high walls and gravel floor was the small cabin Darcy was being escorted towards.

"This is him," the guard said as he opened the creaking door. When no orders came from inside the cabin the old man quickly scurried back towards his stool by the main gate nervously looking up the whole time.

The hut was dirty, and its windows had been boarded up. Its roof was littered with little points, the shafts of arrows that had rained down into the keep. Darcy noticed the faded paint on the wall inside the hut but couldn't help but feel a little family pride — behind his father was a huge motif of the family coat of arms, a sign of the great knights that had come before Darcy.

"Well, it really is you, Darcy," Sir Dean said from behind the table that sat in the center of the cabin.

The cabin was bare apart from a few scattered side tables and old chests that were obviously used for storing weapons.

"Hello Father," Darcy said barely able to believe his eyes.

"Come in take a seat, my lad, and let me take a look at you." Sir Dean stood and pulled out a chair next to his own, which Darcy nervously sat down on.

Darcy had been told several times that he looked a lot like his father, but the man in front of him could very well have been Darcy in the future.

Apart from muscle build and wrinkles every detail was the same. They had same green eyes and hooked nose, an identical beard down to the bald patches at the side of their lips. Their hair even did the same flick behind the ears before cascading down over their shoulders. One large difference was the scar above Sir Dean's eye that ran down his cheek. It looked like he had been slashed open and then badly sown together by a blind woodpecker. It was an old wound that still looked raised and sore.

"Not that I am not happy to see you, my boy, but Darcy what are you doing here?" Sir Dean asked with a smile.

Darcy didn't know for sure, but he could almost feel his father's longing for his son to join the army. In the few letters that had come home for Lady Dean he had often asked if Darcy was growing into a strong man.

"The King is sending me to see the mages, and well, I wanted to see you while we were at Briers Hill," Darcy said sounding slightly disappointed.

It wasn't really the heartfelt reunion he'd wanted. There had been no huge weight lifted from his shoulders, no loving embrace. If he was honest, it was like meeting a stranger... someone famous he had heard of. He respected his father but after years of pining for him, there was no real love. He could feel something near... a spark of emotion but the fire had long faded, and the smoldering ashes were all that was left of what the relationship should have been.

"Well, whatever the reason, it is good to see you again, Darcy. It has been far too long. How is your mother?" Sir Dean asked giving a half-hearted smile. He had once loved lady Dean, but after ten years away from her that love had faded into little more than a distant memory clouded by battle and bar whores.

"I don't really know. She's fine, I guess. The King has her off on diplomatic affairs still. I see her almost as often as I do you," Darcy said in a tone oozing with years of neglect.

Darcy didn't want to blame his father for choosing the army over him. He knew that with Harvey you seldom had a choice, but just being in front of his father, Darcy had so many questions he wanted to ask — too many — that his mind tripped over them and left him unable to settle on one.

"I'm sorry, Darcy. This isn't the life either of us planned for you. It's the war, you understand, right?" Sir Dean said, and he seemed sincere, but Darcy wondered if his father would still have found some way to go off and be a hero, if things had been different.

Sir Malcolm Dean was not a man suited to paperwork and ledgers. Darcy was certain he would have still found adventure — likely taken to the sea and joined the battles in far-off Gologan, or sailed off as an explorer to find the empty corners of the map. Darcy had been alone so long, he could not imagine his father finding any life that was to be had by sitting at home.

"I know. I don't really know what to say to you Father. I have been alone for so long. I've dreamt of meeting you again, but now I have, it hasn't lived up to my dreams," Darcy said with sorrow.

"I'm sorry, son. Much in life doesn't live up to what we tell ourselves, the stories we hold on to keep us going. In the worst battles, I think of you. I draw strength from you, my boy," Malcolm said, but his tone didn't seem to fit his words.

"Aye, stories, I guess that's all its been," Darcy said in defeat.

"Stay a while, share a meal with your old man, won't you?" Sir Dean asked. There was a sadness behind his eyes, and Darcy thought of the caged animals he'd seen when a circus visited the city. Those same cold remorseful eyes the animals had were shared by his father.

"I need to go before it gets dark, Father. I just wanted to see you one last time," Darcy said as he stood and made for the door.

He had waited ten years to see his father and for all that time he had felt alone. In his mind he had built up this impenetrable wall that he thought would crumble the moment he saw his father. However, he realized he felt no different, and Darcy knew he would have to dismantle the wall himself brick by brick and staying there staring at the face of a stranger was pointless.

"Please Darcy, stay a while," Sir Dean called out, but it was too late. Darcy had shut the cabin door and was striding towards the fort's huge door.

The guard by it reached for his weapon, but Sir Dean, who'd followed Darcy out of the cabin shook his head, and instead the guard lifted the latch to open the door.

Sir Dean returned to the cabin alone, a mix of pride and shame washing over him. His boy had grown into a man and he had missed so much, but he didn't feel like he'd had any choice.

Darcy might never understand, but Sir Dean had given up his love and his life to protect that most precious gift, the baby boy who'd just started back down towards Briers Hill. If he would never see Darcy again, then so be it — but Sir Dean would fight through hell and back to keep his child safe from the slaughter of the Poles.

Many people would have gone soul searching or sulked into an empty spirit bottle, but Darcy had never been a normal person. He marched back to Briers Hill, his head spinning with emotions. He remembered just how lonely he'd felt the night of the celebrations and he knew it was all his own doing. He still wanted to blame his parents, but he was old enough to run his own life — he could not keep it on hold any longer. He knew he'd been an empty shell for so long now. Maybe that was why Granny spent so much time with him… she had seen he was still a needy child even at the age of twenty-seven. Darcy had put growing up on hold, while waiting for his parents to finish with the harsh pretentious façades they were living and come home. He had done what was needed to make their lives easier. He had forgone anything that mattered to him, and it had taken leaving the city and seeing things afresh to realize that.

Darcy felt deep down inside himself that he had mourned the loss of his parents years before, and although they still lived and breathed, they could not be part of his life. He could not hide behind his loss of them as a way of avoiding his own life. He had used that for years as an excuse for not making friends, not finding time for them.

Darcy felt horrible for leaving the keep the way he did and turning his back on his father, but he had to do it.

It was on his way back to Briers Hill, with the cool wind clearing his mind and drying his eyes that Darcy decided to start this new life come sunrise. His heart was filled with resolve — he was determined, but he had no purpose. That was something he would have to work on.

If the King's words were true Darcy might never see his father again, but Darcy couldn't see any other way. What good would have been achieved by sitting talking to a stranger that knew nothing but war, Darcy thought to himself. He decided that he would have to stop moping around and start living.

He would deliver the letter for the King and then find his own life. The estate could crumble for all he cared. It was just a mausoleum of memories from his dead past. Darcy would hand over whatever gold he could squeeze from the estate to Granny and head off from Oakenfall and the pressure the King put on him. There had to be something better out there for him, something outside the grasp of the Hansons.

Darcy returned alone to his room at the Dragon's Blood Inn deep in thought. He knew that he had to travel to the mages and drop off the letter, else the King would hound him to the end of his days, but he wanted some purpose in his life after that.

He started considering what he would do when he returned to Oakenfall. He could take sail in one of his father's ships — but that would still be his father's and he would have to wait for it to return from Northholm which could be weeks or even months. The crew, if they did decide to leave with him, would see him as his father's son and would treat him as such. No. He needed something of his own… he needed his own story, but that would have to wait for morning.

The room at the inn was basic, but it was warm and comfortable, nothing like the lice-ridden room Darcy had expected. It was empty, hosting just an empty wardrobe and the bed. The bed was low and basic with linen sheets. Its headboard was plain with none of the decorative carvings Darcy was used to.

Darcy wished he would wake to a bowl of water and mug of warmed milk brought in by Granny in the morning, but he knew the room would be as bare come sunup, as it was in the dark.

Most of the knights from the fort had staggered off sometime around two and the inn finally started to rest along with the creaking of its aged beams. The smell of the clay was relaxing — it was an improvement over the wet grass and cow dung from the roadside of the previous few nights. In the silence of the night and with his thoughts spinning about a new life, Darcy fell asleep to the sound of glasses clinking.

He awoke early as the sound of the horses being fitted back into their harnesses echoed up from below his window. It sounded like the caravan driver was having a bit of trouble with the chestnut mare at the front.

Darcy reached into a satchel at the foot of the bed, which contained basic supplies he'd thought he might need on the road — dried meat, smelling salts, tonics and a sharp blade in a leather sheath.

Memories from the day before washed over him once more and he took the blade to his hair. He wasn't completely sure why he chose to cut his hair and leave it short. It was probably to distinguish himself from his long-haired father, or to signify a new start.

Darcy didn't care too much about the reason and as he stood running his fingers through his cropped hair and looking out the window, he knew that this would be a better day — it was his day. The first day of his life and not just a day he owed to someone else. He would leave his loneliness at Briers Hill with his dead locks of hair.

Chapter Four – Two Souls One Heart

Six days had passed since the Centennial Celebrations and Darcy was due to arrive at any time. The Arch Mage had planned for Calvin to assist Darcy, but Calvin was far from ready to receive guests of any form, let alone lend the aid the Arch Mage expected of him.

Calvin had barely awoken since he was cast into the Spirit Realm. What little snippets he could gleam were a mix of dreams and being carried down from the Arch Mage's room. Then nothing — that was until he finally came too in his bedroom as if someone had snapped their fingers and released him from a trance.

Calvin's eyes had barely opened before he was sent retching to his knees. Vomiting is never a nice process but watching it cascade through a wiry gray beard and splattering against the floor somehow seemed to make it even grimmer.

The aged wood of the tower, as dry as it was, made light work of the moisture leaving only carrot-shaped lumps and the smell of dehydration.

Calvin had always been a sickly child as far back as he could remember, but this was different. He had never felt this wrong. It felt like his insides were burning and his mind was sloshing around like damp cotton wool in porridge.

"Pull yourself together!" Calvin said to himself as he tried to focus on the gaudy curtains fluttering in a gentle breeze creeping in from outside the tower.

The curtains had been a gift from one of his students. Calvin had always hated them, but he was soppy at heart, so he'd decided to keep them. He'd never been a fan of their bright pattern, but the floral swirls on them now seemed to burn his eyes as if he was staring into the sun.

The room was dull and gloomy and should have seemed dark, but Calvin's eyes seemed ridiculously sensitive to light and colors. It was as if he'd spent his whole life below ground and was seeing sunlight for the first time.

His head felt heavy and he let it drop down hanging from the side of the bed, but the view of his explosion from a few moments before made him roll back onto the bed and shut his eyes.

"*Yes, Calvin even for me that was disgusting,*" something inside Calvin said in a chorus of voices that echoed around inside his skull like leaves in a storm.

Calvin went to ask what was happening, but he could feel it all too well. He had known that when the Arch Mage had sent him off to the Spirit Realm, he would end up being possessed to become a Warrior Mage, but he hadn't realized just how literal the experience would be. The demon Rinwid had allowed a small part of herself to join with Calvin's spirt, but she was too weak to hold her own shape within his conscious and for now she crept around the edges of his thoughts like an unwanted hitchhiker.

With her essence shifting to be more like his, Calvin could feel the demon inside his skull becoming part of him. Her gender was not as fluid as it had been within the Spirit Realm. Like water poured into a glass, it seemed to fill the container and take on its shape, so she became a he.

The insides of his mouth tasted like a thousand years of rotting fish. His fingers ached and felt like they were held together with twigs. When Calvin's heart beat it seemed sluggish and labored, as if it was being held in a vice, but all of this would have been mildly pleasant in comparison to being able to hear the demon's thoughts.

Calvin wondered if anyone else could hear the beast's voice… he must have — after all — been looked after by some junior mage over the last few days. If they could hear the demon, what lies could it have told? His concerns were soon answered by the voice in his head.

"Look Calvin don't worry. It's only you who's blessed with me. The bond isn't strong enough for me to speak. Not yet anyway," Rinwid, cackled, obviously delighted by Calvin's discomfort.

Demons are psychotic and perverted, and Calvin had spent the last few days in between brief moments of lucidity sharing the demon's dreams.

They were memories he knew he would never be able to shake no matter how many bottles of strong spirit he tried to use. The dreams had allowed him to learn several new ways of sexually harassing an array of animals and he would never be able to look a weasel in the eye again.

"Is there any way I can get rid of you?" Calvin said to an empty room… but he already knew the answer to that.

That was the reason most Warrior Mages went crazy and killed everyone. There was no way of getting rid of the demon until it wanted to leave, and the longer it spent inside its host the less of the host remained.

Calvin couldn't believe the Arch Mage would stoop to this. He wondered if the rant about dragons was even true or if the Arch Mage was just worried about the rumors that Calvin would be the next Arch Mage. One way to guarantee that didn't happen was to make him insane. <u>Wonderful</u>, Calvin cursed to himself.

"Nope, I'm here until our deal's complete — you destroy the Heart and I'm off. Better hurry if you don't want me to get bored. There seems plenty around here for me to play with. That sweet little thing that tended the

garden with you for a start… say what was her name again?" Rinwid said with a smile from inside Calvin.

Unable to find the strength to argue with his new "live-in*"* lodger, Calvin struggled to his feet.

He stood shakily next to his elm bed, waiting for his strength to return. The curtains blowing in the breeze meant that Calvin could see clearly out of the arched stone window. He was thankful of the clear weather, but the wind had turned and was coming from the south. Normally the smell of the Scorched Lands turned Calvin's stomach, which was one of the problems with the tower being built so close to those desolate lands. When the wind was coming from the wrong direction, it brought with it the scent of ash and death. It had been a hundred years since the war, but so much had died in the Scorched Lands that it was still coated in ash and nothing lived there for long.

That was one of the reasons the tower was surrounded by a huge garden. They used strong scented flowers to help combat the smell. Today the rancid stench seemed to make Calvin hungry, the demon inside him was very strong, and the binding between him and Rinwid was happening fast.

Calvin wondered just how long he had to find the Heart the demon mentioned, before he'd be sucking the flesh off some poor critter out there. Distracted as he was, he could tell from the sun's placement in the sky that it was around noon.

Rinwid flashed an image of the sun spinning around the sky six times and if Calvin's poor interpretation of the demon's display was correct, then it was Nywek the ninth of Nylar and his ward from Oakenfall would be there soon.

Calvin still wasn't overly sure just what he was meant to do. The Arch Mage had said something about helping this person defeat the dragons and that seemed to be what the demon wanted to, but just how they were going to do that, Calvin had no idea.

Calvin decided to clean himself up and head up to the Arch Mage's chamber.

To Calvin's surprise the Arch Mage's room was empty. Well that was apart from the book worms and moths, but they were a staple in the dusty old bookcases of any decent magic tower. You couldn't really call yourself a mage unless you had at least a handful of moth-eaten books.

Calvin wondered for a second why the moths would bother flying up this high. Surely there was food a lot lower to the ground for them without them having to fly a thousand feet into the air?

Rinwid flashed a still picture in front of Calvin's mind of the unknown: a stranger with short cropped hair followed by the Arch Mage puffing his way up the stairs. The premonition made Calvin feel a little uneasy, but it was a hell of a lot easier to handle than the Arch Mage's physic communication — for one, no nosebleed.

The door opened startling Calvin. He could tell it was going to take time — if he got it at all — to get used to seeing the future. The only thing he hoped was that he didn't end up as nutty as the Arch Mage because of it.

"Ah Calvin you're here already, good," the Arch Mage said as he ambled into the room smelling rather strongly of Witches Teeth, a rare herb who's only real use was as a cure for baldness. It was something Calvin had never noticed before. He guessed the binding between Rinwid and himself must have enhanced all his senses.

"Yes, I just woke up after our last little chat," Calvin said through clenched teeth not bothering to hide his anger at being forced into this predicament.

"Yes, yes. We can go over that later, if you really must," the Arch Mage said rolling his eyes. "For now, Calvin, this is Darcy Dean. He's been sent here from

Oakenfall," the Arch Mage said giving Calvin an obvious wink.

The Arch Mage's very subtle don't-tell-the-non-mage-we-knew-he-was-coming was delivered like an elephant into a mouse hole. Calvin guessed that if Darcy hadn't already realized he was expected, he did now. It didn't take a demon inside you to be able to see that.

"A pleasure, I'm sure," Darcy said wondering if there was any point giving the mages the letter. He didn't know all that much about magic, but from the strange greeting he and the caravan had been given when they'd arrived, he was pretty sure they already knew why he was there.

It occurred to Darcy that the mages probably knew a lot more about what was going on than he did. He would have to try to get as much information out of them as he could. It would make choosing whether he wanted to be part of this or not a lot easier. Darcy had decided on the two-day journey from Briers Hill that he might want to be part of finding the Heart, as that could be his adventure. He had after all wanted a fresh start. Maybe this was fate offering him his very own adventure, a chance to make a name for himself that would outshine even his father's legacy.

"Darcy is here as an envoy from the King of Oakenfall," said the Arch Mage, and Calvin could feel Rinwid roll his eyes inside him... a strange feeling but probably one of the more pleasant ones he'd had to cope with since awakening.

"Arch Mage, if you want me to help Darcy then surely, we should be honest?" Calvin said unsure of exactly why they were being so diplomatic and hiding the obvious truth.

"It's bad enough that you put this bloody thing inside me. I just want this to go smoothly, so we do what the King requests inside that envelope as swiftly as we're able," Calvin said very out of character.

He had always been relaxed. If anything, he'd probably argued with the Arch Mage less than anyone else, but he could feel his temper soaring for no reason. He realized it was probably Rinwid's doing but there was little Calvin could do to fight it.

"Silence Calvin! The matters of the Tower are not for the ears of everyone," said the Arch Mage shooting a look through his bushy eyebrows that could kill.

Darcy couldn't help but wonder if he had really needed to leave Oakenfall at all. The mages had seemed to know that he was coming, and they obviously knew about the letter. So, it was not that unrealistic that they knew what was written in it already.

"Arch Mage, he must know he's here to ask us to find something. You know it and I know it, so let's just cut to the chase. I want this over before the Blight even starts," Calvin said, and he knew the bravery to challenge the Arch Mage like this was coming from having the demon inside him, as was the knowledge he seemed to know without ever having been told.

It had only been a few days since the Arch Mage had read the spell that had sent Calvin to the Spirit Realm and already, he could feel something changing in him. He was already not the same man who'd spent his life in the tower. Calvin wanted to get the demon out of him before he changed too much.

"Please, both of you! I had heard that dealing with mages was hard work, but you two make negotiating with the White Flags look like a picnic. At least with them we both start on equal pegs. So, you both know what's inside this envelope?" Darcy said.

Darcy was used to Granny normally having one over him when he spoke to her, but this was different. It was obvious that the two mages could see the future —

well the present in an odd light, at any rate… and it was frustrating. Darcy already had enough on his mind as it was.

"See what you've done, Calvin?! Fine! You two sort it out. I'm going back to see what effect this has on things," the Arch Mage said before storming off into the maze of bookshelves to go play with his crystal ball. He seemed to have forgotten that he was the one who'd put Calvin through this and given him the power of seeing the future among other things.

"Sorry for the bad welcome. This place is a mad house. Magic does strange things to a person's mind. Have you opened the letter? Do you know what we're after?" Calvin asked trying hard to find the nice man inside him and push the demon's influence to one side.

"We? … There isn't a 'we' that I know of. I was asked to bring this letter here… that was it. The King wants your mages to find the frozen Dragon Heart and deliver it to Oakenfall," Darcy said a little taken aback.

"Well, give the letter here then," Calvin said reaching his old but plump fingers out.

Darcy passed the letter and Calvin opened it, silently reading. That moment felt like a lifetime for Darcy. Neither of them knew what was driving the other, but without knowing it, both Calvin and Darcy were being driven by fate — they had both been dealt a hand of cards that they had no choice but to play. Neither one had wanted adventure, but now for their own reasons, neither would be able to avoid it.

"It's as you say — the King is offering us mages amnesty if we help recover the Dragon Heart of old. The Arch Mage has organized things, so I have no choice but to recover the Heart," said Calvin.

"*And destroy it!*" chimed in Rinwid silently to Calvin alone.

"So, that's it? I'm done here?" Darcy asked, in his heart not wanting his adventure to end. He had been thinking for days what he would do upon returning to Oakenfall and had no clue. He had always felt a little lost, but now that was magnified.

"I had assumed you would come with me to stop them," Calvin started but stopped. It was already happening — he was presuming that the young man in front of him knew that he was going to be the one to travel to the Scorched Lands to find the Heart and prevent a second Blight, but obviously that was something the demon had projected from the future.

Calvin's grip on just what people knew and didn't know was slipping already after only a few days of such power. It led Calvin to wonder if the crystal balls were created by demons to torment the mortal world — or perhaps more worryingly — if the Arch Mage had used the same spell on himself.

"Them? The King wanted to stop the Poles, but you mentioned the Blight... I did notice that slip of the tongue. Have you seen dragons from the tower?" Darcy asked, wondering if he would return home as a dragon killer.

Surely that would overshadow his father's name. It seemed the two-day journey had cemented his need to make a name for himself in Darcy's mind. Darcy had had a small taste of adventure by breaking the monotony of decades within the estate, and now he was a man obsessed — petrified, naive — but also obsessed.

"No, we haven't, but surely you can tell something is due to happen. Something is on the brink... a time of change has arrived. There's been a hundred years of peace," Calvin said hoping to change the subject. He was still feeling sick and not up to this. If Darcy hadn't decided to go to the Scorched Lands, then telling him about dragons might change his mind. Changing the future rarely ended well.

"Peace?! Maybe for you mages here, but for those of us in the common population not living in this giant towering fort it's been war pretty much solid. I haven't seen my father in..." Darcy stopped. He didn't like letting people close. In his mind it left him weak and people might use something like his relationship with his father against him.

"I wasn't born in this tower you know. I was from Northholm before it was taken. I lost people too," Calvin said.

"I know all about the war, Darcy. Look. Time is short for me... don't ask why, but I must know. Will you come with me to find this Heart?" Calvin said knowing the answer to that question. The Arch Mage had told him days before that he would have to help Darcy across the apocalyptic ruins of the Scorched Lands and his link to Rinwid confirmed it.

"I can't rightly leave you alone with the King's caravan, can I?" Darcy said with a lame smile.

That night spent watching the fireworks already seemed like a lifetime ago, and maybe it was, as Darcy began intending to make his story one worthy of re-telling. He would make sure of it.

Chapter Five – Wood for the Trees

Out across the ocean and away from the hustle and bustle of Oakenfall as well as Calvin and Darcy's journey, another voyage was starting — that of a young elf named Fintan Flynn.

Alienage Isle, which Fintan called home, was contested territory, but it hadn't always been that way. In fact, the landmass had started out as little more than a soggy marsh-covered quagmire and the island had had little in the way of a chronicle for most of known history — that was until the year of 450DB when the elves fleeing the fall of the Earth Mother had landed there after many months at sea.

Once they'd docked and settled the elves quickly built up a thriving village and planted the marsh with seeds that had been taken from the Earth Mother on the distant shore of Gologan. These seeds already strong with energy from the Spirit Realm, thrived in the rich and fertile soil and grew into a forest that now covered most of the isle.

The trees were sacred to the elves just as the Earth Mother had once been. They were the children of their god and it was the huge roots of the forest that had bonded the shifting silt together and changed the face of the marsh into a deep and flourishing forest.

The elves had joined in the battle against the Dragon Overlords and used their druidic abilities to provide aid to the humans in the many battles against the dragons. At the end of the war, when peace was declared, the first free Hanson awarded the Alienage as a sovereign state to Diadan, the King of the Elves.

However, the peace crumbled quickly. With the continent of Neeska all but scorched, there were no resources for the humans to rebuild their fallen empire with, so they turned their attention across the sea to the coast of the Alienage.

King Hanson ordered that the forest be forested to rebuild the city. Scores of men landed on the Alienage and ripped up tree and root alike, quickly turning the edges of the forest back into cracked marshland.

A war began between the two races. However, both sides had already suffered huge losses and neither wanted to resort to open warfare — many of the soldiers had themselves been healed by the elves they were now sent against.

Reluctantly the Hanson king called his men back and began an embargo against elves, maintaining that they were trespassing and occupying his kingdom. The humans had almost pulled out of the island altogether, but the tensions between the two leaders had been passed onto the next generation.

Even as the lands of Neeska healed and a century passed, the tension between the two kingdoms continued. A lot of the citizens of Oakenfall wanted the war of words to end and felt that the island was the elves' home and should remain that way regardless of what the royal family of Oakenfall wanted.

Some of the most supportive of all were within the noble district of the city, and almost all the attacks planned by the most recent king against the elves were reported to them long before they happened. This led to a long and drawn-out stalemate which had cost the kingdom far more than it had the peace-loving elves.

It was one such report falling into the hands of the Queen of the Elves, Cadeyrn Silverleaf, daughter of the savior, Diadan, which sparked whispers amongst her best knights that one of them would be sent to the human lands. That was something that had not happened since the end of the Dragon's Blight.

The missive that had been delivered in the dark of night was the same as had been delivered by Darcy to the mages. It explained the need to find the Heart and the powers it could unleash.

Ever since the elves first left Gologan, they had been seeking a permanent home, so the Heart could be the key to expanding beyond the edges of the small island they clung to like barnacles.

With the help of her Council of Druids Cadeyrn had concocted a plan to finish her father's work and find a safe place permanently for her people.

The small scrap of paper had barely floated to the tabletop after Cadeyrn had finished reading it before she sent word out across the glade for the best of her elves to assemble at sunset to see which would be the one to travel to the human lands of Neeska.

Cadeyrn could not sit back and let the one last chance she could think of to gather enough power to finally breach the Spirit Realm to save her people from slipping past her fingers and into those of the power-mad human king.

When word reached Fintan's long and pointed ears, he felt in his heart he would have to try out. He was young to be considered, but that did not mean he would not try.

The sun was low in the sky as Fintan arrived at the Glade of the Druids at the heart of the village. The warm breeze had brought out the spring flies early and they buzzed around above the amassed crowd in ever-decreasing circles.

The forest had grown tall in the centuries that had passed since the trees were first planted. They now stood high above the huts and flame-lit lanterns. Their interwoven branches blocked out most of the light giving the town a permanently dim, tranquil form of twilight serenity.

The whole effect was added to by the blue glow of the lanterns bouncing off wisps that darted around playfully. No one knew, not even the elves themselves, just why the wisps seemed to favor them, or how they even came to be on the island.

One theory was that the elves were blessed with such a strong connection to the Spirit Realm that they could manifest little bits of it in the real world using their sacred trees as conduits. If that was true it had little effect on the lives of those that called the mystic forest home aside from making those who lived there feel at peace.

The village was almost perfectly picturesque and barely broke the forest edge with its little huts scattered around like fallen acorns. It didn't have roads or paths as such, just gaps between buildings and trees. The modest huts had glass stained by hand which added a cooling glow to an already rare and beautiful sight. Embers gave off a gentle smell of oak as they smoldered away to ash in large stone jars that seemed as randomly placed as the dwellings.

The village was built in a circle around the clearing at its heart. Each little white sandstone dwelling looked almost identical to the next, with perfectly rounded white walls poking out between the trees that grew freely in the village. The elves' huts were capped with thatched sticks and fallen branches, some of which carried feathers and twig nests, or red and yellow mushrooms.

Without borders or a city wall, wildlife walked freely within the village. It was not uncommon to see squirrels, birds, or foxes trying to enter a home or follow along next to the children. One such squirrel seemed interested in the amassed crowd of elves who had started to gather for the trial of prestige, the chance for one of the brave elven knights to head into human lands.

Since the time of the Dragon's Blight the king at that time, Diadan, had handpicked his chosen to send in to battle the dragons. Since that time the tradition had stuck that only the very best could enter human lands.

It was here surrounded by his peers that Fintan would face his challenge. Fintan was considered a huge outsider at the very tender age of forty-three — the equivalent of a teenager if he were of human heritage — as most chosen previously had at least seen in a century or so. No one would have put their money on the young elf, but it did not seem to sway the squirrel that scampered up to Fintan's nervous feet. The little critter pulled at Fintan's sandal as if it wanted him to enter the ring, but when Fintan did not move the squirrel ran off to harass someone else.

Finding his courage Fintan readied himself to push through the crowd. They stepped aside and let Fintan through to join the five others that stood in front of Cadeyrn. A hushed silence hung over the clearing. Unlike the jeering mob that would have amassed if this had been a human affair, the elves treated violence with a silent regard.

"Children of the Oak," Cadeyrn called out cupping her hands together to project her soft voice, "it has been many years since the last of the chosen were sent into the lands of the humans." She paused taking breath. "There has been no need for the chosen since my father's death and we have had no need to risk travel to the mainland. But the time has now come, so it falls on me to watch over this sacred tradition," Cadeyrn continued and the sudden noise sent a flurry of birds nervously into the dusk coated canopy. "Many of you have heard rumor of why I have called this to pass."

Cadeyrn walked back and forth in front of the chosen and the crowd behind them. The Council of Elves was a tradition that stretched back as far as anyone could remember. It predated her father's rise to power and had always been a honey-pot of whispers. Cadeyrn could not sneeze without rumors of a cold reaching the furthest hut in the village before she'd had time to reach for a handkerchief.

"I hide nothing from my people. My family has always been open and honest and so shall I," Cadeyrn said and there was a slight shake to her voice showing she had still not fully come to terms with Diadan's loss. He had been a hero to her people and a beloved figure to all, but more than that he had been her father. Composing herself and once again cupping her hands she continued. "I have been advised that the humans seek an artifact of power. I know this trinket to be the Dragon Heart which froze during the last battle of the Dragon's Blight."

The hushed silence was broken by some of the older elves who remembered the battle. They had been near enough to see the backlash of the spells that ended the war. They had seen the death and destruction that it had wrought on both sides of the conflict and feared that the power of anything to do with those times was best left to the history books.

The chatter faded quickly, and once silence returned to the clearing Cadeyrn continued. "With the Heart we could finally join our lost in the Spirit Realm and leave this forsaken world," Cadeyrn called out, knowing that not everyone would agree with her dream, and she was right as it was met by a mix of hushed opposing views.

Cadeyrn started pacing back and forth. She was worried the calm of the people would falter. The debate about leaving the world was one that had turned heated many times in the conference rooms of the palace. "Be calm my people. I understand your fear of leaving this place. It is my home too."

Cadeyrn stopped talking and paced back and forth in front of the assembled hopefuls. Taking another deep breath she continued, "I was too young to see the hardship of our kin, yet the pain still flows through my veins and because of this, I, your Queen, as my father's daughter, make you the same promise he would have: that I do what is best for my people… for you. We will find this Heart. We will use it to leave this forsaken realm and we will find true peace as we rightly deserve. With that, I hand to you my knights," Cadeyrn said turning to face Fintan and the other competitors.

"Do not harm your opponents, use of magic is permitted. Wooden blades only and if someone wishes to quit allow them to do so with dignity. No teams may pass this test. You must fight this alone. Each one of you is on his own." Cadeyrn stepped down to join the watching crowd.

"The fight starts when the last ray of sun disappears from view. Earth Mother watch over you," she said and with that silence fell over the glade.

Fintan watched the others around him. He could feel his chest beating like a drum and his mouth was drier than a desert dune. The five other competitors drew their weapons with such confidence that it made the slight shake Fintan found occupying his hand an obvious weakness. His stomach churned with nerves as he watched the sun low on the horizon burning red. The long dark shadows of the trees grew as if stretching out to reach the clearing. The whole of the Alienage held its breath as the last rays began to fade and suddenly as if being sucked into the mouth of a giant, the sun vanished below the horizon.

Chapter Six – Fall of a Hero

Fintan was not the only one who was preparing to battle on the night of Dumon. In the nights that had passed since the marking of the New Year, Briers Hill had stood safely but the giant-like people called the Poles were not known for their peaceableness.

They were naturally barbaric and even in times of peace enjoyed tests of strength and boxing along with other blood sports. If the town had not been raided by the Poles, then the fort should have been, but for some reason things had remained still and quiet.

It was not only the elves who had sympathizers inside Oakenfall. King Ingaild of the Poles had issued an order to the fort on Briers Hill within moments of his spies telling him of King Harvey's plan to recover the Dragon Heart.

Unlike most of the races in the world and particularly on Neeska, the Poles did not carry a surname. This was a law King Ingaild believed in wholeheartedly. He agreed with the belief that each person should make his own fame and not follow that of his parents.

When Ingaild had first got word of what the humans had begun to call his people, he'd embraced the name of the "Poles." To him, his people were weapons! He was the hand of war! His people, the Poles were his weapon! His poleaxe reached across the plains of Neeska and towards the heart of his enemy.

Upon hearing his spy's missive, Ingaild decided to send the full force of his army south, ignoring his advisors who'd recommended searching for the Dragon Heart, as Ingaild did not see the point in trekking after some little trinket that may not even exist. No, he had a better plan! By the time the <u>weak</u> finished scurrying around like rats after a scrap, and claimed the Heart, Ingaild planned to have razed Oakenfall to ashes.

Ingaild would leave Northholm in the morning and join his army within a few days as they made the week-long journey towards Oakenfall. While he traveled, there would be no little raids against Hallows Fort, unlike the ones he'd ordered in the past to keep the soldiers there busy. No. This time they would wait until he sent word and the full force of his men stationed at Briers Hill would clear any opposition and be ready to merge with the battalion of men he rode with when they arrived.

Harvey may have planned to use magic and deception to take back Northholm, but Ingaild would use the sheer power of his weapon, his Pole army to march across Neeska before Harvey's lackey ever found the Dragons Heart.

The courtyard in the Pole fort was empty. Its commander had received orders two nights before to hold fire and prepare the men for war.

It was a task he now eagerly awaited, as he was a man born to shed blood and he relished the prospect of all-out war. He was filled with joy when he saw at around midnight on the sixth, the familiar sight of Ingaild's hawk as it soared over his fort gracefully catching the moonlight on its soft white underbelly.

The men may have been climbing into their hammocks, but it turned out that the only thing that would get to rest that evening was the hawk. The news of King Harvey's plans changed things and the war would not just be waged at Briers Hill, but out across the whole of Northern Neeska. It was an order the commander had been waiting for. The stalemate had been grating on his nerves and knowing that tonight it was finally over was wonderful.

The tired hawk was treated for delivering the news and tucked into the flesh of a fallen Hanson knight, whose corpse had been hung in the courtyard. The hawk ripped free a lump of putrid flesh before taking flight with it up to its roost. The high tower used as a lookout point was one of the main differences between the two forts that outlined the horizon.

In almost all other respects the Poles fort was not all that different to its shadowy image across no-man's land — after all, at one time the two forts would have both belonged to the Hanson Kingdom. The Poles kept a grim museum below the ground from when they had first raided their fort. Its cellar was filled with skeletons of the captured soldiers and their families who'd been stationed there when the Poles first crashed down against Briers Hill.

The raid had happened quickly and before Oakenfall could send aid. The people in the fort had tried to lay down arms and surrender but had been forced down into the lowest part of the keep and left to starve in the darkness. There was little need for anyone to go down into that vile-smelling and damp part of the keep to see the dead now, but if they had they would surely have noticed that many of the dead showed signs of cannibalism by the poor souls who'd lived the longest.

The Poles were notorious for this barbaric and aggressive mentality, and it was the reason that they had once ruled all Neeska before the dragons came. It was with this same bloodlust that the Poles would soon flood out into battle. They had spent the previous two days training inside their fort. The army of Poles knew every stone of it, and thus — because of the similarities — knew the same of Hallows Fort.

They could plan exactly where the Hanson Kingdom's archers would be standing on the wooden balcony that followed along the top of their fort's walls.

They knew the best places to pressure the gate to make it fall swiftly. The fort in which Sir Dean was stationed only a few hundred feet away would have subtle differences, but the Poles were ready. They had however thought they might get a decent night's rest before going to war, but that was not the commander's way. So, the silence that came with the dead of night was broken by the gravel-laden voice of the old commander.

"King Ingaild has given the order. Wake you dogs and arm! We go to war tonight!" the commander, Annar of the East, screamed at the top of his lung startling the feeding hawk who leapt into the sky and made its way back to Northholm. It seemed not even the hawk would rest on the commander's watch.

Annar knew his voice would echo out across the land and warn the Hanson Kingdom and he reveled at the idea of the panic in the other keep as they tried to prepare a defense that would fail. Annar was a seasoned warrior and had led countless battles across Neeska and its northern lands for almost thirty years. He was not worried about the enemy knowing he was coming — not at all! He knew that panic made an army weak. It was second only to starvation for bringing an enemy to his knees.

Annar watched in the open unafraid of an early volley of arrows, while the fort was filled with rushed preparations. By three the army was ready. The fort's huge gates opened like the snarling grin of a demon as its aged hinges creaked.

"Roll out the catapults and fetch our Hanson friends from the cellar," Annar said with a twisted smile disfiguring his face. "Let's return them to their families and show the Hansons just what they can expect by dawn," Annar called out again with a husky cackle.

The enjoyment seemed to be shared by the hundred or so men scattered within the keep who began to carry out his warped order. It took a few minutes to load the long dead into the catapults and ready them for fire, which gave the rest of Annar's army time to suit up in chainmail armor.

The grey looked almost black in the darkness of night in contrast with the white of the bones lying in the cups of the catapults. The effect the commander had hoped for was soon achieved. The twang of the rope releasing the dead cargo to sail over no-man's land and down behind the walls of Hallows Fort was met with screams from inside. Even the strongest knights were brought to their knees as body parts rained down and clattered across the floor.

Most of the bones had been picked clean by rats, but not all. Rotten foul-smelling flesh was cascaded across no man's land. Annar heard Sir Dean shout something from across the night but the sound of cheering from his own men drowned out exactly what it was.

With the catapults empty and pushed aside the battle began. The Poles poured out from the fort like ants from a nest and formed into lines twenty men each. As they marched forwards across no-man's land the heavy fall of armored feet churned up the earth in a cloud of dust and mud.

The grass fell flat, and the animals of the night scampered away into the brush. The large-built Poles carried their huge spear-like weapons high above their heads, the axed edge pointed forward like the teeth of a bear closing on its prey.

The weapon was unusual, but one the Poles had carried for many years. It was like a spear with a long thin shaft about six feet in length, and at its head was a sharp point. Just below this was affixed a huge axe-like blade that could be brought down with enough power to shatter stone. The shafts were always inscribed and elegantly decorated, but you would not have seen that as the army moved forwards in the dark of night.

Clouds shifted above covering the moon and bringing an icy chill to the battlefield. It may have been Nylar, the first month of the planting, but the cold of Winnan had not yet faded.

The Poles approached the middle of the clearing and the peak of the hill that separated the two forts, and the men slowed to a halt. They had planned their attack like a well-orchestrated ballet. They dropped to their knees pulling shields up over their head.

This was not the first time they had pressed against Sir Dean's men and the volley of arrows fell as expected, cascading down and bouncing off the steel shields, splintering and only adding to the litter that already cluttered the ground.

One or two Poles were grazed by broken arrows, but none fell dead or were even gravely wounded. As the Pole army knelt in the mud hidden behind their defenses, the men counted, one, two, and three. The Poles knew they had only a few seconds before the next volley would come so they acted quickly.

The man at the front held his position, spear down and straight ahead to stop any frontal attack if Sir Dean's men tried something new. Each man remembered his task, and so they began, their shields at an angle towards the sky to protect against projectiles if the archers on the fort's walls were faster than expected. Not all Poles carried their namesake weapon or shield, at the back of the ranks those without spears took to their calling. With their mammoth sized muscles, they launched rocks the size of people's skulls clear over Hallows Fort's high wall.

The projectiles did trivial damage to the old stones of the fort, doing little more than knocking old moss free, and the attack could easily be defended against by the archers if they moved quickly enough. An untrained commander might have wondered why Annar had even bothered to get his men to do this, but the Poles knew from previous attacks that many of the archers on the walls would have to retreat inside the main keep to make room for their comrades who had been caught by a falling rocks, and that would buy them valuable extra time to press forward.

This was the moment they had trained for over and over in the keep. The knelt knights raised their spears and begun marching forward again towards the fort's walls before the archers returned to their stations.

Annar had not sent all his men in one raid. His reserve ranks at the fort had readied the catapults a second time and they fired again. More corpses sailed across no-man's land and dropped down behind Sir Dean's walls.

A few slow archers were caught by the falling bodies and dragged off the balconies to crash down into the courtyard below and be pinned there by the bodies of their boney companions, in a grim reunion with death.

Sir Dean's men were losing ground fast. Many of his men had been asleep when they had heard Annar's call and the fear that had gripped them at such an abrupt wake-up had been intensified by the bodies that now cluttered the keep.

Soldiers inside waited with swords drawn for the enemy to come close enough to charge while others clung to the ramparts to avoid the showers of stone and putridity.

The Hanson army had managed to hold the Poles at bay many times before by waiting them out — letting them get close and then cutting them down from the walls, but it seemed the Poles had adapted. Sir Dean would have to try something new.

Satisfied things were going to plan Annar jogged across to join his men as they pressed deep against the walls of the eastern keep.

It was typical of the weak Oakenfall knights to be afraid of the dead. The Poles had two choices now that they had surrounded the walls — try to scale the walls or try to breach the huge doors.

The decision was taken from Annar when the doors swung open and Sir Dean's army sprinted out in a surprise attack. The two armies clashed like the sea against rock.

Bodies fell as steel from sword and spear tore chunks out of limbs from each side. In the heated battle friendships faded as body after body fell lifelessly to the ground.

It was not long before the fighting masses were literally falling over each other. The Poles had height and strength on their side, not to mention numbers, as many of Sir Dean's men were still in the town complacently drinking after of so many peaceful nights.

The huge Pole weapons took time to swing and could be avoided. If the lucky target moved at just the right time, the huge axe head at the tip of the spear would crash down into the mud and get stuck rather than cleave his head in two. That gave vital time for plunging a sword deep into the chest or neck of the giant man assaulting him.

The sheer number of Poles meant that even with them being slower there were still two axes for every sword. If a knight was lucky enough to dodge the falling spear and press his blade into a Pole, another axe was already falling against him.

The battle was one sided and Sir Dean's men soon found themselves pressed with their backs to the wall. The initial onslaught faded and like the waves they had mimicked, the men soon started to fall back away from the rock leaving only red pools to show where they had been.

A few of Sir Dean's men tried to drag fallen comrades back with them, but soon gave in as the Poles pressed harder on them. Seeing their fallen allies wailing in pain demoralized the Oakenfall further, when they were forced back within the walls of their keep.

The Poles gave chase but on entering the giant doors of the fort they were filtered into thinner numbers and a second wave of knights led by Sir Dean himself squeezed their sides, outnumbering the pressing army two to one.

Now the Hanson knights had the advantage. Sir Dean nodded to a younger soldier who stood by him and the young man took to running. He slipped past the fighting mass at the front of the fort. His loose-fitting leather armor allowed him to duck and roll and scramble on his knees when he had to, and it didn't take long before he was out on the open road. He was to make it to Briers Hill and warn them. To call back the drunken guards to support the pinned down Hanson knights.

"Get after him!" Annar yelled out and two men from his rear flank gave chase. The young boy was fast, but the size of the Poles meant their strides were not that far short of a horse's and it was not long before they were on him like a pair of wild dogs.

Annar had to admit that using the bottleneck entrance was a clever plan to make the most of Sir Dean's limited men. Sir Dean may have hoped to be able to hold the raging Poles at bay now with little more than a handful of men — but it would not work.

The narrow alley made it almost impossible for the Poles to swing their weapons and they soon started to falter. As they died, they clogged the alley further and made it harder for the next wave to breach the gateway.

Things started to look good for Sir Dean's army and it almost looked like they might be able to thin the Poles' numbers enough to win the battle if their little envoy had made it, but Annar was not an easy foe.

No — he was a man born for the sole purpose of war, much like Sir Dean but without the worthless need for mortality or the falsehood of chivalry. If there was a war to be found, then Annar would be at its head grinning with a face full of the blood and hair of another man in his teeth.

"You know what to do. Take those men and go now. I'll hold these spineless mice here," Annar said before pushing to the front of his men. His eyes wide he roared and plunged his spear deep into the chest of the first unfortunate knight to cross his path.

Annar was like a rabid bear, biting, tearing and slicing against the Hanson army, the narrow alley doing little to slow him. With the attention of Sir Dean fixated on the mad man, a small group of Pole warriors dropped down over the walls behind him.

They made light work of the few archers that guarded the top and suddenly the few knights that had held the courtyard were being pressed from both sides. They soon lost their grip at the fort's front and the Poles poured in flooding the courtyard.

The Poles had lost a lot of men but still numbered fifty or sixty which was substantial compared to the fort's own rapidly falling numbers. Most commanders would have surrendered but Sir Dean had not got his reputation for nothing.

He screamed until his lungs were sore gathering his men to him. They fought their way inside the small hut hoping to make another bottleneck, but there were too few for it to work.

Sir Dean hoped in earnest that the knights from the town would return in time to win the battle, as he did not know about the brutal way his envoy had been cleaved in two.

With their backs to the hut and standing beneath the faded coat of arms they fought. The battle inside the keep raged on for over an hour, steel crashed against steel. Fist, teeth and sweat swirled around as swords fell and bodies dropped.

There were heavy losses on both sides, but the last of the fort's men fell dead collapsing against the cabin's rear wall.

Sir Malcolm Dean had not held back the Pole army, nor did he have the chance for some grand and final words that would be retold in the history books for years to come.

No. Sir Dean died the way he had always lived… as a knight and one of his men, sword in hand.

As more clouds filled the sky and the night grew darker, the surviving Poles dug through the mounds of dead bodies looking for the weeping and screaming bodies of their wounded. Those that could stand with aid would be taken home, and those that could not were killed as failures.

The few unfortunate survivors from Sir Dean's men had their throats slit and their heads removed. Several of the Poles had dug their long spear-like weapons into the earth at the front of the keep and each one was slowly being loaded up with the heads of the fallen, turning the ghoulish scene into a macabre kebab.

The army would rest and treat its wounds then make its way into town. The few knights there would share the same fate as those at the fort.

Briers Hill was to remain standing but under a new flag.

Chapter Seven – Setting Sail

Dawn came to the seventh of Nyla, but it brought no planting sun as it should have. Instead storm clouds made their way in from the mainland and coated the forest in darkness.

The small collection of huts that made up the Alienage sat like grumpy frogs in the darkness, their sad little faces made up of clattering shutters and rocking lanterns.

Leaves whipped past and branches were ripped out of the trees by the power of the wind and rain. Inside one of these windswept houses Fintan awoke and wished he hadn't. His dreams had been filled with visions of flying high over Neeska like an eagle, the sun on his feathers and the breeze beneath his wings.

The pain had faded but reality was thrust on him as his eyes opened. Fintan went to pull himself up in the small cot-like bed he had been cradled in while he slept.

It was made from a fallen tree hollowed out and filled with blossom — a typical bed for the people of the Alienage who used only things that were cast off from nature — but in Fintan's case it could have been made from sharp spikes and vinegar. Although they had used wooden swords in the ritual last evening, he still hurt all over.

His mind wandered back to the evening's sunset. Some of the other competitors had been so quick to act, that Fintan didn't remember all that much of the fight. He remembered watching as the sun vanished. His heart had been pounding so hard he had felt it beating all the way at the tip of his pointed ears.

Fintan's arms were covered in scratches and his chest was bruised from the several blows he had taken.

They had turned a nasty black and yellow color and felt raised. His nose still had crusted blood beneath it. His long blond hair was matted with blood from a head wound.

It had been a lucky blow that had sent him to his knees with blurred vision. Fintan had trained so hard for the last few years but he was inept compared the others. He'd been an outside bet at best, but still the fight had been humiliating.

Propping himself up in bed, Fintan remembered how he had been knocked to his knees and was left waiting for a blow to the back of his head to finish him off, but the blow had not come.

Fintan remembered how he had prayed to the Earth Mother that he might win the fight. He so wanted a chance to leave the island to find adventure and this might be his only chance to do that. It was then that it happened. Fintan had managed to summon up thick roots from the ground!

He was as shocked as the crowd watching, as the huge roots tore through the soil with such speed that no one could avoid them. They had knocked competitors to the ground and wrapped around everyone, including the assembly of watchers.

It was as if the trees themselves had picked Fintan for the journey! The courtyard had filled with the roots like a giant's spaghetti bowl and at its center completely untouched was Fintan.

He remembered pulling himself to his feet and looking at the damage the roots had done. They'd burrowed through the walls of close-by huts. Behind the thicker sections of roots Fintan could just see arms sticking out struggling to be free. It had taken three hours for the few villagers that had not been involved in the battle to cut the trapped elves out. Thankfully no one had been seriously hurt.

Fintan pushed himself up in bed and sighed as he remembered the look everybody had given him. He was physically hurt, but that was not what bothered him the most. Fintan had trained to put pain behind him. He had spent years as a child working on pushing agony to the back of his mind.

He had always wanted to be a warrior. The thing that he just couldn't shift was annoyance about the truth of the matter — druids were not allowed to the mainland.

Diadan had dictated that at the end of the Blight all druids had to stay and tend to the forest. It had been Diadan's plan to make Alienage as beautiful as the sacred forest of old.

That was an idea Fintan had been all for during most of his life. You see, he'd never had any connection to the forest like the druids. So, it was easy for him to have grand dreams of adventure and let someone else stay home and tend the rosebushes, so to speak — but now it was him who might end up being a druid!

Fintan paused in bed, there really wasn't a "might" to it. No one who wasn't a druid could control the Lifeforce in that way... not even human mages. Some of the older druids could speak to the animals, or make plants grow. The most powerful could shape the trees like Fintan had the night before, but it took years of training and then only a handful could manage to summon roots for a short time which would soon fade back down below the ground leaving nothing but muddy memories.

Fintan hadn't even been very good at maintaining his garden outside his hut — but that was before he fell to his knees and then summoned something so powerful that even now, the following morning, he could still see the blasted thing from his window.

The only creatures not disturbed by them seemed to be the squirrels that had their own carriageway through

Alienage now. Not to mention hundreds of new and exciting places to bury their nuts.

Fintan had fought so hard for the chance to see the world outside Alienage — it had been his dream for most of his life. When he was younger, he had played make-believe that he was off on some adventure for King Diadan and while other children learned what herbs from the forest made the best salves, Fintan was climbing trees and in his mind, he was at the top of a mountain fighting ogres.

This chance had now been stolen from him — the thought circled in his mind once more — druids cannot leave.

Fintan's peace and quiet was interrupted by a knock at the door. He ignored it to start with, thinking it was another falling branch but the second time it came with more of a rat-a-tat-tat, Fintan pulled himself to his aching feet.

He wrapped himself in a pale cream-colored cloth gown made from the bark of the Mulberry trees that grew at the forest's edge and made his way towards the door. Most of the trees in the forest were oaks grown from the seeds of the Earth Mother. When they had started to get taller and more birds had flocked to the island, they'd brought seeds themselves in their excrement and these had since grown in sporadic locations around the island.

Some of these trees had been a blessing from nature when the trade with the mainland had ended, and with it the influx of usable wool or cottons. Without the tapa cloth the people of Alienage would have had to find new ways to clothe themselves.

When Fintan opened the door and saw Cadeyrn standing on his doorstep, he suddenly wished he'd worn something a little less loose as the wind was lifting the bottom up just far enough to make things embarrassing. Either Cadeyrn didn't notice or didn't care.

"May I enter, or shall we speak in this lovely breeze?" she said with the wind blowing through her short hair.

That was an idiosyncrasy in the elven community, as long hair and pointy ears seemed to go hand in hand, but Cadeyrn had always been a little odd. It was a trait of her fathers that would probably be a family trait for centuries to come.

She did not have long flowing locks of hair; in comparison she kept her blond hair short just above her shoulders. Cadeyrn was slender and beautiful, well normally, for now her hair was flat against the side of her face wet with rain and it was only the gusts of wind that gave it any life.

"I'm sorry, come in, come in," Fintan said trying desperately to hold the gown down.

He closed the small door behind Cadeyrn and watched nervously as she looked around his home. Fintan wished he'd cleaned up more. The oven was ash filled and cold. The last fire had not been emptied out for a few days and a couple of dirty plates rested on its top.

His wardrobe was still open from when he'd grabbed the gown and was filled with ruffled up clothes that looked more like rags. His bed was unmade and Fintan suddenly remembered he himself had not bathed after the trial the night before.

There was little he could do now but try to hide the dried blood in his hair and pretend he didn't smell like a wet dog.

"You might try to guess why I'm here Fintan, but I doubt you will," Cadeyrn said as she lifted herself onto the table and rested down gently into a seated position. "Now if you would stay quiet. I do not have long to talk, and you have even less time to listen. That is if you plan to catch the boat," she continued smiling.

Cadeyrn had a smile that could melt ice and it seemed to bring warmth to the cold morning. Her looks were like her mother's, an elf woman who could bring men to her knees, and even wet-through and windswept Cadeyrn was still enticing to look at.

"What boat? You saw what I did! I'll never get to leave here," Fintan said half expecting this was a twisted joke, but the look on Cadeyrn's face showed just how serious she was.

"Normally anyone that showed the kind of skill in druidism that you did last night would never get to leave this island, but that is exactly why you will." Cadeyrn slipped back to her feet.

"I will be telling everyone that you have been sent out into the forest to learn your new skills and find a spirit guide," Cadeyrn said pointing out the window to the tree line that surrounded the village. "But the truth is you'll be catching a boat in one hour from the harbor and racing the storm to Port Lust."

"What? I don't get it," Fintan said forgetting his manners in the confusion. He had barely awoken, and his head was still pounding like a drum.

"They say beauty and brains don't go together and you prove them right Fintan. You've been training for this since we were little. I remember watching you in the forest when mother took me out for walks. You were quite a cute young thing, all scrawny like a gazelle," Cadeyrn smiled as she remembered.

"I am offering you what you have always wanted. Why do you question it?"

"What of the old ways?" Fintan asked. He had always wanted to leave, but from the moment he had summoned the roots he was sure he wouldn't get to.

"As Queen, I make the ways… this is the best plan of action. You have probably seen humans sneaking to the edge of the forest by town and so have I. I don't think for a second it is only us that know what our enemy is planning," Cadeyrn turned to face the window overlooking the town.

"You mean spies, don't you?" Fintan said weakly. The pain washing over him, and the grogginess of sleep had started to fall away from him, and he started to get an understanding of what Cadeyrn might be hinting at.

"Exactly, now hurry and get dressed Fintan," Cadeyrn said turning to look out the window with her back to him. Fintan complied, but slowly at first.

He was not sure what made him more uncomfortable. The fact it felt like a bear was chewing at his ribs every time he tried to lift his arms or that Cadeyrn might turn around at any moment and see him nude but the prospect that he would still be getting to leave the island made him push through it.

"I want you to go in secret. Just as we have sympathetic people in Oakenfall, there are elves here that feel the humans have the right to our forest as much as we do," Cadeyrn paused dropping her head to look at the floor. "Who knows, maybe they are right but not while I live. It's because of these spies that the moment our ship left the port for the mainland someone would send word to the Hanson Kingdom," Cadeyrn continued, watching the weather from the window.

The weight of the rain was making the roots sag in places and it looked like they might start retracting soon. A large splatter of rain carried in the breeze snapped her attention back and she continued.

"Whoever I sent would be apprehended the moment they docked. Brantley will be a diversion, as you will be leaving two days before him and you will be going via Port Lust, and not docking south of Oakenfall as he will be. That way any plan to stop us will be sent the wrong way, and by the time King Harvey gets that information out of Brantley you will be deep inside the

Scorched Lands," Cadeyrn paused and panic flushed through Fintan who half expected her to turn around as he was mid-way through pulling up his brown linen trousers. She didn't but she did giggle softly under her breath. "Relax Fintan. You have nothing I have not seen before," she said realizing why the often chatty Fintan had been quite so quiet behind her.

"You haven't seen mine though, Your Majesty." Fintan said nervously wrenching his belt closed and reaching for a jacket.

"A shame indeed, I fear," Cadeyrn joked — at least Fintan presumed she was joking. "There is always time for that after this is all over. I put my trust in you Fintan to find the Heart. Once you dock, you'll be on your own. You must find out what you can about the Heart and find the humans in the Scorched Lands. Our druids have asked the animals and they know nothing of the Heart. Let us hope this sudden blessing from the Earth Mother last night was a sign," Cadeyrn said once again looking outside.

The foul weather would hide Fintan's departure. She had to put hope in the old teachings and prayed this was the Earth Mother's will. "I must be going now. You have fifty minutes to get your stuff together and be gone. Earth Mother watch over you," Cadeyrn said and began to walk towards the door and was about to open it before she turned back to face Fintan. She stifled a laugh at his back-to-front shirt.

"There will be a suit of blessed armor aboard the ship. It bears our flag and belonged to my father. He wore it during the Dragon's Blight. It was a gift from the dwarves before they sealed up their mine. He was always like you. He never conformed either. You remind me of him, Fintan. Come home safe, won't you," Cadeyrn said with a smile and vanished out into the cold.

Fintan stood in shock as the door clicked shut before struggling to take the shirt off again.

Fintan sprinted towards the secret boat, but not before the rain and foul winds grew even harder. This would aid in him being unnoticed as only the insane or desperate would venture out into a morning like this.

The wind had turned into a full-blown storm and the trees that marked the edge of the forest swayed like drunks. The strong winds that had been battering Alienage village when Cadeyrn had visited were nothing in comparison to the raging torrent they had now become.

The gale inside the forest was weakened by the trees, so the sudden blast that hit him as he pushed out into the marshes staggered him, sucking away his breath and stinging his eyes. As the forest receded into grasslands, the grass at waist height whipped at Fintan's legs like an angry slaver.

The silt-laden mud gripped his feet making moving forward difficult — it felt like muddy hands were clinging to his boots — but Fintan pushed on.

He'd practiced his whole life for just a moment like this, but it was a damn sight harder to slog through weather like this than it had been in his imagination. He had pretended as a boy to be climbing mountains with the wind blowing in gales, but he'd never imagined the burning cold in his lungs or his inability to see.

The rain came down in buckets and soaked everything it touched in moments. The sodden earth had quickly turned into a soup and the marshes hid Fintan's footsteps in a flood of brown sludge. It was as if the world itself was helping the Queen's plan to hide Fintan's voyage. He wondered if it really was the wishes of the great oaks or just a turn of bad luck.

Fintan had expected the vessel he would be travelling in to be small, but he hadn't expected the small two-man yacht that greeted him as he slid down a muddy embankment.

It was a small fishing vessel that would normally only be crewed during fine weather but was now being tossed around next to the small jetty like a gold coin being rolled between a rich man's knuckles.

The "ship's" captain much to Fintan's surprise was a human. The sea sprayed figure was a gruff old-looking man whose beard looked like it could have crawled off his face and lived independently. That was if it was not attached to the bright purple nose that sat like a plum on the old man's face.

The aged captain helped Fintan aboard with his hooked arm — hooked as old, very bony and extremely weather worn, not as in pirate-hooked. Fintan was thankful for the aid as his feet slipped from under him and without it, he would have probably fallen into the breaking waves that rattled the ship.

Once onboard and safely gripping onto a rope the old sea captain had given him, Fintan tried to peer through the rain. The deck of the boat was soaked and bare apart from coiled ropes and a chest that had been bolted down which Fintan presumed held the armor of his dead King.

Even soaked to the bone Fintan tried to edge his way towards the box. The chance to wear the royal armor was an honor Fintan couldn't have imagined.

It was then that it hit him. Fintan had been too busy to really think about anything apart from fighting through the harsh weather. But now that he had a few moments while the captain readied the vessel, and when his mind should have been questioning if he would indeed survive and why Cadeyrn had sent a human to aid him, Fintan's mind floated back to his parents.

He would have loved his parents to know that he, a trader's child, a druid, would wear the King's armor. The memories dropped on him like a ton of lead and obliterated any other thoughts he might have had.

It was a stormy night much like this when Fintan had lost both his parents. They had been traders for the elves taking the wood fallen in the forest that they didn't need to trade with White Isle. That was one of the few boons of the rivalry with Oakenfall — they had formed a strong alliance with White Isle.

The human sharing the rough voyage with Fintan was probably one of those captains. As the sailing ship driven by the aged and probable White Flag pirate pulled out into the open sea, Fintan's mind couldn't help but envision images of his parents clinging to the small ship as it was tossed around and finally overturned in the White Sea.

His guilt was choking, and it was something he had not thought of in a long time. He should have been with them that day, but he had been off playing make-believe and had missed the ship, so they had sailed without him. He had been young, but he'd always felt he might have been able to do something to save them or have at least said goodbye. However, his parents never made it home, and were presumed dead, but Fintan's lust for adventure had not died with them.

Fintan's eyes clouded over as his thoughts faded from his parents to harsh reality as a wave smashed into the side of the ship almost knocking him overboard.

Chapter Eight – White Flags and Empty Bellies

The City of Oakenfall had rapidly fallen into misery and desperation in the week since Darcy had left the city and long before Fintan had boarded his ship. Unbeknownst to them both, they had been one step ahead of the crumbling kingdom since the moment their adventures had begun.

The situation in the city had been bad for many months, but in the days following the celebrations and the start of the unlikely hero's journey, the house of cards had begun to tumble.

Darcy was not the first noble to have been sent out to find the Dragons Heart. In fact, in the months that had preceded Darcy being selected four others had been sent to the Scorched Lands to find it too. As they had failed to find it, or even return to the city, the chances of Darcy being the one to find the Heart were slim. That was why Harvey had reluctantly decided to reach out and involve the mages.

It was very wet the morning Darcy's caravan rolled out into the rainy and mud-laden gullies in the farmlands around Oakenfall that things began to change within the city. No sooner had Darcy disappeared over the first grassy hill, a second convoy was also sent out from the castle. This emissary would not have had such a secret order, as he had the much more easily-noticeable command to ensure that the guards who'd had been protecting the outer reaches of the kingdom were pulled from their patrols.

Even as Harvey wrote the missive and sealed it with wax, he had known that the decision would have ramifications, but time was growing short, and if sacrificing the surrounding farmlands saved countless people in the city, it was worth it. As King, Harvey knew that homes could be reclaimed, farms rebuilt, and commoners compensated for the loss of loved ones, but kingdoms once fallen rarely recovered — and to him, all that mattered was ensuring that the rule of the Hansons outlasted that of Ingaild and the blasted Poles.

By nightfall on the first day of Darcy's journey the first of the soldiers and guards arrived back within Oakenfall from the nearest farmsteads. They were the first of many that would slowly trickle back in towards the city leaving mile upon mile of grassland outside of Oakenfall empty and unprotected.

The lands of Northern Neeska had been a breeding ground for bandits ever since the dragon's dominance had ended, but Harvey could not spare men to guard roads and farms. He needed every trained man aboard the fleet.

At first people within the city were glad to see loved ones returning to the city — the town criers even going so far as to sing of an end to the war — but the jubilee didn't last long, and the city streets were no safer from conscription into Harvey's new fleet.

The last of the guards from the fields finding their way into the city were tasked with ensuring that all city servants, soldiers, knights, or guards stationed within the city were drafted to join the fleet. This left the poorer parts of the city open to the gangs that called the taverns and brothels home.

Harvey's short-sighted actions had more repercussions than he had expected and within the city things turned sour quickly. It had taken no more than a few days for the highwaymen and bandits to hear about the unguarded roads before they started raiding almost every trade caravan that tried to make its way to Oakenfall.

With the roads impassable, and the seas taxed by the White Flags, trade inside the already over-stretched city was strangled, the situation made worse with extra mouths to feed, refugees and soldiers alike. The first of the hungry were even gathering outside the castle by the time Darcy had made it to Briers Hill.

By the fourth day the protests grew more hostile. With food not coming in by land or by sea, with hungry bellies and children to feed, the rioters had turned their attention to the noble estates, which had been left defenseless without guards to stop the would-be liberators.

The worst of the gangs used the opportunity to pillage the city from within, that is, until they learned the truth — that there was no money or food inside the rich and lavish houses to be taken.

The people had no choice but to remain in the dying city. The threat of bandits in the fields around the city trapped the poor inside in a state of civil unrest, as the ships that had sailed would not return for some time. This led to growing tensions, while Harvey sat waiting for the Heart to return. He clung to the hope that the Heart could still turn things around… faith, even blind faith, is a powerful comfort.

Where one man found comfort in blind faith, others saw opportunity. The disorder on the streets would have pulled Oakenfall apart from the inside in only a few days, and signs of the dissent were clearly visible behind the picket lines of protestors.

On the morning of the fifth day, at dawn, ships appeared on the horizon that brought hope for the common man. As it was with the elves and mages, secrets in Neeska spread faster than the breeze and word of Oakenfall and its plight had reached across the sea to Slickrock.

William Boatswain, captain of the White Flags, had sent his first mate to Oakenfall with supplies from Slickrock. He had docked at the harbor bringing with him riches and food to disperse among the people. It was a bold move even for the Flags, but they would have been fools not to take such a colossal chance at gaining favor in the city for their goal of governmental rule.

The crew of the White Flags spread their influence quickly with easy coin at the docks and seemingly asking very little in return. They had connections with the criminal families and almost overnight set up a black-market for food and aid.

The captains listened to all the stories of hardship from the farmers and traders and awarded loot from the hull of their ships to any whose story sounded even partly plausible in return for aid — those taking food would be conscripted to support the White Flags when the time came to forcefully remove the monarchy. Some held out, but after several days of no meals, even the most diehard royalists found themselves queuing for a pirate handout.

William had leapt on the chance to gain favor in such a lightly defended city… it had given the pirates the very rebellion they'd wanted.

At the other end of the city away from the docks, hidden behind the castle walls Harvey waited. He hadn't slept in days and fear began to poison his mind.

His fear was fueled when word reached him of his waning support and the encroachment of the enemy within his own city. As it often does, fear turned to anger. Harvey was angry because he'd given his whole life to the city — spent every coin he owned, sacrificed his reign, his family and his honor for the city — and its people were turning on him for little more than soggy bread and salted meat!

The city was his by birthright, it had been that way since the city was gifted to his family when the dragons had been vanquished. If it was not for the Hansons, there would have been no Oakenfall! The north would have fallen to ruin like the lost City of Old Northholm, Harvey would die before he saw anyone else take his throne and expose the north to barbarian rule.

It was on the morning of the ninth day since Darcy had left Oakenfall, while patrolling the ramparts of his castle and watching the revolutionists gather, that Harvey would receive dire news that would test him to the very brink of his sanity. The test came from a voice calling out from below among the throng of angry faces.

"Sire, I have news from Briers Hill," the young voice called out above the din of the crowd of disgruntled citizens.

The voice belonged to a guard that Harvey did not recognize, but even from his high vantage point, Harvey could see the man was exhausted... and he had the right to be. The messenger was clearly wounded and had ridden nonstop from Briers Hill ahead of the warband of Poles. It was only because of sheer stubbornness that he had not fallen over into the sweet embrace of death.

Harvey too was depleted. He had barely slept now for nine days and his grip on the waking world was slipping. He could barely muster the energy to pull himself up to lean over the wall to see the face of the man who was calling out to him. As Harvey looked down over the parapets, he recognized some of the rioters below.

They swore and spat at the castle walls. Some threw stones and Harvey dared not linger at the wall's edge for long. His voice weakened from fatigue Harvey spoke to the guard who'd escorted him to the rampart via the arched entrance from the keep.

"Bring the messenger to me, but for the love of god don't let that mob inside the keep. You have my permission to do whatever is necessary." Defeat was clear in Harvey's voice as he stepped back from the wall as rocks bounced down barely missing him.

"Sire," the guard replied, bowing just slightly and turning to make his way nervously to the entrance. He suspected that opening the doors to the keep without letting the mob of angry protestors in would be a challenge.

Harvey headed in the opposite direction back up to the throne room. Once inside the familiar safety of the room, he made his way, as he had done so many times in recent weeks, towards the faded tabletop map of Neeska.

Harvey picked up a small wooden figure from the table and placed it into the Scorched Lands. Harvey had been raised by his father to prepare for war. He'd trained most of his life for it and spent countless hours staring at the table planning his next move, but now he was out of ideas, and no amount of moving the pieces would bring him peace.

Harvey was a king who in his own way loved his city, but he would have been better off as a commander in the army. Ruling a city involves taxes, diplomats and trade, but Harvey was suited for war. He hadn't wanted any of this to happen, but he knew of no other way. He was brought up to never to give in and had been born to war.

The world saw Harvey as a harsh and ruthless king, but his father had been worse, even mercilessly beating Harvey when he was but a boy, if he submitted in sword training... sometimes even when he gave the wrong answer while being forced to stare at the map and listen to his father's plans for conquest.

The people didn't realize what had happened behind closed doors and they did not see the sacrifices and pain that Harvey felt... the emotional and physical scars that haunted him. No, they would only see his failings.

Harvey stood staring into space remembering all he had been exposed to, his fingers rubbing against the polished top of the little wooden figurine and in that moment of solitude, Harvey spared a thought for the young nobles he had sent to their deaths.

Harvey knew he was a hated monarch — he made rash decisions, he was quick to anger — but he was not an evil man, though most would disagree. Harvey knew this and wished that the people would trust him to lead them out of all this, wished that they could share his dream of victory and freedom. He would have given anything to have been a hero king, but with his very being, he feared becoming the last of his reign, and a failure.

Harvey took his hat off and wiped his forehead of the sweat that had gathered on it. His eyes were tired and bloodshot. He could not remember the last time he had gone to his bedchamber. Had it been a day or two now? He had no clue. Harvey felt that his stress was already at breaking point and felt like just throwing the crown into the gutter and leaving the city to its fate, but he couldn't. That was not who he was. He <u>was</u> the city and he would die here.

Harvey pushed his hat back on tight and flicked the feathers back and forth as he often did to calm himself. The crown was not the same gold one his father had worn, as Harvey had commissioned one to be made at a local tailor, Spinks & Son, within the city. He was not all that different from Darcy in that respect, wanting to make his own name and not live under the shadow of his father.

Harvey paced back and forth around the tabletop staring at the wooden piece that represented Darcy in the Scorched Lands. Harvey feared that Darcy would not be back in time with the Heart to stop the Poles. The city had become a powder keg and Harvey had to act.

The city was poorly defendable at the best of times. It hadn't needed huge walls to protect it while the dragons occupied it, as no one in their right minds would have attacked it. The walls around the castle were more for show and there was little in the way of siege engines for use.

The only viable option Harvey could think of for preventing internal implosion was to send word discreetly to the White Flags and hope they could muster enough men — cutthroats and brigands as they were— to fight off the Poles.

The Hanson Kingdom would have to deal with one problem at a time and for now that was to survive the week. The debate about his throne — monarchy or republic — could be battled out later.

Harvey was not about to see the kingdom fall under his rule and if it came to allowing pirates to die for his beliefs then that was an easy choice to make, though Harvey knew his father would not have approved.

Chapter Nine – Hope Across the Sea

On White Isle only around twenty-five miles as the crow flies from the hardship in Oakenfall was the town of the pirates, Slickrock.

Slickrock was a masterwork of wooden craftsmanship. It was built in an odd array of ship-like looking buildings and piers rather than as a conventional town.

It had been built on stilts that ran out above the white sandy beach and into the sea. It was a u-shaped multi-story town of oddities with no two buildings looking the same.

Some buildings took on the shape of ships even down to having figure heads attached to the walls, and others looked more like traditional cabins. Some had bigger upstairs levels than they did down below with extensions built for loading cranes. Almost all of them had rigging and rope ladders hanging from window to window.

The long piers at either end of the U were the perfect height for boarding the large pirate ships that often lined the horizon. Barrels dotted the promenade and many of them ended up being used as tables and playing cards or empty tankards littered their tops.

It was a boisterous town that had more alehouses than Northholm or Oakenfall added together and was only around one tenth the size of those two stone giants.

It shared a similarity to the harbor and dockyards of Oakenfall in that it was often changing. As ships mutinied and captains changed, so would the buildings that had once held their crew.

The island itself was mostly covered with high cliffs which seemed to be home to half the seagull population of all Neeska and they often left their tell-tale white glaze on the roofs of Slickrock. The seagulls had grown fat on the gluttony of the island in the same way many of the human inhabitants had.

The island was a smugglers' haven with many of the tunnels that ran through the island large enough for small boats to sail through, and the inner caves were full of hidey holes and lost stashes.

The island was even more attractive to pirates as it sat on the only "safe" shipping route out of Oakenfall — "safe" that is, in comparison to the jagged reefs east of Oakenfall that ran between the mainland and Alienage Isle. Those reefs were sharp, numerous and hidden just below a ship's wake. They forced all ships to sail northwest before they could join the open ocean and the shipping routes of the White Sea. This detour northwest pushed any trading galleon within a few miles of the beach of Slickrock.

White Isle had always been prosperous for thieves and some historians claimed that it was with loot stolen from the Dragon Lords that the dark-skinned sea-faring elves of Gologan managed to set up their harbor of Portsea to escape fiery retaliation.

The risk of the odd dragon reprisal had been worth the payoff and being able to dive into nearby water made the fire breathing giants seem a little less scary, so the many different pirates flourished.

This rugged and often dangerous way of earning a living had earned White Isle a deadly reputation. It was not until William Boatswain, father of the current lord of Slickrock, settled there in the winter of 51AB that the beach had started being built up into the thriving and tavern filled port it was today.

William's father had a charisma that had settled the rivalry between the many different pirates that sailed close to the island, and brought them all into agreement about sailing under one flag and for the most part not openly killing each other. Before his rule the pirates spent as much time killing and stealing from each other as they did from traders. There are stories that survive to this day of lost loot hidden in forgotten caves by pirates who never returned to collect their plunder.

A few drunken pirates had told stories of passing through the caves below Slickrock and seeing flickers of gold beneath the waves and rubies as big as a man's head protected by the spirits of the dead captains — or worse — dragon curses. None of this dissuaded the late Captain Boatswain from building his city and becoming the legend among sea faring folk that he was.

William had been only seven years old when he watched his late father being killed without trial by the Hanson Monarchy. His father's dead body was tossed overboard by King Hanson's fleet just from White Isle and he had waited for it to be washed ashore. That was the moment when the son of the pirate king swore that the Hanson family would not keep the throne.

William believed that everyone should have a say in how the country they lived in was run. How the coffers would be spent and what law and punishment would be handed out should not come down to one man. No man should be killed without fair trial and William refused to rest while bodies like his father's still washed up on white sandy shores.

The small boy was heir to the town of Slickrock and many expected the pirates to start fighting again to claim the land, but they didn't. The boy's dreams made sense to the freedom loving men and women of the Flags. William was barely ten years old when he commanded several ships that sailed under his ideals and the name of the White Flags. Now at the age of thirty-two William commanded more ships than he could count.

The way piracy was carried out on the White Sea had changed even more under his leadership than it had under his father's. Traders could pay a fee either weekly or per ship to ensure they were left unhindered and many lives were saved because of it, both pirate and trader. That was the reason most traders liked the Flags. It was cheaper to pay the White Flags' tax than to hire mercenaries to protect their cargo, which had often been stolen in the olden days.

That is not to say that the seas around Neeska were completely safe, as there were still a few heartless crews that sailed under their own flags, but they could be counted on one hand and avoided White Isle as they were unwelcome there.

As his empire grew the young William remained true to his beliefs many years on from his first promise. William now had the power to directly oppose the new King of Oakenfall openly. His navy was larger and better equipped than that of Oakenfall and his people were more loyal.

Late on the evening of the tenth of Nylar word arrived at the port of White Isle — more honestly… to William's wench-filled bedroom. The message was a short one: that Briers Hill had fallen, and that King Harvey Hanson wanted to meet with him.

As William listened to the report it occurred to him that it could well have been a trap in response to so many households joining the White Flags in the last few days, but William liked the idea of risk in every aspect of his life. That was he had chosen to lie with the married women that lay next to him, rather than with the far less risky courtesans waiting just outside his estate. William was an addict of excitement, actively seeking danger in most aspects of his life.

To say William's tastes were flamboyant would be an understatement. He was rich, powerful, and eccentric, so there was little that was beyond him.

The opportunity for excitement in Oakenfall was too much for him, and much to the annoyance of the lady he'd promised to spend the night with, William left for his ship at once, leaving her waiting atop the covers of his red silken sheets.

When he arrived at his ship, William strutted like a cockerel straight towards the ship's aft and took the wheel. He was still in his night-time attire of a fine silken robe that draped over him in bright green with extremely extravagant gold trim. The robe was embossed with gold leaf and looked ridiculously expensive.

William had had time to change into something more suitable for meeting the King and for the journey ahead of him, but the sensation caused by his strutting up to the castle in his boudoir clothing just added to his excitement — he thrived on people talking about him.

It was warm enough because of its double breasting and lining with a white woolen shirt that was cuffed at the elbow. It was a lavishness presented to William by a friendly trader by the name of Spinks to ensure safe passage for an entire year and was expertly well crafted.

William hazarded a guess that with Oakenfall struggling the way it had been for so long, the robe would be far more expensive than anything Harvey might be wearing. William was used to the finer things in life and his long black hair was soft and smooth even though he lived in the salty air of Slickrock. He bathed it in fresh coconut milk that he had specially delivered by a rather charmingly beautiful and sun-kissed woman from some southern island or other in the Greenstone Isles.

The storm that had been ravishing the north for almost a week was still holding firm and it would take about twelve hours of sailing against it to reach Oakenfall — if the ship did make it over the rolling waves and against the fierce wind. It was a voyage only the insanely cocky would attempt and that was exactly why William did not wait for calmer weather.

He would rather drown in a shipwreck than have anyone think he wasn't brave enough to face the huge waves that rattled the very foundations of Slickrock.

The journey was a rough one and even the more experienced of the crew felt the effects of seasickness as the ship was tossed from bow to stern. The already weather-worn golden figure at the ship's bow looked even more forlorn than normal, as the carved women was dressed in seaweed and dripping white foam.

The waves grew as the night went on and as the moon fell from its highest point and started to make its journey down below the sea, the ship groaned at the hand of waves which reached five to ten yards high and crashed against the deck leaving fish flopping on the well-polished hardwood.

The ship, *Melinda*, had a lonely trek across the treacherous ocean alone with her crew who were a rather motley looking lot. She saw nothing but lightning and rain for most of the twelve-hour voyage. That was apart from one small two-man craft that was rolling on the waves. William watched from behind his ship's wheel, soaked to the bone and with nothing but a rope tied around his wrist to hold him to it.

Even through the fog of sea foam he recognized the flag of Mad Jack, the only captain crazy enough to be out in weather like this in something so small. He was the only pirate William knew that could make him look cowardly and by all rights and reason Mad Jack should have died a hundred times over. The little vessel almost crashed into the side of the *Melinda* before a wave grabbed it and tossed it away towards the west.

William swore for a moment in a flash of lightning that he saw a pointy eared elf aboard the little boat before

132

it vanished from view. Not dark-skinned, and sea-faring elf, but a soft forest dweller. The weather must have been playing tricks on his mind.

The black triangular sails of the *Melinda* held taught with rope were stretched to their limits and the ship battled around against the wind. The three, square windows at the rear of the ship creaked in their frames and threatened to give way as the spray from the ocean shattered against them.

The forty men aboard the *Melinda* sighed with relief when at dawn the clouds began to fade, and the sea settled to a mill pond. William stood at the wheel watching the morning sun light up the pier at Oakenfall. He couldn't help but spare a thought for the other ship and Mad Jack from the night before.

William said a silent prayer to the spirits of the sea that they made safe port somewhere. He had an odd respect for Mad Jack and couldn't picture the day when the craziest pirate of the White Sea finally pushed his luck that little bit too far.

The *Melinda's* crew tethered her quickly to the dock, helped by the locals who'd rushed out with eagerness hoping this White Flag ship held as much free coin as the last ones that had docked.

This was the first time William had seen Oakenfall in many a year and it still looked a beautiful sight to him even with its riot-damage. The narrow roads at the docks had started to be cleaned up under White Flag leadership and William could tell by the singing coming from the local taverns that his gold was rapidly falling into the gutter.

William walked down past the damaged dockyard. Listening to the gentle rattle of ship masts, it was an oddly peaceful calm after the fury of the storm. Within a few minutes of brisk walking the docks gave way to the lower town and the white and black taller townhouses that people called home.

As William crossed one of the many little bridges, he spared a moment to toss a small stick over the edge and watch as it sailed underneath. It never did come out the other side as it got caught on some debris from the night's storm, but it was a game William had always enjoyed, so he was reluctant to leave the trapped stick, but other than climb under the bridge to free it, he had little choice.

William continued taking his time and absorbing the city's temperament… that was until he was met at Celebration Square by two guards from the castle who seemed like they might be loyal to Harvey. The rest of the town had been cursing Harvey's name very loudly and openly. William could tell that it would not have taken much to set off the powder keg that his gold had cooled for now.

"You the White Flag leader we've been expecting?" the one William presumed to be in charge asked. He wore a taller and pointier hat with less rust on it than his counterpart and his beard was bushier.

"I am Captain Boatswain, if that is who you mean," William said purposefully to antagonize the soldiers. After the short and awkward exchange of pleasantries that followed, William was escorted to the castle.

They passed by the crowd which even at this early hour was outside the worn walls, muttering and complaining about the lack of guards. William's thoughts of awe regarding Oakenfall faded quickly as he entered the castle and could see the extent of the damage that had occurred on its inside since the fall of the dragons.

William had for obvious reasons, never been allowed into the castle in his few visits to Oakenfall, but he had seen paintings from when the dragons owned the country.

Once, the castle would have been full of jewels and statues. Now it looked bare and empty. It looked like a massive wine cellar without any shelves or bottles... at least that is how William would have described it if anyone had asked him.

William was even less impressed by Harvey. His unkempt beard looked like a badger had run at him too keenly and stuck. The king was a glutton in William's eyes and his fat stomach was a sign of the self-indulgence that he planned to change. It is true that William indulged himself, but he offered his people no less. If the coffers were bare William would have been the first to break bread with beggars — unlike King Harvey, it seemed, who had sold the kingdom from beneath himself to feed his belly. His people lay starving in the streets only supported by William's ill-gotten gold, while Harvey was still refusing to leave his castle.

"Thank you for coming, Sire Boatswain," King Harvey said as he stepped away from the cloth that he had laid over the map of Neeska. It poked up in places where the wooden and stone figures lay beneath it. Harvey was aware that all the while this war was happening, and he had this unwelcome but necessary guest, William could be making moves on his throne and Harvey planned to keep as many cards close to his chest as he could.

King Harvey wanted to shackle the pirate standing in front of him and throw him into the castle dungeon, but that would not save the kingdom. He would have to plan a way to do that the moment the last Pole ran for the hills.

"I am no royal, so no 'sire' is necessary. 'Captain,' if you want to use any title, or 'William,' if you don't. Besides I could not turn down a chance to meet the King of this lovely city, now could I?" William said in the playful tone that had often gotten him in trouble.

William was a suave man and knew it and his voice echoed with young confidence. It was the confidence of a man who had slept with the wives of some of the most dangerous men in the North of Neeska and shook their husbands by the hand with a smile the very next day.

"I do not try to flatter you, William. I would not have asked you here if it was not important. So please if you will, less of the tiresome games as we have much to discuss," King Harvey said trying to keep things as civil as he could but already feeling the air growing thick with tension. He did not want the pirate "King" here at all.

"Most of the best things in life are tiring, Your Majesty… at least the ones that put a swagger in your step, eh?" William said strutting towards the table with his wet clothes dripping onto the floor. Again, he could have changed on the ship after the storm, but where would the fun have been in that? It was far more enjoyable to have seen Harvey's face as he did just now!

"I have little idea of what you mean," Harvey said feeling a little flustered.

This was not how people normally spoke to him. He knew exactly what William had meant and he would not stand for such depravity inside his keep. Harvey had not met William in person before, but he could already tell that the pirate would say anything just to get a rise out of him.

"Now, please, we do not have time to waste in scoring petty points over each other," Harvey continued, letting William know he was aware what he was playing at and that he was above such childish games.

"You're soaked from the storm last night. Can I get one of the servants to get you a change of clothes?" Harvey asked just wanting to bring some sense of normality to an otherwise rather strange meeting.

Harvey was used to meeting nobles who were either scared of him — or the rare few who were not scared, but could barely breathe as they wheezed their way in and collapsed on a chair, almost shattering it with the weight they carried from their wealthy manor lifestyles. Harvey always had the upper hand. The nobles of the city were all in his pocket in one way or another, but William was not like that. He did not stutter with nerves and showed little regard for King Harvey or his proper place in the social standing.

"I am quite happy with my finery thank you. Your servants can keep their clothes. I very much doubt you have anything in your wardrobe that would be of the same standard," William said trying to find another button to press, but it did not get the rise he'd hoped. It seemed Harvey was not quite as easily rattled as he had heard, but William would not be so easily defeated.

"Why are you so keen to get me out of my robe anyway, Your Majesty? Are your tastes so outlandish? I'd heard that about you, but you're not quite my type. Not bosomy enough I'm afraid," William said making hand gestures that were not describing the coconuts they might have been.

The noise that escaped from King Harvey could not really be described as words. It was a kind of a puff, puff, followed by a squeak.

"Relax yourself, I jest. I am quite fine, thank you. I'm quite enjoying the feel of sand in me nether regions. It lets you know you're alive, when you very well might have a crab or two up your sleeve." William said as he playfully wrung out his jade-colored cuffs and the water oozed out dripping onto the floor in a splash.

Harvey didn't bother commenting. He could feel he had lost track of the conversation. He had been prepared for William to come in blazing threats and demanding this and that. This joker of a man prancing about was not what Harvey had prepared for. If he'd wanted a jester, he would have asked for one! He'd wanted a man who could save the city. It was a mystery to Harvey how this man who seemed intent on buffoonery could command such a formidable pirate force.

"What's under the cloth?" William said trying to lift the corner and half expecting the king to slap his hand away, but it never came. William was kind of disappointed. He'd lied about the sand... well that he was enjoying it anyway. It did feel like he had half of White Shore between his cheeks, but he could see just how uncomfortable it was making Harvey. William smiled to himself. He was enjoying toying with the stuffy and prudish Harvey. All he had to do was find a way to make it worse. With that William whipped the cloth back knocking over a few stone and wooden figures and let it drop to the floor in a tangled mess. That seemed to work.

"Be careful with that! It's a relic from the days of the Blight. I use it to plan the city's defenses," Harvey said, automatically rushing to the table to pick up the pieces and put them back in their correct locations. His red cheeks seemed to almost glow as his blood pressure sky-rocketed.

"What defenses?" William said with a smirk. He had seen how empty the streets were. The city could not have defended itself from an incursion of rats let alone anything bigger.

"Indeed, such as they are at the moment," Harvey bitterly said, the words like poison to him. He had started to wonder if this was the right thing to do. Could this cocky man save Oakenfall or was he just wasting valuable time?

"That is why I had to ask you to come. You understand the importance of Briers Hill falling?" Harvey said giving William one more chance to be of use, before he called for the guards to have him tossed in the stockades.

"That is some relic, that table! I could do with one of them myself," William said ignoring Harvey's final question for the moment. "It would need to be better painted of course and maybe with some little wooden trees and animals. Oh, the fun I could have in the wee hours," William joked trying to find even more buttons to push but gave up when no response came from Harvey.

With a sigh of boredom, he continued, "I understand that it means the Poles will be joining our little get together soon."

Harvey nodded unable to say the words aloud. It had taken a lot for him to admit he needed the help of anyone, and it had hurt him to realize that he had no ally to call on. The only person he could rely on was the leader of the White Flags, the man who had made Harvey's life more than difficult for years.

"Not much time now then. My scouts reported all your ships heading west of my island a few days back," William said as he pushed his thumb down on the miniature White Isle.

"That, I'm guessing, means you have barely enough knights to stop me killing you right here," William said shooting Harvey a stare, which was met with the desired reaction. Harvey abruptly stepped back and scrabbled around the table for something to defend himself with. William had to stifle a laugh at the sight of the fat ginger man holding what looked like a small quill.

"Calm yourself, Your Majesty. It's a shame I left my sword on the ship or we could have tested just how good that would be… just in case, you understand," William laughed alone again.

"Oh, come on Harvey! Relax a little will you! You could hold the city from the farmers and fishwives, but something tells me when the Poles get here, you'll be hanging from your sack by lunchtime, so you may as well have a little fun," William said picking up the figure at

Oakenfall on the board and turning it upside down with a smile.

"Unlike you, I do not have time for fun and games. I must do what is best for my people and as much as I do not approve of the way you said it, that is about it. I do not know how long we can hold out," Harvey said putting down the little feather and realizing his foolishness. But it was not a shock that William was bold enough to threaten him in his own throne room.

Harvey had almost expected it, but it still took him a little aback. William looked toned and he was probably a dab hand with a sword, whereas Harvey couldn't remember the last time he'd even had to hold one himself. Other people had always done the killing for him. He'd picked up a quill and signed a sheet of paper and within days someone was removed from his way. Harvey suddenly felt very alone and unsafe about breaking the silence that had become deafening, but he continued to explain his plans.

He told William everything — about Darcy, the Dragon Heart, and the reason he had sent his fleet to the west. He'd wanted to keep as many secrets as he could, but time was getting shorter and he had the overwhelming premonition he was going to end up dead no matter how things played out. After a little thought and some more awkward silence that William could see was driving Harvey insane, William reluctantly broke the hush, mainly out of necessity.

"Well, you seem to be in a right pickle then and not the nice crunchy kind. I will help you with your little problem," William said placing his hand back on the miniature map and pulling across a tiny boat from White Isle.

"I can have the rest of my fleet here by nightfall, and, let's be honest, my men are better trained than yours anyway, otherwise you'd have killed me years ago, but we need to make it worthwhile for them or they won't come," William said, and he was being honest for once. He might be the so-called "Pirate King," but they were still, after all was said and done, pirates. They did not follow his orders blindly. In fact, they rarely followed his orders at all... unless he could back them up with gold or a title.

"What is it you, I mean they, want?" Harvey asked expecting William to come back with "the Crown", or a ludicrous amount of gold that he knew the city did not have.

"I grow tired of the rivalry between the city and my people. Open trade between us freely and stop all this treason business about the shipping taxes and maybe some of the gold might even start flowing back into your coffers. I do a service for the city and we get the rights for that. Only fair, don't you agree? Of course, you do. So, do I have your word then, or shall I set sail before this city is razed to the ground? I did leave three very voluptuous and very loose women in my bed back at home," William said aware that the king could not really say no and that would make things far more attractive to his men.

It would basically mean that there was no need for the act of piracy at sea, aside for the fun of it, and they would be able to get far fresher food from the farmlands around Neeska to flood the taverns with. Things were at a stage that no matter what William had asked, Harvey would probably have had to say yes. William had thought about demanding the Crown but there would be no fun in just being given it. So, for now, making Harvey ease the pressure on the people and his crew would be enough.

"I have no choice," Harvey gave in. It had become demanding to follow up on the ships that had been paying the tax anyway and the nobles were almost ready to turn against him and join the rebellion, so it might be his saving grace to ease up on this one law, for now anyway.

After leaving the castle and returning to his ship, William turned to an almost unknown pirate among the White Flags. This pirate, Erin Cleat, had been William's cabin girl for the previous two years. William's order for Erin Cleat was to track down the Dragon Heart and steal it from this Darcy. A simple task it seemed for an assassin of Erin's caliber.

Although highly skilled, she had appeared to just pop up in Slickrock one day and had been added to William's private fleet shortly after. The position came with perks that most could only dream of and it was a position that was highly prized and normally took years of greasing the diplomatic wheels to even be considered for. The fact the young girl had appeared and within days been granted access to the inner circle would have led most to question why.

However, the only person who knew the truth was William himself — he alone knew that she was his bastard daughter. Erin had the same slim build and gentle facial features as he did. Her lips were like a slice in the snow of her pale complexion. She was tall for a woman, almost as tall as William. Her hair was a dark red, almost black, and matched the black clothes she wore. Unlike her father she did not opt for brightly-colored clothes. She wore snug cotton tights and body-hugging hooded tops, both as black as the night. She covered her shins and forearms with thin iron shields attached directly around herself with thick leather straps. She was a skilled fighter and an even more skilled assassin. Erin hid a blade, barely, under the shield on her left leg and another longer bronze-colored blade in her belt around her waist.

Standing with her cold eyes staring at William, she smiled and waited. It was not the look of a daughter at her father, as Erin did not know the truth — it was a secret even kept from her. Before her time with William, Erin had worked freelance. She had travelled across half the world and broken into some of the most well-guarded estates and either stolen something or killed someone that was supposedly impossible to reach. So, tracking down some halfwit noble in the wide-open plains of Northern Neeska would be like shooting a sleeping fish in a very small barrel.

Erin was as loyal as a lapdog and as intelligent as a very learned owl. If anyone could do it, then it would have been her. Erin had first come to William when her mother died. She was alone, apart from the drunk who'd called himself Erin's stepfather. Unable to free herself from the drunkard and the memory of her mother, Erin suddenly felt lost.

It was only when she found William's name mentioned often in her mother's diary that she decided to seek him out. Erin hoped maybe to find some aspect of a home with this man her mother spoke so fondly of... yet she didn't even suspect that he could be her father.

William on the other hand recognized her the first time he saw her. She was a spitting image of his mother. It seemed the apple had not fallen far from the tree and Erin's so-called drunken stepfather soon went missing, rather oddly, just as Erin joined William's crew.

William had lavished the eighteen-year-old with gifts. Her cabin in the ship was right next to his. The situation had taken a difficult turn, though, when William was forced to turn down her advances much to Erin's confusion. She was slim and beautiful. Her ample bosom would seduce most men at a hundred paces at the slightest flash, and William was the only man who'd ever turned her down.

That was why she respected him so much, but she had no idea of the truth. William had wanted to tell her he was her father but never found the words. On returning to his bunk one night, drunk, he had found Erin waiting for him under the covers in nothing but a little lace nighty.

That had complicated things, so William had kicked her out of his cabin in a panic and now he could not imagine telling her he was her father — how could he!

Nothing had happened between them and William would never let anything happen, but it hadn't stopped Erin trying and William could not imagine how she would take the news. So rather than complicate things, he treated her like a member of his crew. That way he could protect her and look after her, even raising her as his own without Erin ever having to know she'd tried to bed her own father.

Regardless of their less than perfect father-daughter relationship William knew he could trust her with anything and that was why he asked her to go. As loyal as the rest of his men were, he doubted any of them would come back with the Heart if it was as powerful as Harvey had said.

Chapter Ten – Into the Ash

It seemed half of Neeska would soon be hunting for the Dragon Heart.

It had been almost two weeks since jugglers and drunken revelers filled the streets of Oakenfall and people's hearts had been filled with hope that the new century would bring with it good fortune and maybe — just maybe — peace for the first time in generations, but that was not the way of Neeska.

The days had rolled on and throughout the northern parts of Neeska several stories had started. They all had their own reasons for setting their feet on their paths, and different goals they wished to achieve, but with all these different journeys there was one thing they all had in common — the power of the Dragon Heart.

Darcy and Calvin had left the Mages Tower on the sixth of Nylar unaware of the changes that would happen in the kingdoms they'd left behind, and they had spent less than a day travelling before they reached the border of the Scorched Lands.

What lay in front of them was a sight that would have brought most men to their knees. They were welcomed by ash clouds that floated on for miles and were so dense they blocked out the sun. The darkness so intense that it turned day into night.

The Scorched Lands rolled on as far as the eye could see and was like the landscape of hell. The air was dirty and seemed to steal any attempt to breathe and left a burning dryness in their throats.

The earth was thick with blackened remains. Powdered memories from a war long since finished. The deep ash-coated ground swallowed the pair's steps up to their knees as they braved the border and pressed deeper into the abyss.

The ground was so unstable and the air so polluted that the horses had refused to move, and the pair had been forced to continue alone on foot. The King's Guards had not been paid enough to continue after seeing what awaited them. They would rather risk the King's fury than that darkness.

Shadows hid on the horizon behind clouds of putrid foul-smelling silt that turned out to be burned-out catapults, the dead soldiers cemented in place, forced to work the machines for eternity. They'd turned into statues as grim reminders of the heavy loss of life here, their bones blackened by the heat that must have engulfed the land.

The landscape hid stone farmhouses that were now tombs from a time long since left behind. In some of the less damaged there were places still set around the table waiting for fathers to return for tea, or for fallen soldiers who'd never got to join the battle.

Progress for Darcy and Calvin was slow. The hard slug of shifting through the ash that grew deeper the further into the lands they travelled took it out of them. The aged mage Calvin, although driven by the energy of Rinwid the demon, struggled more than Darcy but neither found it easy.

They thought it was bad at the start of their journey, but it soon got worse as they pressed into the dead wasteland. The ash rose and begun to lap at their waist and like a sea of despair it burdened their spirits as it weighed down the tired would-be adventurers.

The ash of a thousand corpses filled their lungs and dizziness became par for the course as they struggled ever onwards almost blind in the perpetual darkness.

The plan when they'd left the Mages Tower had been to be escorted by the King's Guard and ride comfortably in a caravan, but as with many things in Neeska, plans rarely ran smoothly. The wheels of the caravan had come to an abrupt stop a few miles back and they'd pressed on by foot.

The ever-wavering landscape confused the two soot-covered adventurers as they pressed on alone. They would lie down to rest at nightfall and by morning, after they had dug themselves free from the ash that had settled over whatever hovel they had decided to crawl into, the world around them would have changed again in the choking clouds.

Hills would have sprung up with the wind, and houses or trees that had been buried before would be poking up confusing them. With the sun hidden and darkness hiding any landmarks, finding the path west was far from easy.

Bony hands protruded from the ground as if the dead were still trying to climb to freedom or point to the sky in warning of the fire breathing dragon that had taken their life over a hundred years before.

Skeletons could be seen with rusted armor bearing unknown coats of arms. Whole bloodlines had been claimed and ended in the last Blight, and with so many, dead lineages had been forgotten and few records survived as a reminder of the lost.

Darcy's and Harvey's would have been the first eyes to fall on these forgotten shields in years. They both prayed they would not end up the same way.

Huge sculptures that looked like giant white trees, on closer inspection turned into bones from the giant long dead Dragon Lords that beckoned Darcy and Calvin onwards, teasing them that the Heart might be behind the next shadowy outcrop.

They had each entered the desolate clouds of the Scorched Lands for their own reasons — Darcy desperate to prove he was worth his own name, and not just a shadow following his father; Calvin with no choice but to press on if he ever wanted to be free of the demon forced upon him. Neither was prepared for when the guards had turned their backs on them.

Both Darcy and Calvin had wanted to give in the moment the wheels stopped too, but they were forced on by a sense of determination that had faded quickly when the world vanished. They might have turned back after the first night, if the clouds had not hidden the way out.

They had no choice now but to continue walking and hope for the best. Darcy and Calvin had expected to have been back at the tower within a few days, but time continued to roll on as the pair wandered on lost in the shifting ash.

The eighth became the ninth, and then rolled on in the blackness to the tenth. On their fourth day in the ash, the morning of the Brunwek the twelfth of Nylar the pair struggled on towards what had looked like mountains in the distance. Everything else had shifted with the wind but these outlying shadows seemed to have stayed just out of view for the last few days.

The Scorched Lands covered roughly seventy-five miles by fifty of desolation and hopelessness. Its shape of a sideways boot had taken the two from the longest point where the Scorched Lands protruded out towards the Tower Plains and south-east towards the mountains that marked the worst of the blighted land.

They'd been guided by Rinwid who sensed the power of the Heart from the Spirit Realm using Calvin as a conduit, but it seemed the bond between the mage and his dark secret was not as strong as it could have been, and the flashes of foresight created a map that was hard to read.

The duo was approaching the eastern border of the Scorched Lands, once home to the lesser dragons of Neeska. The mountains they could see were the ones that long ago, before the Great War and before the millennia of slavery to the Dragon Lords, would have been part of the Kingdom of Goldhorn. The mountains belonged to the dwarves who lived east of Oakenfall, but they had been left empty for so long.

The cold winter they had left behind outside of the Scorched Land had little effect inside that putrid place. The ash still held heat from deep below. In places as it shifted it still smoldered and kept the darkness steadily warm.

Darcy and Calvin had spent many dull and eventless days trailing blindly through the ash before they had started to make any progress on finding the Heart, but the fourteenth of Nylar would offer change. The two had struck up a friendship of sorts and had shared many stories from their pasts while they took shelter from the worst of the ash clouds.

They were not all that dissimilar — both carried with them abandonment issues from absent parents, both had been forced into doing something they'd objected to, and both were very sheltered from the real and harsh world they'd found themselves forced to navigate alone.

It was around noon, or it could have been midnight, it was impossible to tell with the darkness... all that Darcy knew was that he couldn't take another step.

"Calvin. Wait a minute will you. I don't think I can go on much longer. I'm so tired," Darcy said staggering forward and almost falling into the ash.

"I know, it's like sludging through old porridge. Quite the 'grueling' journey," Calvin said finding amusement in the wordplay.

The two were hungry, tired and surrounded by a depressing gloom. The Scorched Lands would have driven most men to madness, but Calvin seemed to be holding up well, and it was his occasional lightheartedness that had kept Darcy motivated.

Darcy's clothes were stained gray and laden thick with ash and grime. His once fine noble clothing looked like the worst of blacksmith aprons, his eyes stung, and his breath felt like it was being squeezed out through a vice.

"We've been stuck here for days and I cannot even remember the feel of a good night's sleep," Darcy said missing his cold mattress at home.

"With your incessant snoring, neither can I," Calvin said, again trying to make light of the moment.

"My snoring is nothing compared to your flatulence, old buffoon!" Darcy said with a smile.

"We've eaten nothing but dried salted meat for days — what do you expect!" Calvin replied before his breathe was stolen by a cloud of ash swirling up from the ground below.

Once the torrent of wind settled down and the two could open their eyes again, it was Darcy who was first to break the silence.

"Can't you use that demon to find the Heart? I thought that's why we brought you mages into it. The King said you'd find it and so far, all you've done is run us around in circles. I don't want to die here," Darcy continued as he pulled himself onwards at a crawling pace. The moment of levity had faded as the gloom seemed to choke any hope from them.

Darcy had started to feel desperate as the days moved on and he'd lost the drive to become a hero. The dreams he'd had of returning to Oakenfall as the savior were all but gone and now all he wanted to do was return alive. The gloom surrounding them was toxic. It seeped into their souls and although the pair had only been in the Scorched Lands for a few days Darcy could barely remember what the sun even looked like. The Scorched Lands were threatening to drive him insane before they ever found the Heart.

His would-be guide, Calvin looked more like a grumpy misshaped and discolored gargoyle under the layers of dust, and the pace he was setting was slow. However, he seemed oddly unfazed by the situation. Unlike Darcy who'd grown weaker the longer they spent in the clouds, Calvin seemed to be growing stronger every day.

Darcy couldn't explain it, but the old man seemed to be changing. All around them dead bodies had been loaded with ash, and Darcy had to wonder if they too would become another statue in the drab garden of misfortune, their hands turned to rock clawing for freedom like so many others. The same worry didn't seem to be infecting Calvin.

"Stop your panicking, Darcy. We're not going to die. You're worse than a washerwoman from a slaughterhouse with your moaning," Calvin said as he slugged on leading the way.

His hood had fallen from his head and his hair that flowed down into it had been covered with ash that filled the hood to its brim. It must have held a tremendous weight, but the old man didn't seem to notice.

"Well 'we' might not die, but I don't have the help of a demon, and would prefer to get out of here," Darcy said shooting Calvin a glance through slit-like eyes.

Darcy had been uncomfortable with Calvin's possession since he'd told him shortly after the two were alone together in the Scorched Lands, and they'd built a friendship of necessity. But it had been built on the shifting ashes and was as volatile as the air they were forced to breathe.

Darcy had always thought that he was tolerant person. He'd mixed with many races as a noble, and had even been accepting of dealing with mages or soldiers — but a demon? That was different. Darcy knew little about demons other than the stories Granny had told him when he was growing up, but none of them ever ended well.

"I wish I hadn't told you about Rinwid. I had thought that maybe the other mages were wrong and not all nobles were complete asses," Calvin said with a snarl.

It was not as if he wasn't trying to find the Heart but things within the clouds were difficult and the bond with the demon had made thinking difficult for him. He flipped like a tossed coin now between himself and anger. He missed the tower, the gardens… and he even missed the Arch Mage, which was saying something.

Calvin could feel himself slipping away. Rinwid seemed delighted in the Scorched Lands and Calvin wondered if his companion wanted to find the Heart at all. It was not just Darcy who did not trust the demon, but it was only Calvin who could feel the will of the creature seeping through him like a virus.

Calvin could not remember much from before the time he'd entered the ash. His memories seemed lost, buried. They were still there but it was like trying to find a shard of glass in a desert. If he tried hard enough, he could remember back to things like the orphanage, and the cat he saved but things like what his room looked like, what fresh potatoes tasted like… those thoughts were gone from his consciousness.

Calvin could feel magic surging through him like a waterway, but he had started to feel like that was all he had become. The demon's memories burned brightly like a candle and over-shadowed everything else. Calvin could tell you exactly what the insides of a baboon tasted like and he had never even seen one! He had an urge to let the demon's power flow out of him and was driven like an addict to find an excuse to use his new-found powers.

The dreams came when he was awake now and the premonitions distorted his already loose grip on reality. The way Darcy had spoken to Calvin had changed since he had known about Rinwid, but Calvin had to tell him. After all it was becoming more obvious by the day and Darcy, soft as he was, would have noticed something had been happening.

They were days into the Scorched Lands and could not see a way out. They were no closer to their goal of finding the Heart, but it seemed almost peaceful to think it would soon be over, at least to Calvin. He had been so desperate to get the demon out of him and return to a normal life but the more he lost of himself the less he worried about death — if anything, it could be a release.

After slugging on in silence for a time, Darcy reignited the argument, as the insult must have been playing on his mind.

"You can't paint all nobles with the same brush. Just like we can't say that all you mages are odd-bearded and perverted magic-wielding loons too dangerous to be allowed to stay in the city, but if the pointy hat fits!" Darcy exclaimed unlike himself.

He had been quiet and withdrawn but this place had started to change him. He had wanted to start his life afresh, but he hadn't planned for it to be worse than the isolated shell he'd been in beforehand. As empty as his life had been in the shadow of his father, at least it wasn't full of such torture. Demons, ash, death and what seemed like an endless search for a Heart that Darcy was rapidly starting to think was a myth.

"If you don't like the company, you're keeping you're free to find your own way," Calvin snarled.

"I wish I had stayed in Oakenfall," Darcy said wiping his face to no avail as the ash only smeared and more was blown against it as soon as his hand moved away.

His eyes were bloodshot and burned continuously. Darcy feared he would end up blind because of the dust clouds swirling around them constantly.

It was becoming all but impossible to keep track of the days but if he was right, then he should have been almost back home by now. His mind raced between thoughts of Granny worrying that he should have been there and uncertainties that something might have happened to his father and Briers Hill.

The last goodbye with his father had been unsatisfying, but somehow Darcy knew that was all he would get. It was probably this place making him depressive, but he could not see any happy ending. It weighed heavily on Darcy that his new life would be this. The dullness of his surroundings and the sense of just having to survive that poured over him seemed to attach more levity to his old life. He feared he would never see his noble home again and he almost longed for the hours of loneliness he spent wandering its halls. He was not blind to the irony. He had heard the expression that the grass wasn't green on the other side, but he hadn't expected the grass to be buried under four foot of ash.

"Stop moaning. Do you think I like being here? I'd rather be back at the tower. I don't like this any more than you and I certainly don't like having this Rinwid thing in me," Calvin said.

He could feel the anger growing in him. With a flick of his wrist he could engulf Darcy in a ball of flame — who would notice just one more corpse in that dead place? Calvin battled the feelings knowing it was Rinwid's influence, but it would be a lie to say he was not tempted. It would have doubled his food ration for a start.

The demon seemed overjoyed and eager to unleash the magic that was building inside Calvin. The longer the journey took the more hate Calvin felt inside him. Calvin would hold on for as long as he could, but he had begun to understand just why people feared demons and why the practice of Warrior Mages had been one that was lost to history. He had started to feel like a coiled spring — the magic needed a way out of him. It was leaking into him from the Spirt Realm and wanted to find a way out into the waking world.

The demon was slowly taking him over and when he finally lost all control to it, the horrors the demon longed for would be a reality all Neeska would have to face. The pair continued onwards struggling forward in silence through the dark. It would have been a sad sight indeed for anyone who could have seen them from start to finish.

They had left the tower with brightness in their souls but now there was little more than two flickering flames bickering with each other like children. It was the Scorched Lands that drove them to argue so much. It held something over life and twisted it. It was as if the darkness there could infect the soul.

Darcy wished the King's caravan had made it further into the Scorched Lands than it had. It was a rackety old wagon, but it would at least have been shelter for sleeping in. The last of the surviving hovels were miles behind and all that they could find offering shelter now were huge bleached dragon skulls or the ruins of catapults.

The struggle towards the distant mountains was a little easier after the morning of the fourteenth had dawned. The thickest ash now lay behind them as the earth below became rock climbing up out of the ash. Their journey had taken them clear across the ashen lands to the feet of the mountains.

They still had a long climb ahead of them, but the shifting clouds fell below and to their backs. The air was almost pleasant, apart from the always-present stench. With his feet clinging onto a slightly elevated mound of sharp rock, Calvin could make out the Mages Tower on the horizon. It was a reminder of home and just how far they had come.

With clean air in their lungs for the first time in almost a week and a clear vision of the mountains Darcy and Calvin took the time to rest. They could have made use of the time to travel faster but other than sleeping they had done little in the way of resting for days and they were not sure if they were going the correct way.

"Calvin, can I talk to you about something?" Darcy asked as he sat and pulled his boots from his feet.

The smell that met his nose reminded him of how long it had been since he had bathed. His feet were blistered, and his skin seemed like it was off-color and looked like it was peeling. It hurt like hell to push the boots back on, but Darcy feared if he didn't do it straight away, he would never get them over the swelling.

No reply came from Calvin, so Darcy continued talking, "Creator, I'd give up the family home for a comfy bed and a warm bath," he said as he watched Calvin slide down from the rock he had been climbing on. When he realized the old man either didn't hear him or was more likely ignoring him, Darcy called out again. "Calvin."

"It's been the first time in days we can see the sun and you want to ruin it by talking!" Calvin complained as he dropped back onto the ground with a thud.

The truth was that Calvin felt sick out of the ash. He did not want to sit back and enjoy the sun as it burnt his eyes much like the curtains in his room had when he had first awoken after being sent into the Spirit Realm. He lied, as it made him feel more human. He knew in his heart that he should feel relieved to be free of the death they had been wading through, but he didn't. The demon was becoming more a part of Calvin as each moment passed and things that would have once been a blessing had become a curse. It seemed that Calvin would get no respite at all.

"Well, it's been on my mind for some time now," Darcy said ignoring the old man's complaints. "You told me that the Arch Mage put a demon in you right? So that it could locate the Dragon Heart?" Darcy said.

Darcy waited for a reply as he sat on his haunches pulling apart some unknown meat that had been dried to within an inch of its life and hidden in away in a dust filled bag for a week. It had the flavor of an ashtray and Darcy wondered what was worse, hunger or the feeling of the ashen meat sliding down his gullet like a dog-end roll-up.

"We've been over this. I am trying to find it," Calvin said looking off into the distance longingly. "The images aren't as straight forward as a map. I'm seeing everywhere the Heart has been. We're not the first that have tried to get it out of here. It might not even still actually be here," Calvin said at his wits end.

Since Calvin had taken the time to explain Rinwid's existence, it seemed like every time Darcy opened his mouth that was all he spoke about. Calvin wondered if it was as annoying as he felt it was, or if Rinwid was making it more of an issue than it was.

"No, I understand that. Sorry for the last few days. This place has been getting to me. It's not that," Darcy said with a shrug. The idea of Calvin being possessed did unnerve the hell out of him but that was not what was on his mind. "I remember you mentioning about the Blight when we were still in the tower. You've had a vision haven't you — are the dragons coming back?" Darcy asked.

He had almost forgotten the mage had mentioned it until they were sleeping inside the mouth of one of the larger dragon skulls they'd found. Darcy had originally thought about returning home as a dragon killer once they had the Heart, but after being able to curl up inside the head of a dragon that thought soon vanished. He'd read books on dragons and was fascinated by them as a child, as most children are, but the sheer size of them had never come across from the worn pages of the history books.

"No, they're not coming back, because they never truly went," Calvin said, his brow wrinkled as he stared off into the sky.

Calvin felt his mind swirl like a soup being stirred. The demon flashed images of the battle past Calvin's inner eye. He could feel the heat of the flame. He watched as the people ran screaming. He could see the dragons soaring high above and the catapults firing at them. He could feel spells coming from mages and druids alike. Calvin could feel the rumble of the ground as dragons crashed into the earth crushing men below them.

That was not all he could see... Calvin could see those ancient times, but he could see the time that came after. The period between the end of the Blight and the moment he was in. Young dragons had crawled around and taken flight. There had been only a handful of them, but then something else came. It had the Heart. It went towards the mountain, and it called to the young dragons.

"What do you mean? They have to have gone or Oakenfall would still be enslaved?" Darcy said gruffly.

Darcy was getting sick of being confused. King Harvey had misdirected him. His father had misinformed him and now the historians had got it wrong too... is that what Calvin was saying?

Two weeks ago, Darcy was a lonely noble stressed about what taxes to pay and what ships to send out and now he was knee deep in crap and getting more frustrated by the day. There was only so much a person could take before he said enough is enough — and for Darcy that had been the moment the caravan had ground to a halt. Everything afterwards had just been gravy.

"I suppose you're right, but I see them, babies, travelling towards the mountains. Oh, there is a Heart and the biggest of the dragons did fall along with hundreds of others. Still it was a small loss compared to the hundreds of thousands of humans who died," Calvin said pulling himself from the vision.

The real world slowly melted into view. The clear green grass and bloodied bodies vanished into ash and brimstone.

"You know something more don't you. Please tell me. I know I'm not a mage and your Arch Mage swore you to secrecy, but please? We're probably going to die here anyway. Don't let me die for nothing," Darcy begged just wanting to relieve his mind.

"We aren't going to die. We can't. This is too important to just sit down and stop. Dragons have hordes, gold, loot, treasure, but that's not normally all of it. They normally have corpses, livestock and eggs. The dragon children would have been kept safe in the mountains. The visions showed these dragons coming back and trying to reclaim their throne from the humans," Calvin said.

He felt Rinwid try to replay the images past his eyes once more, but he forced them shut. He would not go through it again. What he was seeing couldn't be right!

"You mean the dragons didn't all die? They retreated to the mountains? The same mountains we're heading towards?" Darcy asked, the realization hitting him like a millennium of slavery. He dropped the stale meat back into his pouch suddenly losing his appetite.

"Yes. I didn't have a clue where the Heart was until we started getting close yesterday, but since then the visions have been getting stronger. I almost feel like I am at the battle. I can see the dragons darting above us in the sky. I can hear the battle cries. I can feel the pull of the Heart's memories close by and there is something else, something powerful. Darcy, can we talk about Rinwid?"

Calvin asked pulling himself back from the premonition once more.

"Of course, what's on your mind?" Darcy had been alone for so long with Granny as his only real company, so he was not good at heart-to-hearts, but even he could feel this one needed to come out.

"He's strong even by demon standards. I didn't realize it at the time, but he summoned me to him when I was in the Spirit Realm. I don't think he is the one the Arch Mage meant me to meet," Calvin said. As the bond with Rinwid had grown, things the demon had kept hidden to start with opened like the sky after a storm. "I don't think I can control him for much longer. I'm losing myself. I need to know that if he takes over, you'll finish me. I don't want to become an abomination," Calvin said and Rinwid expressed his disapproval.

The headache that washed over Calvin brought him clean to his knees. His hands shot up to his head and he buried his fingers into his grey hair pressing hard against his skull.

So, you plan to go back on out deal, do you? Rinwid said to a concussed Calvin.

His body lay face down in the ash, his heavy frame barely moving through labored breaths. Darcy by his side tried hard to turn Calvin over, but it was as if Calvin was beneath an enormous weight.

That invisible force was not what disturbed Darcy the most. No... that honor was given to Calvin's skin that seemed to alter as if it was filled with worms. Darcy could see movement beneath the skin. It looked like tendrils surging through Calvin's veins.

The demon's voice echoed out from somewhere inside Calvin as if projected from a being inside him. The voice was not Calvin's, it had hints of Calvin's accent to it, but it seemed deeper, and yet higher pitched at the same time. It gave Darcy the impression he was listening through water at the bottom of a very long well.

"Our deal was that you would leave once we destroyed the Heart," Calvin's body said in the real world and Darcy could hear the difference between the two beings arguing inside the same frame.

In Calvin's mind he was back in the fiery cavern the demon called home. He could feel nothing but the demon's presence. The real world seemed like a distant memory and Calvin wondered if he had ever actually been in his body — had he been a prisoner in the Spirit Realm ever since he'd been first placed there?

And I would have. I am good to my word. Most demons are. It's you humans that break yours and blame us when we punish you for it. You will not destroy the Heart, so I will not leave. Your little friend Darcy plans to take it back and I know others are coming for it, Rinwid said.

Calvin's body twitched as he tried to fight himself free and Darcy watched as his skin pulsated as if it was being pushed free from the bones and sinew inside.

They think to use something of powers beyond them to save this world, but that is foolish. They will fail as you will, old man. So, once the dragons deal with you humans and tear Oakenfall from the world, it will be as I promised you — no longer the time of dragons! The demons will rise! Rinwid said exposing his true purpose for merging with Calvin. *See old man, I have kept my promise, just not how you figured it.*

"You're wrong demon. We will stop the Blight. I will die before I let you into this world," Calvin's body called out in the real world while he shook like a fish in its death throes.

Darcy pressed down hard trying to hold his friend still, but he was tossed aside like a rag doll. Darcy crashed down on his back only being saved from broken bones by the soft ash that still lay in a thin layer over the sharp rocks below.

You know you can't kill yourself. You've tried that several times in your pathetic little life, haven't you? So lonely, can't take it, little orphan boy. No one wanted you, boo-ho! Rinwid taunted.

I don't think our little posh pants would actually be capable of killing either, do you? There is no point asking him again. So, unless you have something else up your sleeve it will not be too much longer before the link to the Spirit Realm is weak enough for me to come through,' Rinwid said before receding back to his realm.

Calvin's eyes opened, and he rolled onto his back gasping for air. The prison of the Spirit Realm faded, but he could still feel its presence as he stared up into a warm and clear sky.

"Are you ok?" Darcy said after getting to his feet with some difficulty.

"I'll be alright. He's gone for now, but see what I mean? Rinwid's getting stronger. I can use his powers for now, but it won't be long before he uses me," Calvin pulled himself up onto his knees and wiped his face against his sleeve setting off a cloud of dust from his beard.

"Come now, we have more pressing things to worry about… dragons for one. We need to get that bloody Heart," Calvin said, and he begun to hobble up the rocky path leading towards the mountain. He didn't share the last truth Rinwid had whispered before leaving. The conversation had faded to a memory and Rinwid had seemingly remained silent as the fourteenth came to an end.

Dawn brought with it warmer and still weather even on the sloped mountain sides. The duo had not discussed the events of the night before, as neither one wanted to broach the subject of what had happened with Rinwid.

Darcy had thought about it a lot over the night though and he had no choice but to face what Rinwid said. The demon was right — he knew that if it came to it, he probably wouldn't be able to kill Calvin. He had never killed anything… he felt guilty when he swatted at flies or stamped on spiders. The demon's words had hit hard because they demonstrated to Darcy that his big dream of killing a dragon and returning home a hero, had been just that — the dream of a sheltered mind. The thought was far easier than the action.

The pair toiled onwards towards what looked like a graveyard of dragon bones mostly in silence. Exhaustion was winning the battle and each step was agony. It would only take another day to reach the mountain peak, but the mountains were far taller than they'd looked from the distance and they hid valleys full of sharp rocks. Hundreds of small fissures and tunnels lined the steep face of the mountain's many curved sides.

Broken statues could just be made out high above them and served as a reminder that these outcrops had once belonged to the dwarves, a group of small humanoids who lived below ground. They were short, dumpy and had an aversion for bright lights. They'd been the ones who'd carved most of the great temples of the Dragon Lords, and their skills with stonework was unmatched by any other race.

Pulling himself up by using the stone hand of a statue made by a long dead mason, Darcy's hand slipped and knocked off a few loose stones. The chorus of clattering echoed back from the mountain walls around them. The area had been so quiet, silent, as not even birds sang this close to the Scorched Lands. The noise of the stones echoed around the various valleys until finally it faded.

Taking a break from the slog, Darcy stopped and strained his head looking above. The mountainside was steep and made up of small ledges much like the low one he had pulled himself up onto. The ground was loose and made progress difficult.

Darcy turned and offered a hand to Calvin to help the aged man clamber onto the outcrop, when an echo rang out from above.

"What was that?" Darcy said as he pulled Calvin up onto a ledge that was blocking their path between two slopes up the mountain path.

"I'm not sure," Calvin said, his voice adding to the chorus of echoes now flooding the mountainside. When the echo died down Calvin continued, "I thought I saw something run down from the valley over there."

"I think something is coming," Darcy said as a showering of small stones and dust trickled onto his shoulder from above. "You better have a fireball or something useful ready," Darcy jested light heartily expecting to see a bird flutter past and tried to calm himself.

"Sounded big, stay behind me," Calvin said, the hairs on his arms standing up. He didn't know if he was scared, or excited. If something was coming, it meant he would finally have a chance to turn on the faucet of his powers and see what Rinwid could do through him.

"Fine," Darcy said, but he wasn't going to take any chances and stopped slowly, placed his satchel onto the ground, and without making a sound, slipped his hand inside feeling around for the cold bronze of his knife.

Darcy hadn't seen anyone cast magic and didn't know what to expect. He had heard stories, but just in case it was a bandit or wild cat, maybe even a wolf, and the mages weren't as powerful as the stories, Darcy wanted to be ready.

Darcy was shaking, as he knew in his heart that he wasn't a hero and didn't really have any clue how to fight. He hadn't even owned a sword before… the knife had been given to him by one of the guards before they'd parted ways.

It was plain with a simple tube-like handle. It had rusted to a dull green-gray finish, but it was light to carry and well weighted. If Darcy had known anything about daggers, he would have known it was a throwing knife, probably one that had come from White Isle, but he didn't, and he held it loosely like a small sword.

The dagger might have had some value to it once, but none of that was of any consequence as from behind an overhanging rock-laden ledge a growl roared out in a deep boom. Darcy barely had the time to leap back falling onto his backside in the dust before a young dragon dropped down sinking its claws into the very rock where Darcy had been standing just moments before.

The pair froze in shock as the beast slithered upwards in an almost snakelike motion to its full height. The dragon was young, far from being an adult and stood at about the height of a horse. Its wings opened in a display of aggression and its amber green scales glinted in the sun.

The young dragon stood as a massive blockade to the mountainside behind it. From the tip of the creature's long and scaly tail to its teeth-filled and snarling mouth it was around two yards in length.

Its head was the size of Darcy's torso and smoke trickled from its nose, a sign of the heat inside the beast. As the dragon stalked towards Darcy in an almost catlike motion, its huge claws dug into the rock as if it was butter. Its eyes fixed on Darcy menacingly.

"Calvin, why are you looking at it? Do something," Darcy screamed as he scrambled to his feet holding out a suddenly rather weak looking blade in front of him. The cutting edge was only about twice the length of one of the dragon's fangs and Darcy didn't have two rows of them. The dagger felt like little more than a letter opener.

The dragon's snake-like eyes shot from Darcy towards Calvin and the beast turned expectantly. It arched up back on its hind legs and for the first time Darcy could see the beast's soft underbelly. It was a lighter green, almost olive.

Darcy thought for a moment about leaping at the dragon and sinking the point of his weapon into its underside, but he had no clue as to where the creature's heart was! Or even if he had the strength to rip through the thick blubber and scales... plus fear had rooted him to the ground like a tree.

"Stand back," Calvin called out and he let the power of Rinwid surge inside him. The surge of power was incredible, and Calvin felt the energy grow in his stomach. His eyes clouded black and he felt Rinwid awake. Clouds circled around Calvin and loose stones and dust swarmed into the sky in a tornado in the vacuum being created. Sparks flickered across the hairs on Calvin's body and the excitement was palpable. The dragon arched ready to pounce, but it was too slow.

Calvin shot his arm out extending his fingers towards the snapping dragon. His gray hair writhed about his face like an angry octopus as the wind churned. The clouds seemed to be being sucked into the void created and the ball of energy conjured itself at first into small sparks that seemed to drip off Calvin's fingers and singe the soil at his feet.

The energy was so intense that it turned the sand into glass and crystals before the sparks seemed to grow and condense into a bluish gold ball in Calvin's hand. It shot out as a lightning torrent. The blue, white and golden tendrils smashed against the rock shattering it. The dragon caught between the fingers of electricity wailed in agony as they scraped away flesh and burnt it from the inside out. The beast managed to let out a pitiful puff of fire before it slumped lifeless to the ground.

"You did it! That was… that was… that…" Darcy stuttered. He had known Calvin was a mage. He knew he would use magic, but Darcy had not been prepared for that!

The two stood in awe, neither having the words to express what they had just witnessed. They had seen the first dragon in a century and Calvin had, with little more than an outstretched hand, turned it into ash.

Darcy wiped the blood and scales from his face that had been sent flying free in the backlash of power as the lightning had discharged itself. Calvin's eyes faded from black to white. His hand dropped to his side shaking and was reflected in the perfect mirror at his feet.

"That was incredible. The power was more than you can imagine. It felt like I could have moved the mountain if I'd wanted," Calvin said as he looked down at his wrinkled fingers.

The power was intoxicating. It was way better than any of the illicit drugs Calvin had tried as a junior in the tower. He could see why the old stories were full of mages who had turned to demons for power. The bargain was almost worth it. If only he could find a way to control Rinwid, but that was a dangerous thought he dared not think.

"It looks like you'll get more chance to use it. Up there quick!" Darcy said as he pointed to the higher of the two ledges that lined the entrance to the valley.

Three more dragons that were slightly smaller than the last one peered down snarling. Although they were smaller, they were still dangerous, and it was Calvin this time who had to leap backwards. Not for a leaping dragon this time, but from a blast of scorching orange flame that rushed across the rocks barely missing him.

Calvin could feel the heat of it. The hairs on his beard curled with a sizzle and the bottom of his long beard vanished into nothingness. The closest of the three dragons sucked air into its huge lungs to fire a second blast at Calvin, but Calvin took the chance to scramble on his knees to hide behind the rock he'd used to view the sky a few minutes before.

"I can't yet. That took too much out of me. If I use it now, I will collapse," Calvin said.

He wished he was younger. He knew there was more magic to use but his body was just too weak. That was the thing with magic. The more you used, the more energy it took out of you. Simple spells that the mages normally used in the Tower used no more than a brisk jog would — whereas the power that Rinwid had unleashed through Calvin had made him feel like he had not slept for a month.

It was unlikely that they could outrun one dragon let alone a pack of three, but it was even less likely that Darcy with his little bronze toothpick would be able to kill the dragons, so it left only one choice.

"Run!" Calvin called out and without looking back he hitched up his robe and slipped down the mountain making a beeline for the Scorched Lands. A blast of flame bounced off the stone behind him barely missing him for a second time. Darcy gave chase, followed by the dragons.

Chapter Eleven – Sacrifice

By the time Darcy and Calvin were fleeing back into the perpetual darkness of the Scorched Lands, hundreds of fires dotted the dusk filled streets of Oakenfall making the air thick and ash-filled there too. William had wasted no time in starting to prepare a defense when he'd left Harvey's castle. William knew that time was of the essence and it was a resource he didn't have much of. He rigged the city into a weapon, using its structures to make the most of his fleet that had set sail already.

In the days that followed he had used the small stone arched alleyways in the noble district to create blockades, with upturned carts and barrels of gun powder. Fruit crates, wagon wheels and even furniture from the nobles' homes added to the blockage. It created a bottleneck in the city making it all but impossible to enter straight into the southern parts of the city. The castle walls and steep hills made the northern route an unattractive prospect for the enemy.

Even for the strongest of men it would take minutes to clear the clogged alleys giving the militia time to ignite the gunpowder. If the Poles tried pressing in from the south, they would be filtered down into a single line of smoldering corpses, so it left them one option, circling the city and coming in from the coast or the city's midriff. They wouldn't come in from the middle for fear of being flanked on both sides, so it was a fair guess they'd come in from the open but maze-like dockyards and port.

That was where stage two of Williams plan came into being. With the noble district blocked all the way from the castle to Celebration Square, only the ever-shifting maze of the wooden homes of the dockyard streets remained.

The dockyard was filled with archers by nightfall and the maze of roads blocked at strategic points made navigating them a nightmare. The alleyways sent people in circles and through trap-rigged houses and hovels. Roofs were rigged to fall; archers' aims were trained at gunpowder barrels. As the Poles pressed through they would be being picked off by the White Flag archers. Those that made it through the circling alleyways and into the houses would set the traps off and thin their numbers even more.

Many people might lose their houses, but the explosions would block the cluttered roads even further, so the only option would be to clear the path of debris. That with the smoke and collapsed buildings would just add to the confusion and hopefully some of the Poles might even pick off their own men in the panic.

This would give the White Flag archers even more time to snipe them one by one. The plan was to weaken the Pole numbers enough, so that by time they made a move on the castle where the main bulk of the citizen army was hiding, they had a less than fair chance.

That plan relied heavily on the fact the Poles wouldn't want to risk a direct assault on the keep. William hoped they didn't know just how weak the walls were or that his men would be stationed at the wrong part of the city. William's most heavily armed ships had arrived in the early evening just as the sun was setting and they now waited just off the coast ready to bombard the shoreline.

The cannon fire would pick off a few more Poles as they circled the city before they even entered the deadly maze. All William and Harvey could do was hope that the blatant blockades and stone walled buildings and cleverly placed guards made the southern road look too fortified, so the Poles took the bait of pressing through the city first.

The city had prepared itself for the siege that was making its way towards them one slow step at a time. The militia had been pulled together from brigadiers, wrung-out farmhands, and disgruntled nobles.

The city, normally a hub of trade had grounded to a halt. The dockyard and harbor looked like shadows of their former selves and were filled with motionless gloom. Hidden in the shadows that led up from the water's edge ran the maze of common wooden houses that had been filled with frightened youngsters, each clinging to their bow as they waited for the signal to begin the fight.

They citizens of Oakenfall had been preparing and things looked like they were going well, but when the Pole army appeared on the horizon, they formed into ranks on the distant hill. The huge and iron-clad men of the Pole army stood taller than anyone from the Hanson Kingdom and in the dull light of the thirteenth their weapons held aloft pointing to the sky made the shadowy horizon look like a forest was marching towards the city. The wind-calm carried the shouted voices over the plains adding to the fear that strangled the city.

The two armies that had set out from the Western Reaches and Briers Hill had joined into one under the leadership of Ingaild. They numbered only around four hundred strong. It was a small number of men to besiege a city, as it would be unlikely that they would have the numbers to breach the walls of the keep, even as weak as they were, and things looked promising for William's plan.

The heavy fire of the White Flag archers and the gauntlet of the city itself should obliterate the Poles. The city, although not walled as such, had used the stone houses of the noble district and blocked alleyways between them to force the Poles down and in from the North on the opposite side to where they'd gathered — but they had seemed reluctant to move.

Watching the lurking army from the top of the castle was Harvey. He had left his throne room for the first time in days and stood atop the castle. The cool wind blowing against him ruffled the feathers in the cap he wore. He leant over the battlements for a better look, the masses of gold necklaces around his neck sagging and shining slightly in the dim light.

"Why do they just stand there?" Harvey asked.

"Waiting us out it seems… that's unlike them," William replied.

"Indeed. Something is wrong. Can't your ships reach them there?" Harvey asked.

"No, they're holding just out of reach. We'll be ready when they make their move. Let us just hope the men hold steady," William said acknowledging that the assembled army was less than optimal. "Some nice little trinkets you have there," William said as the king's jewelry caught his eye. He could tell the medallions had been enchanted with something and were probably worth more than the rest of the castle put together.

"They were my fathers. They bring safety to the royal blood line. They will not work for anyone else," Harvey said as he cupped the golden circle in his hands. It showed the Hanson family crest encircling a red gem that looked like it held a thick liquid.

"That's blood magic, isn't it?" William asked. He could already tell it was by the odd glow and the blood inside the gem that sloshed around in thick glop-like waves. William had seen enough bodily fluids in his time to recognize them and he had had the fortune to have come across a few magic items.

"I'm not a mage, William. I have no idea what enchantment is in this. All I know is it saved my grandfather and it'll hopefully do the same for me today," Harvey said fighting the draw of the medallion. It had an odd power over him, but Harvey was more concerned with the huge machines that the Poles were pushing towards the west. "What are they doing with those trebuchets?" he asked with dread settling in his stomach like an old friend. "Don't tell me they're planning to push them all the way through the city to get here!"

"They would never make it. They would realize, though, that they could shoot the things from the south of the castle," William said as he stood overlooking the grass plains around the castle's battlements.

This was far from the first battle that William had overseen, but they were normally out at sea, and with ships you could plan your moves and those of your opponent more easily. Ships could only move in certain ways. If the wind was against them, they would slow or turn. The only wind that seemed to be on Williams mind now was the wind of chance.

"You're right. Why aren't they bombarding us already?" Harvey asked, and the warm breeze filled with shouting brought no answers. "There are so few too. I had expected so many more."

"This could be easier than I first thought," William said lying to himself. He truly wanted to believe it would be just the case of adding a few bodies to a pile at the bottom of the ocean, but he had no idea what the Poles were planning. The way they were moving the war machines along to Sea View Hill made no sense and their army just sat there like a cyst on the landscape.

"The majority of their men must still be holding Northholm against the ships I sent," Harvey said in his finery next to William. He had adorned himself in his finest golden and red fleeced jerkin to try and outdo his pirate counterpart. He wanted the people of the city to know who their King was. He'd been hidden away for so long, but now, this was the time he wanted to be remembered for… he wanted it to be remembered in the history books that he stood with his kingdom for the final battle and pushed the Poles from their lands.

"I don't think they're planning on assaulting the city, you know. They're camping by the trade road there. That's what I would do if I wanted to stop trade to you by land. Let's be honest. It's almost identical to what I've been doing from the island for years," William said with a nervous smile and it was true. He had put himself on the only route out to sea and had control of anything that made it through into the city. The Poles were mirroring this on land sitting comfortably on Oakenfall Ridge.

"At least you admit you're a common thief," Harvey commented with a snarl. He had held his tongue for days while William had brought his men into the city and the work to prepare the defense was underway, but he felt at the time of sitting on the roof that he could finally say what was on his mind. There was no backing out for the White Flags now.

"I never said I <u>stole</u> your stuff. I said I <u>stopped</u> your trade ships. It's your cowardly tradesmen that hand over their goods. Wait…" William paused holding a hand up. "The trebuchets are being pulled up the hills there. Only reason I can see for doing that is to be able to reach the ships," William said as he pointed to the west where four trebuchets were very slowly being dragged uphill by some of the biggest men he had ever seen.

"It's not liked the Poles to play tactfully. They rush in. They pillage, and they leave. What the hell are they up to?" Harvey said and then he realized…

The Poles intended to strangle the city itself. They would stop trade getting in from the farms and the sea. The city would run out of food in no more than a few days… a week or so, if they'd been well stocked. The people would have two choices. Eat their pets and each other or choose to fight the Poles and die.

"What supplies do we have, Your Majesty? How long can we last?" William asked and for the first time since he'd arrived at Oakenfall, real concern coated his face like a pale mask. His men were skilled at fighting from still positions. They would be useless in an open combat against trained ranks. They were pirates and bloody good ones at that, but they were not soldiers. Harvey had noticed the slip in power and took full advantage of his regained standing.

"We have enough stored for perhaps three days. We're mid-planting. Most of our supplies are all but gone. We're bringing stuff in by ship from the south and waiting for the orchards to start fruiting in a month or so. The fields have started to bear shoots from the wheat, but they're no good for harvesting for months yet," Harvey explained, his mind racing as he thought hard about a way to survive another stalemate but this time one much closer to home.

The rumors of the hidden labyrinth flashed through his mind and it could be worth a go. That was if it wouldn't take a week to clear the huge marble slabs that had been used to deck Celebration Square. If only they'd left it open! They could evacuate the city into the catacombs and pray they led somewhere.

"We might be alright. We got word out. The people of Port Lust will be heading this way. They'll stop at each of the two forts between here and the town. How many men will that be?" William said asking for more than one reason. It might be their saving grace now to have reinforcements arrive in a few days, but he also wanted to know for when he tried to claim power from Harvey — for they too might be reinforcements against him when the time came.

"You're right. They should number a couple of hundred and we'll have them flanked. We only have to hold out until they get here," Harvey said suddenly feeling cocky about his idea of bringing the pirates into this. If nothing else, they got word out quickly and if King Harvey could win this battle with little bloodshed for the city then keeping his throne would be easier.

"We can't just sit here though. They'll be expecting us to realize what they're doing. If we just sit tight then they'll know we have reinforcements coming. Not to mention I can see them turning those siege weapons on us just for the fun of it," Harvey said.

"We need to throw some lives at them and sadly Your Majesty, it'll be your men. None of mine are going to die willingly no matter how much gold you offer them when they get back," William said with a wink.

William did not feel comfortable with anyone having to die, but if it had to fall on someone to give the order, Harvey being that person, made the decision almost bearable. Harvey had no choice but to agree. It was a hard decision to make. Harvey would have to send his knights out into the open plains and enough of them to make it look like they were launching a defensive strike. It was obvious that they would be cut down by the Poles before they even broke the front wall of their ranks, as his so-called knights were made up of farmhands who had switched their forks for swords.

It was a move that would destroy the last of Harvey's respect among his people. Harvey felt the seesaw of power rise back up in Williams' direction. The average person would not understand the reasons Harvey had sent men to their deaths — all they would see was the needless slaughter of their loved ones.

"William. Go get the Captain of the Guard," Harvey said, as he physically sagged. "I'll give the order."

Harvey lifted his cloth crown and dropped it over the edge of the battlements watching it float down and rest gently on the soft grass that had started to sprout with the calm weather that had followed the heavy rains.

The night of the thirteenth was filled with sleepless beds, disturbed dreams and taunts from outside the city. Behind shut blinds families gathered, collectively sharing their last few hours together before father or son would be sent to his death.

The hushed sound of sobbing was matched by a few poorly aimed shots that had been sent into the harbor from the thumping machines hidden in the darkness to the west. The deep thuds splashed into the ocean for the most part, but some unlucky ships found their final resting places at the bottom of the White Sea. The Creator seemed kind enough to grant them a tide washing towards the shore and many them would make it to the golden sands.

The sailors could have made for the city, but few did. Instead they escaped east and made their way towards the fort that overlooked the reef. It was a strange hand of fate that could lead to more reinforcements, but no one knew if it would be in time or not.

When dawn came on the fourteenth of Nylar, an expected air of anxiety bathed the streets of Oakenfall. The militia cleared the blocked alleyway beside the empty Dean Estate and said their last tearful goodbyes.

The shoddily-armed and sleep-deprived men readied their assault into the open land between them and the Poles. The battle would be a hard one and every man, boy, and grandfather had said his goodbyes to his family. Staring death in the face, they all moved slowly, not wanting the last of the fruit crates to be moved and the alley to be free, but time seemed to toy with them and the hour it took to completely clear the debris felt like minutes.

Behind the amassed militia of soldiers, the sobbing of family members, women and children alike rang out like a forlorn bell calling the hour. Women pulled younger children back as they tried to cling onto the cold metal chain-linked legs of their fathers. Wives begged husbands to stay with them cursing the king and dooming the city, but their cries fell on deaf ears.

The cleared passage gave the men at the front of the crowd a view of the lush hill in the near distance. The sun only low in the sky had started its ascent and its long golden fingers silhouetted the hundreds of spikes poking into the air from the Poles weapons. The men of Oakenfall took a deep breath and one by one they set off to a trot in the warm morning.

The morning would have been a beautiful one if it did not bode to be the last for so many. Each footstep that landed on the hard earth took them closer to the embrace of the Spirit Realm and further away from the loving arms of the people they would leave behind.

The rustic walls of the nobles' houses made for a picturesque backdrop to the rushing Oakenfall army. The younger ones were easily recognizable by the poorly fitting armor and some tripped or slipped out of their breast plates. Yet still they continued holding swords out in front of them, some longer than their young and scrawny arms.

The older men took the lead, their strides wide as they roared. It was a sound meant to send fear into the enemy and shake the very fear out from their own souls.

The world seemed to hold its breath as it had many times before. It paused at the brink of such battles in utter amazement at the mortality that would follow.

Their roar may have made them feel more confident, but it mattered little as the first few lines of tin soldiers did not even reach the Poles front line. They were cut down and laid lifeless at the mercy of stones that fell in a heavy rain from the sky.

The militia was not a well-dressed army and the stones tore through them like water through a strainer. A few had armor, but most wore leather jerkins that they would have used to protect themselves while working at smiths, butchers or taverns. One had even forgotten to take his blacksmithing hammer out of the chest pocket. This forgetful act went on to save his life as a large sharpened rock that would have otherwise punctured his heart shattered off the iron head and splintered into his shoulder.

The old gruff smith fell to the floor bleeding from the several large splinters that had pressed into his shoulder. He would not get to see the rest of the battle, injured only a few feet from the ivy walled garden of a noble estate. He was dragged back by a grey-haired woman and fell in through the crisscrossed wooden gate.

The army was made up mostly of tradesmen and farmers and Harvey had picked the oldest trying to keep the young safe. That is not to say a large number were not in their teens, it was only that he had tried to find older men who were fit enough to fight first.

He had even gone as far as fitting out those he could with the decorative suits of armor from inside the keep. It was old, weak and rusted but it may save some lives.

Harvey was not leading the charge, instead he lay on his bed unable to watch the faces of those he had sentenced to death this time. He remembered wishing that the battle went well, that there were heroes born and the kingdom was saved... but there were not.

It was a blood bath and only that one old smith who'd collapsed in a rose bush would see the next dawn.

The Oakenfall army crashed against the hard tips of the Poles spears and wave after wave found their journey to their maker. The battle was not purely one sided and many Poles did fall too, but the ratio was around three Oakenfall to one Pole and within half an hour of the alleyway being cleared the last man was dragged screaming into the clearing between the Poles and run through.

It was a slaughter but a needed one. The lives lost would at least hold the Poles back long enough for the reinforcements to arrive. Harvey had stood still in his chambers, his head in his arms. He had known that the men he sent would die, but he had not planned for their deaths to come as swiftly as they had.

To make it worse the ships in the harbor were making a break for the open sea under the fire from the trebuchets. Harvey had watched from the keep as his loyal men's corpses were desecrated and held aloft on spikes to taunt the city. His stomach reminded him of the choices he had made, and nausea swept over him as he stared into the cold lifeless faces gawking at him from the horizon.

Harvey turned to look at William who surprisingly was down on his knees praying and even more strangely Harvey decided to bend down onto one knee with him and beg the Maker, the Creator of it all to spare the city. Together Hanson and the Pirate King prayed to make it through the night.

The rest of the fourteenth had been a blur.

Chapter Twelve – A Chance Meeting

As the militia of Oakenfall were laying down their lives for the kingdom, Darcy and Calvin were dashing away from the mountains back towards the shifting clouds of ash.

The dust had barely settled from the thud of Darcy's supplies sinking into the ashen ground before he had turned on his heels and followed the aged mage who was rapidly disappearing into the distance.

The three young dragonlings chased them relentlessly. Their huge wings were beating the ground and stirring up clouds of powder that engulfed the fleeing duo as the dragonlings dropped into the ash behind them.

They were toying with the two of them, chasing close and then dropping back to let their prey get a little further away. They were calling out between each other in little playful chirrups, and much like kittens playing with twine, they swiped at Darcy's legs and body, as he was still lagging behind the surprisingly swift Calvin.

The three dragons chased them for what seemed like a lifetime to Darcy and Calvin. The dragons scratched at them with their huge claws tossing either Darcy or Calvin across the ashen grounds. Neither one dared stay down for long for fear of the dragons' playful swipes killing them.

They rolled to their feet between blows. At one point the larger, and presumably the leader of the dragonlings, had grabbed Calvin by the robe and lifted him kicking and screaming into the air. The crunch that had echoed out into the night as Calvin hit the ground had made Darcy freeze.

He could remember just staring at the still figure of Calvin, who lay lifeless and bent double. Calvin's legs were snapped out in different directions and even with no medical training in his life, Darcy could see that at least one of them had been broken.

When their toy seemed not to be getting up again, the dragons grew bored. They did not leave Darcy alone for long, as he froze watching his lifeless friend, and they began to surround him.

A whip from the strong tail of one of the beasts knocked Darcy to the ground. The dragons had circled him while Calvin lay on the ground gasping for breath. The tail whip had winded Darcy… his chest heaved, and he was in agony. He wanted to run but couldn't find his breath. It was then that he had heard the murmur from Calvin. He was still alive! Calvin went to stand but fell flat back into the earth with a wail. His leg was broken but at least he was alive.

When Calvin hit the ground, it was obvious that he would not be able to outrun the dragons and Darcy began to fear the worst. He didn't know for sure, but he was all but certain he would not be able to overpower the dragons in a feat of heroics and, just when all hope seemed lost, a shadow appeared above Calvin.

It was Calvin's shadow, but it moved in the air and seemed alive. A sense of cold foreboding fell over the whole area and even the dragonlings froze staring at the shifting shadow. Their excited chirrups fell to silence as they stopped nervously.

Darcy had never faced a demon before but somehow, he knew it was Rinwid. It might have been the cold that ran through his back or the way the hairs stood upright on his neck, but Darcy knew he was looking at the shadow of the demon inside Calvin.

The dragonlings turned on their heels and started to scarper. Their fear was obvious in their scaly features. Darcy did not know what came over him, but as the last dragonling was bounding over him Darcy pressed the knife up into the air almost by reflex.

It connected with the fast-moving animal and sunk in deep slicing it from chest to anus. The beast made it another few feet before sailing through the air with its innards showering down before it collapsed behind Calvin and next to Darcy.

Darcy awoke panting. His head was killing him and the pain in his shoulder was not much better. His nightmarish dreams had been filled with the horrors from the day before, replayed in the distorted theatre of his subconscious.

The chirrups that echoed from the snarling teeth still chilled Darcy to the core as he pulled himself up onto his scraped elbows and woke in a cold sweat and shock. The memories dropped from his mind, but he could feel his heart still beating like a slaver's drum.

The stone hut they had sheltered in was dark. The roof had collapsed and was only a few feet above Darcy's head. It was being held up by loose rubble that looked weathered and weak and it would not have taken too much for it to collapse in on top of him.

The walls looked like they should have had weeds and moss growing between the cracks, but this was the Scorched Lands, so the sad sight remained as bare as a newborn child.

The bricks had started to turn to powder in the constant cloud battering its outside and Darcy was thankful that it had remained standing at all. The ash on the floor inside seemed finer than that outside and managed to coat everything in an oddly white shifting residue, that showed imprints of wherever Darcy had been.

An aged wooden table that had survived the years of neglect sat warped against the far wall of the room. Its top, aged and flaking, still had faint ring marks in from the person who used to live there. It was a reminder that the Scorched Lands had once been a lush and prosperous part of Neeska before the dragons had turned the very ground into lava.

Under the stone debris of a collapsed wall scattered planks hinted at where a bed would once have rested. Torn white linen danced gently in the breeze that pressed in through the many gaps dotting the hut.

Through one of the larger cracks in the southern wall Darcy could make out the shape of the dead dragon slumped against the side of the hut. It had been a miracle that the weight of the dead beast had not brought the wall down and sealed the inside off completely, but it seemed on this occasion that lady luck had given Darcy a helping hand.

The pain flashed back through Darcy's arm as his wounded elbows grew tired of his weight and forced him to move and pull himself up with difficulties to a sitting position. He looked down at the blood that filled his hands. It had dried and congealed against his white sleeves staining them. He knew some must have been his, but it was hard to tell what blood stains were from his wounds and what belonged to the dead dragon.

The memories from the night before replayed once again as Darcy tried to scrape the gruesome dried lumps off onto the torn linen scraps next to where he'd lain.

Darcy sat staring around the dark hut and looked over at Calvin. He was breathing gently, but he was still out cold. The old man's skin looked paler than normal. Deep blue veins could be seen under his skin and the same odd shimmer that had disturbed Darcy when Rinwid spoke was very noticeable.

Calvin's brown robes were now as stained with blood as Darcy's own clothes. Darcy had done his best to fix Calvin's leg last night using his own belt and a table leg from the wreckage to make a splint. That was before he himself had collapsed and fallen asleep.

Darcy had thought that he would never waken again. He had been prepared to die. He pulled himself across the hut on his hands and knees. His shoulder was still in agony and he wondered if he'd torn something, when the dragon had wrenched his arm back while the blade had sunk in.

It only occurred to him then that they had lost all their supplies. He had dropped the bag back at the foot of the mountain before the dragons started chasing them. He hadn't had time to think, and its weight would only have slowed him down, but it was gone now. Darcy's mouth was dry, and he wanted to wash the blood from his hands not to mention that Calvin looked like he was about to pass away. But there was little Darcy could do unless he fancied heading back out and hoping he ended up going the right direction back to the mountains.

Pushing through the pain Darcy made his way towards Calvin, but he stopped as he approached Calvin's side suddenly feeling ill at ease. Calvin's shadow looked normal, just like any other shadow but Darcy had seen it when the dragons were about to kill Calvin. It had risen into the air with such ominous intent that it had scared the dragons enough that they'd fled like mice. Then as if it had never happened, the shadow seemed to settle back down onto the ground where it should have lain.

"Hello," Darcy whispered praying the shadow did not answer back.

When no reply came Darcy gently shook Calvin trying to stir him. Calvin remained unresponsive. His breathing was shallow, and he barely had a pulse. He was either dying or the demon was coming through and neither option seemed that great to Darcy. He didn't relish the idea of trying to find his way out of that place on his own, but he dared not face the demon.

"I'm... I'm sorry Calvin," Darcy said. He felt terrible about leaving Calvin, but he had no choice. He would die if he waited with Calvin. They were still a couple of days walk at best from the edge of the Scorched Lands and probably further from a good meal and fresh water.

If Darcy waited around for Calvin to recover, he might not make it out of the Scorched Lands at all, and if Rinwid came back Darcy wanted to be as far away from the shadow creature he'd seen as he could get.

Darcy was about to crawl out from the hut when a spluttering of ash and dust fell in through the half-filled doorway scattering across the floor and landing on top of a similar pile Darcy had made when he'd pushed Calvin into the same hole.

"Who's there?" Darcy called out startled.

He was too weak to fight off anyone and his shoulder felt like it would pop out of place if he swung the little dagger too swiftly. The only blessing was that the hole was too small for a dragon to get through, but that did not mean that the young dragonlings had not come back and would not dig down into the hut... or worse — collapse the hut in on top of Darcy.

"Were you with the caravan?" Darcy asked scrambling around for the bloodstained dagger. He hoped maybe that one of the guards had decided to come with them after all, and that the caravan and supplies were up top too. He hoped, but knew it was a fool's hope.

"What caravan?" Fintan called out as he slid down into the gloom. The silver-colored armor he was wearing was filthy and showed signs that he had been travelling through the Scorched Lands for the few days he'd been tracking Darcy and Calvin.

Darcy could not have been more relieved to see that it was a humanoid dropping down into the hut and not the snarling face of a young dragon… or worse — its adult counterpart — but that did not mean he was safe.

"Who are you?" Darcy asked not releasing his grip on the dagger. It was amazing to Darcy that he even found the strength to hold the weapon up. A day before he could not willingly kill a fly, but after the sickening feeling of his own mortality and what he'd felt as he executed the dragon, Darcy knew that if it came down to it he could kill again, if it meant getting out of this place.

"The name's Fintan. I presume you're Darcy from Oakenfall?" Fintan said.

There was no point in hiding the fact he knew the name of the man in front of him. He had after all been tracking them both for days and it didn't look like he would be much of a threat. Fintan eyed the young human noble, Darcy, and the weak way he held the dagger.

"You may as well put the blade down human. Your skills are no match for mine," Fintan said, as he did not need to be diplomatic. He had practiced all his life for an adventure just like this and his journey from Port Lust had given him all the time he'd needed to find his sense of confidence.

"You're so sure of that, green skin?" Darcy said eyeing the elf. He didn't fancy his chance against the newcomer, who it was easy to see, was more athletic than Darcy had ever been in his life. He sighed and reluctantly dropped the blade to the ground by his side. "What do you want then?"

"I'm here to take the Dragon Heart from you," Fintan said not taking his eyes off Darcy.

The noble might have been scrawny and now unarmed, but Fintan did not fancy having to fight him off if he was lunged at in the confined hut. It was small enough and weak enough that if they began to fight the most likely outcome was the roof coming down on top of them.

Darcy laughed. He'd always known Harvey had sent other people into the Scorched Lands to find the Heart, but he hadn't expected that another kingdom had joined the bandwagon too. It was even funnier that the elf wanted to rob them for it after the hopeless attempt they'd made of getting it.

"You're as out of luck as the rest of us! We don't have it," Darcy said, and he could see that Fintan believed him by the way he sagged. "You have water in that bag of yours?" Darcy asked nodding towards the satchel that Fintan carried on his back.

"I do. Some," Fintan said offering nothing up. Most of the supplies he'd gathered before boarding the ship had been swept overboard. What little he had left had been rationed beyond the point of desperation.

"Please. We lost our supplies. My friend is wounded," Darcy said, and he stepped aside so Fintan could see Calvin clearly for the first time.

He knew it was a long shot to ask this would-be bandit for aid, but it was the only option Darcy could see in the moment.

"What happened... I saw the dead dragon up top?" Fintan asked as he slid the bag from his shoulders and offered up his water skin to Darcy.

Fintan knew it would leave him short for the journey home, but he was a kind person at heart. Probably too soft, if he was honest with himself, for the adventuring life that he longed for. Then again, here he was living it, and to keep living it Fintan guessed he would need to know what the story was with the dragon. After all they were supposedly extinct.

"It's a long story," Darcy said before he struggled to drink from the skin. The water was warm and tasted stale, but it could have been urine and Darcy would have still drunk it, his throat was so sore from the gulped breaths that had been laden with ash during the escape the day before. "How'd you find us?"

"It looks like your friend needs some healing. While I tend to him, I'll tell you the story," Fintan said.

He had been practicing his newly discovered druidic skills as he tracked Darcy and he had begun to control his new-found powers. It was still a long shot, but he might be able to help Calvin.

"I came by ship. The ship barely held together by time we reached Port Lust and I felt as sick as a dog. The crazy old captain even looked a little green, but I didn't have too long to recover. I found a horse by the edge of town and rode as fast as I could this way. That's when it got tricky," Fintan said as he passed his hands over Calvin again hoping the druidic power would flow through him.

Fintan had been practicing with the powers since he arrived on the mainland and had managed to get small shoots to sprout from the ground at command, but the gift was still very weak. It was something he'd have to work on, as people would expect him to be able to use his powers to aid Alienage when he returned.

"Tricky... how did you even track us through the ash?" Darcy asked interested in how it was Fintan had managed to find them in the ever-shifting clouds of ash that hid their footsteps.

Darcy watched Fintan as he continued to pass his hands back and forth over Calvin occasionally touching the old man's chest or head. Fintan had been sent to steal the Heart from them, so Darcy was understandably hesitant about the suddenly helpful and open nature Fintan was showing.

"To be honest it was down to luck. I relied on the Earth Mother's blessing and kept walking straight. That was until I saw the clouds swirling overhead yesterday, so I started to head this way. And if it wasn't for the dragon up top, I would probably have walked straight past the entrance to this place," Fintan said making another pass with his hands.

He wondered if his power would even work here. He hadn't trained as a druid, but all elves knew a bit about the lore of it. The whole thing was a blessing from nature and there were no living things in the Scorched Lands. Fintan could barely manage to get green shoots to grow in the open grasslands, let alone heal a man in this desolate ash-clogged place.

"Yes, the dragon," Darcy said with a shudder that ran through his aching body like woodworm through a library. "The clouds you saw would have been Calvin. He used magic to kill the first of the dragons," Darcy said.

"That explains why I can sense power in him," Fintan said still focusing on the old wheezing man in front of him. Fintan wasn't sure if it was power, he could feel, or if it was just his imagination. He couldn't shake the feeling that something was watching him — and it wasn't the continual untrusting stare of the well-spoken Darcy.

"What are you doing?" Darcy asked, changing the subject of power and growing tired of nothing happening.

He hurt all over and had planned to be halfway towards the edge of the ash by now, but instead he was sitting in the cold watching as Fintan waved his hands around slowly.

"To be honest, I'm not sure. I only found out recently I had any power at all, but I should be able to cure him a little. Druids can often tend to the sick," Fintan said pressing his hand against Calvin's clammy forehead.

"So, you mean this might not even work?" Darcy said in frustration.

The shadow might have scared the dragons off, but they would be back, and he didn't want to still be here when they did return.

"No, it might not," Fintan replied with annoyance. "Look by rights I should have just left you the minute you said you didn't have the Heart. It's going to be hard enough to get back to my island as it is with the Poles making their way to Oakenfall."

"What?" Darcy asked taken aback. Things had looked peaceful at the fort when he had left it only a week or so ago. His mind raced between his hometown, the little inn with its pretty barmaid and his father. Oh, Creator his father! If the Poles were on their way to Oakenfall, then his father must have been captured or worse. Darcy slumped, the shock dropping onto his shoulders like lead weights. If he wasn't so exhausted, he might have cried.

"When I arrived at Port Lust, they were sending men to aid at Briers Hill, as the Poles had taken it. By now they should be at Oakenfall," Fintan said flatly.

He could tell the news had upset Darcy, but he could not afford to get too attached. He had to keep himself detached from these humans, if he planned to take the Heart from them as soon as they found it.

"My father was at Briers Hill," Darcy said solemnly. He'd been thinking it was the last goodbye, but now it was confirmed he wasn't prepared for it.

If only he had stayed at the fort! He could have sent the caravan onto the Mages Tower alone and stayed with his father. The mages could be out in the place looking for the Heart and Darcy could have done something — anything — to save his father.

"I sense you feel you could have done something. Do not let this grief cloud your mind Darcy. I have never seen a Pole, but I have heard the stories and you, one man, could not have turned the tide of battle," Fintan said turning to face Darcy who, he could tell, was fighting back tears.

"You're right, but there's still a chance. We have to get the Heart. There is still time to save Oakenfall," Darcy said trying to force down his sadness. He could not and would not let depression creep back into his life. This was his new life. He could not mourn for a father he'd lost in his old life.

"Do you have any idea where it is?" Fintan asked as he slumped to the floor giving up on the old man for now. He was getting nowhere, and he was tired too.

"No. Calvin was the one able to track it, though to be honest he didn't seem to have much idea. I don't even know where we are or how far we would have to go," Darcy said in defeat.

He rubbed his face with his hands hoping by time they passed over his eyes he would wake up back at home to Granny bringing in a warm bowl and this would all be an overly-real nightmare… but as the dull light hit his eyes again, he knew he was still in the hovel.

"Well I walked in from Port Lust to the north. I travelled towards Northholm to avoid Briers Hill and came down almost directly south," Fintan said thinking. He bent down and with his finger drew the crude boot shape of the Scorched Lands into the dust.

"Then I had to turn west to head for the clouds you made while fighting the dragons. So, we should be about here," Fintan said pushing his finger into the lower right corner of the upside-down boot in the area that would have been the tongue, or laces.

"You say that like it's meant to mean something to me," Darcy said looking at the scrawl.

He could tell it was meant to be a map, but he had never had much need to learn how to read maps, and unless the dust showed where the Heart was, he couldn't really care much either.

"You came in with a mage, right? From the tower? So you came in about here," Fintan said tapping the top of the boot where the hole would be. "So, you walked how?"

"How? With difficulty and straight mostly… at least I think so. For about two days or so and then we saw the mountains and started heading towards them," Darcy said unsure of exactly what the elf was getting at.

"So, you must have doubled back about there to get here," Fintan said marking an X into the dust. "That must be where the dragons come from. So, that's likely to be where the Heart is!" And Fintan felt excitement for the first time since he'd landed on this god forsaken place.

It was short lived though, as the realization that they did not have the supplies to make it there and back hit him like a pinecone falling from the tallest of trees.

"So? We have a map?" Darcy asked. "What happens when we get there then? I can't let you take it from me," Darcy said feeling for the dagger at his side. He had picked it back up while Fintan had been distracted with Calvin.

"We couldn't make it now, not without supplies. We've gone far enough southeast though, that we're barely a day's walk from the Goldhorn Mountains. We should make for them and restock with the dwarves," Fintan said drawing out the path towards them in the dirt.

"How is it you know all of this?" Darcy asked suspiciously.

It seemed almost too convenient! If life had taught him nothing else, it was that it never went smoothly and anything that seemed too easy always ended up going wrong.

"I always wanted to be an adventurer as a child, and we had a map left on the Alienage from before the war started. I used to keep it with me whenever I was out in the forest, and pretend I was adventuring in here, and now I am," Fintan said truthfully.

He had spent so much time playing that he was off in the mountains that he knew the area almost as well as he knew which branches to grab on his favorite climbing tree.

"I guess I'll have to trust you for now," Darcy said defeated.

He had known the moment that Fintan quite literally slid into his life that he would either be his savior or his end. As he hadn't outright killed him, Darcy felt his best chances meant following Fintan's hand drawn map.

Chapter Thirteen – Second Hands of Silence

The ships that had broken for the sea had dropped over the horizon to the east of the city, and with them gone and their cannons no longer pointed towards the shore, Oakenfall was left exposed. In the days that followed the grassland slaughter of the battalion of old men, farmhands and children, the Pole force sat patiently in their makeshift encampment. It was a stalemate with William and Harvey on one side of the chess board, and Ingaild and Annar holding the line on the other.

The gods had not seen fit to move any pieces in the game for days, but each army was so close that as he watched from the parapets, Harvey could see the shadows that flickered behind campfire lights on the hillside. The brash sound of the barbarian tongue echoed out over the silence of the night, while the city was trapped in fear. When dawn came on the second day of the occupation, some civilians had loaded up wagons, or overburdened donkeys, or set off in small fishing boats trying to flee the city.

In comparison, Ingaild's men had set up tents, campfires and even carried out training drills just outside the city walls in the days they were stationed at the city's edge. They were raised from birth to believe that dying in battle was the greatest honor they could achieve, so they would not flee.

The Oakenfall defenders were few in number and many were not even trained soldiers, but they did their best, taking it in turns to guard the city perimeter, firing the occasional volley of arrows into the lands around the city in a show of strength, that was growing weaker with each day as more and more refugees risked the unguarded roads, or the harsh mistress of the sea rather than the ever-present army at their door.

Under the cover of darkness, it was not only civilians that fled. Come sunrise it became clear that posts that should have been manned were left empty as the city's defenders had slipped away under the cover of the moon. It seemed that all hope was gone — that was until the morning of the fifteenth, when hope for the petrified city was briefly re-ignited, because reinforcements had come from Port Lust.

Harvey was almost jubilant from his perch watching over the lands below his keep, but as the shadow of the marching army grew closer, his heart sank — it was a lot fewer in numbers than Harvey had hoped for. But what more could be expected? Oakenfall had been on its knees for years and the little money that had remained in the treasury had not been travelling to the small villages surrounding the sleeping beast. When it came time for Oakenfall to call out for aid, many of its people had little love for it anymore and few would die to save it.

"Charge!" a commander from within the pack called out and the lightly armored soldiers began to trot towards to the enemy. They numbered less than fifty men, and were already tired from the march south, whereas the four hundred Poles had been resting in the fields. Harvey considered sending men from the city to join the men, but he had so few and it would take too long to organize them. They would arrive after the reinforcements were already drawn and quartered.

Harvey was right. Swords clashed against poleaxes, in a flurry of blood and fury. The reinforcements' swift charge had caught the Poles' unaware. It was a brave move, but a foolish one. Even though many of the Poles had not had time to suit-up into their armor or form ranks, enough did. They clashed against the small battalion of hope snuffing it out like a used candle. The Poles were brutal, and Annar and his berserkers were at the heart of the battle tearing at the flesh of the Oakenfall defense. With each swing of their weapons they ended bloodline after bloodline, turning families into little more than memories.

The skirmish was over quickly and with next to no losses for the Poles. The small regiment from Port Lust broke ranks and retreated within hours of first being sighted coming over the hills in the distance and they showed no signs of regrouping for a second assault.

Harvey had been frozen within his keep, and his people would notice this. They would not forgive that their king had been watching another defeat from the castle roof top.

Harvey was alone in his prayers this time... he wasn't sure where William was. He had last seen him heading to Celebration Square with his men who were trying to hold the entrance to the noble section of the city when the Pole army turned.

It had happened so quickly. The intrusion from Port Lust had had seemingly awoken the sleeping arm of the Pole from where it had remained still at the edge of the city, and with the reinforcements gone, it marched on the city.

The front line approached slowly, their feet drumming into the grass hills and flattening the foliage, with Annar and Ingaild at the forefront, their dull armor casting shadows as the midday sun glowed like fire behind them.

"Ingaild?" Annar queried, his face dripping in blood that was not his own, his voice so powerful it could be heard from the roof of the castle keep clear across the grasslands.

"It is time! Raze the city! Take the keep!" Ingaild proclaimed as he brought his poleaxe down severing the whimpering head from a young man's shoulders that he'd pinned to the ground. The Pole army gathered its ranks, forming line after line and began to march towards the city. The archers from the city began to fire into the grasslands but too few found their targets and within minutes the barbarians were pressing against the noble district.

Harvey watched as the army grew closer. He could see William standing with his men as planned. The city rallied and those men who'd not fled began to take their posts. The Pole army split trying to take the city in a pincer movement, and the lower parts of the city began to light up as the traps were triggered. The view of the ocean from the castle was hidden behind clouds of smoke as the sounds of battle became deafening.

The Pole stone throwers retaliated against the traps and archers, by launching a barrage of flaming shrapnel back onto the roofs and balconies forcing the White Flag archers to retreat. The debris spread the flames, and the slums of the city turned to kindling and, even after their saturation by the recent storms, the streets turned into infernos.

Ingaild led a battalion of hundred men towards the northern city, under the cover of the chaos. Once there they cleared the blocked alleyways of the noble district. There were losses and the beautiful gardens of the noble homes would be the final resting place for many a man, but the sheer brutality that drove the Pole army forward succeeded and soon the two regiments rejoined in the heart of the city crushing what little resilience the Oakenfall regiments had managed to muster.

"The keep! Press on!" Ingaild snarled from behind the men who'd gathered around him as they fought the brave Oakenfall soldiers who had not fled in terror and still had strength to draw breath. Harvey watched in horror, knowing that there were only a handful of men, and a rundown wall standing between Ingaild and his goal now.

The battle had raged on for several hours and the city was awash in flames and blood. The hope that had been sparked in the early light when the reinforcements had arrived had all but faded as the sun turned red and began the final part of its descent.

The Poles made it to the keep's large dwarfen-carved gates and tossed ropes around their tops. Once the ropes were secure the barbarians lined up twenty men at a time and began to pull. Their brutish bodies pulled like horses dragging a wagon and the aged wood creaked, splintered and then gave way. Once the dust had settled, the Poles poured into the inner keep and with them, all hope for Oakenfall died.

Harvey sat defeated in his throne room waiting for the doors to give way. He had barred the ramparts and barred the door, but it would not be long until it gave way to the thuds that beat against the aged wood like the second hands of the grandfather clock. It reminded him of the clock in the lower castle — he wondered how many ticks he had left. Harvey was certain that it was all over. He couldn't believe they had really lost the war. Great Oakenfall, Jewel of the North, home to the people who'd repelled the Dragon Overlords, now sat defeated and waiting for the final blows to sunder it.

Harvey walked over to the window to take one last look out across his city in the setting sun. The weather had become pleasant and the season of the planting was almost ready to begin. The city should have been calm. The sounds of traders and music should have been filling the air. Smells from the tanners, bakers and smiths should have been meeting his nose. The streets should have been full of tradesmen and workers preparing for the slump of Winnan to end, and the business of the good weather to start… but that seemed like a distant dream now. Instead, the sight that met him was one of horror. Flames could be seen reaching into the sky from as far away as the harbor, and black smoke coated most of the city in a choking blanket. The stench of death permeated the air.

Celebration Square was a mess of bodies and its black marble looked red. The stone heroes of another age stood in dismay at the sight strewn around them like offal on a butcher's floor — it made the litter of the Centennial Celebrations look tidy in comparison to this putrid sight of the dead. Harvey's eyes were drawn closer to the castle where a few private guards of the noble estates where still fighting the Poles in the street and the noise of battle sounded out like a muted chorus hidden behind the thumping at Harvey's chamber door.

People had been dragged out into the street and beaten for trying to save their homes. Women and children lay dead as the army pushed onwards. Harvey could see a young man lying still in the furrow that ran through the main Oakenfall road. He recognized him as one of the serving boys, his pet dog lying next to him. The dog had gone for a Pole soldier who'd grabbed its owner, and because of the animal's bravery, both now lay together to wait out eternity.

Harvey could only be thankful that they seemed to be letting those who surrendered live and even let some retreat from the city. It was a good sign that the Poles planned to leave the city standing at least. If they'd planned to annihilate it completely, they would have let no one escape. As it was, they would need workers to rebuild the city and that would mean there was a chance to rebel. It had taken only four days from when the Poles had first been sighted for the city to lie in ruin. The ships bombing Northholm were due home soon but what would await them? Harvey dared not think. Instead he shut his eyes unable to take any more of the horror. Letting his mind wander he thought about Darcy, who should have been back with the Heart by now. Harvey could only guess that he had met the same fate as the others he'd sent. The Scorched Lands had claimed yet another victim. Harvey truly felt that he'd done what he could to make the city strong. It was all for them. It really was.

Harvey screwed his eyes even tighter. He had wanted to be remembered in history — and he would be… as the king that failed the city. He would forever be known as the last Hanson to sit on the throne before the civilized world fell. When his eyes opened, the sun stung them slightly. He looked out to the right from his window and could see the fallen gates of the keep. They lay shattered on the ground and the courtyard itself was filled with the enemy. That same adversary now pounded away at his chamber door splintering the ancient wood and buckling the brass seals. Harvey wondered if they would kill him outright when they finally got through. He hoped they would, as that would be preferable to facing his people. Sighing he walked towards his favorite table and with deliberate significance knocked over the small wooden figure that sat at the location of Oakenfall. "Checkmate," he muttered.

Harvey was ready. He walked to the doors by the corridor and lifted the beam locking them shut. With the next thud, they opened inwards knocking him to the ground. The seventeenth of Nylar would forever be remembered as the day the Hanson era ended.

Chapter Fourteen – Wrong History

As the door splintered to the floor within the Hanson castle, Darcy was still many days away, lost within the shifting gloom of the Scorched Lands. At least he was not alone, and Darcy held his end of the makeshift stretcher with difficulty, for the old man Calvin was heavy and even between him and Fintan, who was assisting in holding the tabletop transporting Calvin, it was still hard going.

Of the two of them, Fintan looked more comfortable holding the weight, but even the strong elf had difficulty as the trio waded onwards through the ash. The weather was still holding nicely, and the temperature was on the rise. This would normally be a blessing in an otherwise desolate place, but when struggling knee deep in ash and carrying an extremely well-fed old mage, the hot weather wasn't best.

"Are you sure it's this way?" Darcy said panting. He could feel his arms shaking and he wasn't sure if it was from the effort of carrying Calvin or from hunger. The only thought that seemed to persist was the longing for food. He couldn't remember the last time he had eaten. It might have been yesterday… or even the day before that. His stomach churned continually echoing like a wasp in an empty ballroom.

His dry hands struggled to hold onto the rough wood of the stretcher and Darcy could feel his fingers growing more and more tired. It would not be long before his grip weakened completely, and he could not face having to backtrack if they'd gone the wrong way.

"Yes… at least as sure as I can be," Fintan said leading the way. The sun was on its descent from the sky and was at their back, so they should be heading east and the mountain path they had slowly been climbing up would hopefully lead out of the Scorched Lands and eventually on towards the dwarfen Kingdom of Goldhorn.

Darcy didn't bother replying — it was an effort he didn't have the energy for. He didn't understand why but he thought back to the story Granny had told him of when she was driven in the slave caravan across the Western Reaches. He couldn't imagine how hard that must have been for her young legs. His own felt like lead and had grown numb, so numb in fact that he hadn't noticed that they'd been gradually gaining height out of the ash as the rocky road climbed higher. It would not be long before the path became too steep for carrying Calvin up on his makeshift bed, but he showed no signs of waking.

With erratic shallow breath Calvin's chest moved only little. It was labored as if the old mage was beat. His skin looked pale and dark blue spaghetti-like veins showed like a map across his skin. Dark circles surrounded his eyes and his lips were blistered and dry from the ash that whipped at them constantly. It seemed that whatever spell or blessing it was that Fintan had tried to cast in the little hovel had not done Calvin much good.

However, had anyone looked closely at the aged table they would have noticed the condition of the wood had improved. It was not as splintered as it had been. It looked fresh, as if it had just been cut. It was still rough around the edges, but it had a color to it, some life. If they'd looked underneath it, they would have seen small green buds poking their heads out from its grooves. The Earth Mother's blessing Fintan had been praying for had started to show, but it would take time, time Calvin may not have.

After another fifteen or so minutes of gradually climbing out of the debris of the old war, Darcy had had enough. "Can we rest?" he asked.

He was well-aware that they still had a long way to go, but he could feel his grip loosening and if he dropped Calvin now it could kill him. The slope had grown harsher and the earth was almost solid beneath their feet. If he had dropped his end of the stretcher then Calvin could slide halfway back down the mountainside and back into the deeper ash.

"That shoulder still giving you grief?" Fintan asked, feeling the strain himself but not wanting to admit it. Fintan was thinking ahead. They had planned to restock once they reached the dwarves, and then return to find the Heart. Fintan wanted to maintain the upper hand just in case Darcy was any good with that oversized letter opener that he kept at his waist — demonstrating weakness would complicate things.

However, Fintan was tired, more than tired. He was exhausted and was still feeling a little nauseated. He had a mission to do for his queen and he would not let anything stop him. This was his one chance at becoming the adventurer he'd always dreamt he could be. He had grown fond of Darcy quickly, but whatever bond of friendship was forming it would not stop him returning the Heart safely to the Alienage.

"Yes, something to do with that," Darcy said looking to the sky. He'd forgotten that his shoulder was wounded. He should have hurt, but for some reason he just felt numb. It was like his brain was a sponge that was drying out. He could feel himself inside like a passenger on a ship, he was within himself somewhere, deep below the surface, but his edges had grown hard and callused.

"Do you think we're far enough away from the dragons here?" Darcy continued as they slowly put Calvin down onto the ash. The tabletop sunk slightly as the ash compacted a little, but slowed to a stop before Calvin disappeared below its pale surface.

"I'm not too sure. I'd guess from the young ones, sure," Fintan said remembering the sight of the beast slumped over the roof like a fallen bird. It was bigger than he'd imagined dragons were when he was a boy fighting them with a stick in the forest. He didn't know how far they travelled or how fast — for all he knew they could be only moments behind them, or they may never leave the mountains again.

"How do you know they were only young? I thought no one had seen a dragon in over a hundred years," Darcy asked.

"They were only young. You can tell from the softer scales on the underbelly … at least if they're like the lizards from the Alienage. They change color when they mature," Fintan said sliding down onto his haunches.

It was funny really. He didn't miss home that much at all. He was out on an adventure and the King's armor still managed to shine even through its thick coating of ash. The silvers and blacks glinting in the low sun made Fintan feel like he was a beacon of elfishness in this desolate place. He could feel something in the wind. There was a tie to this place. The Earth Mother was watching over him. He would return home successfully… he just knew it.

The few minutes that Darcy and Fintan had planned to rest turned into hours as sleep had taken hold so quickly that neither of them realized their slow labored blinks had become slumber. Fintan was the first to awake with a start. Something was coming. His long ears could hear it in the distance moving quickly. He slid silently across the ground barely moving a stone. When he reached the still snoring Darcy, Fintan gently rocked him by the shoulder, his hand hovering above his mouth. He waited poised as Darcy started to stir, and before Darcy could make a sound Fintan pressed his hand down covering Darcy's mouth.

Darcy struggled to fight free, but Fintan pointed silently towards the sky. Darcy soon realized the elf was not taking the chance to assassinate him in his sleep, as he'd first thought, but was instead warning him of something much more dangerous. The shadow that soared above in the night sky was huge. It was easily fifteen or twenty feet long and its wingspan more than that. It flicked in the air and darted back as if it was searching for something. From the ground Darcy could see the glimmer of the beast's armor even in the darkness. Panic choked Darcy and he couldn't have made a sound even if he'd wanted to... Fintan gagging him or not.

Darcy's eyes darted around the makeshift camp looking for what he did not know. He had an overwhelming urge to run but his legs had turned to jelly, and the breath had vacated his body. They had only meant to stop for a while, but they'd both been so exhausted. Darcy had lain down just to rest his eyes for a few minutes and he had no idea how long he'd slept. The glow of the sun had faded and by how dark it was, he guessed it'd been for at least four or five hours. That had been more than enough time it seemed for the adult black dragon to have tracked them down in revenge for the death of its offspring.

Darcy's pointless search of their campsite was cut short as his eyes were drawn to the sky once more, as the huge black dragon made another pass, this time lower. The dragon's huge wings beat with such force that ash and stone from the ground was sucked back into the sky in huge clouds that clattered down around them. The wind was strong enough that Fintan's long blonde hair flicked in the breeze as if trying to reach up to the beast in awe.

Fintan's eyes were more accustomed to the dark than Darcy's and he could see the thick armor the beast wore. It looked dwarfen in craft, old and sturdy. Either the dragons had kept some slaves alive to dress them, wherever they had been, or this dragon must have been wearing the blackened steel since the time of the Blight. Neither option brought Fintan any solace.

With the beast fading into the shadow once more Darcy pushed up and Fintan moved his hand but barely. He did not move back far for fear his footsteps would alert the dark dragon to their location. Darcy could see fear on Fintan's face for the first time since he had met him. That was almost more terrifying than the dragon itself. Darcy did not know Fintan well, but he had seemed so solemn and stone-faced. He had barely shown any expression since he'd slid down into the hovel, but now his face dropped in fear, his wide eyes and his mouth drooped low.

"Calvin," Darcy whispered barely making a sound. He couldn't see if the mage was safe or not. Before he had gone to sleep Calvin looked as if he was on death's door, but the last thing they needed was him waking up now and drawing the attention of the huge beastly dragon that seemed to be hunting in the sky.

Fintan's eyes widened as the words left Darcy's mouth. He knew why Darcy had called out. He understood he was worried for his companion, but to risk talking! That was something Fintan could not understand. He did not reply. The screech came like thunder from the darkness. The huge dragon appeared once more. It must have heard the whisper even from its distance. Fire lit up the night sky as the dragon appeared in view. The torrent of flame barley missed the camp.

The dragon landed with a thud as it crashed into the ground sending vibrations strong enough to knock rubble free that then slid down the mountainside. After a short pause it staggered towards Darcy, its huge head bigger than Darcy's whole body. Its cat-like eyes focused on him fixedly. The world seemed to fall silent apart from the gentle clinking sound that came from the aged joints of its armor. This was followed by the sound of rock splitting below its massive feet as they slammed into the ground as it moved forwards.

"Run," Fintan said to Darcy. At least he had meant it to be to Darcy, but he knew deep down in his heart that he had said it for himself, but he couldn't move, his legs were frozen in fear. He had heard of the majesty and power of the Dragon Lords of old, but he had never expected to see one this close. Fintan recognized the emblem — faded as it was — that adorned the dragon's chest plate. It was the symbol of Oakenfall during the time of the Blight. This dragon would have been one that had called the city home. Fintan was not sure if that boded well for them or not. They may escape with their lives but being a dragon's slave was barely a life.

Darcy had not even heard Fintan. His mind had shut down in panic and he was fixated on the huge black dragon that was now right in front of him as it raised itself above him. Its neck seemed to extend, as it faced Darcy with a snarl. Darcy waited for the blast of heat. For the white hotness that would end the nightmare, but it did not come. Instead to his surprise, the dragon spoke.

"So, this is the little one that killed one of my children," roared out a voice that sounded like an earthquake and knocked Darcy onto his back. "I can smell its blood on your hands. This is surprising, I had expected more," the dragon said almost sounding disappointed.

It had wanted a challenge, something to test its strength again. It had been a century since the beast had had a worthy battle, so it wanted to cut its teeth again and it would not get that from the whelp that cowered below it like a cornered mouse.

Noticing for the first time the rest of the camp, the dragon turned to look at Fintan.

"Ah… a pointy ear is here too," the dragon said sniffing the air around it. Darcy could feel the sudden intake of air even from so far below the beast's head. The smoke that trailed from its nose vanished inwards before returning as the beast carried on talking.

"And magic, you have a mage! Quite the alliance, isn't it... just like the old days."

"Please?" Darcy said in shock. A millennium of slavery and fear of dragons was buried in his genes. It awoke when he looked at the creature in front of him and it was all he could do not to faint. Darcy's mind was awash with every scary story he had ever heard or read about dragons. Oakenfall history was one of slavery to dragons so they had been an ever-present part of his childhood, but the stories did not equate to the fear he felt now as he stood in front of the gigantic flame throwing and intelligent creature.

"Please?" the dragon said imitating Darcy as best it could with its deep booming voice that sounded like the roar of a volcano. "You slaughtered my child, and now you expect to live?" the dragon asked.

"We... I... had no choice," Darcy stuttered in absolute terror.

"No choice! I guess I could let you live, if you bow and serve me... after all, we ruled you for millennia and we will again," the dragon said with a laugh. "You think you won't. I can see that in your eyes. Your little city still thinks it won its freedom from us," the dragon lowered its head so that its foul breath and pointed teeth were at ground level. "Maybe for a time, that might have been true, but you have drawn the first blood and now you will pay."

"You should be dead!" Calvin said sitting up for the first time in days. His outburst stunned the whole camp, the dragon included. He had been awoken as the dragon had landed. It had taken him quite a few minutes to discern whether this was real or another dream, but by the shocked faces of the others, he knew he'd finally awoken.

"Calvin," Darcy said turning away from the dragon to see Calvin sitting bolt upright on the stretcher and staring past him at the dragon. Something was different with him. He looked fresher. His hair was still matted with ash and his clothes looked like rags tossed over him in a strong wind, but his skin had a life to it, that Darcy had not seen since they'd left the Mages Tower.

"I should have died. Is that what your history books tell you?" the dragon said, his attention seemingly pulled away from Darcy by the audacity of the outspoken old man. The dragon moved forward bearing down on Calvin and knocking Darcy away as if he was a rag doll with a swipe of his huge claw and barely breaking his stride. Darcy landed with a thud a few feet away from where he'd left the ground. His chest felt crushed by the dragon's claw that had swatted him like a fly to the side. Agony swamped Darcy's whole body as the numbness he'd felt when the fear that had been gripping him washed away like the edges of a riverbank in a storm. He could barely breath. The night sky grew brighter, until nothing but whiteness filled his vision, and with a flash he passed out.

"I am a god. I cannot be killed by the likes of you, no matter how many of you turn against me and my kind," the dragon said as it walked towards Calvin. It didn't seem to have noticed what it had done, or barely acknowledged that Darcy had even been between him and his new interest, the mage Calvin.

The dragon's stare was so solid nothing could break it and the dragon didn't even seem to perceive Fintan as it strode forward. Fintan remained still as the beast passed him by, the creature's huge muscled legs pounded into the earth, shaking it and cracking the rocks beneath. The dragon was a powerhouse of muscle, armor and flame.

Fintan was looking for a weak spot in the dragon's armor as it passed him. When he was a boy, he'd imagined a situation just like this, and he had leapt into the dragons' belly and pushed his wooden stick sword into the imaginary Dragon Heart thus saving the kingdom. However, the real world was not like his fantasies, and there was no way he could have done that now even with all his might, seeing how strong the dragon's scales were and how well fitting its armor was.

Even with a real sword it would be like stabbing a cliff face with a toothpick for all the good it would do. Calvin climbed to his feet never taking his eyes off the black-scaled creature. The wooden tabletop slid down the slope. The dragon's foot dropped down onto it and splintered it, as if it had been made of straw.

"The Arch Mage destroyed you," Calvin said remembering everything he knew about dragons. Whatever daydreams he had been having before were gone. He could only see one time and that was now. It was all crystal clear. Rinwid had removed the smoke screen he had placed in front of Calvin. He was no longer torn between images of times during the Blight, but to the misfortune of all of them — the dragon was still there.

"Ah! That blast that shook the Mages Tower and razed most of these lands to ashes?" the dragon laughed again. It was entertained that the humans had forgotten the truth already. "What! You thought that was us? You thought our fires blackened this land? We would not have ruined our own land and our own feeding grounds." The dragon was right on top of Calvin now. "The mage had consorted with a demon to be rid of us, but he didn't know the truth of it — though I sense you do. You know of the Dark One."

"The one locked away?" Calvin said remembering what Rinwid had told him. He couldn't believe this was the same dragon that had ruled over Oakenfall, but he had to. He could feel the Heart he was seeking so desperately inside its massive chest. He could hear it beating with a drum-like thud. The demon had tricked him. There was no way they could get the Heart. No way that they could use it. Rinwid had known all along that the dragon had survived — that he would have no choice but to kill the dragon and destroy the Heart.

"Yes. You understand more than most ticks. They killed most of my kind, but a few survived. The Seal that binds the Dark One is still in place. Together, we dragons rebuilt our numbers in the mountains. My horde has grown. They grow restless, tired of the dark. It is time to retake what is rightfully ours," the dragon said and let out a roar so loud that larger rocks were shaken free from the mountain side before it leapt up into the sky. Then with two beats of its wings it was gone leaving the confused group staring into the night sky.

The rumble from the mountain side continued for a few minutes and then slowly stopped as the landslide subdued. They waited for the dragon to circle around and engulf them in flame, but it didn't come and after a few moments of not knowing if they were about to die — that seemed like a lifetime — it was Fintan who was the first to speak.

"What was he talking about?" Fintan asked from the shadows, his heart still dancing to its own tune and his hands wobbling like tree sap in a storm.

"The Dark One, a demon of sorts… he is something far worse than dragons," Calvin said trying to take his first step in days, his leg still weak and broken. Fintan had banded it with old cloth and one of the table legs.

"I'm confused. What do you know Mage?" Fintan demanded as he looked at the mage who appeared to be the healthiest of the three companions now.

"I wasn't sure. I couldn't see it clearly until now… the demon tricked me, but I now know what Rinwid really wanted. There is a Demon God sealed by Seven Magical Seals. One of them is here, deep below the earth," Calvin started, as he could see the story now as clearly as words in a book.

"Rinwid —?" Fintan went to ask but was cut short.

"We do not have time to explain. Just know that the dragons weren't the enemy. They had stopped human greed from breaking the Seal, but demons — like the one in me, Rinwid — used magic to blister the land, to twist the truths that we know, all in the hopes of opening the lock. But it didn't work and now the dragons have returned," Calvin said finally clear of the messages, that Rinwid had been trying to hide.

"The armor the dragon wore, I know it," Fintan said.

"Yes, that was the same dragon that ruled over Oakenfall. He didn't die during the war. We were all sent on fools' errands, there never was a Heart to find. This has all been for nothing and now the black dragon and his horde plan to take back Neeska. We'll all be enslaved again, but the alternative could be worse," Calvin said half explaining it to Fintan and half just clearing it all in his own mind.

"We have to do something," Fintan said.

"It took all of the Northern Kingdoms and the might of the demons before," Calvin said flatly. He knew he should have been scared, angry, or at least hurt after everything that had happened — and knowing it was all for naught — but he felt nothing.

"The dwarves! We were going to the dwarves. Even if we can't get the Heart, we're still close to Goldhorn. Perhaps we can convince them to join us like they did before. We beat the dragons once right, and there were a lot more of them back then."

"A second Great War or we face the Dragon's Blight again. I don't fancy either option. Getting the dwarves to join us will be one thing… uniting the north, that'll be another challenge," Calvin said.

"What choice do we have, Darcy? … Darcy? … Where is Darcy?" Fintan said suddenly realizing he was missing. Fintan scrambled down the uneven path towards the deeper ash that Darcy had been knocked towards. He kept low encase the huge black dragon made another pass.

Calvin was not far behind, but he did not bother bending down, that is, not any more than he normally did with his aged body and heavily-beer-bellied stomach pulling him down. Calvin knew the dragon was gone. He could sense the Heart pulling further away. There was no risk of flame erupting into the night sky.

"Darcy are you alright?" Fintan called out as he stumbled closer. His flat leather soled shoes slipping on the debris that had been shaken loose. They were of top-quality elven craft, but they were designed with the forest floor in mind. Twigs and damp leaves were a different kind of slippery to the jagged rolling stones that hid themselves under the blanket of ash and sent Fintan onto his knees more than once in his haste.

No answer came back from Darcy's motionless body to meet Fintan's words. He had been tossed hard against the rocks before landing in a particularly deep pile of ash. It barely looked like he was breathing as Fintan closed in. Darcy's white shirt was colored gray with dirt and dust that should have shifted and fallen free with each breath. It remained still like the dust on the many wine bottles that had filled the cellar of Darcy's home.

Fintan struggled to come to a stop next to Darcy as the rolling stones slid onwards. He laid his hands onto Darcy's chest and froze — it was as he feared. He had known it before he had got to him. It was not hard to see that Darcy had stopped breathing. Fintan had just been hoping that Darcy's breath was so shallow that he could not see it, but now the touch of his already cooling shirt confirmed his fears. "He's not breathing," Fintan said flatly confirming it to himself more than saying it for the benefit of Calvin who had caught up and was now standing just behind Fintan.

"Move aside," Calvin said pushing the stunned Fintan to one side with a gentle nudge to his shoulder. "Move will you, boy. Let me have a look at him," Calvin said feeling frustrated.

The anger the demon had been pouring through him seemed to have subsided for now, but seeing his companion of the last eleven days lying unconscious wasn't productive of a good mood… and it would not take Rinwid's interference for Calvin to boil over.

"Is he alive?" Fintan asked in the same frozen tone. Millions of people had died in his adventures, but that had been different — they had been faceless nobodies, and when he grew bored with the game it had ended, but in this is place death was still around him. It didn't all fade away back into beautiful forest and mischievous squirrels. No. This was real and not make-believe — death here felt different to how he had imagined it.

Fintan had lost people before… elves lived for a lot longer than humans, but they did die. He'd often found dead animals in the forest while out exploring but for some reason this was different. It was not nature. It was not from old age or sickness. Darcy had been in the prime of his life and set for something great and he had just been snuffed out like a candle in a strong breeze.

"I don't think so," Calvin said as he tilted Darcy's head back and leaned in to listen for any breath too faint to see. Calvin could hear Fintan starting to whimper behind him.

"Be quiet. Let me try something," Calvin said calmly. He looked over Darcy and how he'd fallen. The crick in Darcy's neck was definitely not normal. It looked like it was broken, and blood had already begun the pool under his skin. It would take a fair bit of power to bring Darcy back now, and Calvin wasn't sure just how much more juice he had to give. He hovered over Darcy's body deep in thought. *Rinwid if you can hear me, I need you to help me save this young man,* Calvin thought to himself.

The words floated through the empty space that was his thoughts. "Rinwid," Calvin said aloud hoping it would have more effect, but it seemed like the demon had little interest in Calvin for now.

Annoyed as he was, Calvin saw the look of confusion on the elf's face. It reminded him of Darcy when he'd first been brought into the tower and the muddled conversation, they'd had explaining about the Blight to start with. That seemed so long ago. The strange life of the Scorched Lands had become the norm, but he could tell by Fintan's face that he would need to explain it all to Fintan later. Now was not the time and Calvin began the spell.

Calvin could feel the white light growing inside him, as if someone had lit a candle in the middle of his chest. It started off small like a tiny glowing marble but grew and grew. The gasp that came from Fintan's direction must have meant it was working. The glow continued growing and protruded from him as Calvin concentrated on Darcy. His hands shook much like they had when the electricity had flowed through him when fighting the dragons, but this energy felt different. It almost felt calm and dreamlike. The vision blinded Calvin as his mind hunted for Darcy — he could feel the body was empty... the spirit had left.

It was in the stream, the flow that washed around the world bringing life to everything. Darcy had joined it. Calvin could feel his magic waning. It would not be long before the spell failed. He hunted in the light. There, in the distance he could feel him. Darcy was with someone... a man, who felt the same, yet different. The word *father* flooded through Calvin's mind as the magic snapped back like a spark from a flint and was gone.

"It's no good," Calvin said sinking to his knees. It would have taken more power than he had to bring Darcy back. He was gone.

Darcy had passed into the Spirit Realm. The door between that world and this had been closed before Calvin could even call out to Darcy. Calvin would never know it himself, but the man he had seen Darcy with would guide him well into the heavens. Darcy had finally come to terms with his father in that place and now they could be together uninterrupted by war or duty until the life-stream saw fit to send them forth from the Spirit Realm to bring new life to the planet.

"He's really gone?" Fintan asked knowing the answer but needing to hear it.

Calvin just nodded.

After a few moments silence it was Fintan who spoke again. "At least it was fast. That's all we can ask for sometimes. We should bury him and move on." It sounded heartless, but it was the only sensible thing to do. Their rations were all but gone and Fintan did not know how long the mage's newly found strength would last before he ended up collapsing again. They would have to mourn Darcy another time.

"You're right," Calvin said still hovering about the dead noble's resting body.

"How did you come to be travelling with us, Elf?" Calvin asked turning to face his new companion. He felt angry about the young noble's death and if the elf had anything to do with the dragon finding them, he would pay with his life.

"A long story, as is yours, I guess," Fintan said calmness coming back to his mind.

"Once Darcy is laid to rest, we can both tell our stories," he said picking up a broken plank of wood from the shattered stretcher that had rolled down close to Darcy, and with it Fintan begun to dig.

Chapter Fifteen – Showdown in Celebration Square

Unaware of the danger that would soon be upon them, Harvey took a moment to make the last few minutes in his mind clear, as he was led through the city blindfolded.

It had all happened so quickly. He had been thrown to the hard-stone floor much like the fallen figure he had so deliberately tumbled himself but — unlike the figure that showed no remorse about falling — Harvey felt pain as he hit the hard stone floor and it had stolen his breath.

There was a taste of blood as the huge brutes pouring into the throne room surrounded him. A boot came first, then another, and another. Finally, a fist had caught him across the jaw, and this was followed by another thud to the side of his head. He was expecting to be bludgeoned to death, as darkness overtook him.

Harvey was not sure how long he'd blacked out for — nor for how long they had continued to beat him once he had — but when he came too, he was dragged to his knees. A sword had been pressed against his throat. Someone had said something he couldn't understand but it had seemed to spur a debate. It was ended by another hard blow to his stomach and a bag being pulled over his head.

Harvey was gasping for breath as strong arms dragged him down and out through the castle to the dungeons. It was there that the stocks were forced over Harvey's neck and arms. He was led still blinded by the bag through the city. He heard muttered conversations in both Oakenfall and Pole, but his mind could not focus on them.

When the bag had been ripped from his head Harvey recognized Celebration Square instantly. After all, for years it was the only place in the city, he'd spent any real time in other than the castle. Harvey and several others had been lined up facing southwest towards the towering noble residences. It seemed like Ingaild had amassed everyone left alive within Oakenfall to Celebration Square and every foot of the black slate floor was covered with people.

There was an odd quiet to the event as Harvey lifted his head from the stocks he had been shoved into. The fires subdued and the battle over, calm was returning to the city. The white domes looked pretty against the sky's blue backdrop. It was cool, a typical spring morning, and the familiar mist Harvey had loved as a boy rolled in from the canals and cooled his aching body.

Harvey remembered fishing the same canals and feeling the same mist when he was a boy, but back then he had been guarded by several soldiers and felt safe. Now he suspected he was minutes from his death, and as abusive as parts of his childhood had been, he longed for those times, times which had lied so much about the city's future promise… a promise that had been stripped away and laid bare by years of war and corruption.

Smoke from the ransacked buildings seemed to have calmed and it looked like the last of the fighting had ended. The battle was over but still upturned carts and bodies littered the streets and pigeons had already started picking through the debris and carnage for food.

A huge and mostly bald man stood in front of the assembled captives. He had straggly long brown hair that grew from around his ears but seemed to have vacated the top of his head. His face was red and hidden behind a beard that reached his chest, where it met with a fine thick wolf-fur jerkin around his barrel chest. The jerkin showed he was important in Pole society, and Harvey soon realized it was Ingaild, King of the Poles.

Ingaild strutted back and forth silently taking in the faces of his captives, the crowd behind him matching his lack of noise as the supposed heroes of Oakenfall lay bound and ready to be executed. Harvey struggled to look to his side to see who else was confined with him. He was chained down and his arms wrestled with the restraints as he distorted his head to look to his right.

Through blackened eyes he could see two young men restrained in the same way. He had no idea who they were, but they had cheap rusted armor on from the castle, so they must have been in the keep when it fell. Their reward for trying to save a king who failed them would be death it seemed. Harvey sighed and looked to his left, where he recognized the outlandish clothing of the man he saw there.

"William," he whispered his jaw aching from the effort. The bruising had swollen, so the words slurred. Harvey tried to move but behind him a giant-like man was holding the chains still. Harvey gave in to the restraint.

"Silence you pit dog," Ingaild said spitting in Harvey's direction. "Your days of talking are over."

Ingaild walked over to Harvey and grabbing him by the hair yanked his head up almost to breaking point. "See people of Oakenfall your precious King kneeling in the wreckage he brought on you!"

"I don't think it was him that fired the bloody trebuchets you know —" William said defiantly from his stocks next to Harvey. His words were cut short by a sudden thump to the back of his head from his own giant-like jailer wielding his chains.

William regretted the words, but he couldn't help himself, as William was a pirate and it was in his blood not to take to authority.

"No! You're right in that. He did not release the spring of the mighty trebuchets, but he stole our lands — fields that belonged to the barbarians — and reclaimed now by my arm, my might, and my Poles! Northholm is in our lands and should have been ours, but thieving Hansons stole it. The Hansons are no better than dragons enslaving you all!" Ingaild boomed with the confidence only victory can bring.

"It is you that keeps slaves not Harvey. Mind you, I understand why. What with the entire dome-polishing crew you must need, I can understand your bald bas—" William's taunt was cut short by another thud that sent him crashing into the floor, its hard-black slabs doing nothing to break his fall.

He was already in a lot of pain from his capture and didn't think he had anything left to ache, but it was novel that the Poles were finding new places to hurt him. He wished he could keep his mouth shut, but that was a skill he had never developed.

"If that one speaks again cut his throat!" Ingaild said pointing his bear-like hand towards a bleeding William.

"Your city lay in ruin saved only by my choice, my kindness," Ingaild said pounding at his chest. "All of Neeska belongs to the Poles, not just the wastes the dragons before you drove us to. This was our land, a land where a man is judged by the might of his arm. A land where you can claim what is yours, if you have the will to fight for it!" Ingaild turned to the crowd placing his huge spear like weapon down in front of him.

"The Hansons were brave once. They fought back the dragons — and I will not deny this — but namesake alone does not make one a leader. I ask you now, why a son or anyone else should be given the throne unless he fights for it? I killed for my seat and I throw down my spear for any of you Oakenfall-dogs brave enough to fight me to take it," Ingaild said and as expected the crowd remained silent.

Their spirits were broken and those who had been brave enough to fight to the end now lay dead in the streets. The spear rattled against the hard stone pavement before coming to a stop. Desperate women looked to their husbands among the crowds begging them to step forward to give their children a chance of freedom, but none were brave enough. Death was all around them and their fighting spirit had fallen with the castle walls.

"Free me and then I will," William said to everyone's surprise, but his injuries were so bad he fell to his knees again without the need of a thump from the jailer. He winced in pain and waited for the blade, but it never came.

"Wait!" Ingaild said stalling the jailor that would have ended William's life otherwise. "You have spirit," Ingaild continued as he turned back to look at William. "You should have been King not the fat redhead."

"Oakenfall needs no king," William said coughing at the blood congealing in his throat from his broken nose. He wished he hadn't tried to make the jump from that roof, but it had been either that or give up. It had turned out that giving up would have been less painful. He had crashed into the ground, was captured minutes later and had woken up in chains.

"William... no... if anyone is to fight him it should be me. He plans to execute us anyway. As the rightful King of Oakenfall, I challenge you Ingaild to single combat — the prize... freedom of the city," Harvey said hoping to buy more time.

He still hoped deep down that reinforcement would come from somewhere to save the city. It was fruitless, but a fool can find hope even when all likelihood has long since faded. He could feel the blood in the necklace slosh around. Whatever magic was in there was being stirred by something. Maybe it really would protect him.

"I had hoped you'd say that," Ingaild said with a wide smile. "Executing you would have little worth to me. Whereas killing you in battle — that will be a namesake. Unchain him. Feed him. Arm him and return him to my throne room on the hour," Ingaild ordered.

"In one week, we meet here again. Until then go! Rebuild!" he said to the watching faces of the desperate citizens of Oakenfall.

"What about the rest of them?" Annar of the East, Ingaild's general asked his weapon ready. It was no surprise to anyone that he'd survived the battle and even less of one that he would be the executor.

"Take the mouthy one to the castle dungeon. He has earned his chance to live. As for the others, kill them," Ingaild said turning and without another word walked towards the castle closely followed by a dragged and defiant William and a silent Harvey.

Chapter Sixteen – Reluctant Steward

As Darcy's body was being laid to rest, William was given the chance to avoid the same fate within Oakenfall.

William found this visit to the throne room much more uncomfortable than his first, only a few days before, when he'd come to see Harvey for the first time and had known what to expect — civilized royalty is one thing, but barbarian leaders tend to kill first and forgive later.

William was a confident and cocky man for the most part, but he did not feel on the top of his game now. This was largely due to his broken nose and the bruises that riddled his body like mold on cheese, but that was not the only reason. William watched in silence as the massive bull-like man Ingaild, took the place of Harvey in front of the miniature map of Neeska on the worn tabletop.

"Strange thing to have… toy soldiers and painted maps. It is no wonder Oakenfall fell so easy. Real men do not waste time on toys. They train hard. They practice," Ingaild said turning to face William for the first time since they had left Celebration Square together.

The guards that had escorted him had left now, but William felt no freer without them holding the chains. Try as hard as he might, William was in too much pain to think of a witty retort. His nose was bunged up with his own drying blood and he could feel it swelling to what felt like a watermelon-size. For the first time in his life, he remained silent.

This would probably be William's last and best chance of escaping with his life. The guards were no doubt not far away and judging by the scars on Ingaild, he was not afraid of a fight. It wouldn't be easy, but William liked a challenge. Ingaild had given him a chance "to earn his freedom," as he'd put it, but William was almost sure it wouldn't be an offer he would want to accept. So instead his eyes slowly took in the room in a new light. This time he was not judging the decadence. No, he was looking instead for anything that would help him break free of the chains that bound him and a way to overpower the bear-like Ingaild… that would be stage one. Escaping a tower full of Poles and fleeing a city under occupancy could be stage two.

"Not so brave or chatty without your crowd it seems. No matter. It is in front of them that I intend you to be of use," Ingaild said running his hand through his beard and obviously thinking of something. "You see. I could kill Harvey Hanson and prove my strength, but I am not a stupid man. It would give Oakenfall an idol, a fallen king to use for raising a rebellion. You rats would flock to it as if it was mulled cider," Ingaild said, surprising William.

William had not expected the Pole leader to be so far sighted. Stories about the barbarians were not about clever plans, but of brute force. The fact Ingaild possessed both made him more frightening.

"Do not mistake my sparing your life or your possible usefulness to me as allowing you freedom, worm. I will slit you from ass to ear and hang you from my pole out the window without remorse," Ingaild said pulling his trusty weapon from the tabletop and thrusting it so it barely missed William's cheek.

"My offer is a simple one so even your little brain in that tiny head will understand it. If I kill Harvey, I make a martyr out of him, but if you, another Oakenfall, kill him. Well, he's just another victim of the war and it shows how easily you can be turned," Ingaild said still holding his spear against William's face.

It went someway to showing Ingaild's tremendous strength that his arm didn't shake at all even from holding such a big weapon at such an outstretched position for such length of time.

"What if I refuse?" William said certain of the answer. A week before he would have relished the idea of killing Harvey. It would have been the justice he deserved for killing William's father, but not like this. The man had been disgraced. He had already lost everything. It was pitiful. William could not take pride in this and it would not be a true victory, if another dictator took the throne. It would not bring the freedom he had been seeking.

"Then you never leave this room," Ingaild said unemotionally, his cold stare confirming he was not bluffing.

"Now, will you be my champion? Fight and kill Harvey, and I will let you get on the next ship out of Oakenfall, a freeman so long as I never see you again. Lose or refuse and I will end you myself," Ingaild said never taking his eyes off William. The pirate restrained in front of Ingaild fascinated him. He was outlandish and had taken a beating that would have made most men turn into whimpering children, but William remained defiant until the end.

"I see no choice then… I'll do it," William said. He hated himself for saying it. He'd wanted to tell Ingaild to stick it where the monks keep their pencils, but his slow search of the room had not revealed any magic way to escape and he really, really didn't want to die.

"Good. Then the meal I promised will be yours and your wounds will be treated." Ingaild pulled his weapon back slowly, pulling it upright so the rounded base could drop to the stone floor with a loud and satisfying thud. This was seemingly a signal someone had been waiting for, as the broken door that had been pulled back into place was slid aside.

"Do not show mercy when you fight Harvey. Only one of you will survive the fight — and if it is not you, I promise you that your death will not be painless," Ingaild said turning away and walking to the small wooden throne.

Chapter Seventeen – Emotional Climb

"Well Fintan, it looks like your Queen is going to be as out of luck as the Arch Mage is," Calvin said glancing over his shoulder. "It would be funny if it wasn't so bloody depressing." Calvin turned back to face Fintan who had taken to following as they made their way up the mountain path.

Fintan had started off leading when they'd first left the site of the dragon attack, but when the pecking order had been sorted out between the old man and the elf, without the need of words, Fintan had ended up at the rear even though Calvin walked with a limp from his broken leg.

"I can't believe the Heart isn't real. I just can't," Fintan said trying to take it all in. Calvin had explained everything to him the best he could. All about Rinwid and the search for the Heart but it all seemed too farfetched for Fintan's sheltered-island-mind to take in. It was less believable than any of the adventures he had made up as a child.

"Well it's not that it isn't real Fintan. You see demons have an odd sense of morality about that. They won't tell a lie — at least not a straight lie — in a bargain, so the Heart had to be real for Rinwid to come to a deal with me to destroy it. It just turns out that the bloody thing is still in the chest of the dragon itself," Calvin said struggling to pull himself onto the edge of a boulder that blocked the ever-thinning path. His little crooked legs kicked against its side like a turtle trying to mount another, until finally after catching his beard from under his arm, he managed to pull himself up.

"Let me get this right. So, if we can somehow get the dwarves to help us kill the dragon, then the demon will use you to break the Seal and release the Dark One as they call it?" Fintan asked.

"Yeah, so seems we're screwed either way," Calvin said panting. "I need to rest a moment. I'm not as young as I once was," Calvin said feeling more himself… which was not a good thing in this case.

Rinwid had given him the energy to traipse through the miles of churning ash and battle the dragons, but that was all at the expense of Calvin's own spirit energy. He had not been a young man to start with, but now he felt much older than his sixty-three years.

Calvin did not know for sure, but he wondered if that was why Rinwid seemed to have gone dormant for now… in fear that he might use up all of Calvin before he could achieve his plan. The journey from the Scorched Lands had been easier than either of them could have expected. Once they'd laid Darcy to rest, they'd headed almost due east and began climbing higher. The ash had fallen away quickly giving way to more solid rock and earth and it was not long before they could even start seeing small shoots of plants trying to push back the decay of the Scorched Lands.

As the days had moved on, they climbed higher, but it seemed like Calvin needed to rest more and more often. He had refused to eat or drink to start with, but after Fintan's continual nagging, had given in, though it seemed to barely increase his vanishing strength.

Stopping on the outcrop behind the mage, Fintan looked out over Neeska. With the sky still clear and the ash below them they could see the horizon for the first time in over a week.

"Look at that view," Fintan said joining Calvin in sitting on the crest of the boulder. He had gotten used to the time it took for the old man to rest up enough to continue their journey and at least now they had clear skies over them while they waited.

"You can see most of Northern Neeska from here," Fintan continued, amazed by how far he could see. Life on the island had meant views were not something he had really come across. The Alienage was flat and covered in forest or marsh. The furthest he had really been able to see while growing up was the edge of the clearing of trees.

The view was indeed amazing. If they had not lost Darcy on the way, it may have made it all worth it — the shortness of breath, the aches and pains and the many lost days and sleepless nights — just to gaze out and see all that lay before them. With their backs to the ash they could look out across the northern part of the continent. To the west they could see a slim black line pointing into the sky, the Mages Tower at the heart of the Tower Plains.

Stretching out from it in all directions were lush green lands filled with valleys, dales, hills and crests. The odd tree even managed to blemish the otherwise perfect view. From the high point they could make out small flocks of deer that gathered not far from the foot of the mountain to feed in the warming sun.

It had been two days since they'd buried their friend and Oakenfall had fallen and only four more days remained in the month of Nylar, the New Year month. Olar the month to sow would soon be on them and the planting season was finally turning pleasant, as it should. The last of the Winnan storms and cold had been cast aside. Although the wind still blew with an icy blast on the mountain side, the sun was warm.

"It's incredible to think we've come so far. The tower has to be fifty or sixty miles away easily and your island is there to the north behind those mountains the dwarves live in," Calvin replied in awe himself.

He had seen a lot of the lands from the Mages Tower. Looking out from the top windows watching the fireworks or just looking down over the garden, but for some reason he could not put his boney old finger on, this just seemed more beautiful. Maybe it was the silence, the only noise being the gentle whisper of the wind as it fluttered past the mountain and the distant sound of bird song.

"That must be over a hundred miles. How do you feel being so far from home?" Calvin asked feeling oddly at peace with it himself.

"I haven't really though that much about it," Fintan lied. He didn't know why he'd lied, but he did. The truth was that he thought about it almost non-stop, and he didn't miss it! He felt some strange draw to keep travelling the same as he always had, but he missed the people he had grown up with — but he didn't miss the home part of it really.

"I guess you haven't really had the chance to think. It couldn't have been easy to face the Scorched Lands alone before you found us," Calvin continued.

Fintan was young and Calvin couldn't help but feel like a teacher again. The druid might have been in his forties, but for an elf that was the same as a human teen, which on its own would have made Calvin feel parental towards the youngster, but the fact he had only just discovered he had magic! That was just the same as those Calvin had taught before all this had started… which made it impossible for him to feel like anything other than being a tutor again. Calvin grabbed at the small fragment of his old life that he could remember.

"I only did what my Queen asked of me. No more, no less," Fintan said keeping true to the loyal appearance that the bright armor he wore demanded of him. The truth was that when he'd arrived at the edge of the Scorched Lands after leaving Port Lust, he'd almost turned on his heels and gone back the way he had come, but he couldn't face a life of tending to the trees in the forest like a druid should. He'd wanted something better for himself and so he'd forced his feet onwards.

"That's honorable to be sure. I can't knock you on that, my boy, but what now? You can't get the Heart, so you might as well head on home once we're done with the dwarves. There is no need for more needless death," Calvin said unable to shake the image of Darcy from his mind. The young noble had seemed too bright and full of life, if not a little odd, when he had come to the Tower. It seemed unfair that he should have been killed, while Calvin himself trudged onwards at his advanced age.

"You're right and that is why I have to join you. Humans cannot face this alone. I must represent the elven people and I plan to save them from what would happen if the dragons ever made it to our island," Fintan said, aware that the peaceful elves would pose little threat to the dragons if they commanded Oakenfall again.

The elves would lose their home once more and even though Fintan had not been born when the Whispering Woods fell, he knew the story well and would die before he let anything take his homeland from him, even if he himself did not actually want to be there.

"Fair enough, my lad. Well, we've still got another couple of miles along this path before we should start seeing dwarfen carvings and then god only knows how long until we can actually get an audience with the Dwarfen King, so we might as well start moving again," Calvin said dropping from the boulder back onto the thin mountain path with difficulty. He still felt worn-out, but the sun was almost midway across the sky, so they had only four or five hours of daylight left, and he didn't fancy his chances on the mountain path after dark.

"Do you think Darcy is happy wherever he has gone?" Fintan asked ignoring Calvin's request to get moving for the moment. The question was a little out of character for an elf, as that was something they tended not to think about.

"I don't know," Calvin said pausing to help Fintan down from the boulder, which was unneeded, but Calvin felt almost responsible for the young pointy eared student he'd acquired.

"I felt him when I tried to bring him back. He went to the Spirit Realm for sure. He was with someone… an ancestor it felt like," Calvin said stepping back as he realized he was impeding Fintan's descent more than he was helping it.

"So, you believe in the Spirit Realm then?" Fintan asked, wondering just how much of the Earth Mother's teachings had passed into human knowledge in the many years since the elves had arrived on Alienage Isle.

"I believe in what I can see and do, young one, and I know my magic comes from the Spirit Realm. I know that the energy there comes back here, and I know some weird old things can happen because of it. Why do you ask anyway?" Calvin asked, as he started to scuttle forward carefully trying to find secure footholds in the shifting stones that made up the mountain path.

"I don't think I'm dealing too well with it. I…" Fintan paused. "I know it's been a couple of days now, but I'd never actually seen anyone die before. Have you?" Fintan took his eyes off the path for a moment to look at Calvin for comfort, but it didn't come. The old man was too engrossed in where he was putting his feet.

"Don't get to my age without losing a few people, lad. I guess you become numb to it, at least a little. I try not thinking about it too much. Not a pleasant thought when you get over sixty. I have twenty years in me at best, likely a lot less than that," Calvin said. He wasn't sure what would kill him first now — old age, falling down the side of the mountain, exhaustion, hunger, Rinwid, the dragon. Hell, the list seemed to just go on and on.

"How do you deal with that?" Fintan asked, taking the lead up the mountain for the first time. If they left it to

Calvin's slow progress it would have added another day to the journey.

The mountain path had grown thin. It was not the main road that most people would have used to get to the dwarves. No… that would be on the other side of the mountain and be wide enough for a horse and cart to get up for collecting the ore. The path they traversed was barely wide enough for a mountain goat to clamber up. It seemed like the only thing keeping the shifting stone together they were walking on was the feathery Anemanthele Grass that poked out like the mountain's very own moustache.

"Same way I deal with a class full of students. Ignore it most of the time and avoid it where possible," Calvin said joking and he followed it up with a husky laugh that echoed out across the mountain tops.

Calvin knew he should be sad about the loss of Darcy and he was, but he had to be strong for Fintan, and joking just made it a little easier. That and with Rinwid's recession, Calvin felt more himself than he had for days. It was like part of him was returning. The two carried on making slow progress as the sun began its descent from the heavens. If they were lucky, they would make it to the dwarfen Hall of Goldhorn by nightfall.

Chapter Eighteen – So Many Heirs

It had been exactly a month since the celebrations and the north had changed beyond recognition, but the world never stands still and as it spun onward, Oakenfall continued to rebuild unaware of the gathering forces of dragons in the mountains. Calm had returned somewhat, and people had begun rebuilding their lives under the ironclad foot of the Poles, but normality would not be known again for some time. The Poles continued to stamp their dominance on the city and the final blow was yet to happen — the death of the old King.

The day of the fight had come around all too quickly for William. His wounds had been treated as promised by the tyrant Ingaild and his belly had been filled. He had been kept in the dungeons since being removed from the stocks — apart from one fleeting moment of enjoyment in the company of a young Oakenfall-maid who'd been given the pleasure of mopping down the dried blood from William's wounds, and bandaging them with torn sheets that had been taken from the keep's laundry. However, it was all he could do not to pass out from the agony that riddled his body, so that was where the luxury ended.

Darkness became William's companion quickly. He only saw someone once a day when some foul-smelling ogre of a man that must have been in the employ of Ingaild brought down a bowl of slop, which judging from the teeth marks in some of the meatier chunks, were leftovers from the royal table.

William had a lot of time to think, rarely broken in the hours of darkness between disturbances from the odd mouse or rat that scurried past. William had wondered how it was that Ingaild could eat so heartily, the city being in the state it was. The only thought that seemed plausible was that the assaults on Northholm had not been as damaging as Harvey had hoped and that the supply lines had been reopened already for the first time in fifty years.

Oakenfall may have been about to fall regardless of the Pole invasion, but it seemed that across the grasslands in the occupied City of Northholm the Poles had been doing well for themselves on the spoils of conquest.

William heard lots of noise from outside the high and small slit of a window providing his only source of light. It sounded like carts were rolling in almost on the hour. Ingaild must have been bringing in supplies from Northholm and the reconstruction of the city had begun already. William could not see but shouting and hammering sounds seemed to be plentiful. He was not sure but hazarded a guess that more Poles must have arrived… or at least some Oakenfall slaves had been returned to the city to start construction.

When William had been escorted into the keep barely a week before, the streets had been devoid of life. If more Pole warlords had arrived, then the nobles of Oakenfall would have been pushed out from the south-west end of town to the common houses. They would have been unlikely to do so kindly and the commoners would have been forced even further down towards the docks.

Other than the loss of life, at least from his position, William could not see Oakenfall being in a worse state than it was before the battle. If anything, it might even be better for the city with access to the Northholm mines now reopened to the people. That would open jobs and would explain the sudden supply of stone that William could hear being hammered away on. Not only that but it would bring an influx of ore that would bring commerce and trade, leading to gold and power, so the nobles might have more time for arts and crafts. The city might just reclaim its title as Jewel of the North.

If the Pole army could integrate or command successfully, it might even be the best thing to have happened to Neeska in recent history. It would not bring the freedom that William had wanted, but peace would do for now.

William pulled himself up off the hay pile he'd taken to sleeping on and wiped the slumber from his eyes. His nose still ached and felt swollen but at least the bruising seemed to be on the turn now and showed some signs of healing. His ribs had been bandaged but the itching suggested the wrapping needed a clean to evict the lice that had decided to call it home.

Ingaild's gorilla of a jailer had taken all of William's finery when he had been cast into the dampness. Other than the now filthy bandages, all William had to maintain his dignity was a pair of off-brown drop front woolen trousers, that judging by their stiffness and stench had probably belonged to the previous occupant of the dungeon.

William was thankful that the body had been removed. It was common for Pole prisons to be waist deep in macabre former inmates — so, it was likely the cells would only get worse now that the Hansons were not the ones tending them. William's throat was as dry as a blacksmiths apron. He hoped he'd get a drink before the fight, or he would probably collapse from dehydration before he could even lift a sword from the ground... if he was given one, that is.

His head ached but William was not sure if that was because of the smell in the dungeon — a putrid mix of urine, excrement and stale unmoving air — or the lack of light. Even with help from the midday sun the cell seemed unable to brighten. It was either that, or it was because of the wounds he'd sustained while trying to fight off the

Poles. He prayed it was one from that list and not something worse. Mice and rats often seemed to dart around in the darkness and William knew from his time on ships that a single rat could lay waste to a whole fleet if it carried the plague with it. All he could hope for was that when he got water, he would feel better.

William wondered what treatment Harvey had been given. If this was what the Poles considered treating a captive well, it would not be a surprise if Harvey didn't show up to the fight half dead. It would make William's victory all the easier, but it would lack even less prestige.

A grinding sound at the door snapped William from his worry and thoughts. The ogre-like man had returned and it was time to face the music. William pondered for a second just where that expression had come from and what it meant. After all, was facing a musician really that scary? He had often sung and danced with them during drunken nights back on Slickrock and found them if anything to be a little fruity, and as far from as intimidating as a field mouse would be to a lion — regardless… the music he would face.

"Face the wall. Don't even think of trying anything," Annar growled as he stepped into the room clutching a brown sack that looked like it had once held potatoes.

William's tired mind fell from his thoughts once more. He didn't bother trying to speak to his jailor. He had tried a few times over the course of the week and had never got anywhere. Even his sharp wit had fallen on death ears. Instead he did as he was instructed and faced the wall arms behind him. The sack was pulled down over his head with such force William thought he might rip through it and end up wearing it like a shirt. Moments later the cold clasp of irons gripped his wrists, the wooden beam was slid around his throat and the stocks were closed.

"Come with me," Annar said again tugging at the chains and almost pulling William over backwards onto his rump. William somehow managed to turn in time and staggered on blind behind his escort.

"Slickrock!" William swore to himself. He would do whatever he had to get back there. He'd planned to only be a few days when he had rushed away from it, leaving his many lovers panting at his bedside. William wondered if he would ever feel the warmth of another woman again.

After being dragged in darkness for a few minutes, William was met by the sound of a cheering crowd. The smell of ale was strong in the air and mixed with cooked meat. The city didn't smell like the smoke and death he'd experienced the last time he was outside the dungeon.

William was pushed to his knees, and the sack was whipped from his head to a cascade of rowdy ovations, and once his eyes got used to the sudden blast of bright sunshine, he took the time to look around at Celebration Square. The first thing he noticed was the stage he had been dragged to. It sat next to a ring of sorts, much like that used by the bareknuckle boxers back in Slickrock. William knew that this was the place he was meant to kill Harvey in — they were planning for him to pummel the King to death! A brutal way to go... no doubt to send a message to any would-be resistance.

However, on looking around further, to William's surprise the Poles had brought in granite slabs to replace the statues they had torn down and smashed, and someone had already started to sculpt figures into the stone. It would be sometime before it was clear exactly what they would be, but it somehow comforted William to know that the city would not lose everything it had once held dear.

The fight was a spectacle set up to draw attention and the wooden ring that had been constructed temporarily at the execution site had been done quickly, but with care. Thankfully all the bodies had been cleared from the streets and crowds and jugglers now stood in their place. They had turned the ruined city into a carnival. The market had returned, and bunting hung in bright colors. A band could be heard in the distance and a crier was calling out in the Oakenfall common tongue about the upcoming fight.

It was as if the city had already forgotten the horrors from only a week before and had even stooped as low as celebrating Ingaild's horrific end to King Harvey. William had hated the man for most of his life and had plotted to free the city from its monarchical dictatorship, but even he had never wanted Harvey's end to come like this. He had wanted him to stand down, leave the city and never come back. It was not in William's nature — flamboyant as he was — to create such an exhibition of horror to celebrate a murder like this.

William shook himself from his sorrows. This was not how he'd wanted it to happen, but he could not change it. It was out of his control. The city would be freed from the Hansons and he would finally get revenge for his father's death. He would have to hold onto that thought to get through this.

William continued looking around the city that had changed a lot in his absence. Scaffolding had been erected and work had been begun to repair the damage that the mighty trebuchets had wrought on the city. The ash and debris from the dockyards had been swept into massive piles and the roads cleared. William could just make out a few ships' masts in the harbor, none seeming to carry the markings of the White Flags. It would seem like a swift and daring rescue was out of the question. William only recognized one banner from the many and that was of the *Cassandra*. It seemed that the King's fleet that had passed by White Isle just after New Year had returned to the city. That ship would serve the city well. William envied her captain… he had planned to take her as his own, if he'd succeeded in freeing the city.

It was then that William saw him, Harvey. It looked like age had taken him forward years in just a week. His beard was wiry and had grown long, as if it had been trying to protect him from the beatings, he'd obviously had. It was no longer groomed and trimmed and looked like a wild red badger matted with dried blood. Harvey's skin seemed loose and hung from his features like a cloth thrown over an upturned chair. He looked almost delirious with glazed eyes that seemed swollen and fixated on the ground. The dirt on his face almost made it hard to see the bruises and broken skin, but they were so deep they could not be concealed completely. Harvey had lost a lot of weight, easily twenty pounds or more, and he shook continuously.

William wondered if Harvey had had anything to eat at all since before the siege of the city. William knew that Harvey had lost his appetite after sending the people out to their deaths. He could not remember seeing him put anything in his mouth after that, and it looked like the Poles had not offered him anything in the time since they'd been apart.

Harvey too had been stripped of his normal lavish robes and wore similar trousers to William himself. They revealed Harvey's bare back that had been torn like a sail in a storm. Red trenches lined his back marking the torture he had received from his captor's whip. William suddenly felt extremely lucky for his treatment. A child could win a fight against Harvey in this state. This would not be a fight — it would be a slaughter — but what choice did William have? The crowd blocked his escape routes. If he chose to run, he would have to fight through them, and risk being taken down by one of Ingaild's men. If he could somehow avoid the spear in the back and get past the crowd, he would still have to make it through the maze that was the harbor and dockyards to get to a ship. And then he would somehow have to prepare it to sail on his own and get safely out to sea. No — his only choice was to do as Ingaild asked. Kill Harvey and hope Ingaild honored his words again and turned William free.

"Quieten down! Calm down!" Ingaild roared as he pushed his way into the ring drawing both the crowd's and William's attention.

The ring had been made using ropes from one of the ships at the dockyard and some of the wood used to create the frame even had barnacles clinging to it. The stage of sorts had been quickly built next to the ring, and gathered around it, like flies to shit, were spectators waiting to see more bloodshed only days after the city had fallen. It was an odd time for the thought to occur to him, but William wondered if the people of the city were really that different at their core to those they labeled as "barbarians."

"As I promised to you on the day of occupation…" Ingaild paused… "No… on the day of liberation," he said correcting himself for that is how he saw it. The north had once belonged to the tribes before the time of dragons, and before the Hansons. The people had grown weak and the country struggled. He would thin the herd of its lame and make Neeska strong again.

"Exactly one week since I stood here victorious and told you to begin rebuilding our city, look what we have achieved! The markets are full. The taverns are rowdy. The stones are being re-laid. There is but one act left to cut the cancer from this city — the execution of the traitors to Neeska! Today your champions will fight against each other. The Pirate King here…" Ingaild proclaimed as he pointed to William, "who fights for the honor of us all, the Poles and our people. He is no Northman, but he will die for our cause, so strong is the might of our weapon."

To William's surprise Ingaild's speech was met by glee, like milk being lapped up by a kitten. Oakenfall had been in recession for years and people had tightened their belts beyond the point of acceptance. Although many of them had lost neighbors, or even loved ones, the promise of food, gold and peace was a hard to resist.

"Harvey fights to redeem the cowardliness of the Hanson lineage," Ingaild continued and pointed towards the shell of a man that had once been Harvey.

"This will be a fight to the death. I hope you see it as I do — as a fitting end to our incursions into this place and its return to its rightful heirs, namely all of us assembled here," Ingaild proclaimed and to William's horror the people seemed to be loving it. Some were even cheering him, and they did not appear to be of Pole descent. These were Oakenfall people who'd turned coat.

"For years we have been portrayed as villains, but this land was ours long before the dragons came and long before they made this city with the blood of slaves. Those slaves then refused to return it to its rightful owners and my people remained pushed back to the harsh and cold mountains." Ingaild paced back and forth showering himself in the admiration of the boisterous masses.

"Yet you see what I have done for you. I've returned, and I'll let you live, as long as you live under my rule — and more! I'll return this city to the glory it lost during the Great War," Ingaild proclaimed and his words made sense even to William.

It might have been the lack of decent sleep, but it seemed like Ingaild was talking sense. The city was looking the best William had seen it and the people looked happy. It didn't even feel like the same city he'd docked at. The buildings were being repaired and improved, the streets re-laid. It did hint at a richer city, but the city that had been rich during the time of the dragons was not necessarily the best as the people's city.

William would not meet Harvey in battle, and Ingaild would never get to finish his speech. There was not much that would have stopped him from enjoying that morning basking in his victory, but his fate had been sealed by Harvey long before Ingaild had reached Oakenfall.

Most of the city had gathered in the center of town, and there was nothing that gathered crowds liked more than the spectacle of brutality. A hanging would normally bring out half the city, a bloody brawl to the death of a king... well that would draw the other half.

Ingaild had frozen during his speech, his eyes fixed on the horizon. A flock of birds, sparrows, darted above the gathering crowd as if fleeing from something. The sound of the music faltered and suddenly the silence was deafening. That was until in unison, a scream ran through the crowd like a ripple through a pond. Human nature is supposedly built on fight or flight — to stand one's ground or to flee in terror — but on that day, they all seemed to become statues, unable to move. William was facing away from the direction the amassed crowds were staring at in absolute terror, so he strained to turn in his bindings.

William had felt a moment like this just before the Pole army had attacked — a moment when the world held its breath — and then as if fate itself had exhaled, the gathering started to scatter and run. People clambered over each other like ants in spilt jam. The clearing begun to empty in moments as people fled, scattering the market stores like bric-a-brac marbles. The jugglers dropped their balls and torches and joined the fleeing masses.

Ingaild turned and William saw his eyes open wide. He could not imagine what could scare the Pole King, but the look on his face showed that whatever it was, it had petrified him — but he was still a Pole, and Poles did not run.

It was then the shadow passed over William engulfing the whole of Celebration Square in darkness. The clap of the dragon's wings rattled the chains binding William and Harvey. The black dragon swooped low before landing, clinging to the side of a noble's home and shattering the brickwork of the Dean Estate before leaping back into the air, where it hovered with its huge wings crafting the air below it into a cushion.

"You did not run like the rest of the rodents scurrying back into their holes. Who do I address?" the dragon said, as it settled onto the ground landing as softly as a cat leaping from a tree.

"Ingaild, Hand of the Pole, King of the North," Ingaild said, feeling fear for the first time in his life. He had been apprehensive before a battle, but he had never known fear until now.

"There are no kings of the north aside from my kin. This city was gifted to us!" the black dragon continued as it eyed the human standing across the street from him.

"Gifted? Enslaved!" Harvey said speaking for the first time since William had been led into the clearing.

"You call it enslaved. We call it a trade. A treaty was signed in 1625DB when my forefathers left Lashkar Gah to come here as agreed to keep the Seal safe and banish the Dark One," the dragon said affronted by the very idea that the humans did not owe their existence to it.

"Silence, Harvey. What do you want? The city will not lay down its arms to you, Dragon," Ingaild said, his eyes looking around the clearing for his men. They had started to gather but none wanted to make a charge against the dragon, and they would wait for the word of their King before striking. The dragon turned looking at the men starting to circle it, but quite disinterested and unafraid it turned back to Ingaild.

"We lived peacefully until you maggots sided with the very demons, we protected you from! Your rebellion, your war… they almost killed us but enough of us escaped into the ash."

"You're lying! We would have seen signs of you. We'd have known if you'd stayed there. This is a trick, a conjuring by mages, you cannot be real," Ingaild said but he could sense the creature was real. He was not magical, but the animal was exactly that — bestial and real — it was a creature of raw power and muscle.

"It is not my kind that spins untruths… no! Your usurpation failed and now the ancient treaty of peace will be honored, or blood will be spilt. My time in the ash is over, my brood regrown and now my children come to call this place home. You have seven moon risings and we will return. Accept us as your gods, prepare a feast for our forgiveness… or we will show you the true power your ancestors feared," the black Dragon King roared before beating its wings once more and knocking even more rubble loose from the nearby buildings before vanishing up into the sky.

Ingaild remained motionless, as did his army. The crowd was full of whispers and panic but Ingaild would be remembered for standing his ground when most men had fled. If any had doubted his right to claim Oakenfall, they were silenced.

William knelt staring at the still crumbling Dean Estate. He had wanted a diversion so he could escape but he had not been prepared for dragons to return. It would have seemed unbelievable to him had he not seen it with his own eyes.

William had heard rumors from his fleet in the past about dragons swooping down and stealing their haul of fish, but he'd always put it down to the empty kegs of rum that returned with said ships. Dragons were not real. They'd all been killed off — or so the stories had said. It seemed William's perfect chance to escape had been missed as by the time his thoughts returned to him, Annar, Ingaild's second in command, had appeared in the clearing blocking his escape.

"Looks like you two have had a turn of luck. Ingaild will want all able-bodied men to fight that thing. We have not forgotten the power of dragons. Men, get these two back to the dungeon!" Annar called out glancing at the damage the dragon had caused in only a single pass.

William could see fear in Annar's eyes. He hid it well, but it was there. Annar had fought every kind of soldier Neeska had to offer, but not the dragon. That would be a worthwhile challenge.

Chapter Nineteen – Going Underground

There were only two others that could claim to have seen the Dragon King and lived, and they were now deep below the snowcapped mountains drinking their misfortunes away and filling their bellies after what felt like a lifetime of slogging through the ashen wastelands.

Once the shock of the black dragon had left them and they had buried their friend, Calvin and Fintan had fought the mountain's biting cold and made their way to the Goldhorn Kingdom, where the mountain path had opened and eventually led to the city's huge stone doors.

The dwarves had been reluctant to let humans into the city but when talk of dragons was mentioned, they eventually retracted and escorted the pair to a tavern to await a council with the elders.

The technology the dwarves kept very much to themselves had not reached the outside world and was something to behold. Pressed in between the colossal pillars and tunnels were huge pipes that ran along the low ceilings churning with the sound of water rushing through them after being pumped up from beneath the dark. The dwarfen race was hundreds of years ahead of the rest of the world when it came to their technological prowess — they had running water, steam powered electric generators and industry based on their huge humming machines.

The tunnels were lit with lights not fueled by flame but from some whirring source not even the elder mage Calvin could name. The heat from the pipes warmed the air around them and in places steam escaped in short sharp jets. The muddle of tunnels opened into an enormous underground cavern that could have easily housed Oakenfall and this was where the city of the dwarves had grown. It was made of mine shafts and more gloomy tunnels branching out randomly from its edges, and a thick choking smog almost as unbearable as the ash of the Scorched Lands filled it.

Calvin and Fintan had been greeted by a steward, the equivalent of a noble in human lands, almost as soon as they'd entered the city limits. He seemed to appear from nowhere running up to them as they came down the stone steps that led in from the main tunnel, and this swift response had given them false hope. The pair were overjoyed that they had seen the steward so quickly, but then things had taken a bad turn. They were offered free lodging while they waited to speak to the king as he was "otherwise engaged." That had been four days ago.

The days seemed to have passed slowly in the continual murkiness of the oddly buzzing lights that seemed to do little to battle the darkness. They found it hard to breathe and both Calvin and Fintan were at their wit's ends. They had buried a friend not long before and then tried to outrun the wings of a Dragon Lord and every second they spent trapped waiting gave the dragon time to continue its conquest across Neeska. Calvin could not feel it anymore as it was too great a distance from them, which was a blessing and a curse both.

They had grown accustomed to the continual gloom but every shadow seemed to hum with the same constant noise from machinery that Fintan and Calvin were now habituated to sleeping through. The many buildings joined the thumping mess of noise that seemed to be generating the smog that filled the warm wet air. Calvin and Fintan's amazement faded swiftly the longer they spent in the smoke-filled tunnels, however. The gas used in the lighting made their throats sore and the dwarves seemed less than happy to have the pair there at all.

The two felt unwelcome and racism for the two topside races was ever present and barely masked. The dwarves had sealed their city many years before and after suffering persecution by humans and had now grown sour towards them.

The last of any awe the village-born Fintan might have had faded with the fat drunkard sitting next to them that evening, as he had with every other night they had been unlucky enough to be stuck in that inn.

"So, I told her my uncle was Chief Miner of the Second Tunnel Lead Operative and then I slapped her on the arse," the drunken dwarf announced loudly to the bar in general as no one seemed to be listening to him, least of all Fintan.

The dwarf had latched onto Calvin and Fintan when they'd entered the tavern. They'd been in the dwarfen city for a few days and had spent most of that time in the crowded bar growing more resentful of the dwarves that offered them a kind of hospitality normally saved for stray dogs.

The drunkard met every stereotype that gave dwarves a bad name. He was short, fat and bearded. His breath smelt of cheap tobacco and stale ale. He was stinking drunk and barely coherent about anything but his stories of conquests in the darkness which he repeated loudly over and over regardless of anyone paying any interest or not. His beer belly protruded as if he was hiding a watermelon under his jerkin and his rather fine-looking red clothes were stained with homebrew and shards of broken peanut husks.

"Look. I've politely asked you more than once now to leave us alone," Calvin said, his patience having all but gone.

"Leave you alone? Leave you alone?" the pot-bellied dwarf spat in reply to Calvin's request for some peace and quiet. "I'm doing you a favor I am. Not many down here that would sit and share ale with a long-legged old coot and a pointy-eared tree monkey," the gruff and rotund dwarf slurred through a mouth of froth.

He tried to guzzle down more of the foul-smelling brew while still talking. It amazed Fintan that the dwarf didn't choke. If it wasn't for the fact it would take next to nothing to set the powder-keg that was the tavern off and have a bar full of short but stocky dwarves brawling with them, Fintan would have kicked the noisy dwarf clear off his stool. That was another thing that had made their time underground even less pleasant. The chairs were tiny, about the size of children's chairs in the nursery and the beds were not much better and even dumpy Calvin had gotten used to his legs hanging over the edge from the knee down

"Brill you tired old windbag shut up and leave our guests alone," a new voice piped up from the general area of the tavern's low doorway to the surprise of the drunken dwarf now known as Brill.

The newcomer was a woman. She wore a similar style of fabric as the drunk but hers looked far less stained and more lavish. The regretful and depressed look in her eyes showed it was highly likely she was married to Brill.

"Woman, who do you think you're talking to? I'm your King!" Brill slurred, and Calvin almost fell from the short stool he was struggling to clamp his aged knees against.

"You're the King?" Calvin coughed in shock. They'd seen the drunken dwarf at the bar every night since they'd arrived in Under City. They disliked the bar, and its company didn't seem too keen on the travelers either, but it was the only place that seemed to serve anything that wasn't made of rat or bat. The whole time they'd been here eating and waiting to see the King, the drunken fool had been dancing, singing and falling all over the place night after night. At one point he'd even taken to dancing on the bar while trying to strip before he was escorted out by the barkeeper and his son. Calvin had been barred from a few taverns in his younger days for a few drunken party tricks and couldn't understand how this old fool was allowed in night after night, especially as he didn't seem to pay, but now it was painfully clear. Brill was the blasted King.

"King of the halfwits, aye, that's him," Brills wife said rolling her eyes. It was very apparent that her love for this man must be strong or she would have never put up with him, but that didn't mean she wouldn't clip his ear if he spoke out of turn.

"Now if you don't want me to take a rolling pin to the side of your head, Your Majesty, I'd suggest you get your worthless hide back home," the oddly muscular dwarfen women said, and the King obeyed.

"Sorry for him gentleman… he's a good dwarf but the drinks got the better of him ever since the mines collapsed. So, I hear you were wanting to see the King?" she asked with a smirk.

"Well sorry to say he won't be able to help you much, not until he sobers up and if the last few years are anything to go by, I'd get yourself comfy on that one," Joani said not showing any of the shame she felt because of her husband's downward spiral.

"Anyway, we don't trade with outsiders any longer. Us dwarves can't afford to get dragged into another pointless war," Joani Goldhorn Queen of the Goldhorn Dwarves said as she flicked one of the long darkened brown snake-like dreadlocks from her face.

She was a pretty — in a certain light. — but butch-looking woman. Her hair was long and plaited into unwashed dreadlocks. She didn't wear a crown or anything else to mark her as royalty and looked uncomfortable in the fine clothing that she was wearing. Her defined and toned arms showed she either trained as a warrior or worked in one of the mining tunnels. Her stance demanded people take notice of her and it was plain to see that she was the true governing force of the dwarfen people, by fist and by voice it would seem.

"We don't want to trade but it is war that is coming. The dragons are back," Fintan piped up from his own shrunken stool by the bar. He looked even more out of place than Calvin did. At least Calvin was shorter, and fat and he even had a beard. Fintan looked like a shiny metal-wrapped bean pole compared to the inhabitants of the Under Dark, but he remembered the stories he'd heard as a boy. They'd been about the dwarfen heroes and he couldn't believe they were all as useless as the drunks in the bar.

"So, the stories are true then," Joani said flatly. "I'd heard as much…" She paused in thought. "Some reckoned it was dragons that collapsed Mining Shaft Four a few months back, baby ones set fire to a few barrels of blast powder and brought the whole shaft down. I'd put it down to smoking while working but couldn't prove it either way. I'll need time to think on this," she said nodding to the barkeeper and preparing to turn and follow her drunken husband, who hadn't made it all that far down the corridor taking as many steps sideways as he did forwards.

"You haven't got time to think. We need your husband to send troops to Oakenfall the same as in the Great War," Fintan said rather naively and Calvin shot him a look before shaking his head slightly. The old mage had a fair few years on Fintan and he'd seen women like Joani before. You needed tact to get what you wanted from them. It had to seem like it was their idea. Giving them demands was a sure-fire way to find a frying pan in place of where your teeth had been.

"What my young friend here meant, Your Majesty, is that we need you to tell His Majesty he must help us. Time is of the essence," Calvin said trying to save the conversation from heading down a needlessly violent route

"We don't have much of an army to send anymore. No need for one. We have a few archers and the mountain itself lined with enough blasting power to sunder the rock to dust. It would only take a handful of sober dwarves to lay waste to the biggest siege you could get up the mountain," Joani said half to herself. She didn't have the army she once had to send to aid topsiders. There had been no need for one for almost a century.

"Are you saying you will not lend any aid to us?" Fintan asked. Dwarves had come to the aid of elves at the fall of the Earth Mother. They had been the turning point in the war and were hailed as heroes in his home of the Alienage. He could not believe the mighty yet short warriors he had heard so many stories about would turn out to be no better than humans.

"Now, I didn't say that. I just needed time to think," Joani said, her shrunken features curling as she thought hard. "Our doors have been closed to your kind for many a year now."

"How long once the dragon's retake Oakenfall before they come hunting here for food or sport? Can your traps and explosives clear them from the skies!" Fintan said, not hiding his annoyance. He had not had a decent night's sleep in weeks and all he wanted to do now was get this over and done with and he did not want to wait for Joani or her drunken husband Brill to "think" for too long.

"My people cannot help you. This is not our fight," Joani said and turned to walk from the bar, when the candles flickered, and the room grew dark.

"Joani Goldhorn you will listen. Your kind more than most knows what would happen if dragons claimed this mountain." A new voice echoed out from inside of Calvin and the bar fell silent.

"The Under Dark would not take long for an army of slaves to clear... for the pathways to reopen. The dragons would spread feeding on your kin, every kingdom belonging to dwarfen kind would fall. It almost happened once before. You know of this and no doubt you already realize what I am and my goals. Yet you will help," Rinwid gurgled out from inside Calvin's throat shocking him almost as much as it shocked the rest of the bar.

Silence fell over the drinkers — not even the clinking of glass or tankard could be heard — as they all stopped motionless. The barkeeper himself had frozen. He held open the tap to a massive keg that lay against the wall spilling a fine golden flow out across the floor.

"So, Mage, you brought a demon in here with you?" Joani said her hand sliding down her side slowly clutching the staff at her side. The look in her eyes showed she would hold no quarter if it came to killing the old man standing in front of her.

"I mean no harm and Rinwid is under my control... for now," Calvin said, feeling all eyes in the bar on him. Rinwid had remained absent for days. Calvin had even started to forget about the ordeal expecting that Rinwid might just leave them alone, but it seemed he was less asleep then Calvin had thought, and, in that moment, the rushing memories started slurring through his head again. The coppery taste returned to his mouth. Rinwid was still as much a part of him as the beard on his face. He may have chosen to withdraw but he had not released Calvin.

"I should kill you both now where you stand and drag your bodies back to the surface," Joani said and a few of the nearby dwarves dropped to their feet ready to brawl. "But that demon is right. I will have to do what my husband is unable to. We can't risk the old tunnels being opened," Joani stopped obviously deep in thought.

"I will travel with you to Oakenfall and make the arrangements. We will bring as much ore for weapons and blast powder to bring the beasts down as we can," Joani stopped and took in the risk of the old man.

"You two are never welcome in my city again. Bringing a demon here is treasonous and if you step within the city again, my people will see to it you never see daylight again. Now get out of my sight, go topside and wait for me. I will come by nightfall," Joani said never taking her hand from the club-like staff.

Neither Fintan nor Calvin dared question her orders. They would not have left the city alive if they did. They made haste to gather what few belongings they had and made their way up and out of Goldhorn Halls to sit in the sun of the last day of Nylar waiting for Joani Goldhorn Queen of the Dwarves to join them. That night they would continue the journey back to Oakenfall. Not with the army they had hoped to raise, but hopefully with enough arms and explosives to turn the odds in their favor. With his second quest again failing to deliver the outcome needed, Fintan was not being as successful an adventurer as he had been when he was a child.

It had amazed both Fintan and Calvin how swiftly the preparations had been made. Within hours the first horse-drawn cart rattled out from the huge mouth of the mountain. It was loaded up with barrel after barrel, stacked five high and bound by rope. It had enough explosives to level half the city when they reached it and it was not alone. Moments later a second and a third cart rolled out carrying the same. The fourth cart held nothing but pristine ore ready to craft into weapons. A fifth and final cart rolled out and at its reigns Joani sat in a fluffy white shawl that looked like it had been taken from a mountain goat.

The shawl matched her short skirt that was made of the same material and sat just above her tree-trunk-like knees. She looked much more comfortable in what was clearly warm but minimal fighting attire. Fintan's eyes were drawn instantly to the glint of the golden dagger that sat nestled in Joani's belt. It was of elven design, but the gold used was dwarfen. It hinted of a time long ago when elves must have called this continent home, before even the time of the Earth Mother. It must have been millennia old, but it still looked as sharp as a cat's claw.

"Unless you boys plan to walk the whole way, I suggest you get aboard," Joani said seemly in a pleasant tone. She had calmed down once Rinwid had left the city and was a little excited to be leaving the mountain. Joani had always been a bit of a wild-child and being from a peasant background should never have been royalty, but her take-no-nonsense attitude had been the thing that had made the king fall for her to start with. It would later be the thing that beat him into submission and left him at her whim, but it was this aggressive spark of life that would lead the dwarves to aid the topsiders one more time.

"How long will it take to reach Oakenfall?" Calvin asked as he struggled to pull himself up into the rear of the cart. His legs had decided to go to sleep while they had been waiting and at his age it could be days before they decided to wake up again.

"If we can drive the horses at a gallop and they don't tire too swiftly, a couple of days no more. We should arrive on Duwek or Midwek at the latest," Joani said as she offered Fintan a hand to help him climb into the cart.

The main path down the mountain was much wider and less difficult to traverse than the path Calvin and Fintan had taken up. Its slow and steady decline would take them towards the Tower Plains. However, they had not taken off far down the mountain before being forced to stop.

"Whoa!" Joani called out pulling back hard on the reigns of her horses in a desperate attempt not to plough into the rear of the cart in front.

"What in the nine hells are you doing stopping like that?" she called out seemingly uninterested in the wellbeing of the two others sharing her cart who'd barely managed to hold on as the cart jolted to a stop.

"There's a girl in the road. She looks hurt... maybe bandits or something. We'll need to move her to continue," the dwarf who oversaw the cart at the front of the convoy said loudly through a thick mesh of beard.

"Move her?" Calvin exclaimed. "We need to help her. Is she still breathing?" he asked sitting forward and trying to see over the mounds of supplies and horse backsides that blocked his view.

"Is she with you?" Joani asked shooting Calvin a glance that could kill. She'd been in two minds about helping Calvin ever since Rinwid had reared his ugly head and she would not tolerate any more surprises.

"No, she isn't, but I still need to tend to her wounds," Calvin said and took his chance to slip down onto the rocky mountain road with a clatter of loose stones.

"You have five minutes old man. I think I've already been more than patient enough with topsiders and surprises today. If you can't get her on her feet by then, we leave her to the elements," Joani said not hiding her dislike for humans.

It is true that dwarves and humans had once been allies but the incessant thirst humans had for conquest had over time weakened relations to the state they were now.

"That'll have to do then," Calvin said grumpily as he slugged his way slowly past the front carts until he could see the wounded women clearly.

She was young and white. Her pale flat features suggested she was Oakenfall and her red hair, that was revealed by the falling back of her hood, backed this theory up. She was slender but looked well fed and showed no signs of dehydration, which ruled that out as a reason she may have collapsed. Her blackened outfit had been stained by ash, lots of it and it looked like she must have come through the Scorched Lands or close by it at least, but if she was being pursued by bandits, then why had she continued past the dwarfen kingdom? It made no sense.

As Calvin examined her further, he could see no signs of her being attacked. There were not any visible bruises or knife wounds. Calvin bent down to listen to see if the women had a heartbeat still, but before his ear could press against the tight cloth that covered her, the cold of steel clipped his throat.

"Don't move a muscle old man," Erin Cleat said as she opened her eyes and looked up into Calvin's startled face.

"It's ok young lady. I'm here to help," Calvin said trying his hardest to sound friendly, which with the demon inside him stirring at the imminent danger wasn't particularly easy.

"Help me, you old fool? Aye, s'pose you might just do that. You see I need to be taking the Heart you found in the Scorched Lands and I need to be walking away nice and quietly without one of your short friends there causing any hassle. We have an understanding?" Erin said slowly slipping from her back onto her haunches and never once taking her eyes off Calvin or moving the blade from his throat.

"I was trying to help you. I thought you were injured," Calvin said trying his damnedest not to swallow. He was infuriated by the betrayal and wanted to let loose the power Rinwid was offering, but he could not risk it. He didn't know how many more times he could resist Rinwid taking over. No — he would have to deal with this without magic.

"That was the idea really. Poor pretty girl wounded on a mountain. I knew you wouldn't be able to just walk on past. I didn't plan for half the dwarves in the bloody mountain to follow you down, mind, but I'll adapt. Now the Heart… where is it?" Erin said looking around the gathering dwarves, who'd dropped down from the carts and started to move towards her and Calvin.

Fintan was with them. He had been so easy to track leaving more clues than a blind hippo through a wheat field. He had been more interested in making flowers grow and talking to the horse he'd stolen after making sure he was alone. When he let the horse go and walked into the Scorched Lands, he'd become even easier to follow. The only time Erin had almost lost him was during the heavy winds that had hidden his footsteps. Fintan's vanishing act didn't last for long as Erin easily picked his track back up when the mage had cast the spell and drew her attention that way. At times she had been so close to Fintan she was sure he should have heard her footsteps, but he had been oblivious to her.

"The Heart, is that what you're after? Then you're as out of luck as we were. The Heart is still in the dragon," Calvin said deciding to be as honest as he could. Maybe it would put this would-be assassin on the backheel enough for him to make his move. He was old but far from small and this girl was no more than eighteen or nineteen and didn't look like she had seen much real battle. Looks can be deceiving though and her accent hinted she'd spent time around the White Flags, so Calvin was taking no chances.

"You almost look like you're telling the truth. Shame they might be the last words you ever speak," Erin said pressing the blade against Calvin's neck and drawing a thin sliver of blood.

"Look you skinny little poke-reed. Kill the old man if you really must, but he's telling the truth — the Heart is still in the blasted dragon and that is why we're heading to Oakenfall," Joani said seemingly running out of patience and forgetting she didn't actually give two hoots if the demon carrying old bastard took his last breath.

"Who are you calling a poke reed?" Erin said flabbergasted.

"Look girl, I've taken out shits bigger than you, so either get out of our way, or join us and help, or kill the old man. Either way I don't really care but do one of them quickly as you're slowing down our trip and it'll be nightfall soon," Joani said stepping forward and leaning against her walking stick.

Joani had no need for the stick as she was probably the strongest person among the group, but she liked using one. She felt it gave her height.

Erin lowered her knife. What choice did she have really? At least joining the caravan would get her back to Oakenfall quicker than on foot and she was tired.

"If the Heart's not here, I guess there is no reason no one's got to bleed. Where shall I mount up?" Erin asked pulling the blade away from Calvin's neck and offering him a hand up.

The carts rolled on down the mountains without further interruption and the weather held true. It felt like the planting season was well underway and as soon as the caravan of carts passed down under the blanket of cloud, the skies opened back out into the view that had taken Calvin and Fintan's breath on their way up. They could no longer see the Tower Plains or out over Briers Hill as they made their descent on the north side of the mountain, but opening up in front of them was the City of Oakenfall and the glorious sight of the sun shining back from White Sea behind it.

On the horizon low and green was the silhouette of the Alienage. It was the first time Fintan had seen it since he'd set off in the rickety old boat with the crazy old White Flag captain. It was somewhat ironic that his journey home was in the company of another pirate.

"Why are you so glum then, me old chum?" Erin said elbowing Fintan gently in the ribs as the carts rattled on gaining speed in the descent.

"It's nothing," Fintan replied. In truth he was still a little in shock from Darcy dieing in front of him. It had been days since they had dug the shallow grave in the ashes and laid his body down to rest. They had used the broken tabletop to make a marker for the head of the grave and scratched Darcy's name into it. It was an image that would never leave Fintan.

"Doesn't look like nothing to me. I seen barnacles on the side of beached boats that looks happier than you," Erin said tilting her head to look up into Fintan's drooping face.

"We lost someone back in the Scorched Lands. I don't think the boy's dealing with it all too well," Calvin said from the rear of the cart. He couldn't believe he had been pushed into the back to let this pirate tart sit up front, but then at least he could keep an eye on her from back there.

"First time you seen someone die is it?" Erin asked, and it seemed to Fintan that she was honestly interested.

"Yes, it was sudden. There was nothing that could be done. We tried but we lost him. He was young, his heart seemed pure," Fintan said staring off into the horizon watching the sparkle of the sun on distant waves.

"Never met none that heart's pure, but aye, it can be hard the first time. S'pose I just got used to it in my line of work. Sometimes it's either them or us, and sometimes it's just their time."

"How can you ever get used to something like that?" Fintan asked.

"See it enough, it's no different to skinning a rabbit, but I saw the grave you dug the noble while I was following you. Not many would have bothered. You did right by him. Tell me then, what was it that got him — the ash in the end?"

"A dragon," Fintan said not taking his eyes off the glistening golden reflection on the ocean.

"Dragon! ... You actually saw one then — I thought you were pulling my plank on that one. So, the Dragon's Heart is really still inside a big fire-breathing city-pillaging dragon?" Erin asked mainly just to make conversation.

"I told you as much," Calvin added from the back as he shifted around uncomfortably in the piles of ore that moved about with the rolling of the cart, and then they began to level out.

The ground started to flatten into a low slope. In an hour or less they would be officially out of the mountains and on the brittle heather lined roads that made up the highlands.

"I know, but I never believed you. Creator's arse, dragons! No wonder you're in shock pointy ears. I'm just glad I wasn't with you when you saw them," Erin said bluntly.

"Will you help us when we get to the city then? We'll need everyone to help us fight them," Fintan said not trusting Erin as far as he could throw her but knowing it would take every human on Neeska to repel the Dragon Lords.

After a moment's thought about the prospect of dragons returning and having to tell William she had failed him for the first time ever, Erin replied hesitantly, "I guess I'll have to. I just can't believe it... dragons!"

"Best start believing quickly then. Not too many more days until we'll arrive in the human city," Joani said breaking her silence for the first time since she had reluctantly picked up the "hitchhiker" and continued driving the cart onwards.

The convoy of carts rolled on for the next few days in almost perpetual silence with everyone deep in their own minds as they passed down the mountain and out across the plains. The only exception was when the carts pulled to a stop to rest the horses at night and the fires were lit.

Erin who was sitting up front for most of the journey thought of home. The week of tracking a hapless elf had been dull in comparison to the adventurous life she was used to, and she wanted to get back out onto the open sea as quickly as possible. That is not to say she was not a fan of the thick dark stout the dwarves brewed and shared when the caravans made camp at night.

The ale was also appreciated by Calvin, who serenaded the camp until the last flames died and the kegs ran dry. The dwarves had been kind enough to share their food and the group shared stories over the smell of roast goat. As the smoke curled into the night sky Calvin thought of his students and the large lunches he had enjoyed at the tower. His heart grew heavy knowing that he would never get to taste them again.

Fintan resided within himself and during the day sat silently next to Joani. When the carts pulled up and the rest of the convoy gathered for drinks, stories, and song, he found himself sitting on the outskirts of the fire watching the moths that were drawn to the flicking lights, the weight of Darcy's death playing on his mind. Fintan longed for home, for his little hut and the squirrels. He thought of his Queen, and the battle for the right to leave the island. He had been so unprepared for the world that had awaited him on the mainland, and his adventure had been nothing like he'd planned.

Joani too kept herself to herself on the most part, only sharing whispered conversations with the other cart drivers. She had left the city so quickly and some would have questioned why, but she had always longed for the open road. The boredom of the court and the heartbreak of seeing her beloved consumed by the bottle had grown too much to bear. As she steered the cart onwards during the long days she thought about her husband, the drunken buffoon alone in charge of the city while she was gone. She thought of the coming battle. She feared the darkness, the deep secret darkness hidden in the tunnels below the mountain — the dragons could never be allowed to find it.

As the days passed and the songs grew quieter, the highland heathers eventually gave way to ferns and grass, and pine trees lined the road as the convoy approached the flat lands that made up the Hanson Kingdom. The smell of the sea replaced the crisp air of the plains and the sound of the city began to overshadow the song of the crickets.

The carts pulled to a stop for the last time before they would reach the city. Their makeshift tents were pulled down off the carts and the sleeping rugs strewn around the clearing. It didn't take long for the fire to be started and even less time for the keg to be tapped.

"Still looking glum pointy ears," Erin said as she walked around the campfire to sit next to Fintan. He was the only one of the convoy riders that seemed to speak to her with civility.

"I'm just worried," he replied looking down from the stars. He couldn't help but notice how they reflected in Erin's eyes.

"It's still that Darcy fella?" Erin asked. It surprised her that she wasn't just making conversation to kill time and pass the boredom; she had an interest in the elf. She didn't know why but something was drawing her to him.

"Partly, I think... but it's everything. Queen Cadeyrn Silverleaf sent me to find the Dragon Heart for my people... I failed her... I failed to save Darcy... I'm a failure," Fintan said holding back the tears he could feel fighting to free themselves.

"Being a bit hard on yourself, fella. Not much you could do about the Dragon Heart... not much any of us could have done. And that noble, well you did more than most... I'd have left him in the hut where I found him," Erin said remembering back to the story Fintan had told her the night before. She realized then that she had sought him out each night the carts made camp.

"The armor I'm wearing, it's meant to mean something. It's a hero's armor — I don't deserve to wear it. I don't even know how to buff it to keep it shiny," Fintan said with melancholy.

"No one wants a knight in shining armor, it just means they haven't seen any real hardship. What you want is a knight in some rusted chain. Fancy a drink?" Erin asked as she pushed the tankard towards him.

It was Fintan's first ale of the evening but not his last and Calvin sang, the crickets chirped and between these two unlikely travelling companions an unspoken spark was born.

Chapter Twenty – A Council Reborn

The dwarfen carts' arrival on the cobbled slabs of the City of Oakenfall marked the first week of Olar, the second month of the year. The first few days of Olar had come with an uneasy peace. The city was busy when they arrived. The group had expected the arrival of a convoy of dwarves, humans and elves to draw attention, but it seemed few had interest in their arrival. They would eventually learn that they were far from the first unusual guests to have arrived in the city in the days following the dragon's warning.

By the time the dragon was out of view Ingaild had sent his white plumed falcons off into the sky with word for his spies — a new enemy had come, one fiercer than anything the Poles had faced before. Ingaild would need more than his weapon, his Pole army, to push the dragons from the north. The first missive had been sent out from Oakenfall to the Poles' capital of Northholm.

Another similar white plumed bird was sent out to Slickrock for the White Flags to come to the aid of their leader William. He had been spared death considering the dragon's return. Word had even been sent to the elves of the Alienage who Ingaild suspected were a longshot for lending aid. It seemed unlikely that they would once again take up arms for a city that turned on them after the last time they'd helped it, but he had to muster what aid he could, and by the time the dwarves arrived at the city's edge on Bruwek the fourth of Olar, the gathering of the Council was almost ready to begin.

This would be the first time all the kingdoms of Northern Neeska would gather peacefully since the end of the Great War just over a hundred years before. They had only four days until the dragons were due to return to the city. That left little time to prepare an army let alone for airing and settling the petty squabbling that had torn the races and kingdoms apart in the first place.

It had been surprising how quickly the elves had answered the summons, but it seemed like they remembered the bloodshed of the dragonkind better than most and a ship had docked in the harbor the very next day to the bird being sent. It was almost as if they had known about the dragon's appearance in the city during what should have been Harvey's execution. That was something Ingaild would have to investigate once this was all over. He would not make the same mistake as Harvey and spread himself too thinly by fighting petty wars on each front.

The gathering of the Council would be a chance to calm the contested north and proclaim the rule of the Poles and bind it into law. Ingaild had planned for the finest of the noble homes to be available for the diplomats to stay in. The castle was cleaned, and the hall prepared for the visitors.

By the last golden ray of the setting sun, Ingaild stood at the head of the tabletop model of Neeska.

"When I freed the city from Hanson rule, I never expected that within the month I would be entertaining the old Council," Ingaild said.

He was honored to be at the table surrounded by so many powerful people. There were stories of times before the dragons came, before even humans occupied the continent of Neeska, that far overseas the first of the races met in councils much like the one Ingaild headed today to settle peace in the world. To think that Ingaild now took part in such a ritual was empowering, but he would not have long to bask in its magnificence. With each passing hour the time left before the dragon's return was shrinking.

Gathered around the table were the most powerful faces in recent years. William Boatswain, the Pirate King who represented the White Flags, had been freed from his debt and prison and his finery returned to him so that Ingaild could count on the many blades of the pirates to aid in saving Neeska.

Next to William Erin Cleat was sitting. She would not have normally had any reason to be a part of the Council, but fate had crossed her path into that of the dwarves and when they had rolled into the city, they had been escorted immediately into the castle grounds bringing her with them.

Once inside the walls of the Hanson castle Erin had spotted William instantly and had not known what to expect, but he had been pleased to see her, even with her failings. Erin didn't understand why William had been so forgiving. He had not left her side as they had been led inside the keep proper.

Opposite Erin glaring at the rest of the crowd sat Joani the Queen of the Goldhorn Dwarves. She had not been happy about being manhandled by the Pole guards and led into the castle. She had come to help the city only to protect the dwarves of the mountains she'd left behind, and as far as Joani could see all they were doing now was wasting time that could be spent bending the ore she'd brought into weapons.

To Joani's right a still weak-looking Harvey Hanson sat. He had been more than lucky to survive two attempts on his life and a beating that would have shattered most men's souls, and he was a husk at best. His only reason for being kept alive was to banish any chance of a rebellion until all the dragons were dealt with. Ingaild had not wanted to turn Harvey into a martyr.

At the foot of the table sat both Fintan Flynn and his Queen Cadeyrn Silverleaf to represent the peaceful yet powerful elves of the Alienage.

The last seat taken at the head of the table was that of Calvin Drake, who represented the mages... unbeknownst to the rest of them. Calvin was going to decide for the Tower and none of the mages living inside it probably even knew he had left or that this danger was being pushed upon them, but as the only magic user to openly admit it within the city he had been proclaimed the Tower's spokesmen. It had surprised Calvin that the Arch Mage had not made his way to the city, but perhaps he had seen the proceeding in his crystal ball and assumed he had already attended.

To Calvin's side was Ingaild himself who completed the table and represented the united humans of Neeska, both Pole and Oakenfall born.

"You freed nothing," Harvey said retaliating to Ingaild's opening speech.

Harvey was obviously feeling uncomfortable in his old throne room. He knew he was only there to make the proceeding easier. It would make things smoother if Ingaild could be a fair leader and not for the ruthless brigands that he was perceived to be at the head of, the Pole army. Harvey felt like death. In fact, he felt worse than death. Death would be a respite from the agony he felt. His insides burned with the lack of food and his head ached, but he had been dressed up like a prize peacock to be dangled out by Ingaild like a center piece for the table. That did not mean he had to play along.

"Please Harvey. This will not help anyone now," William said from his place next to Ingaild, and he had to wonder if the choice in placement was with purpose. William understood the loss Harvey was feeling, but this was not the time.

The fight for the throne could be dealt with later if any of them survived long enough to sit upon it. William didn't like being a puppet to Ingaild any more than Harvey did, but he had more to lose. Even more since Erin had been poured into the mix.

William would do whatever Ingaild wanted if it meant getting Erin out of the city alive. He had put her in danger once chasing down the mythical Dragon Heart and would not do so willingly again.

"Look I couldn't care less which topsider stakes claim to this city. All I am here to do is set up the explosive powder and stop the dragons reclaiming Neeska," Joani added to the conversation. She was growing more and more annoyed with humans in general the longer she spent topside. She found it ridiculous that they would waste time like this bickering about who owned the city when in a matter of days, the dragons would turn it all into dust anyway.

"Your powder is ludicrous. We would risk blowing up half the city and our own men. We tried a similar tactic when Ingaild invaded and look how that panned out," William said remembering back to the failed attempt to filter the enemy down through the dockyard. If it didn't work for an army of humans that had no choice but to walk on the streets, what hope would they have with dragons that would just fly over them? William had not wanted to upset the dwarfen Queen any more than she seemed already, but his men had laid down their lives once in the maze of buildings and William did not think they would do it again.

"I did not invade, Master William. I reclaimed," Ingaild said shooting William a look that confirmed his freedom was a fleeting thing and William should watch what he said a little more closely. "But you're right… it would be pointless to fill the city with explosives," Ingaild said reclaiming control of the conversation.

It was clear from his demeanor that he would try to stake entitlement over the Council after the battle if they did win against the dragons. Ingaild's hunger for power really did not know any end. He had set out from the Western Reaches with the sole purpose of reclaiming the land that he believed was rightfully his, and now he had done that. The rest of Neeska suddenly looked appealing and he would have to put himself at the head of the race for power.

"These ideas seem futile. My people have been driven from our homes once before. My father united a continent to push back against a dark force much greater than the dragons we face," Cadeyrn said standing up to get the full attention of the Council. "Let me lead the people into battle and we will claim a victory as great as that," Cadeyrn said confidently.

She believed what she said with all her conviction and she had a right to. The elves had almost managed to stop one of the Seven Seals being broken in the Whispering Woods. They had directly opposed the demon responsible for it and then after months at sea they had landed in Oakenfall. If they hadn't, things in Neeska might have been very different. The elves had made the pivotal difference that had won the Great War against the dragons the previous time.

"My Queen... if I may. We did do as you say, but this is different. The city is divided at best. The dragons built this city to serve them. We would not have the blessing of the Earth Mother and we do not truly understand what we face," Fintan added, while thinking on just how far he had come in just a month.

He had been so nervous of his Queen before when she had with the help of the wind burst into his hut, but after all he had seen now, he felt her equal. If anything, he knew better than anyone other than Calvin just what the dragon's anger would mean. They were bickering and making plans but none of them had faced a dragon. He had felt fear paralyzing him, so if anyone was to plan it should be himself or Calvin.

"We're missing something that won us the victory once before," Calvin added. He was scared to suggest it, but it was true. Dragons were beasts of the old world, from the time of the Creators. It would take magic to win this fight.

"Mages, Warrior Mages," Harvey whimpered from his seat, with exhaustion clear in his voice.

"Demon worshippers! Can't believe I'm hearing this. Mind, look at him! He looks half-starved and as crazy as a hare," Erin said speaking for the first time which was unlike her, but she had been keeping quiet with purpose.

Erin knew that she did not belong in the Council, but it did not mean she would not make use of the opportunity. She was after all a pirate at heart and when would she ever get a chance to see the wealthiest and most powerful people in Neeska around one table again? No, Erin had been taking in those around the table while they all flapped their lips. Erin might have been young, but she was not as naive as some would think her to be.

William had shunned her once too often and his sudden forgiveness of her failings on her return showed a weakness that the King of the Pirates should not show. He had lost a lot of his hold on the White Flags since the battle ravished its numbers. When this was all over, Erin planned to take them as her own. The faces around the table would be those who would oppose such a move, so she sat quietly waiting, watching, and learning.

"Mayhaps you're right," Ingaild agreed.

"So, what then? You would have us send word to the mages and they would get here Duwek of next week at the earliest… by then it will be too late," Cadeyrn said.

"The process of making a Warrior Mage takes time. They would have needed to have begun already to have gathered the power we would need. The risks are not worth it either… I speak from a place of knowledge on that matter," Calvin added to the conversation.

"Then we take the battle <u>there</u>," Ingaild said thinking aloud. The table of faces all turned to look at him as if he was mad... all apart from one Calvin.

"Yes. The dragons will fly past the lands close to Briers Hill. The Tower can cast that far, and we can be there within three days. That would give time to prepare — not Warrior Mages but magic," Calvin said as Rinwid gave him a premonition of the battle.

The tower was in the background and standing on it was Calvin. This would change a lot. Calvin didn't understand how, but he could sense it in Rinwid's forewarning. Rinwid was hinting at a new future. That did not mean it was for the best, but Calvin had come to realize that Rinwid had seen this all play out long before he had met Calvin. He had been waiting for this to come to pass and was probably the only one who knew how to come out of this successfully. As much as Calvin hated the idea, he would have to go along with the demon's plans that happened to match Ingaild's.

"That would give us a day, no more to get the blast powder set up across the battlefield. It's going to be tight, but my dwarves will get it done," Joani said half trying to convince herself there was enough time. It would not give them time to press the ore into weapons, but they should be able to arrange the barrels into some-kind of formation strong enough to catch low flying dragons if they left now.

"Then what are we waiting for? Send word to your men respectively and we leave as soon as we're ready," Ingaild said standing and stepping away from the table.

"Send your fastest to the Tower. I will have the might of the Pole army waiting," Ingaild said.

He did not plan to give the Council time to start bickering again. A plan had been weakly agreed on and that would have to be enough for now.

"I trust you can all see yourselves out?" he added before walking to the doorway in which Annar had been waiting.

The two Pole leaders vanished into the corridor outside leaving a slightly stunned table of faces behind them. Cadeyrn was the first to break the newfound silence.

"Fintan, my precious Fintan! You must be exhausted, but can I ask that you leave now to alert the mages? I do not trust anyone else to get word to them in time. While you do, I will travel to the harbor and let our people know we move," Cadeyrn asked feeling the weight of her request. She had already put so much pressure on the fresh-skinned druid. She could see the change in him, the callus he'd built to protect himself from all that he had seen. He was not the same man full of hope and adventure as he had been. The Scorched Lands had aged and changed him, but she could not let him rest yet.

"I am tired Your Majesty, but if that is your wish," Fintan said not relishing the idea of leaving again so soon. He had wanted time to rest, he had wanted to see the Alienage again. It felt like his life had been one long rush since Cadeyrn had first entered his hut and told him to leave for the ship. He couldn't remember a time he had been at rest since then. The time with the dwarves came close but he was now dead on his feet, feet that would again have to leave the city shortly.

"I'll go with your elf. I can ride faster than you and I might have more luck speaking to mages than your kind," Erin said. She wanted out of the city more than anything, not to mention she had started to get a soft spot for the whimsical would-be-hero, Fintan. He was so different to any man she had met in her time with the Flags. She didn't know why, but he had caught her eye sitting brooding by the firelight on the trip down the mountain.

One night catching him alone after one too many ales, she had promised him that she would help him find the elves that might be his parents and for the first time in her life she planned to keep her promise.

Chapter Twenty-One – Dragon's Blight

In the days that followed caravans rolled out of Oakenfall once more and the world shifted — the tremors could be felt throughout the ripples of time. The first to leave had been Erin and Fintan. They had been given two black stallions from the royal stables, and at a gallop were making quick progress, some hours after the armies of the kingdoms began to move.

Feeling exhausted Calvin had left and travelled at a slower pace with the rest of the army, but something had changed in him since leaving Oakenfall. A dark shadow hung over him and he looked pained. The horses that had led the caravan containing him whinnied and pulled away from the reigns making the journey rougher than the gullied roads should have. The veil between the waking world and the Spirit Realm was weak and a dark sensation seemed to emanate from the aged mage.

The army made it to the edges of Briers Hill, and it was there that Calvin had continued his journey alone, to join with Fintan and Erin who now waited within the tower's high garden walls. Calvin's departure was well received among the ranks of the Pole warriors and the soldiers of the many other flags, who for a reason they could not place, felt nothing but discomfort around the old man. With the eerie feel dissipating the further Calvin got from the battle-readying men, they calmed and now they waited.

The temporarily united army had gathered seven miles southwest of Briers Hill in between the surrounding fields and the Mages Tower. They made ready as best they could in the short time they had been given by fate. The dragons were due to fly into Oakenfall that evening and would pass close by to the fields they waited in sometime around midday.

No one had any idea how many dragons the Dragon Lord had amassed in his horde in the mountains. It could be ten or ten thousand, so every man, women and child standing ready to defend the north knew they might not make the journey home.

All the people of Neeska could do was to wait and pray to the many gods that would be watching over this moment that they had settled their squabbles in time to have retained enough strength to win.

A pandemic of fear ran through the crowd like a plague, spreading from person to person. The clattering of steal could be heard as soldiers worriedly fidgeted, while never taking their eyes of the sky. Tempers ran high and to describe it as a powder-keg was an understatement. Men who had been at war for as long as they could remember had to stand side by side waiting to face a mutual enemy.

It would have taken little more than a look in the wrong direction to tear the peace apart and Pole and Oakenfall would be at each other's throats once again.

Noon came and went, but with it came no sign of dragon shadows in the sky above. Some people even began to think it had been a magic trick, a spell of some kind, an illusion and that no dragons would come. Small arguments broke out between fractions, but their leaders did their best to maintain a peace.

Even the new ruler of the Northern Kingdoms, Ingaild, knew that he would have to keep his men in line. Ingaild was not a stupid man and the tensions that ran around like wind through rustling leaves told him of what would happen even if they did somehow win this battle today.

Ingaild had prepared himself for death as he could not see anyone walking away from the coming bloodshed, but he was the Lord of the Poles and could not turn his back and run like a measly Oakenfall dog. On the small chance that they did win, once this battle was over and the dragons were routed, it would fall to Ingaild to decide how to set the country to rest.

He could guess that things were far from over in his plan of conquest by invoking the old alliances. The dwarves and elves would expect recompense and no doubt it would awaken the mages to the plight of Oakenfall.

If Ingaild was not careful then his actions would cause wars to spark up just as they had at the fall of the dragons the previous time and Ingaild did not want to end up like his predecessor Harvey fighting never-ending skirmishes on each front… but for now that did not matter.

Ingaild swallowed and returned his gaze to the sky. He paced back and forth looking out over the fields. The dwarfen Queen was still out with a couple of others doing something with the odd-smelling powder and wagons they had brought with them. Ingaild had little understanding of the technological advances that the dwarves seemed to prize so much, but hopefully whatever they were up to would be of some use when the time came.

In stark contrast to the busyness of the dwarves was the stillness of the elves. Cadeyrn stood at the front of her flanks just behind the Poles. Unlike the Pole army who bickered and seemed in a permanent state of ruckus the elves seemed silent. This was after all not their fight and it had been the second time that they had been dragged into it. Ingaild had had hardly any dealings with elves but he was struck by just how beautiful they were, even clad in their golden-colored armor. Maybe after the battle he would have to get to know this Cadeyrn a little better.

Ingaild's thoughts snapped back to the front of the ranks at ten minutes past two when shadows appeared on the horizon. The dragons came, with wings beating so hard that they still carried a cloud of ash beneath them. At the head of the flock, for want of a better word, was the Dragon Lord, his battle armor shining brightly in the low sun.

He roared to the others with him as he spotted the army waiting. He remembered these lands and would not make the same mistakes that he and his kin had made the last time they'd met humans in battle.

The dragon army numbered no more than ten strong, but that would not make them any less formidable. Ingaild had expected the dragons to speak or demand a retreat before they launched an attack, but that was not how it happened.

The Dragon Lord remembered the pain he'd felt as he watched his kin almost stricken from the world on these very fields a hundred years before. He would hold no quarter this time. The Dragon Lord snarled something in an ancient tongue none left alive knew and the younger dragons pulled in tight.

The dragons flew straight above the amassed army as if continuing towards Oakenfall. With their flight nearing the front of the ranks they let out swift jet-like streams of fire indiscriminately into the ranks of the Neeskan army. The dragons' breath scorched the ranks of humans loyal to the Poles before they could even raise their sheepskin slings to return fire.

The heat blistered flesh from bone and turned the earth below into a mirror of red and black. Ranks of men died as they ran screaming and aflame before the dragons reached the end of the clearing.

The tight ranks that had been setup fell to chaos. Ingaild watched horrified as the dragons cleared the men and continued. They would reach Oakenfall to find it defenseless. He had known the plan to march out would be a dangerous one, but he had not planned on the dragons not even joining the battle. The sudden shock froze some men as the huge beasts flew above bringing a blackening cloud of ash that hit them like sea-salt. Elf archers stood ready, but were unable to fire with their hands quivering on the string of their bows.

"Fire! Damn you! Fire!" Cadeyrn screamed, her eyes wide as the last dragon passed on overhead. A volley went up from the elves close to her. The arrows cascaded into the sky, soon joined by human shots from a thousand or more bows, but too slow for the dragons' swift flight they fell harmlessly into the grasslands below like a heavy rain of steel and iron. They became a shadow of would-be-death that killed nothing more than ants and grass.

As the dragons reached the end of the lines of soldiers everyone expected to see them disappear off into the horizon but instead, they turned in the air with a flick of their tails and began to fly lower. It seemed they were not heading to Oakenfall just yet.

"I offered you a chance at peace," the black Dragon Lord called out as he soared above the terrified faces. "But you have chosen to die."

With that the battle for Neeska begun.

The dragons made another pass back the way they had first come spewing out more plumes of molten breath that crystallized the soil below and incinerated anyone unfortunate enough to be in their path.

They moved with such speed that the Pole catapults were too slow to even come close and the odd spear that was thrown sailed into open air behind the huge scaled beasts.

The dragons had almost made another clear run, but they were not so lucky to make a pass unhindered this time. They had managed to make another sandbank of smoldering corpses in the sea of soldiers, but it was soon filled in by men desperately trying to put out and save their companions.

With the Pole and elf weapons proving almost futile against the dragons, it fell to the White Flags and William. They had brought with them machined harpoons they used to catch whale meat out at sea — it was something that would turn out to be genius. The wooden contraptions were manned by three men, one to load and aim, and two to twist the huge cogs that ran at the sides tightening the ropes to fire the harpoon at breakneck speed… in this case into the air.

The huge harpoons tore at a handful of the slower moving dragons' wings and they fell crashing down like meteors into the ground below. It took almost no time at all for the beasts to roll back onto their feet, but flight would elude them now.

Pole, Oakenfall and White Flag Pirate lunged at the downed beasts with everything they had, but even downed the dragons were not an easy prey. The dragons were not as young as the ones that Darcy had fought in the Scorched Lands and were about a third bigger. Their armor-like scales made piercing their skin almost impossible, even if the brave soldiers could get in close enough to them.

Between their razor-sharp claws, fiery breath and the tree-like thud of their tails the dragons held scores of men at bay. Soldiers circled the beasts waiting for a chance to lunge in to try and puncture the scales and soft meat below, but they were often met with crushing blows that came from a swinging tail or slashed almost in two by white bone claws.

By the time the remaining seven flying dragons made it to the end of the clearing for a second time three hundred lay dead, a mix of human and elf. The grand cities of the north would be a lot emptier if the battle was ever won.

"Ready and light the buggers up," Joani said to the cowering dwarf next to her. The fuse shot off into the field like a snake after a vole. The blast powder exploded into life sending chunks of earth high into the sky ahead of the bright white flame. Another four dragons were grounded in the blasts and one of the smaller young ones was killed outright. A cheer went up from the ranks.

"That was incredible," William said as the smoke began to clear, and he could see the dragons flailing on the ground like wounded flies.

"You haven't seen nothing yet," Joani said pushing her small knife between her teeth and running at one of the grounded dragons.

The blast powder had been successful, but it was all gone in a single blast. Now Joani would show the humans the might of a dwarfen arm. The dwarves accompanied by humans ran in swords ready to lunge into the dragons.

Many were sent airborne by the dragons' powerful tails and crashed into the ranks of soldiers behind them. If they were lucky, they were killed outright by a burst of flame that followed, but the battlefield echoed with the agonized screams of the unlucky.

Only two dragons remained in the skies now, the two fully grown black dragons, the previous Lord and Lady of Oakenfall. They would not be as easy to kill as the young horde. They moved so swiftly it seemed impossible to hit their wings as they darted around in the skies like swallows. Even the harpoons of the White Flags trailed limply through the air behind the beasts as they darted back and forth spewing out flames.

"We can't bring them down," William said trying his best to hold the ranks amongst the panicked men.

Dead bodies lay smoldering, scattered around like chess pieces. Two of the young dragons that had been grounded in the blasts were still alive and held the attention of a large proportion of the army not far from Ingaild, who was accompanied perhaps surprisingly by Harvey who had been allowed to join the battle. He had been armed and fought not far from Ingaild. It was a sign that even the squabbles over Oakenfall were a fleeting shadow when confronted with slavery to Dragon Lords. However, Harvey felt too weak to even lift his sword to strike them let alone find the speed to get past the slashing claws.

"You didn't expect it to be that easy, did you?" Ingaild said with an uncomfortable grin. He had decided to fight alongside Harvey. It was safer to have the man who wanted you dead — and more to the point — his sword facing the same direction as your own sword rather than at your back.

"We're losing too many men. At this rate there will not be anyone to return to Oakenfall," Harvey said. Even in the heat of the battle and after suffering the loss of everything, he still held the city's needs first. He would rather see it in the hands of a dragon than empty. His family's name had to go on… the Hansons had to be remembered.

"Harvey, fate spared your life for some reason. Do not let yourself become a coward now. You're not too much different from me. Battle is in your blood. We'll find a way to bring these overgrown lizards down," Ingaild said showing his old enemy a respect, he did not even know he felt for him. After so long at war with each other it seemed that they may become sword brothers after all.

"Look out!" Harvey shouted instinctively as the huge female dragon made another pass. He grabbed Ingaild by the top of his breast plate and shoved him back before trying to make the leap himself, but Harvey was too slow, he was too tired, and the flame caught his lower half melting his clothes onto him in an instant.

Harvey screamed in agony. The fire started to spread up his body pressing its amber fingers over the top of his chest plate. Harvey tried desperately to shake it off, but it was too late. The fire took him. Rolling in anguish his vision blurred to red. His skin blistered, and his blood boiled.

Ingaild stared motionless — he had felt the blast of heat but had been saved by Harvey. He could not think straight but did not have time to collect his thoughts as he was dragged to his feet by another soldier and found his spear pressed firmly back into his hand. Now was not the time to think — thinking could come once the war was won or lost. With that, he threw his spear down into Harvey ending his pain.

"Find peace in battle, my friend," Ingaild said turning away. Harvey had not been the coward Ingaild had always thought he was. The man had saved his life and Ingaild intended not to squander it.

"Give me another spear now," he ordered to the heaving mass of men that moved around the battlefield. "I'll bring that bastard down with my teeth if I have to." However, the beast was not impressed by heroic deeds and cared little for Ingaild's claim as King of the North. With snarling teeth, it fell from the air and raced towards Ingaild. The two kings would meet but only one would walk away.

Away from the battle, the conversation with the Arch Mage had gone about as well as any discussion with him ever had. Fintan and Erin had somehow managed to successfully gain agreement for the mages to help in the crusade. Reluctantly, the students and teachers had left the Tower and began to march... well, meander, towards the battle but they would never arrive in time.

After resting for the evening Erin and Fintan were about to leave, when Calvin had arrived. He barely acknowledged anyone and seemed more distant than even Fintan had grown used to. He began to climb the tower steps without speaking. Fintan, concerned for his aged friend followed, Erin tagging close behind.

The climb to the very peak had been crippling for Calvin, both physically and emotionally. He hadn't thought he would ever get to see the tower again but now he knew he would never leave it. Rinwid flowed through him like water through an open faucet and his footsteps sent sparks across the stone steps as he climbed out onto the open rooftop.

The daylight that had shone in through the windows seemed to pale in his shadow and as they'd made their way up the spiral stairs; the tower turned to blackness, as if midnight had found its way into the day.

This was what the demon had been planning all along — a second chance to cast the spell that the demons failed to cast during the Great War, to end the dragons and breach another of the Seven Seals.

Standing at the top of the tower Calvin's beard blew in the strong and freezing wind and his robes whipped at his legs. Fintan and Erin could barely hold on to the edges of the doorway looking out at him.

"What do you see? Are we winning? Are the mages almost there?" Fintan asked squinting towards the towering smoke that could be seen on the horizon.

"No one wins here today — the mages will not make it in time. It is too soon for them," Calvin said unblinking. His eyes had blackened as they flooded with power from within. The very tower itself seemed to vibrate along with his heartbeat.

"Damn it, I'm going back. I am no good here and you bearded old farts don't seem like you're going to be much help," Erin said abruptly turning away from Calvin. The truth was that Calvin was scaring her. She'd seen plenty of frightening men in her time as a cabin girl, but she'd never seen the clouds circle above one man… and for that matter, she'd never heard what sounded like a hundred voices trickle out of one person's lips either.

"You would do no good. Rinwid knew this all along — that when the time comes it would be me that would find the Heart and destroy it," Calvin said smiling bitterly. It wasn't his smile though. It felt cold and lifeless.

"What are you on about old man?" Erin snapped back wishing she had let Fintan make the journey himself.

It turned out she had been of little use in the negotiations for getting the mages to help anyway. It was Fintan's supposed connection to some old alliance or something that the nutty old Arch Mage had mentioned before agreeing to send aid.

Erin had feelings for Fintan and had made him a promise — one she'd planned to keep — but she couldn't just sit there with Calvin and his demon. She would come back once all this weirdness was over. At least that was her plan, but she would not get the chance to escape and join the battle.

"Calvin, what can we do?" Fintan asked reaching out for his friend but unable to let go of the brickwork for fear of plummeting to his death.

"This!" Calvin said throwing his head back. The blackened clouds spun into a vortex that poured down around the Mages Tower shaking loose bricks and mortar.

"Grab my hand!" Fintan called out from the walled edge. He pulled Erin towards him and together they barely managed to hold onto the quaking brickwork before the wind tried knocking them free.

Calvin seemed not to notice the storm raging around him as the blackness grew inside him pulsing from the depths of his soul. His hair whitened and started to fall from his head into the torrent of air. His black eyes sank into his body and his skin seemed to retract as if it was shrinking.

The power was so intense that it made anything Calvin had summoned before seem like cheap trickery, little more than the equivalent of pulling a rabbit out of a hat. Calvin's blood turned to ash within his veins, his very soul was pulled from his body as the Spirit World tore open.

The shadow of Rinwid appeared surrounding the decaying frame that had been Calvin, as if it had stepped out of his shadow. With the door open lightning filled the sky and crashed into the tower where the aged mage had stood. The energy absorbed, it was followed by a sudden blast that shot out from Calvin like dynamite exploding. Bricks fell from the tower and it swayed threatening to fall under the pressure, but as the discharge of darkness took flight shooting out across the sky, behind it, the winds stopped churning and then — just like that — it went calm. Calvin's body fell to the floor.

"Are you alright?" Fintan asked as he slowly let go of the brickwork, fingertips bloodied from the effort of holding on.

"What was that?" Erin managed as she looked over at Fintan. She had held onto him so tight that his armor had come loose. The belts holding it across his shoulders had slid and Erin knew that if he hadn't managed to hold onto the wall, they would both be dead.

"I don't know," was all Fintan could muster as he looked down at the old man he had travelled with, his body lying so lifelessly, not just dead but void. It looked like he had died years before and had decayed.

"We need to get down," Fintan said not letting go of Erin's hand and together they began to descend the fractured stairway away from the horrors they had just witnessed.

The blast of power shot across the Tower Plains uprooting what few tall trees were still dotting its landscape. It soared through the air like a meteor of darkness, the swirling vortex at its front parting the atmosphere and leaving a vacuum at its back as it gathered speed. The landscape below was torn by its power as it made its way across the plains. It flew high into the sky tearing thatch clear from the rooftops of any farmsteads unfortunate to lie below its path before it arrived at the battle for Neeska.

The battle below raged on with the races of Neeska fighting the dragons. The flames were either extinguished by the jet winds or sucked into the vacuum to join the darkness. The dragons spun in the air losing the thermals that had kept them afloat. They watched as the arc of the spell seemed to have been traveling on ended and the unforgiving meteor slammed into the ground missing the dragons completely, as it burrowed deep into the earth creating a sink hole the size of the Dean Estate.

This was true blood magic and as such held dark power. The ground shook and vanished into the nothingness. Plant, earth and stone turned into nothing more than a memory. The dark tail of the meteor descended into the gloom of the cold soil. The air stilled and the world waited.

Seconds later a blast of darkness exploded sending clouds of loose stones and soil up and high into the air. The clouds of smoke brought with them shade, and it was then that the gathered army noticed it — the silence. The battle seemed to have stopped. The two huge dragons stopped beating their wings and slowly drifted to the ground, as the remaining seven hundred or so living people of the Neeskan army watched immobile and with bated breath.

The spell was so powerful that it turned day into night. Even the wind discontinued, and not even the ants hidden within the grass dared move. A sphere of blackness sat deep within the hole and from the silence came the sound of scratching, clawing and movement.

"Retreat everyone! Run now!" Cadeyrn screamed, the blackness striking something primal inside her blood.

Humans, dwarves and elves scattered like mice, but some were too slow. Calvin had opened the door to the Demon Realm, and from the shadows skinless, bloody raw claws pulled the creatures up from the very pits of hell. The shadowy creatures climbed up with inhuman speed and tore at anything in their way, as if everything was nothing but paper.

The dragons went to take flight but before even they could beat their wings a sea of the creatures clambered over them like piranha over a buck's corpse. The screams of delight from the demons echoed out, only broken by the anguish of the beasts they devoured. Once the blackness passed over them like a wave, the snarls of the agonized dragons ended. All that remained was rusted armor rocking on the ground and slowly settling to a halt.

The last dragons of the world lay dead. It seemed the spell had worked, and the dragons would not get to reclaim Oakenfall but there was no time for victory between the screams. The scuttling shadows gave chase to the fleeing masses but seemed to slow as they got further away from the crater, the connection to the Spirit Realm weakening, and they eventually faded to dust.

It seemed for now, the demon's power could only stretch so far. All that was left on the battlefield were the lifeless signs of a war. No bodies remained. No bones. Just empty suits of armor. With Calvin's lifeforce spent and the energy all used, the blackness faded, and the sun's rays began to push back against the night. With it the shadowy demons were dragged back to the Spirit Realm. The breeze returned, and the world sighed a breath of relief. The door had closed.

Those who'd been lucky enough to survive the rush of Calvin's spell fled without turning back. If they had, they would have seen her, the woman sitting alone at the craters edge — the door might have closed but not before Rinwid had stepped through.

Rinwid sat weakened by the ordeal. She had promised to return to the Spirit Realm if the Heart was destroyed, and a demon does not lie… but its deals are not ever black and white. She had done what was promised. She had saved Oakenfall from the dragons and in return Calvin had destroyed the Heart. She would even one day return to the Spirit Realm but that would not be today.

Standing Rinwid stretched and took her first step in the human world. The Dragon's Blight was finally over, but Oakenfall had more stories to tell — she would make sure of that.

Chapter Twenty-Two – The End or the Beginning

The days that followed the implosion of dark energy and the fall of the last dragon were oddly peaceful as families made their long journeys back to their homelands and the loving embrace of those they'd left behind.

The dark crater remained silent and whatever dark force had crept out from it ravishing the dragons seemed to have fallen silent. The grasslands remained empty and those who'd survived the battle fought off their nightmares with prayers.

Funerals were held at Celebration Square for all those who'd not returned. The most shocking of names to be scribed into the stonework was that of Ingaild, Lord of the Barbarians. With his death the barbarians lowered their weapons and returned to their original name.

The mighty Weapon of Ingaild was no more. The Poles would be laid to rest until a time when war would once more spread over Neeska.

The continent broken and with a new threat looming in the darkness, whispers of demons rising from the crater sent panicked gossip through the solemn taverns of Neeska. No one could believe the dragons were really gone. The City of Oakenfall remained open to both Oakenfall and barbarian, while many refugees from both sides spread to the four corners of the map hoping to get as far away as they could from the memories of the shadowy demons.

Not everyone had left the great city of the north though and word had been passed out for the Council to meet. Three weeks would pass before they were all ready to look at the walls of the Hanson castle once more and face the fact that the dragons' death had released something far more horrifying into the world, but on Nymon the eighth of Solar, the summer month, the dignitaries arrived ready for debate.

"Thank you for coming," Annar said from his seat at the head of the table. It was not surprising he took leadership of the barbarians upon Ingaild's death and the fall of the mighty Poles. Annar had always been the next in command and no one would have dared to raise a sword against him to challenge his place once Ingaild had died. His son, Lucien sat by his ankles intently listening to the events that transpired.

Annar had been badly wounded during the battle and seemed crippled down one side. His head hung slightly to the left and the white glaze to an eye showed that he had been blinded. A dragon tail had made a direct hit against him, and most people would have died from such a battering but Annar's reputation was well earned.

The first to speak from the gathered Council inside the familiar settings of the Hanson throne room was Cadeyrn. She had come representing the elven people. Cadeyrn had been lucky enough to come away from the battle unwounded and remained as beautiful as ever, though sadly not all her kind had been so lucky.

They had suffered losses just like the humans of Neeska but unlike them, the elves were fewer in number to start with and Cadeyrn was not stupid enough to think they could hold the stalemate for dominance of the Alienage any longer. If war returned in the aftermath of the dragons' deaths, then Alienage Isle would fall. With the promise of the Heart to send them safely into the Spirit Realm removed from her grasp, Cadeyrn had no choice but to put her faith in diplomacy.

"We are eager to discuss what will happen now," Cadeyrn said trying to show a willingness to move forward as a mutual ally.

"Perhaps we should wait for the Dwarfen King?" Annar wondered, looking at the empty seat around the table. It had impressed Annar that the different races of Neeska had managed to sit together at all previously — let alone discuss what to do about the dragons without tearing at each other's throats — but he was even more surprised that they had all returned, when he had summonsed them again. Well, most of those who'd come when Ingaild had called them still lived, and again they sat at the table to decide the fate of Neeska.

William of the White Flags had returned, somewhat surprisingly considering his swift disappearance at the end of the battle. Cadeyrn had made the journey back across from the Alienage. The Arch Mage of the Mages Tower even made the journey and sat intently digging something out of his tooth.

Two names of note that had not returned were Erin and Fintan but their parts in the legend of the Dragon's Blight were over. They were not leaders of people and could have returned peacefully to their previous lives — they could have but did not. Erin and Fintan were travelling into the Tropical Bounding and the precious Green Stone Isles. It would seem Fintan's adventures were not yet over and Erin would be at his side… but that is a story for another time.

"The Dwarfen King isn't likely to come unless we move this Council to the nearest tavern. Leave the dwarves to their fate for now. They'll shut themselves off as they always do," William said, remembering his brief conversation with Fintan when the Council had last met.

"If the old Council is to remain as it is, then we need to include everyone… dwarves as well," Cadeyrn said trying her best to steer things towards the diplomatic peace her people so desperately needed.

Ingaild's sudden death at the hands, or rather the mouth and crushing bite of a dragon, had allowed a peaceful way forward that would have not existed otherwise. However, fear and panic of the spell they had all witnessed crashing into earth and creating the crater had made everyone aware that it would not take much to send the continent into war.

"I have no interest in making this a Council," Annar said, and the room fell quiet. They all had known it was unlikely things would go smoothly, but no one had thought the barbarians would continue as they had before. The continent was too weak to support another conquest and although Northholm had been largely unaffected by the dragons' return surely even Annar would not ignore the risk the demons posed to them all.

"Then why are we here now? Ingaild died and with it so did his grip on this city. We fought side by side. I would probably be dead if he hadn't tried to take out the dragon, we were fighting. Now you plan to push us back out of the city, to claim Neeska for the Poles?" William said. A lot of his bravery had returned upon his homecoming to Slickrock. Things there had largely been unaffected by the trials of war aside from the heavy losses the dragons had wrought.

"The name of Pole died with Ingaild. It was he who led my people to raise our weapons against the Hansons. When the great arm of war is resting, we are humble barbarians, North Men, as we have always been, and you misunderstand me," Annar said staring at William with his one good eye.

"I cannot lead my people like this. You see me. I am crippled, weak, and my wounds do not heal. I will not survive much longer. I plan to return home. I brought you all here to suggest peace," Annar said to the surprise of everyone. It seemed the haggard old war general had more to him than anyone suspected — it could have been because he was facing death, or it could have been the loss of his mighty King.

"Many of your wounds can be healed with a little magic," the Arch Mage said seemingly focusing on the room for the first time since he'd arrived. He had been deep in thought since Calvin had died. He knew it was his doing that gave the demon the opportunity to break the Seal and it would mean that things for the mages of Neeska would no doubt become worse than ever.

"No. That is not the Pole way. My time is done," Annar said abruptly, but with such devotion no one in the room dared argue it. He would not have magic cast on him and would happily go to the hunting grounds of death.

"William you were to be Ingaild's champion and fight for the city. That chore is not yet finished," Annar said staring across the table as best he could.

"I as the rightful ruler pass command of Oakenfall and Northholm to you — on the condition they remain open to my people."

"I... well... what do you mean?" William said taken aback. He could feel all the eyes in the room fall on him. The warm stares and hushed silence meant that no one objected.

How the average man on the street would react was another matter — and what it meant for the White Flags was something else — but those gathered around him had all had dealings with William and his White Flags and knew he would bring a peace that no other man could. William could scarcely believe it. He had been striving for this for years. When he'd arrived in the city a month or more before, he had thought it might be possible then but when the city fell to the Poles, William had almost given in to the idea that it impossible... that his plan for a republic would ever come to being.

"My men know my wishes and have already sent word throughout the people. I do not envy you trying to tame the two cities, but they must remain open to both people elsewise another war is guaranteed," Annar said wheezing. No one had really noticed it before — as they were too shocked by his appearance — but Annar's breathing was labored. It sounded slow and shallow. Talking so much was obviously taking a huge toll of his damaged body.

"I don't know what to say," William said honestly. His boyhood dream had come to fruition. The first steps to a new future had been opened and for the first time in his life William had nothing to add. His mind raced as he tried to think about how he could calm the streets from clashes between Oakenfall natives and barbarians.

Oakenfall had hope and this time the Dragon's Blight was over.

With the signing of the treaties, the death of the last dragon, the laying down of the mighty Pole army, the Battle of Neeska and the Dragon's Blight passed into the chronicling of the world.

In the months that followed, William took to his role as governor like a fish to water.

He awarded the Scorched Lands to the now honorary Baroness, Queen Cadeyrn on condition that the elves used the Earth Mother's blessing to return life to those destitute lands and that they traded wood with Oakenfall openly.

The people overall adored William and the peace he stood for. That is not to say there were not clashes between North Men and Oakenfall natives, but with the mines reopened and trade flourishing, the once royal guards soon held the twin cities securely.

Commerce was re-initiated with the dwarves, but they kept themselves pretty much to themselves. The war had passed them by with only a handful of tons of lost explosive powder, and Joani decided it was best for them to remain separated from the power struggles of the topsiders. The only change to their long segregation was that a shipment of stone was sent once a month to the city to help the humans rebuild in trade for food sent to the mountain once a month. However, greed is greed, and it would not take long for the first of the cart drivers to sneak plans for one of the dwarfen steam driven machines out from behind Goldhorn's gates. Life in Oakenfall returned to a peace it had not known for generations. Trade routes that were lost and forgotten reopened and under William's fair hand promise of a bright future for the city and everyone who lived within it became the talk of the taverns.

The plans put in place by Ingaild to repair the city continued and more plans for the future of the sleeping beast took up William's every waking moment... well almost. He was after all a pirate at heart and being Governor brought many new treats and a city of women he had yet to meet.

Annar returned to the City of Northholm before passing away in the arms of his loving wife. He had left her before being called to take up arms as a Pole and it seemed just to him to spend his last days back in her arms. His favorite hawk is said to still be circling the city looking for him, but no one is sure if that's a fairy tale or not — several people, on their way home from the pubs late at night swear they have seen it.

Not all the elves left Alienage Isle, but many did and under Queen Cadeyrn they begun the painstaking task of reclaiming land from the scorched earth, but almost as soon as they planted Earth Mother's seeds into the warm ash they could feel it — a closeness to the Earth Mother that they had lost during the fall of the Whispering Woods. This land held great promise for them, if only they could take it.

No word was heard from Erin or Fintan and people moved on with their lives almost forgetting those two, whose adventures lay elsewhere, a tale for another time.

Epilogue – Under a Starry Sky

"You said you'd keep Darcy safe!" Granny said as she wrapped a woolen cloak around herself. The Dean Estate had been quiet for the last few weeks, but Granny had been waiting for the arrival of the woman on horseback for decades.

"He is happier now with his father," the cloaked women said as she stretched out a hand to pull Granny onto the back of her horse.

"Come now, we have work to do," Rinwid said…

For more Oakenfall Chronicles head over to
https://www.facebook.com/OakenfallChronicles/

A Tailor's Son Preview

Chapter 1: The Queens Tavern

The night that would change Harold's life forever started normally. It was a fortnight before that wintery night he spent in the darkness writing his notes. The date was Nymon the 16th of Thresh, the end of a harsh autumn and one that hinted at an even crueler winter just around the corner. The day had brought with it an icy breeze that kept the rats off the streets and sent them scurrying into people's homes and cellars.

The fall had been the worst anyone had seen since the poor harvests of 100 AB. That combined with the ban on imported food from Gologan due to the damnable potato famine, meant that everyone was feeling the pinch.

Which much of the farmlands still recovering from the war with the dragons, food prices were the highest they had been in centuries. Most people took on a second job just to make ends meet. Starvation had begun to claim the lives of the poorest in the city, and Harold was as much at risk as anyone.

Although his family did have some inheritance and had been comfortable enough during the Dragon's Blight, funds were not limitless. They were far from nobles. They were not as poverty-stricken as most but would still be classed as some of the poor souls the city came to know as "the unfortunates."

His family were positioned as upper working-class traders, not as desperate as those worse-off that worked the streets and docks around him, but only barely. His family managed to scratch together enough to buy clothes and eat while the nobles continued to live off the rich pickings from their broken backs.

The promises made by Lord William at the end of the war had started with potential. It seemed like times could be changing, and innovation came quickly, but men's greed had not taken long to manipulate his intentions and corrupt his government. The nobles that had become rich under the monarchy soon found footholds in political positions.

This had turned William's promise into dismay for many, but Harold's father was very tight with the purse-strings, As he had lived through the war that almost brought Oakenfall to its knees during the first century. He had learned not to spend a single copper where it was not needed, a trait that had been passed on to his thrifty son and allowed them to keep their tailor shop open where many would have folded.

Harold had just finished working at the little shop on East Street to make more coins that would doubtless hibernate in his father's moth-filled wallet.

His father had taken on an order from one of the local factories, two hundred aprons by the end of the next month. Harold had argued with his father that they could not finish the order in time. He was more realistic and accepted that one of the sweatshops with clanking machines the Dwarfs had traded would have been more suited to handling it. However, his father ignored his concerns, as always, and took the work.

Harold was not sure if he did it for the money, or if he feared giving work to the machines that drove the industrial revolution forward would speed up the inevitable end of their little family business. They had gone from a time when black iron and the might of a smith was at the forefront of technology to strange steam-driven machines in barely a generation – coal had become the new black magic.

Whatever his reasons, in his blind hope, Harold's father saw the massive order as a challenge and, as usual, wanted to face it head-on. He knew Harold would do everything he could to make sure they succeeded.

Harold should have left the shop a few hours earlier, but they had already been running behind on the day's work, when his father had rushed home sick with the flu.

Harold had to admit that he was worried about his father's health. He was in his fifties, and his age had begun to weaken him. The flu was a known killer, and over the past year, Harold had seen the huge mountain-like man of his father shrink.

Harold did not have time to linger on his worries for not long after the last stitch had been pulled tight, he left the shop for the night.

With the shop locked up, Harold was off to the Queens for his second job. The Queens was a little smuggler-run tavern down by the docks. Harold had started working there once or twice a week in the evenings to help meet the cost of the family estate and make up for the shortfall in earnings coming from the tailor shop.

That particular night Harold was running late, but he knew that no one would notice. They never did so long as Harold was there before the kegs ran dry. The money was good for the hours Harold worked and for the menial tasks he was required to do, like lugging empties from the cellar onto a cart or unloading full ones that just arrived and tapping them ready to keep the foul-smelling grog flowing.

The money was much more than the work was worth, but the reason it paid so well was that it was hush money to avert his eyes from things going on there.

The smugglers and criminals of the city had always had strong ties to the White Flag pirates, and the Queens was a real den of iniquity. Gambling, fights, prostitution, and other unmentionable acts that should never be carried out by decent Oakenfallian men and women were stock and trade for the little back alley boozer.

The tavern was favored by the worst Oakenfall had to offer. Still, Harold was left to do his job, and he was the kind of person to go unnoticed, so he did not let himself worry about what went on inside its walls. His only worry was the amount of liquor that used to go in and out.

Harold was a tailor, so he was not used to heavy lifting, but thankfully, he did take on a little of his father's shape and was bulky. Not overly muscular like some of the brawlers that he saw fall in and out of the Queens of an evening, but he was not a reed pole.

All the same, the full kegs almost tore his arms from his body and with the number they had going in and out of the place, it was not unreasonable to think half the harbor had gills.

Harold walked the quiet streets alone on his way to the tavern, not eager for the weight of the kegs awaiting him. His body had begun to yearn for sleep, although the sun was only just setting.

He had walked this same path many times before and knew each loose cobble, rise, fall, and slope that beset his path. For just that moment, Harold could relax.

He did not need to think as he passed the high buildings all around him that helped to block out the sound of hustle and bustle.

As usual, as Harold walked along the canals, he was daydreaming. It was a good pastime for him, which he had used most of his life. The trait had started back at school when Harold was just a boy and had caused a fair few chalk rubs to be thrown at him by his teacher, old Macgregor, not to mention the cane once or twice.

Harold had hated Macgregor. He was from the Western Reaches somewhere and seemed to detest all children. He was the headmaster of the school, and ran the place more like a prison, often taking some of the more poorly behaved children and locking them away in his room for hours at a time. Those he took would always come out crying, followed by a red-faced Macgregor.

Harold had been lucky enough never to enter his room. Macgregor was a Pole, not an Iron Giant as they were known in times of peace, but a cold-blooded warrior, a giant-like barbarian, and there were rumors that he had slaughtered children during the war. Harold never found out whether that was true or not, and he did not wish to know. Harold was a coward at heart and just did his best to block out the memories of his school days.

Continuing to walk deep in thought, Harold stepped around a flock of moulted pigeons. He was contemplating how, although his family lived on the edges of the more common parts of the city, he had been sheltered from the worst it had to offer for the most part – that was until he started working for the smuggler family known as the O'Briens. Harold had then started to see a lot he never wanted to.

His thoughts faded from logic to dreams as he walked down Harbor Path. It was the same dream he'd had many times before, ever since he was a child – normally centered around the coast.

His mother and father had taken Harold to Port Lust when he was young, and the sights and smells of the sea stayed with him all his life.

Harold remembered staying in his grandmother's little cottage and he remembered the gulls that flew overhead. They were a beautiful white, not the dirty black-gray of the pigeons that painted the rooftops around Oakenfall.

Harold swore to himself that one day he would go back there but the house was in ruins; it had decayed with years of isolation. His father had always been too busy to travel down and maintain it, and his mother was unable to manage the Oakenfall home let alone a faraway holiday cottage that was rarely visited.

The painted walls of the seaside retreat began to flake, and the once pure green grass of the expansive lawn was now little more than a jungle of weeds.

However, in his daydream, it was still as perfect as when Harold was a boy. Small and full of character, it had some small birds nesting in the thatch roof – swallows, Harold remembered. They used to dart back and forth through the air as he sat on the cliff top.

Every morning Harold used to travel down the stairs that lead from the garden straight down to the shore and spent the day at the beach pestering the crabs that called the rock pools home, and chasing clouds. Then at night they slept with the sound of the ocean as it brushed the rocks, stealing pebbles as it went.

The little windows had wrought iron bars in the shape of perfect crosses. The shutters themselves were engraved with flowers. Harold felt happy and safe there, both as a child and now in his dreams as an adult.

Harold remembered finding a fossil of some long dead creature at the base of those pure white cliffs and still had it to this day, sitting above the fireplace. For him, it was a last memento of his childhood, a memory of innocence that seemed so rare in a city full of beggars and thieves.

Still daydreaming Harold came down from the bridge that crossed one of the waterways on Harbor Path. The sound of the waves in his dream married well with the very real sound of ships' bells that rang out from within the haze of smog. The changes to the harbor had brought in a lot of work and made money for those that already had it, but those that did not were suffering even worse than they had before the century celebrations. They now worked longer hours in hot, smoke-filled, and cramped factories that were run by oppressive managers who had little care for them and worked them to death.

The end of the Dragon Blight had opened trade with the dwarves for the first time in many years and below ground they had built things centuries ahead of the humans.

The trade catapulted industry forward but at a price. The clouds they produced seemed to mix like an unhealthy stew with the smell of the canals. The thick clouds seemed to grow denser with each passing year and now covered most of the city.

On some days, the cloud was so thick that it seemed almost pliable and the buildings around that area of Oakenfall had already begun to take on some of its blackness and were quickly losing what little charm they used to have.

The city had become overcrowded with multiple families being squeezed into each hovel like wharf rats. With the promise of yet more money to be pulled out from the secrets the Dwarfs were finally sharing from behind their huge stone doors in the Kingdom of Goldhorn, there would be need for more people to come to the city – and the overcrowding only promised to get worse.

The sun was falling over the horizon as Harold's daydream was broken by a husky and desperate voice close to his left ear.

"Looking for a good time? You look clean enough, so I'll do it for a halfpence. What do you say?" the young woman leaning against a nearby wall asked him, as she staggered out of the shadows looking like a scarecrow.

She instantly made Harold feel ill at ease. She sported two blackened eyes, no doubt from an unhappy client the night before or from her pimp or, worse, her husband. Her ginger-red hair was pulled tightly into a ponytail and was thick with grease. The few hairs that escaped the grasp of the ribbon clung to her forehead as if glued in place.

She gave Harold a smile full of remorse and the smell of cheap bourbon hit him. Harold watched, unsure whether he should risk aiding the poor girl as she almost lost her grip on the wall she had taken to holding. She had been drinking. Harold suspected it was to keep out the cold or to block the thoughts of what she would have to do for her meal that night. Harold could not say for sure which.

It was a world he didn't understand. He skimmed along its edges and in his naivety, he even went as far as blaming the poor girl for letting her life end up that way. He did understand that having to work the streets could not be an easy task, but didn't understand that for some single women it was the only life they had ever known.

Taking a closer look at her, Harold noticed that she was young and not one of the leathery-skinned old hags he normally saw at that time of day. It was a horrible thought, but Harold knew that some of the girls working the streets were as young as twelve or thirteen years of age. It sickened him to his core to think that this poor girl might be that young.

Harold could tell she was nervous. She clasped her hands together, all the while fiddling with the pocket of her blouse which hung loosely from her young body. She did not seem to carry the same hard-edged attitude as other bangtails that Harold had seen throughout this area of the city, but being young, she had not long been on the streets. That made the whole situation worse for him.

Harold had no love for whores or their trade. He didn't understand why they didn't leave the city and go tend to the farms or head off to one of the southern cities away from the reach of the Poles or criminal families and start again.

Harold thought for a moment about what would make such a young girl turn to a craft like this and his disdain for his employer at the Queens flashed through his mind once more. Whatever the young girl's story, O'Brien would have had a part in it. Harold's anger was due to the fact that O'Brien was no doubt her pimp. Harold was prone to flights of imagination, and in the moment, he imagined her life story.

He dreamt up the story that her mother died in labor – as was common – and her father – a drunkard like most men from the wooden built part of the city – had abused her. She had finally collected enough courage and run away, just for O'Brien to find her begging on the street somewhere, no doubt asking for nothing more than a scrap of bread.

O'Brien would have spoken to her in his charming accent and offered her to come back to the Queens for a meal. He would have given her a bed for the night, no doubt treated her well, all the while getting her drunk on free ale.

Then, like a spider trapping the fly, he would change, demanding payment for the ale, threatening her, and finally when she couldn't pay, putting her out to work, the bastard. The workhouse would have been better for the poor girl, although Harold did admit, only barely.

O'Brien put her out to work but she was not bringing in enough money, so he taught her what happens to those that did not deliver what O'Brien wanted. He beat her, not enough that she would be permanently useless to him, but no one cared if a prostitute had a few bruises and before the blood on her nose had even had time to dry, he'd sent her back out on the streets to stand in front of Harold.

His heart sank at the thought and as if she sensed the sorrow in his eyes the girl looked away. She brushed her front down, loosening the rags to reveal more of her young bosom. Small freckles dotted her chest that mirrored those around her nose and cheeks. Harold could imagine from her small trim jaw that she would have been attractive but for the swelling on her face. One eye was almost closed and yellowing from the bruising.

It was then Harold noticed the filth on her, so much dirt on her clothes that calling them clothes was too much of an honor. They were more like rags that had once been a cheap cotton dress, but all shape had fallen from it so that it hung loosely over her small shoulders.

One sleeve of her blouse was torn, and Harold wondered if that had been an overzealous customer. Harold looked at the unfortunate girl in such sadness. She approached him with the same statement as before in her brittle tone as his glance met hers.

"Halfpence, what do you say?"

Listening past the cold she carried and the slur from the alcohol, Harold could hear in her voice that although young was likely to be a little older than he'd first thought. It was hard to tell under all the dirt.

No matter her age, she was desperate and that was for sure. If Harold had thought of it at the time, he would have wondered why she hadn't moved toward the ships with the rest of the whores who wanted easy coin, but Harold guessed she had some reason to avoid sailors.

It saddened him that there were so many nightwalkers along the docks. The place was littered with them, all hoping to make an easy penny from the sailors coming in from their long voyages. There were plenty of nameless young women or old hags for them to satisfy their urges while they visited the shore. Most of the poor women received a black eye or a bloodied nose from their swift visit lovers.

As much as Harold hated the sensual crafts, as he called them, he hated the men that abused such desperate women even more and it pleased him that fate would have the last laugh as the cowardly bastards had no idea what they would carry back with them onto their ships. They would have a rash, and a vile one at that, but it served them right, no doubt, as the scurvy took them and sent them mad.

Harold stood there awkwardly deep in his own thoughts unaware of the moments passing. He did not want the services the young woman offered but he felt obligated to do something to ease her pain or be as bad as those that caused it.

"How much do you need to earn for a room tonight?" Harold asked, feeling around for the loose change in his pocket. He didn't have much to give as most of what they earned went straight to his father. The little he had, he had reasons for not wanting to carry on him after sunset in that part of town.

"I only need a halfpenny more. I will do whatever you want and I'm clean too. No warts or anything," she replied trying to sound provocative but was clueless about achieving it in her drunken state.

That might have been enough for some of the potbellied pond-scum that had somehow managed to get a handful of coins to bed her, but Harold had no interest in anything other than getting her off the street. Whatever he planned to do, it would need to be quick as he had to be at the Queens before the kegs ran dry and O'Brien turned his anger toward him.

"Anything I want? You promise that?" Harold asked, her as he pulled the lint out of the handful of small coins he'd found at the bottom of his pocket. It was his whole earnings for the day, but Harold knew he would still have food waiting for him when he got home, more than could be said for the redhead.

"Yes, for sure, mister no matter how weird, less it's magic. No magic," the young girl said, eagerly snatching the small handful of coins from him. "Cor-blimey, there's got to be almost two pence here. What weird stuff you after?" she asked, and suddenly her face changed.

It seemed darkness had seeped into some people's hearts ever since the demon Rinwid had broken through the Spirit Realm into the waking world and there had been talk of working girls going missing. It was clear she was worried just what Harold would expect for such a pay-out.

"I want you to get home, get off the street. A young girl like you shouldn't be working like this," Harold said with a smile.

Suddenly his attention was diverted as a coach rattled by passing between him and what he would loosely call a woman, and almost knocked them both over.

Harold took his chance to trot on quickly leaving her behind. The near collision had startled him, and it took him a few minutes to notice a leaf that had entangled itself in his cropped brown hair. As Harold removed it, he began to daydream again.

He had needed the money really, but not as much as the girl did, and it was worth it for the thought that for just one night she could sleep peacefully, just as peacefully as Harold had in the bed at his grandmother's cottage.

Continue reading in 'A Tailor's Son' the second Oakenfall Chronicle Novel.

Printed in Great Britain
by Amazon